TENDER JUSTICE

A Novel

by

James J. Mulligan

This book is a work of fiction with reference to numerous historical characters. Insofar as possible they have been placed in the book in the same context in which they were at the same time historically. However, their interaction with the fictional characters is clearly non-historical. Beyond that, any resemblance between the characters in the book and real persons living or dead is purely coincidental.

All rights reserved. No part of this book may be reproduced or transmitted in any form by any means, electronic, mechanical, photocopying, recording or otherwise without the prior written permission of the author.

Copyright © 2013, James J. Mulligan

A very learned and compassioned Judge in Texas, on passing sentence on John Jones, who had been convicted of murder, concluded his remarks as follows: "The fact is, Jones, that the Court did not intend to order you to be executed before next spring, but the weather is very cold, our jail, unfortunately, is in a very bad condition; much of the glass in the windows is broken; the chimneys are in such a dilapidated state that no fire can be made to render your apartments comfortable; besides, owing to the great number of prisoners, not more than one blanket can be allowed to each to sleep sound and comfortable... In consideration of these circumstances, and wishing to lessen your sufferings as much as possible, the Court, in the exercise of its humane compassion, hereby orders you to be executed to morrow morning, as soon after breakfast as may be convenient to the Sheriff and agreeable to you."

The Carbon Democrat
Mauch Chunk, Pa.
Saturday, February 10, 1866

CARBON CO. PA.

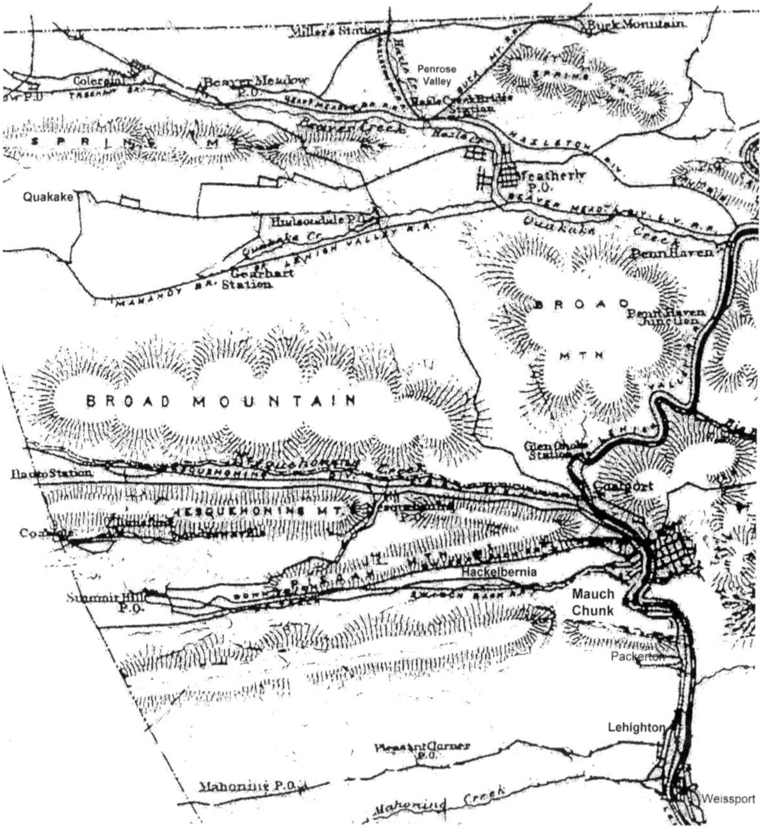
Miller's Station
Buck Mountain
Penrose Valley
Colerain
Beaver Meadow
P.O.
Spring Mt
Beaver Creek
Hazleton
Weatherly
P.O.
Quakake
Quakake Cr.
Lehigh Valley R.R.
Gearhart
Station
Quakake
Creek
Penn Haven
Broad
Mtn
Penn Haven
Junction
Broad Mountain
Coalport
Hackelbernia
Mauch
Chunk
Summit Hill
P.O.
Packerton
Lehighton
Pleasant Corner
P.O.
Mahoning P.O.
Mahoning Creek
Weissport

The Diarist

July 23, 1860 — I must kill her again.

He stopped writing and reread the words in the copybook, a book like all the others he had filled the last few years — the same rough paper, the same flimsy pasteboard cover, the same loosely sewn binding. All the same. Book after book, all stored in boxes, all recounting the events of the past decade, none of them intended to be seen by anyone but himself. He seldom referred back to them; but he knew that he could and that sufficed. He was quite the diarist. Indeed, that is how he had begun to think of himself. The Diarist.

He wondered sometimes at the handwriting. It was his, of course, but by no means the strong, confident hand that he had so carefully cultivated and of which he was so proud. This was the loose, irregular scrawl of his childhood. The childhood he had so successfully expunged from memory that even with serious effort (an effort he all but never exerted) there were parts of it that he could no longer recall even vaguely. It was as if they had never existed.

He closed the book, set down the pen, corked the inkwell and, for the space of ten minutes or more, sat staring into the candle's barely flickering flame. He liked to write his thoughts by candlelight, to avoid exposing them to the gaslight's harsh, white glare.

He blinked, as though suddenly awakened from a dream, and sat up straight. Not the faintest breeze stirred the curtain, nor had it done so all evening long. He rose, snuffed out the candle, and walked the few steps to the open window.

The street noise three floors below had begun to die down for the night. A few neighbors still sat on their stoops, prolonging the time before they must go back into the stifling heat, the oppressive humidity that turned the effort to rest into a fitful struggle destined to drag on until morning. Now and again a voice was raised. A lone word spoken. The muffled fragment of a sentence, trailing off into an unintelligible murmur. A child cried softly next door, a hushed voice spoke to comfort it, then both fell silent. The old man across the street sat in the darkness, alone as always, his face appearing and disappearing as he puffed on his pipe making it glow and then exhaled the fragrant smoke, its aroma detectable in the still air even this high above the street.

It was incomprehensible. There had been subtle hints — the similarity of stature, the color of the hair, the familiarity of the gait. Meaningless, really. Things like this had happened before and had signified nothing. Then he saw and stopped dead in his tracks — so quickly that the well dressed gentleman behind him trod hard upon his heels and drew himself up as though to lodge a complaint. Then he saw his face, mumbled an apology, and went on past.

At another time the Diarist might have been amused at arrogance reduced so rapidly to apprehension, but at the moment he had felt no satisfaction. He was preoccupied. Devastated. As though the whole world had been overturned and he was suddenly dumped into a place he had never been before.

She was there. Not ten paces in front of him. She had just turned her head, her attention caught by someone or something on the far side of the street. He saw the profile, the full lips, the rounded curve of the cheek, the tilt of the head in silhouette against the background of the parasol's white expanse, and he knew. How could the years have changed her not at all, when they had changed him so much?

He realized that she had moved on while he stood there blocking the pedestrian flow and making a spectacle of himself. He could not wait. She was already about to turn the next corner and he could not risk losing her. Had she seen him? Was she hoping to get away? He quickened his pace, but common sense prevailed and he did not break into a run. It was hardly likely she had recognized him. It was his own careless haste that might draw her attention.

He turned the corner. There she was. Her pace bespoke no urgency, no special destination, just a casual stroll. He settled down to keep step with her and again melted easily into the anonymity of the other strollers. Just one more idler, swinging his cane, enjoying the day.

Their surroundings changed from the last of the small businesses into a purely residential area unfamiliar to him, the streets much less frequented. Would she see him now that he lacked the camouflage of the other promenaders? But almost before he had properly formed the thought, she was at her destination.

This was not the hovel of ten years past. Even the thought of that place revolted him. This immaculate white brick structure was not her former style. It stood upright between its neighbors, its door framed by graceful columns surmounted by a modest arch. The door's highly polished brass knob and knocker glinted in the bright sun.

Her return must have been expected, for, before she could touch either knob or knocker, the door was opened and the smiling maid said, "Welcome back, Miss. Did you have a nice walk, then?" Both disappeared within and the door closed.

Now what? He stood there, wondering, knowing that he could not long tarry without himself becoming the object of others' curiosity. Then the door opened and he was assailed anew by fear that she might see him, perhaps recognize him in spite of what common sense told him. But it was the maid, apparently on her way to the market.

He caught her eye, tipped his hat and smiled, pretending to admire the architecture of the house. He asked who lived there and she responded with a suspicious frown. But his smile was, he knew, quite pleasant, and she could not resist responding with one of her own. He was well practiced at this. She told him the name. It was the wrong one, but he was not deceived. It was starting again and he must not allow that. He had all he needed, all the warning he was likely to get, and he would heed it. Oh, yes... he would prepare for the day. It was coming. He would be ready. And then he would kill her again.

PART I

JANUARY, 1866

Chapter I: Brogan's Back

The cure for this ill is not to sit still,
Or frowst with a book by the fire;
But to take a large hoe and a shovel also,
And dig till you gently perspire.
    Rudyard Kipling (1865-1936)
Just So Stories (1902)

[Monday, January 8, 1866]

The sulfurous smell of smoke, the flickering flames of dim lamps, the constant drip drip of muddied water, the clang of iron tools, the muffled murmur of voices, and the dense black haze as thick as cobwebs in the stale air could have graced the portals of hell. A far cry from the cold, crisp air with its hint of impending snow that prevailed above ground, the sort of atmosphere that impels one to breathe deep and revel in good health. Not so here. The dreadful dust-laden air of this dark hole filled him with the urge to cough or sneeze with each breath he took. If he had one particular fear, it was probably this — this boxed-in feeling, the sensation of walls and roof about to close in and crush the breath out of him.

Nothing was visible beyond the few feet in front of him. He should have been familiar with this; but he wasn't. In spite of the fact that he'd spent most of his twenty-three years in Carbon County, he had never before had reason to enter these domains, so much a part of daily life for most of those with whom he'd grown up. Still, he had undertaken his present position knowing full well that this occasion might arise. A contract physician with the Penrose Valley Coal Mining Company undertakes the care of its employees and their families, and most of those employees spend their waking hours deep beneath the earth.

The faces and hands of his two guides were black as those of any of the former slaves he'd seen in Virginia during the war. The dull coal dust coated them head to foot, reflecting nothing of the light of the lamps attached to their hats, leaving the wet gleam of the whites of their eyes to hang disembodied in the blackness as they pressed deeper into the tunnel. It had been a gray afternoon above ground, but not even the darkness of night could have rivaled the gloom which descended once the canvas cover of the adit had fallen shut behind them.

The dense atmosphere under the timber-supported tons of earth oppressed him with the irrational fear of sudden collapse. His throat constricted with a sense of suffocation, though he knew full well it was but the fruit of imagination. The tunnel was large, built for the passage of the mules, men, and cars which brought the coal to the mouth of the mine, thence to be hauled to the breaker. He knew it was ventilated to ensure sufficient oxygen and the necessary circulation to carry off the inevitable traces of the blackdamp that could smother you or the firedamp that could blow you to smithereens. He was still not consoled.

His two companions strode the flat iron band tracks with all the nonchalance of a stroll down Broad Street in Beaver Meadow, their pace, from long practice, spaced to accommodate the width of the wooden ties. They'd said that the distance was no more than seven or eight hundred yards. Less than a half mile — a distance insignificant on the surface, but here already endless, though they had yet gone no more than two hundred yards at best. He felt foolish. He knew he was slowing them down, stepping gingerly from tie to tie, unused to navigating the tracks in the dark. But they showed no impatience.

The cave-in could not have been serious. No whistle had sounded to alarm the town. The mine's work went on as normal: More than once they were pressed against the walls to allow passage of the coal-laden mule cars, their advent invisible until long after the warning clip-clop of iron shod hooves and the rumble of heavy wheels in the dark. Boys of no more than eleven or twelve years urged the mules on — boys undaunted by the stubborn beasts towering far above their lanterned hats. Neither the boys, the men, nor even the mules paid the three of them the least attention. In the dark they were but one more gang of laborers headed back to their dig.

"Are ye all right then, Doctor Dougherty?" the taller of the two inquired.

"I am," he said, and said no more. Even voicing those two words revealed his shortness of breath — not for lack of oxygen but from groundless anxiety. He had been in far worse situations during the war, but none that so quickly and effectively sapped his spirits.

"Ye'll be finding two o' them needing yer ministrations," the short man said, "They was partly buried, but the boys was digging them out as fast as they could. They have to be careful, ye know, seeing as how they don't want to start another slide."

Left and right from the main tunnel the narrower gangways led off into the veins, to the breast where the coal was dug.

"How did it happen?" Dougherty asked, switching the leather bag to his other hand and realizing just how unnerved he was. It wasn't heavy, but he'd been clutching it so tightly that his fingers ached as he straightened them. He hid his hand at his side and opened and closed his fist to rid it of its stiffness.

"Ah, sure, who's to say," the tall man said. "We was loading the cars. The blasting was done fer the day. I guess a timber was bad or slipped or something, and brought down the roof. It happens often enough."

His guides were common laborers, not the skilled miners who did the blasting in the first half of the shift. These merely supplied the muscle to load the cars for the breaker. The miners might know more about the cause of the cave-in, but they were done for the day and not here to be questioned.

The tall man was right. These accidents happened often enough. Lately they had been happening all too often throughout the coal region. Mining was never a safe occupation; but ever since before the war the small operators had been scooped up one after another by the big companies whose owners never even saw the inside of a mine. They sat in their New York and Philadelphia and Boston and London boardrooms, and, to keep themselves in fine cigars and good liquor and the other simple necessities of life, took risks with rotting timbers and poor ventilation systems. Occasional cave-ins or firedamp explosions were the cost of turning a profit. Too bad for the men who died, but there were plenty more where they came from. Immigrants rolled in day after day, full of hope and ready to start at the bottom —

never suspecting how deep that bottom was and how sparse the hope of moving upward, especially if they were Irish. Still, this was a new mine and the timbers should have been far from rotting. That bothered him.

He was glad his guides had thought to supply him with a pair of gum boots and a heavy coat. The footing was treacherous with the puddles of water between the ties of the rails, and more than once he slipped, but caught himself before he fell into the black slush. At least this far inside the mine all they had to contend with was the water. Nearer the adit it had been sheets of ice which the mule boys had been breaking up all day long as it constantly refroze. His guides pretended not to notice his lack of experience, but still stayed close enough to catch him before he could go flat on his face.

"We'll be at the vein soon," the short man said. "Have ye never before been in the mines, doctor?"

His shortness of breath and unsteady gait must already have answered that. The man was merely being polite.

"I have not," he said.

"D'ye mind being under like this?" the tall man asked.

"Not really," he said. At least, he thought, not so much as actually being buried alive, but he didn't say that.

He had tried to sound confident earlier, too, when the knock came to the door and he opened it to the breathless little mule tender, black-faced with coal dust and shivering now that he had stopped running and his perspiration was cooling him all too rapidly. Some men were hurt bad and could the doctor come help? Dougherty had put on his best face for Jen as he gathered up his medical bag. Her eyes said that she knew better — but she made no comment, just kissed his cheek and said she hoped he would not be gone long.

There was no quaver in her voice, but he felt the tension as her hand squeezed his. Six months. Time enough for the pain to have lessened somewhat, but it would probably never be gone entirely. She had always been sensitive, but now more than ever. His nervousness at going into the mine must have communicated itself more strongly than he'd realized. Yet, beyond that slight tremor in the tips of her fingers, she gave no sign of her fear for him.

"It ain't pleasant the first time under," the short man said, "but ye get used to it."

He sincerely hoped he would not have to.

Up ahead the sound of voices and the clank of iron tools grew steadily louder, but they saw no light. Maybe the tunnel curved or it could be just the constant dust keeping the light from penetrating. They plodded on.

"We're almost there," the tall man said at last, pointing. "They're just ahead."

It was another hundred feet until he saw the first hint of light, so faint that without the tall man's comment he might not have seen it even then.

"We'll turn there," the short man said. "They're right inside that gangway."

The light was closer than he'd thought. It came from a lantern suspended from a beam. Voices came from the gangway on the left but no sounds of mining, although the clink of tools from deeper in the mine never abated.

From the gloom of the narrow gangway two men emerged supporting between them a man shocked and dazed, his arms draped over their shoulders. The area was too narrow for all three to proceed abreast, so they sidled crabwise like a line of clumsy dancers each hearing a different tune.

"The doctor's here," the tall man said.

"So I see, Johnny," said one of the rescuers. "Manus here ain't so bad off. A little groggy maybe. Some cuts and bruises. But he'll be fine once he's caught his breath. We've bigger worries with the other."

Dougherty confirmed their diagnosis. Manus was weak from shock, but he was already recovering as they propped him against the dank tunnel wall. He mumbled his thanks, then hunched over, his elbows on his drawn up knees, his head cupped in his hands. He would be fine.

"What's wrong with the one still in there?"

"Don't seem to know where he is, Doctor, and he can't move his arm right."

"Why don't you take me in and I'll examine him there?" Movement might mean more harm to the man, and that outweighed Dougherty's fear of entering that suffocatingly narrow passage.

"Sure," the man said. "By the way, me name's Frank O'Laughlin. We're glad ye come. It ain't every medico I've known who'd be willing to do it."

Dougherty shook the rough, grime covered hand. The comment surprised him. He'd taken it for granted that a company doctor was obliged to come down here whenever called. It was just as well he hadn't known there was an option. It might have given him an excuse.

O'Laughlin's partner was introduced as Will Shannon. The two who had led Dougherty into the mine were Johnny O'Rourke (the tall one) and Charlie Shea (the short one). The man still in the gangway was Ned McGinley, and the one nursing his aching head was Manus O'Donnell.

"C'mon then, I'll take ye to him," O'Laughlin said and headed into the gangway.

It was oppressive, barely high enough to stand upright, and it curved as it proceeded, amplifying the dreadful, hemmed-in feeling. The dust was thicker here and Dougherty was coughing again. He forced his mind back on the patient. Ten or fifteen yards inside a man lay against the wall next to a lantern. His eyes were open, but it was impossible to tell if he was aware of their approach. His lips moved slightly, but the only sound was a feeble groan.

"He's coming round," O'Laughlin said. "They was both under, but we dug them out before they smothered. They must'a been coming out o' the gangway when it started to go. Good thing they was, else they'd'a been on the other side o' that rubble. It goes a good ways back."

Beyond the injured man, rock and timber littered the area and all but filled the gangway. Its far end was where the day's mining had taken place and it was from there that they had been carrying out the coal.

Dougherty knelt beside Ned McGinley. The right side of his forehead bore a nasty cut. A mere trickle of blood now seeped from it, but the coagulating mess on his face and clothing bore witness to profuse bleeding. He had a magnificent lump beneath the laceration and, if he survived, should have an impressive black eye by morning. That blow probably accounted for his stupor. His pulse was steady, but rapid. He closed his eyes as if to gather strength, then tried to speak.

"Wh... wh..."

Even that almost undid him, and he drew a deep breath to try again. Dougherty waited, knowing that to try to dissuade him would serve no purpose. He had seen this all too often among the battlefield wounded, convinced that what they had to say was of utmost importance and they would not be deterred. Far better to let him try and then get his cooperation once he realized that he could not yet do what he wanted to do.

"Where... where..."

This time his eyes did not close, but were pained with the effort this was costing him.

"Where... Brogan..."

"Where is Brogan? Is that what you want to know?"

Again his eyes dulled, but, with great effort of will, he moved his head in a shallow nod.

"Do you know who Brogan is?" Dougherty asked O'Laughlin.

"That I do," he answered. "That'd be Charlie Brogan, but he ain't here t'day. He's been took sick since Saturday and he ain't reported fer work neither day."

McGinley shook his head, agitated, his face full of frustration. He tried to speak, but merely moaned. He turned to his right, trying to get up. He failed and relapsed into his former position, tears of agony eroding two white trenches into the coal dust on his cheeks.

"McGinley," Dougherty said, "like it or not, you'll have to let me examine you first and see what I can do to help. Maybe then you can tell us what you want us to know."

He nodded, resigned to his fate. O'Laughlin held the lantern and Dougherty probed McGinley's head with his fingertips, looking for an irregularity or a soft spot or more bleeding. Apart from the cut on his forehead, there was nothing. His legs were not broken and he could wiggle his toes.

The left arm was not broken and rolling back the sleeve revealed no cuts, just scrapes and reddish patches that would blossom soon enough into full fledged bruises. The front of his unbuttoned coat covered his right arm, and when Dougherty pulled it back, he elicited a sound of agony and the patient's eyes glazed.

There was the source of his pain. His upper arm jutted out from his body, not in the normal manner, but as though it grew straight out below the shoulder, not properly joined to it.

He took a scalpel from the medical bag and, gently as he could, cut away both coat and shirt to lay bare the shoulder and upper arm. Sorry for the pain he was causing, Dougherty tried to distract him with talk. All he got in return was another moan, but for the moment McGinley's eyes were back in focus.

Just below the acromion, that point above the arm where clavicle and scapula meet, was a depression where none should have been. In the axilla was a bulge — the head of the humerus, which had slipped from its socket. There was no discoloration, no other lump or swelling, so the axillary artery had likely not been damaged.

"Do you feel my touch?" Dougherty gently brushed his fingernails along McGinley's forearm.

"No." Even the one word took effort.

The numbness came from pressure on the axillary nerves, typical of dislocation. The outward direction of the arm indicated a downward dislocation, probably the easiest to correct. From the bag he withdrew a clean linen napkin and a small bottle of chloroform.

If only Sean McBrien could have been there to help! But he had gone to Beaver Meadow and was not yet back. O'Laughlin would have to do. They moved the patient out a little from the wall and O'Laughlin inserted himself into the space provided, so that McGinley could lean back against him. Dougherty folded the napkin into a narrow cone and poured about a fluidrachm of the chloroform into its cavity.

"McGinley, can you hear me? I want you to take a deep breath and hold it until I tell you to release it. Can you do that?"

He nodded, and inhaled. Dougherty waited until McGinley could hold the breath no longer, then told him to exhale. As expected, the exhalation was followed by a deep inhalation just as Dougherty lowered the cone to within an inch of his nose. The effect was rapid. His eyes rolled back and their lids closed. His breathing eased. Dougherty set aside the napkin, ready to work quickly, hoping to avoid more chloroform. He had no assistant to watch McGinley's color and breathing. Still, the amount of anaesthetic he'd inhaled should be sufficient, but not enough to do him harm.

"All right, Mister O'Laughlin, keep your hands firmly upon his shoulders, just on the collarbone, and don't let him slide upward when I begin to pull on the arm."

Kneeling on his left knee close before McGinley, Dougherty lifted his right knee to a position in McGinley's axilla. The head of the dislocated humerus pressed upon his leg. He pulled firmly on the arm, the outer edge of his own leg thus a fulcrum across which he drew McGinley's humerus as a lever. In spite of his outward confidence, he'd never done this before, but he knew what to expect. It was like pulling McGinley over his knee by the arm, but he could not follow the pull because O'Laughlin was holding him firmly in place. His arm moved until the steady pressure produced a loud snap. The upper process of the humerus was back in place. It had gone smoothly, with no tearing of tendons or muscles. He would be fine in a few days, provided that he put no great strain on the limb until he gave it a chance to heal.

"Can we get a plank to carry him?" Dougherty asked O'Laughlin, who was all queasy, even though the patient happily slept the sleep of the just.

"I'll get it straightaway," he said, glad to have his first experience as medical assistant safely behind him.

Dougherty was left alone with the sleeping McGinley. He looked about in the gloomy light of the lantern. Deeper in the gangway was nothing but debris. A toppled wooden upright lay just outside the area of piled earth and stone. He went to look at it. It had a deep gash, the white gouge in stark contrast to the black coal dust that covered the rest of its surface. It was not rotted. This was a young mine. The timber was new, perfectly strong. If the other timbers were of equal quality, then no one could fault the mine owners for inferior wood. The cave-in may have come from shoddy workmanship in the placing of the beams, or even from some reason beyond anyone's control, but not from rotted wood.

He moved deeper into the gangway. Gingerly he poked in the rubble, half fearful of starting another slide. His fingers contacted something soft and he dug deeper. Even in the dim glow of the lantern there was no mistaking that he had uncovered a human hand, attached to a body still buried under the rubble. There was no hurry about digging this one out. The hand was limp. There was no pulse. He thought of McGinley's incoherent comments and wondered if this was Brogan — the man who wasn't there. Unfortunately, McGinley was unconscious and likely to remain so for some little while. He would be answering no questions just yet.

He turned at the sound of footsteps. Frank O'Laughlin and Charlie Shea were there with a plank and a coil of rope. He pointed to the hand.

"Well, who the hell is that!" Shea said. "There was only the two o' them here."

"D'ye think," O'Laughlin asked, "it could be Brogan?"

"The thought had occurred to me," Dougherty said. "Why don't we get McGinley out of here first and then dig for this one?"

"Doctor Dougherty," said O'Laughlin, "I hope ye'll not take this amiss, but why don't ye go out o' the mine with McGinley and O'Donnell? Me and Shannon'll find out who this is. God be good to him, ye can't help him now. Besides, clever as ye are at snapping an arm in place, I think — no offense meant, mind ye — I think ye'd be totally useless at moving that rubble."

A reasonable concern, Dougherty thought. He wouldn't want O'Laughlin poking around in his innards any more than O'Laughlin wanted him poking around in that unstable pile. They tied McGinley to the plank and got him to the main tunnel. From there the procession set off — O'Donnell leading the way, O'Rourke and Shea carrying McGinley on his plank, and Dougherty bringing up the rear, full of relief when at last he felt the touch of fresh air on his cheeks and saw the traces of outside light around the edges of the adit canvas — no longer so bright a light on this winter's day. It was near on four o'clock.

The cold was dreadful. The morning's temperature — 20° below zero — had earlier risen, but now had plunged again, as scattered flakes of snow drifted down from the rapidly darkening sky.

All around was the uproar of men at work — utter chaos to the casual observer, but to the worker the movement of parts in a well oiled machine. Mule-drawn cars emerged from the mine, creaking under the weight of coal destined for the breaker almost a half mile away — the breaker, whose dust and din dominated the lives of those who spent their days in its shadow feeding its insatiable appetite, their livelihood dependent upon its unbroken output of black boulders crushed into marketable portions of the precious anthracite. The steady thump thump of its steam engines and the squeal and shriek of the smashing coal were audible even at this distance.

Back in the shelter of the storage shed Dougherty put on his own boots and coat. Shea and O'Rourke laid McGinley and his plank across the tops of two barrels and headed back to the mine to finish their shift. The patient moaned, less from pain than from the temporary confusion of the anaesthesia. Dougherty lit a lantern. Manus O'Donnell was himself again, all over his brush with death and thankful to be alive — already indicating how much more thankful he would be once he could warm the inner man with "a drop o' the real stuff" — which he had earlier, no doubt, been swearing off for life, provided only that he survived. With a handful of kindling and a shovel of pea coal from the scuttle, Dougherty started a fire in the pot-bellied stove, then sat on the bottom of an empty nail keg to wait, in the sure and certain hope of McGinley's resurrection.

"Did you see Charlie Brogan down in the gangway before it caved in?"

"Brogan?" O'Donnell said, "That I did not. He was off sick. That's how come Shannon was working with O'Laughlin today. Me and McGinley was all by ourselves in that gangway. We was bringing a load out in a push cart — me pulling and Ned pushing — and I heard a great crack and the start of a rumble, and I turned to look behind me fer Ned, and then we both took off fer the main tunnel. Ned yelled something and then everything come down and there wasn't nothing to see but dust. We both went flat on our faces and started to get buried, but most o' the fall was behind us then, thank the dear Lord, but we ended up with a snoot full o' dirt and might'a laid there and died but fer O'Laughlin and Shannon. Ye've no idea how hard it is to move once the dirt starts to pile up on ye. Ye'd think it'd be easy enough to start digging yer own way out, but it ain't. Ye just can't move nothing enough to get any purchase. I seen it happening and I seen Ned going down, but divil a thing did I see o' Charlie Brogan ner nobody else."

"Maybe it wasn't Brogan," Dougherty said, "but there was somebody there. I saw him. I guess we'll find out who when they bring him out."

"It don't make no sense," he said, annoyed at being contradicted. "There wasn't nobody there! That's the fact of it."

Sensible or not, annoyed or not, he was wrong, Dougherty thought. That hand had been no illusion.

McGinley stirred, but the ropes held him in place. Dougherty left him that way — safer than rolling over and hurting himself again. He placed a hand on his shoulder to calm him. Eventually his eyes opened, out of focus at first and then, little by little, with increasing comprehension. He strained against the rope, but gave it up with a groan when he tried to use his right arm.

"Don't struggle," Dougherty said. "You're tied to keep from falling off the board. How do you feel?"

He relaxed his struggle, comprehending and ready to cooperate.

"Me head's full o' hammering and me mouth feels like it's stuffed with somebody's dirty socks. And me arm aches something awful. Where in the name o' God are we? How's Manus?"

"He's right here and he's fine." Dougherty said, stepping aside so McGinley could see O'Donnell. "You're out of the mine. Do you want to get up?"

"So I do," he said. "Can ye git the rope off'a me?"

"We can. But first tell me this. How many fingers am I holding up?"

He went through the routine. He counted Dougherty's fingers, touched his own nose with the tips of his fingers with eyes opened and then with eyes closed, tolerating the doctor as if he were some sort of idiot putting him through his paces before doing the obvious. Apart from the residual effects of the chloroform and the pain in his arm, McGinley was doing well. They undid the ropes and helped him sit up.

"Can you answer some questions?" Dougherty asked.

"I can."

"What were you trying to tell us about Brogan?"

He screwed up his face in puzzlement, then it all came back.

"Charlie Brogan! Did ye find him, then? He was in the gangway and he shouldn't'a been. He was sick as a dog since Saturday."

"Brogan in the gangway? What the hell are ye talking about? I never seen him there," O'Donnell said. "And that's a fact. Are ye sure ye wasn't dreaming it all up, Ned. I've heard o' things like that happening to people in cave-ins. After they come out of it they think they seen things that wasn't there. Ain't that maybe what happened?"

"No, it ain't!" McGinley was indignant. "Ye know damn well I saw him there before the roof ever come down. Ye must'a heard me call him. Ye can't deny that, now can ye?"

"Well, ye yelled something I couldn't make out, but that don't prove nothing. Ye was in the middle o' the dust from the fall. Ye might o' seen something or ye might o' seen nothing a'tall. Why would he'a been there, then? Answer me that. Ye said yerself he was too sick fer work."

"Ah, Manus O'Donnell, ye just love to argue, don't ye?" McGinley was getting his strength back. "Ye just love to hear the sound o' yer own damned voice, whether ye got anything to say or not, don't ye? Well, let me tell you something fer a change. Just when the roof was coming down, I turned and seen him leaning against the wall like he was ready to fall over. He wasn't even trying to get out from under. He was just leaning like he was about to slide down and lay there. I couldn't understand it... not why he was there and not why he wasn't trying to get out like any sane man would'a done. And it was Charlie Brogan and none o' yer damned silly blather is going to convince me otherwise!"

The discussion went no further. There was a bang as the door slammed open to another procession with a plank. This time Frank O'Laughlin led the way and Will Shannon held up the rear. It was already dark and the wind and snow had increased.

"It's poor Charlie Brogan, all right," O'Laughlin said.

"What did I tell ye?" said McGinley to O'Donnell, "Ye always have to be right, and ye damned well never are. Ye never learn! Why d' ye never listen to me?"

"McGinley, ye sound healthy enough to be off that plank, so just move outta the way and we'll put this one in yer place. Instead o' arguing, ye ought'a be glad it ain't you we're putting there in this condition."

O'Laughlin spoke with authority and McGinley hadn't another word to say; he stood up, a little wobbly at first, and then moved nearer the stove with O'Donnell. Interesting, Dougherty thought. O'Laughlin is the man to listen to. A small man, perhaps five feet seven inches, but with all the confidence in the world. He gave orders with the self-assurance of a man who does not even imagine that what he says will be disregarded. Even disguised beneath the layer of coal dust O'Laughlin was still a handsome man, with regular features and inquisitive, intelligent eyes. The sort of man with an infectious smile for his friends and a glare that would stop others dead in their tracks. He would have made a good sergeant in the army. Maybe he had, for all Dougherty knew. With a grunt of relief, they set down their burden and began chafing their hands, numb from the cold and the strain of carrying the body a half mile.

Brogan was, like all the others, covered in coal dust and dressed in the same rough work clothes. Atop his lifeless chest was his hat, to which was still attached his lamp, its body crushed and punctured so that almost all the oil had flowed out. The little that still dripped from it soaked into his coat.

"Has he a family?" Dougherty asked.

"None here," O'Laughlin said. "He come into the valley a while back looking fer work. He'd no talent to use above ground, so he hired on fer the mines — a laborer, o' course. Ye didn't have to know much to know he'd never been a miner. He's been boarding with the Widow Corrigan. I just sent one o' the boys over to her place to let her know about Brogan. She's not family to Brogan, but she's a good woman, and I know she'll be upset."

Dougherty knew Catherine Corrigan. She'd been sick when he and Jen first came to Penrose Valley. One of her boarders had sent for him. It was fever and it was all she could do to care for her boarders while she recovered. A few days later he went to see her again and Jen went with him. The two women took a liking to each other and still visited. Catherine Corrigan had two boys, one five and the other six years old. She'd had another who died shortly after birth. Maybe Jen had heard her speak of Brogan. He'd have to ask her.

"Let's clean him up before we do anything else," Dougherty said. "We may have to wake him at Mrs. Corrigan's, and I don't think she should see him as he is now."

But Dougherty was thinking of more than cleaning him up. What, he wondered, was the actual cause of death? It would come as a surprise if it were anything but asphyxiation or the crushing weight of the cave-in, but as a medical student in Philadelphia Dougherty had worked for Carl Gustavus Brownson, a doctor at the Jefferson Medical College, who was also a police medical examiner. He had no reason for suspicion, but old habits are hard to break.

Palpation of Brogan's limbs and rib cage revealed nothing. The skull was not damaged externally; there were scratches but no excessive bleeding. Almost certainly a case of asphyxiation. Still, he should look. O'Laughlin helped lift the upper half of the body, leaning it forward against himself, while Dougherty pulled back the coat to slide it over the shoulders and down the arms. His hand was flat against Brogan's back for a moment and he touched wetness. Hard to tell, but perhaps too viscid to be mere water. He brought his hand nearer the lantern. It was covered in mud and wet coal dust, and a barely discernible trace of red.

Outside a horse clattered to a halt near the shed. He barely adverted to it, his full attention now on the coat — more specifically, on the little round hole right in the middle of the wetness. A chill went up his spine. He set the coat carefully aside.

O'Laughlin had lowered the body back onto the board and was opening the heavy wool shirt, beneath which was a long-sleeved undershirt gray with age, the four buttons at the neck all carefully closed. He opened those as well, and again lifted the body forward so that Dougherty could remove the shirt. It too was damp with what now was clearly blood. Like the coat, it had a hole in approximately the same position — a hole which, no longer to his surprise, was matched by another in the undershirt, which they untucked from the trousers and pulled upward to reveal at last the condition of the body beneath.

It was at that moment that a booming voice thanked someone for his kindness in pointing the way. The door opened and a blast of cold air swirled past the edges of the man whose bulk all but filled the opening. Well over six feet tall, broad shouldered, blue of eye, and red of hair and beard, it was the one person whose presence Dougherty could not have been more pleased to see.

"Ah, there ye are, Major," said former army medical steward Sean McBrien. "I got back not long ago and yer lady, Mrs. Dougherty, asked me to come see what's holding ye up."

Dougherty did not immediately answer. His attention was riveted on something no longer a surprise to him, but still hard to accept. He had seen more than his share of them in the war. He was looking at a neat, round bullet hole right in the middle of Brogan's back!

Chapter II: No Least Concern for Life

Awaiting the sensation of a short, sharp shock,
From a cheap and chippy chopper on a big black block.
    W. S. Gilbert (1836-1911)
    The Mikado (1885)

[Tuesday, January 9, 1866]

He opened his eyes a slit in the pre-dawn darkness, not even the first streak of gray yet perceptible through the window. It may have been a sound or mere force of habit that had awakened him. In either case, he had no desire to get out from under the covers. The tip of his nose was so cold that he knew this day would be nearly as bad as yesterday, and all he wanted was to roll over and go back to sleep.

Jen called from downstairs and he groped sleepily toward her side of the bed, the coldness of the sheet telling him she had already been up for some time. He answered her, rubbed the sleep from his eyes and steeled himself to throw back the warm quilts. Then it all came back in a flash and he recalled that McBrien had promised to come early for breakfast.

For everyone in the shed, the bullet hole had been the first real shock. There was the conventional somberness of mood, of course. After all, someone had just died. But death in the mines was all too familiar — not a daily visitor, but hardly a stranger. Then too, everyone, with the exception of Dougherty himself had known Brogan, but none of them all that well, unless it had been O'Laughlin. And there were five years of war to consider, years that had left no one untouched by death. Dougherty could not even begin to count the number of the dead and maimed who had passed through his own hands these past years. Indeed, he wouldn't want to. Sometimes that worried him. Had he become callous? He hoped not, but he had to admit that his response last night to a cave-in death had been more intellectual than emotional.

But it was the bullet hole in Brogan's back that had done it. That belonged in the war, not in the mines of Penrose Valley. That changed things. This was neither accident nor casualty of war. This was murder and so, if Penrose Valley had a victim, then it also had a murderer, and therein lay the real horror. Their conventional somberness became something else. Accidents and warfare produce victims, but much as the result of blind chance, with the survivors secretly blessing their own good fortune. But cold blooded murder? Why? And who else might become a target?

"Shot!" McGinley had gasped.

"Ach! Ye're daft! It can't be!" O'Donnell was true to form. "Who'd'a shot him anyway? Hell, he ain't even been here long enough to have an enemy!"

That, Dougherty thought, may have been the most telling comment of all. If there had been no time for making new enemies, then had he found an old one already here? If so, who? And why?

O'Laughlin, oddly enough, had been the only one to say nothing. His expression, beneath its coating of coal dust, had been hard to read. Disturbed? Thoughtful? Dougherty couldn't tell.

In any case, there would be no preparing of Brogan for burial that night. An investigation would be required.

"So, what'll we be doing now, Major, sir?" McBrien had asked, simply assuming that Dougherty would take charge. So he had. He arranged for the body to be kept in the shed overnight. With the fire in the pot-bellied stove kept low, just enough to stave off freezing, it would be cold enough to preserve it for medical examination in the morning.

He invited McBrien home with him and Jen gave them supper. He had dreaded having to tell her about the death, even though she probably would not know who Brogan was. One more death would only bring back painful memories. He had even entertained the notion of not telling her about it. Utter foolishness, he realized.

He saw the sadness in her eyes, the trace of a tear. But it was only when he mentioned the man's name that the reality hit her.

"Oh, James, no! Not Charlie Brogan!"

"You'd met him?" Dougherty asked.

"No, not yet. But Mrs. Corrigan spoke of him so often that I was beginning to feel as though I had. He'd made a great impression on her."

"What has she said?"

"Well, now that I think of it, nothing very informative. It was just that she mentioned him so often. I don't mean that there was any romance." The trace of a smile came to her lips, and then she remembered why he had asked. "At least not yet. But she is a widow with two boys to raise and I know that she took him for a responsible sort. Oh, James, she will be so crushed by this! And her husband died in the mines, too. He owned the boarding house, but he wanted the extra income. Poor Mrs. Corrigan. She is so full of remorse. She thinks that she should never have allowed him to go back into the mines, when, in truth, how could she have stopped him? I must visit her tomorrow and see if there is anything I can do. She must be in such pain."

After supper he walked back to the pharmacy with McBrien and then had gone on to fetch Owen Williams, the telegrapher, to have him open the office and send a message to the county seat at Mauch Chunk. Williams had already heard of the death and of its apparent cause, but that still did not dispose him to go back out into the cold just to please Dougherty. He was not a man inclined to do favors for anyone, unless he felt he had something to gain and he had never much liked Dougherty anyway. But he was inordinately curious, grasping any bit of news as avidly as a miser does gold and just as avaricious at hoarding up his little grudges. This inconvenience would be one of them. With alternating grumbles and silences he did as asked and was visibly disappointed when Dougherty's telegram to Judge Barrett produced no more than the curt answer: "AWAIT RESPONSE A.M. BRODHEAD." He closed up and walked away mumbling to himself.

Dougherty smelled the aroma of the coffee and heard the subdued tinkling of dishes being placed on the table and pans being set on the new cast iron stove that dominated their kitchen. He smiled as he descended the stairs.

Jen had a rack of warm buttered toast in the heating cabinet over the stove, the table was set for breakfast, and the eggs and bacon stood ready for the big black iron frying pan as soon as McBrien arrived. It was already a little after six o'clock. She had placed two kitchen chairs in front of the stove, its oven door open to cast some extra heat, and she sat with her stockinged feet propped up on its edge. He stood behind her, his hands resting lightly on her shoulders, and she tilted her head back to look up at him. He kissed her and she patted the seat of the chair next to hers. He poured himself a cup of coffee, refilled hers, and sat down.

They sat at first in comfortable silence, their usual early morning ritual. The sharp pain of loss had started to dull and would, with time, recede still further. The seeds of hope may even have begun to germinate. She sipped her coffee. His eyes caught hers and she smiled.

"Will you have your answer from Judge Barrett first thing this morning?" she asked.

"I hope so. I'd like to do the postmortem right away. Barrett must have been out of town last night since Brodhead answered. If he is still not back, then I hope that Brodhead or another of the associate judges will authorize me."

Dougherty held no public office in Carbon County, but he expected to receive the authorization. It was highly unlikely that a doctor from Mauch Chunk would undertake the hour and a half train ride to Penrose Valley in this frigid weather. The telegraph office opened at seven-thirty, and he intended to be there when it did.

In the meantime he would enjoy this moment with her. They'd met in Maryland four years earlier, when she was Miss Genevieve Collingwood, nineteen years old and, in his opinion, still a child (although he was only a year older). Then he'd seen her with her mother caring for the wounded and his opinion changed. Now she was Mrs. James V. Dougherty and here she sat in her plain house dress, warming her feet at the oven door, and all he could think of was a candlelit September night and the joy of their first meeting. He had just reached out to take her hand in his, when there was a knock at the door.

He opened it and a gust of arctic wind blew McBrien into the kitchen. He pushed the door firmly shut as McBrien hung up his coat and hat on the rack and headed for the stove, rubbing his hands briskly together and holding them palms down over the hot lids. Jen got him a cup of coffee and a minute later the kitchen was full of the comforting sizzle of crisping bacon as the grease got hot enough to do the eggs.

Dougherty had joined the Sixty-ninth Pennsylvania just before Antietam and there had first met McBrien, a veteran of the Mexican war who had rejoined as a medical steward when the rebellion broke out. What began as a chance encounter had led to mutual respect and then to lasting friendship. As they ate, they discussed the killing.

"Well, there's no mystery about what killed the poor devil," McBrien said. "That hole in his back's a sure giveaway."

"All we need to know now," Dougherty said, "is just who put it there. That may be quite the mystery. If O'Donnell and McGinley are to be believed, then neither of them could have killed him, unless they were in it together and are lying. And if they were, you'd think they could have come up with a better story. But they both claim that no one else was there."

"Someone was," Jen said. "He certainly didn't shoot himself in the back."

"Yet neither of them heard a shot."

"Don't ye think it's possible," McBrien said, "that the sound of it was covered by the rumble of the cave-in?"

"I suppose so," Dougherty said, "but I doubt it. Even a small caliber pistol should have sounded like an artillery piece in the close quarters of that gangway."

"Could it'a been fired from the main tunnel into the gangway, do ye think?"

"I don't see how," Dougherty said. "That gangway is narrow and curves just enough so that anyone in the main tunnel couldn't have seen back to where the body was found. Then there's the dust. Even with a lamp you can't see more than a few feet in front of you when the mine is in operation, and it was in full swing yesterday when the cave-in happened."

"Leaving aside the problem of the sound," Jen said, "isn't it possible that whoever shot Brogan could have been concealed from McGinley and O'Donnell by the dust?"

"Unfortunately," Dougherty said, "by the same token the killer couldn't have seen them either, and from the positions of all three, Brogan was even deeper in the tunnel than the other two when the cave-in came."

"Maybe the killer was behind them in the gangway..." McBrien began, then stopped. "Sure, that don't work neither, does it? If he'd'a done that, he'd'a been trapped in there when the roof come down, wouldn't he?"

"He would," Dougherty said. "We'll see what else turns up when they clear the rubble today and shore up the roof, but I don't think we'll find the killer in there."

McBrien took out his watch and flipped open its cover.

"Getting near a quarter past seven," he said, "Have ye yer bag ready?"

"It's in the office," Dougherty said and went to get it. He had packed it with the paraphernalia of the postmortem: Cartilage knife, scalpels, rachitome, enterotome, scissors, Hey's saw, trephine and all the other odds and ends — sealing wax, sheet-caoutchouc, bougies, note cards. In a pannier he had gathered a number of wide-mouthed clean glass jars with tight fitting corks for wet tissue samples.

Dougherty carried the bag and McBrien the pannier, much as they had when they had gone to set up a field station for the wounded. As the regimental surgeon used to do, Jen gave him orders to bring back a full report. She followed that with a kiss on the cheek: Something the regimental surgeon had regularly omitted. Bundled in coats and mufflers and gloves, with hats pulled low over their brows, they marched off into the snow.

* * *

It was precisely seven-fifteen when Owen Williams bade a curt goodbye to his wife and ventured out into the winter weather. It was dreadfully cold as he looked up at the pearly clouds that blocked out the sun entirely. Another miserable day. There was bound to be more snow — as if they hadn't had enough already. Almost every morning as he left the house, he looked at the sky, found it wanting, and began his pre-work soliloquy with one version or another of why today was a miserable day. Too hot, too cold, too dry, too wet... It never seemed to occur to him that by his criteria there never had been and never could be a day that was not miserable. Life was an endless round of sending and receiving urgent messages for people who were so intent on the usually paltry content of their communications that they had no time for the one who made it possible. Without him there would be no messages, but they never thought of that, did they? Why should the day not be miserable when it was always filled with the same old round of useless people?

The job did have its hidden advantages. Williams had a constant and unrelenting curiosity about the business of every one of his neighbors, an overriding desire to know their secrets, to be able to sneer at their foibles. This was one of the things that had attracted him to depart from the years of working in the telegraph offices of big cities and to settle here, in a town that was only a few years old and where he could get to know everyone. And that he had done quickly. There was not a person in town he did not know, and know something about. The flow of telegrams in and out of his office was a fertile source of information. Nor was it entirely without its own possibility of profit. Arkwright himself had shown his appreciation for the odd bit of news from time to time, and he was convinced that eventually Captain Maddock might be willing to offer some more tangible rewards for the same. That remained to be seen.

Williams was a skinny little man with a perpetually sour expression and all the good cheer of an undertaker with a toothache. His upturned coat collar and its surrounding muffler hid the thin-lipped, down-turned mouth, the tuft of graying moustache, the sneer that seemed to be his only expression. The frowning brows above the sly eyes were all that presently could be seen below the brim of the hat that cast its shadow over the whole face and made it look as though he were a rodent peeping at the world from within a dark hole.

He had been seriously tempted to move more slowly today, to arrive late for the opening of the telegraph office. He had no doubt that Dougherty — and probably McBrien as well — would be there on the dot, expecting him to be at their beck and call. He couldn't stand either of them, a couple of micks that no amount of education would ever transform into anything else. No sows' ears to silk purses there. His dislike for Dougherty was usually kept in check by a degree of grudging acceptance that he was, after all, the only physician in town and might some day be needed. But he neither felt nor showed any respect for McBrien who was nothing but a one-time medical steward, now thinking he was a pharmacist. It never occurred to Williams that this was an attitude more than a little improvident. After all, Dougherty might need some day to write him a prescription, but it was McBrien who would have the last word on what it was that Williams actually swallowed in the dose.

It was tempting to make them wait, but their annoyance had to be weighed against his own pride in doing everything to the letter, everything on an undeviating schedule. Their annoyance wasn't worth the slight to his own pride.

He looked about him, expecting to see nothing new and not being disappointed. Main Street had a few small businesses, three saloons, two churches, the livery stable and blacksmith shop, McBrien's pharmacy, and the railroad station. The only possible point of interest was the building near the station. The "mystery building" people were calling it, but it was no mystery to Owen Williams. A substantial edifice built of new red brick with a stout oak door, its rear windows were high up on the wall and protected by bars. He knew that it was connected with what was going on in Harrisburg these days. A year earlier the legislature had legalized "railroad police," making it possible for the railroad companies to carry out their own law enforcement. Now they were going to pass a law giving the same authority to every "colliery, furnace, and rolling mill." This building was, he was certain, the new home for the protectors of the Philadelphia mine owners from the constant agitation of the miners for more money. Money for what, Williams often thought. For more drink? What else did they have to spend it on? Do them good to stay in their God-given place in the natural order of things and not get too far above themselves.

He put his hand into his pocket and felt for the office keys and from the corner of his eye he saw Dougherty and McBrien headed straight toward him. He would not be hurried.

* * *

It was dreadfully cold. Little droplets of vapor froze on their beards and moustaches as they set out on their way. The town was quiet. There were lights in the kitchens, but little other sign of life. The miners and laborers were already underground and the slate boys had gone their frigid mile to the breaker. When they got to Main Street there was a light inside the three-story office building of the Penrose Valley Coal Mining Company, but a cardboard sign in the window announced that opening was not until nine. The office building dwarfed the plain wooden structure just down the street, the company store, the true symbol of company power — the supplier of food, clothing, equipment, blasting powder, tools and endless resentment.

Their brisk ten minute walk brought them to the telegraph office just as Owen Williams arrived to unlock the door. He studiously ignored them as he fumbled with the key, apparently preferring the momentary clumsiness to the discomfort of removing his mittens.

"Doctor Dougherty, McBrien... right on time, eh?" he said as he pushed the door open and walked in ahead of them. He pronounced the word "doctor" as though it were an insult.

"Ah well, Mr. Williams," McBrien said, "ye're always such a bundle o' smiles and morning cheer, we'd not want to undermine yer mirth by being late. Besides, we're in a bit of a hurry, ye might say."

"The trouble with you, McBrien, is that you think you're still in the army, always in some infernal hurry and full of orders for the rest of us. Well, the war's over, my boy, so learn some patience."

Williams set out to show just what he thought of their hurry. He hung up his coat and hat. He chafed his hands and stirred up the fire in the little stove behind his desk and added a bit of coal. He snapped the elastic-edged cloth cuffs over his sleeves to protect them from ink. He settled himself at the desk and shuffled things about. He lined up sheets of paper in precise little stacks. He arranged a veritable parade of pens and pencils into rigid ranks and files, checking to see that each pencil had a pin-sharp point, using a small pen knife to dress up those that failed to pass muster. He looked to see that the inkwell was full. He checked his batteries and his telegraph key. Owen Williams was a man who thrived on detail.

When at last he could find nothing else with which to annoy, he tapped the key to let them know downline that he was ready to receive. For a time nothing happened, then his machine sprang to life as a steady stream of clicks and clacks poured out and he wrote furiously with his newly sharpened pencils, cashiering each as it became battle worn and replacing it with the next in order. Then, as abruptly as it had begun, the clatter stopped and their ears rang with the loud silence. He shuffled the stack of sheets into the same military precision demanded of the pencils.

One at a time he transcribed the messages into a fair hand from his jumble of penciled scrawls. Every few words he gingerly dipped the nib of his pen into the inkwell, made a test line on a scrap sheet, and wrote some more. He completed each page, tore it from his pad, waved it gently to dry the ink, and went on to the next. He said not a word, but it came as no surprise that Doughety's telegram was the last he did. He tore it from the pad and handed it over. It was not from Judge Barrett.

```
TO JAMES V DOUGHERTY MD STOP JUDGE BARRETT IN
PHILADELPHIA STOP AUTHORITY GRANTED STOP WILL
CONFIRM BY LETTER STOP SEND POSTMORTEM RESULTS
STOP A G BRODHEAD JR ESQ ASSOCIATE JUDGE
```

The sarcasm in Dougherty's thanks was wasted on Williams, who smiled his thin-lipped smile, satisfied that he had won his little victory. At the livery stable they saddled up and left for the mine, the horses full of life in the cold, blowing out vast clouds of steamy breath with each snort, enjoying the activity.

Even on this winter's day, there was no letup in the mining, and the breaker's noise increased with each step they took. Once at the mine they put the horses in the mule stable and set out to accomplish the task that to many seemed little short of ghoulish.

They expected the shed to be cold, but not unbearably so, since their fire of the night before should have lasted for some hours. What they found was a blast of hot air. Someone had tended the fire and added too much coal.

McBrien put a bucket of snow on the stove to heat, while Dougherty removed the burlap sacks that covered the body. The warmth had accelerated the progress of rigor mortis. It had already reached its peak and begun to dissipate. They laid out the tools on the bottom of an overturned box and lit a lantern. McBrien used the melted snow to clean the single window — all the outside illumination the shed had to offer — then put the refilled bucket back on the stove. They would need it again.

Dougherty began with the victim's physical appearance. Brogan had been a tall man, almost exactly six feet, probably between thirty and thirty-five years of age, in good health. The musculature of arms, shoulders, chest, and upper back indicated considerable physical strength. Patches of deepening *livor mortis*, the purplish marks left by blood settling after death, were diffused over the skin of the back, along with older bruises of varying size and age on arms and legs — congruent with what one should expect to find on the body of a mine laborer.

With the warm water, they cleaned the body. The coal dust on hands and face came away easily without trace of residue. Most men who worked in the mines for any length of time had black dust worked into their pores as a permanent, bluish discoloration of the skin, especially in the wrinkles and folds around neck or wrists or the palms of the hands and the knuckles. Not so with Brogan.

He had not shaved in a few days — probably since the start of his illness. His dark hair was fairly long, his countenance pleasant, his complexion as pasty as that of a corpse should be.

"Look at his hands," McBrien said. He had cleaned them and now held the palms up to the light. "It looks like he'd not had an easy time of it down in the mine."

The palms bore signs of recent hard labor, with no time to form calluses. There were the remains of bloody blisters, burst open and not yet healed. Dougherty felt them. They had been treated with a layer of grease or lard.

"That would fit with what we heard," he said. "O'Laughlin said he'd had no experience as a miner."

The backs of the hands told another tale. They had seen heavy use, with knuckles hard and knobby. The index and middle fingers of the right hand had once been fractured and knit crooked. They were large hands, those of a working man, had it not been for the softness of the palms.

On his torso were earlier cuts, not made by sharp instruments but more jagged, rougher abrasions now turned to whitish scar tissue, none of them significant. The face, too, had seen some abuse. The nose was slightly crooked, as though once broken and set imperfectly. Above the outer corner of the left eyebrow and running across it was another jagged scar about an inch in length. His right ear bore marks of trauma, again not recent. The pinna was mildly swollen and distorted, as though from a hard blow. Otherwise, the condition of the body was unremarkable — provided one excepted the small matter of that bullet hole which had yet to be examined and explained.

Dougherty pulled open the jaw, its rigor mortis almost gone. He had a full set of teeth, except for the past loss of the second upper left bicuspid. McBrien brought forward the lantern. There was dirt not only in the mouth but also in the throat and nostrils. About the lips and just within the mouth were traces of a frothy mucus.

They turned him over. The back revealed nothing new, but they examined the bullet hole more carefully than had been possible the night before.

"What do you think of it?" he asked McBrien.

"Ye mean the size, I suppose?"

Dougherty nodded.

"Well it sure ain't the kind o' bullet hole we've been seeing the last few years. It's small, ain't it? Something like a .22 caliber maybe, wouldn't ye say?"

"I would. But big enough to do the job."

The hole was just to the left of the spinal column at the level of the third or fourth rib. A bullet there could result in a quick death, provided it penetrated deeply enough. Even if it did not hit the heart, it would probably have done irreparable damage to the left lung. In either case, there should have been considerable blood. There was not. Dougherty reexamined the clothing to be certain. There was dried blood, but not enough. He would see why once the body was opened.

Dougherty gently probed the wound with the tip of his little finger, but was unable to penetrate, even where the bullet should have broken the ribs. From his bag he took a flexible gum-elastic bougie, a thin one, and inserted it, pushing hardly at all, not wanting to risk distorting the wound before he had seen its results within the chest cavity. It would not penetrate, but turned slightly leftward. The bullet must have been deflected before it penetrated. They took a last look to be certain they had missed nothing, then they replaced the body on its back and Dougherty made the incision from shoulders to sternum, thence down to the pubis — the cut that made new medical students re-taste their last meal and turn a pleasant shade of green.

He cut away and removed the front of the rib cage and opened the parietal and visceral pleura, expecting to find in the left lung signs of the bullet's passage. Nothing. Either the bullet had stopped within the lung before penetrating the anterior surface, or it had lodged in the heart. Further dissection revealed no such damage. The lungs were mildly congested with blood and there were bits of dirt in the trachea. The distribution of blood within the heart was unusual. The left chambers contained so little as to be almost empty, while the right were congested. The abdominal viscera showed dark patches of ecchymosis.

There was no bullet. Where had it gone? It was only once the organs were removed from the chest cavity that he saw the bruising in the posterior intercostal musculature, where blood had flowed between the layers. They turned the body onto its side and again inserted the flexible bougie into the bullet hole. He probed the path of penetration more deeply until he met a resistance that was probably the bullet. The path extended to the left, following the ribs and ending in the deltoid muscle. The tips of his finger detected beneath the skin a hard lump next to the tip of the bougie and there he made a small incision. The bullet lay just below the surface, a .22 caliber pellet, its shape barely distorted.

Bullets do not always do what one expects. Variations in cartridges or in the powder may change their velocity. The angle of contact with a bone may send even a large bullet off in a direction neither intended nor foreseen. A moving target makes for even more unpredictability.

"So there's no doubt it was murder, is there, Major?"

"Actually," he answered, "there is now considerable doubt. Brogan did not die from the gunshot wound. It must have been painful and the bullet might have done lasting damage to the nerves near the spine, but it was not fatal."

"Ye mean, Major, that it was the cave-in killed him after all?"

"Yes," he said, "The frothy mucus in the mouth points to asphyxiation. So does the dirt in the mouth and nose and trachea. For it to penetrate that far, he must have been breathing when he was buried."

"So he was still breathing when the roof come down?"

"I am sure of it," he said. "The blood distribution in the heart shows that and so does the ecchymosis of the abdominal viscera."

"Well, I'll be... So it ain't murder after all?"

"Not technically. It was most likely a case of attempted murder and that must be investigated, but the bullet did not kill him. The direct cause of death may be accidental."

"So what now?"

"We still need to know who shot him and why. We'll finish here and then we'll think how to proceed. I'll write up a report and have Williams wire it to Mauch Chunk."

For over an hour they packed tissue samples in jars, labeled and sealed them, and put them in the pannier. They sewed up the abdominal cavity. It was past noon when the body was ready for burial. By then the snow had begun anew and was falling in earnest.

They bundled up and were ready to get the horses, when the door flew open and O'Laughlin came in, shaking off the snow, all excited.

"Ah! There ye are, doctor. We heard ye was here, doing fer Brogan. I'm glad I found ye. It looks like ye was just about to leave."

"We were, but we are in no hurry if you have something you want to see us about."

"Aye, that I do. And I knew ye'd want to know about it. Yesterday when ye went looking in the gangway and come across Brogan, d' ye recall seeing the beams that was laying on the ground? The timbers that come down in the cave-in?"

"Yes," he said. "That concerned me. I thought the cave-in might have been due to bad timbers, but it wasn't. They were black from the coal dust, but still new and solid."

"True enough," he said, "but there was more. Ye may'a noticed that one o' the timbers had a deep gash where ye' could see the white of it? Well, I looked, and there was nothing there that could'a made a cut like that. In me own opinion, there's no explanation fer it save that somebody done it on purpose. He must'a used one o' the big drill bits or a crowbar or something else to pull that timber out and make the slide happen."

And suddenly they were back where they had been. It was murder after all, and perhaps a more heartless murder than they had suspected. That block had been chopped without a thought for the other men in the gangway, with no least concern for life.

The Diarist

> October 20, 1860 — For days I have sat before this blank page unable to write. Not from foolish remorse, but from exhilaration, a heretofore unknown ebullience. It is done. The expectation had become almost unendurable as the proper occasion came nearer and nearer at its own damnable snail's pace. Then came the day and I marveled at its ease of accomplishment. At the joy of its completion.

A sense of displeasure flared up and just as quickly subsided as he very nearly made an inkblot on the page. One thing he could not stand was slovenliness. Neatness, efficiency, precision, punctuality... those were things he prized.

He set down the pen and held his hands before his face, examining them dispassionately, as though they were the hands of a stranger. There was a decided tremor. Slight, but real. But even as he recognized it, it began to subside and within seconds he was again rock steady. Excitement is what it was. It encompassed him each time he went back in his mind to the glorious day. A beautiful autumn day, so unlike the sweltering July afternoon when he had made the discovery.

Once he had seen her, she became an obsession. Every chance he got he found himself somewhere near that white brick house, appearing in a variety of outward appearances so as not to be too obvious. How fortunate that his mode of employment made this possible. Its hours were variable and its demands such that his presence almost anywhere in the city would be plausible to those who knew him. But he could have saved himself the worry. No one saw him and no one ever asked. Even she had more than once passed by so close that she might have touched him, but he may as well have been invisible. Even that last time, when she had finally looked at him with full realization, it was as though she had never seen him before.

For almost three months he planned and waited, and was surprised to find that, protracted as those months had seemed, they were not without their reward. There was a pleasure in the completion, but there was also an unexpected pleasure in the anticipation, in the attention to detail, in the ever growing promise of fulfillment. The chase was in its own way as exciting as the kill. He had not expected that, but it was true. She had been right after all. Patience, Sammy, patience, she'd told him time and again.

But how boring these three months must have been for her. Her days so well regulated, so tediously the same. The strolls, the daily visits to her circle of friends and acquaintances, the occasional carriage ride with her father, the contacts with milliners and tradesmen. How insufferably dull, her dreary little life. How relieved she must be to be shut of it.

To the world it was all a great mystery. Who had done it? How had it been possible? What could be the motive? The newspapers made much of it at first, but then let it drift away as their interest waned. But even when they were most interested, they still had the thing all wrong, missing its beauty, its purpose and seeing the whole thing only with the ugliness that was the result of their own lack of vision. Nonetheless, he carefully clipped out all the articles and put them away to examine later. They would be part of his memories.

The deed had been simplicity itself. It was a perfect day for a stroll, and he counted on that; nor was he disappointed. He had acquired the use of the carriage without its owner knowing that he had done so, and he would just as easily return it when he was done. Just a nondescript old carriage, nothing ostentatious, nothing memorable.

Never had his senses been so alert. Each least sound was as clear as the note of a symphony, each complementing the others, none muffled or lost. Every color was startling in its clarity, each object in perfect focus. The clear air still held the fragrances of late blooming flowers, unsullied by the more offensive odors of the city. Time itself seemed suspended, each second an entity all its own to be savored and fondled and released only to be replaced by the next.

He parked the carriage in the most likely spot and waited. The minutes passed and he felt in the back of his mind the first faint tickle of doubt. And then she appeared, walking directly toward him. The street was, for the moment, all but deserted. He prepared to descend from the carriage. Then a woman with a baby appeared across the street, coming from the other direction and he hesitated. She didn't seem to be aware of him or the carriage, her whole attention focused on the babe in her arms; she cooed and smiled, oblivious to everyone and everything else. He was sure she wouldn't be a problem. He stepped down just as his prey arrived.

The silk of her visiting gown was as yellow as the sunlight itself, and she walked as though the world was hers, lost in her own thoughts and not attentive to him, until he placed himself directly in front of her, tipped his bowler and begged her pardon. Even then it took a second before she responded, hesitant but not alarmed, even at being addressed by a strange man. He called her by name — her new name, the one the maid had given him those months ago — and her expression changed to one of mild surprise and curiosity. Clearly she wondered if she should know him, if she should be able to greet him by name.

It's your father, he told her, he's taken ill and wants to see you. He even gave her his own name and occupation, knowing that it wouldn't matter. She would be telling no one else. Your father was taken faint, he said, and a family took him into their home. He sent me for you. And so she came with him. After all the planning and concern, it was just that easy. She climbed into the carriage full of appreciation to him and concern for her father. He had to control his distaste for her pathetic little smile as she thanked him over and over again for coming to get her. This is so kind of you, she kept saying. She did not suspect just how kind.

He took her directly to the house, its occupants only recently gone to visit a relative in another city. Her mind was clotted with thoughts of her father and when he handed her down from the carriage, she almost ran up the steps of the house he pointed out to her. He held the door and it was only when they were inside that she began to look puzzled. He could see in her face that she had begun to sense the emptiness of the building. She wanted to say something, began to open her mouth, then saw his eyes and her words dissolved into the beginning of a scream. He had no time for that. It could ruin everything. He silenced her, pleased with himself that he had so efficiently wiped away her fears.

He'd been through this before, but this time he had every intention of making sure. It was harder than he had anticipated, but he never for a moment doubted his capacity to carry it through. The cord was more than sufficient, as he had been sure it would be. It never broke, even when it drew blood, and that pleased him. And then he made her smile. A real smile this time, full of joy at what he'd done for her. He was at peace. And even later as he sat at the table thinking what next to enter into his diary, the Diarist could picture it all again in its every minutest detail, and he was satisfied. He had made her smile. And, after all, wasn't that what she had always wanted? She should be pleased, at last.

Chapter III: A Simple Social Call

If the duties of a family do not sufficiently
occupy the time of a mistress, society should
be formed of such a kind as will tend to the
mutual interchange of general and interesting
information.
    Mrs. Isabella Beeton (1836-1865)
    Beeton's Book of Household Management (1861)

[Tuesday, January 9, 1866]

The house was so quiet once they were gone. Jen smiled, thinking of how they had headed off into the cold as happy as two little boys who've discovered an unattended cookie jar. Well, perhaps happy was not quite the word. Enthusiastic maybe? Eager? Anyway, it reminded her of what she had seen so often in the war. Men setting off to do what needed to be done, difficult as it might be, ready to face some challenge and conquer it. It was not a feeling totally unfamiliar, now that she thought about it. She'd felt it herself when she and her mother had set off each day to tend to the wounded. Dreading it, yet eager to do it.

For now, however, her duties were quite different: She washed and put away the breakfast dishes, set out the day's supply of kindling and coal for the kitchen stove and the small fireplace in James's office, made their bed, swept and straightened up the kitchen. And then she was done. Not exactly a day of excitement.

She withdrew to the little room next to the kitchen that was hers for sewing and reading and sometimes just for thinking. It was a pleasant room with a lovely wide window, a small desk, two comfortable chairs, and a mahogany bookcase with glass doors, atop which was a framed photograph of her parents — both rendered stiff and stern by the photographer's art, when in reality he was strong, quiet, with a droll sense of humor, and she softly feminine but with a backbone of steel when it came to doing what was right.

The room was delightfully warm from the heat of the kitchen stove and through the window she saw the branches of their young apple tree bend and sway before the winter wind. Snow was on the way again.

She sat at the desk and her eye fell on the letter she had received from her mother on Friday. It was some months since she had visited from Maryland — just when Jen had most needed her. She took the next half hour to write and reassure her — without making a great point of it — that all was well. And what she wrote was mainly the truth; she could honestly say that she was beginning to recover. At least she hoped so.

But today her thoughts kept going back to Charlie Brogan, the sadness of his death taking her mind off her own sorrows as nothing else had been able to do for months. Catherine Corrigan had been wonderful to her during the hardest days, and Jen hoped that today she might repay at least some of that kindness.

It was still far too early to go calling. Penrose Valley was not the sort of community whose female population traipsed the livelong day from friend to friend, leaving a trail of *cartes de visite* and sipping tea in each other's parlors as they recounted the petty scandals of the moment or discussed the frivolities of fashion.

She would spend the rest of the morning, she decided, baking. The oven's heat would be as welcome as would the aroma of fresh bread. While it raised, she could pass the time mending clothes and darning stockings that had been sitting in the basket for two weeks now. She would bake enough bread for home and two large loaves to take to Mrs. Corrigan.

It was well past one o'clock when she set out with the bread tied up in brown paper, its warmth coming right through the wool of her mittens and its delicious, yeasty fragrance wafting away on the wind that now blew snowflakes against her cheeks. She still wore the plain brown house dress with its small white dots. To have changed into something more would not have been expected — indeed, would only have seemed pretentious and served to create the impression of a distinction between herself and Mrs. Corrigan that she neither felt nor to which she had any desire to pretend. She switched the two loaves over to her left arm, leaving her right hand free to clasp closer the neck of the blue Hispania cloak. It was now a few years old, but one of her favorites — out of fashion for the city, but perfect for a snowy day. Its voluminous folds let her toss an end across her shoulder for warmth and its ample hood shrouded her face from the sting of the icy bits now mixed with the softer snow.

* * *

Catherine Corrigan was a pretty woman, barely into her thirties and seeming sometimes much younger, a bit over five feet tall and with a figure not quite girlish but perfectly capable of drawing an admiring glance from her boarders when they thought she wasn't looking. She gave no notice of being aware of their admiration, finding it more flattering than offensive and harmless enough, all things considered. She had the fair skin, blue eyes, and dark hair of her Irish heritage, as well as the soft brogue that most of the Irish maintained even in America, being, as they so often were, left to themselves. Her hair had a curl to it that refused to be constrained by any effort to comb it flat and gather it at the back as current fashion favored. Wisps always managed to escape, falling down in front of her eyes and causing her, when her hands were full, to purse her lips and blow the strays out of her way, emphasizing all the more her attractiveness.

Today she felt like Martha in the gospels, busy about many things, but Catherine Corrigan had no expectation that anyone would come along and raise up Charlie Brogan as had been done for Lazarus. She was busy, but it was getting her nowhere. Her mind was so distracted that she moved from one chore to the next and went back and did the first one all over without even realizing it. Yet she was afraid to stop, afraid that if she did she might collapse into a fit of crying that would do no good for herself or for the boys.

And it wasn't enough, him dying. Being murdered. It was what she found when she went to clean the room and look for his burial clothes. What would she do about that? Who could she talk to about it? She'd been growing fond of Charlie, she had to admit it, and apparently he'd been fond of her, but she didn't know what to think now. She stopped in the middle of the kitchen, forgetting what it was that she had been about to do and instead looked out the window at the increasing snow.

* * *

It was not far to the boarding house and Jen had no need even to knock. Mrs. Corrigan must have seen her from the window; the kitchen door opened as she approached.

"So it's yerself, is it then?" she said, "Sure and I didn't recognize ye at first, all wrapped up as ye are like a Christmas present and just as welcome to me home. It's pleased I am to see ye, Mrs. Dougherty. Come in and get warmed."

She bustled about, hanging Jen's cloak behind the door and clucking with pleasure over the bread, breathing in the aroma and putting the loaves in the tin bread bin. She pointed Jen to the kitchen table, to the chair nearest the fire. Her boarders were still at work and her boys were out, so there was time for a visit.

Her greeting was warm and her smile sincere; but all her apparent good cheer could not hide the vestiges of red in her eyes nor the puffiness of their lids. She had been crying, and Jen knew that it would take little to make her cry again. The catch in her voice she covered with a cough as she turned to take two cups from the cupboard and put the kettle on the front lid of the stove. She spooned some tea into the teapot and then, her composure restored, sat to talk while the kettle came to a boil.

"I was so sorry," Jen said, "to learn of Mr. Brogan. Is there any way I can help?"

"Ah, Mrs. Dougherty, I thank ye kindly fer the asking and I appreciate it, but I'd guess there's nothing more fer us to be doing now. They sent fer his burial clothes and I gave them his Sunday best. They'll put him in his casket and get him ready to be waked. That'll be here tonight. It's the least I can do. Father McGuire'll read the funeral Mass in the morning, and I'm hoping they'll have the grave dug in time, never mind the snow."

"Has he any family to be notified?"

"None I know of. Charlie didn't much talk about family. He did once say he'd neither wife nor child, but more than that he never said."

She was hesitant, choosing her words carefully. Her eyes flitted from cupboard to stove to table and back again, the lids lowered, never directly meeting Jen's gaze. She was the living paradigm of the uneasy evasiveness of a person not accustomed to evasion. Mrs. Corrigan was holding something back, and that piqued Jen's curiosity.

That was when the door flew open with a mighty bang, a blast of cold air, and the joyous whoops and shrieks of her two boys, each shouting that the other was chasing him to put snow down his back. They slid to a halt at the sight of a visitor, but came back to life when they saw who it was. They'd seen Jen often enough these past few months and liked her, as she did them.

"Glory be to God! Ye're both soaked through! Putting snow down each other's backs, is it? Get outta them wet coats and boots and let's see what else ye need to change. Sometimes I don't know what I'm to do with the two o' yez."

Coats were hung near the stove to dry, boots kicked off and turned upside down to drain. But the snow down the back proved no more than a mutual threat. A change of warm woolen socks repaired all the damage. The boys took it in stride as she fussed and fumed — that sacred duty of mothers — but Jen noted that she also took advantage of the distraction to defer any more talk about Brogan.

She gave her full attention to the kettle, now at a rollicking boil. She poured the water into the teapot and set it to steep. Finally she poured four cups, the ones for the boys half filled with milk. The passing of sliced soda bread and the pot of elderberry jelly put the severest strain on the limits of their endurance. They waited, almost sitting on their hands in impatience, as their mother offered their guest the plate first and only then gave them their chance.

Daniel, the six year old, was the quieter of the two; never totally silent, but always taking a moment's thought before answering. He had his mother's blue eyes and dark hair, with its unruly curls. The five year old Michael, dark eyed and brown haired (perhaps, Jen thought, favoring his departed father), was usually all smiles and chatter.

Between her boarders and the sewing she did so skillfully for the people on the hill, Catherine Corrigan nourished the hope that her boys would have the start of an education and a way of escape from the mines — not impossible, Jen thought, as witness what her own husband had accomplished.

"And we didn't even do nothing and they hollered at us and chased us away. They even threw a stick, but I was too fast for them, wasn't I, Danny?"

The two boys had been going on about their day's adventures as Mrs. Corrigan and Jen chatted, still avoiding the topic of Charlie Brogan. It was not so much Michael's words as his righteously aggrieved tone that caught their mother's attention, which until then had been focused on the account of a gown she was altering for one of her customers.

"Who was it threw a stick at yez?" she asked him, "Who are ye prattling about?"

"The man at..." Michael began.

"Nobody," said Daniel. "He's going on about nothing. He's just a baby."

"I am not a baby! He did throw it. It wasn't nothing and you know it." Little Michael wiped his eyes and Jen's heart went out to him. He couldn't even take refuge in tears, not if he wanted to belie the insult of being called a baby.

"Ach, Michael, ye know he don't mean it. And you, Danny, don't tease yer brother. But I still want to know who done it. Who threw something at yez?"

There was a long silence, both boys looking downward, their tea and soda bread now forgotten. Mrs. Corrigan waited, no longer smiling. Finally, Daniel broke the silence.

"It was the man at the building." His voice was subdued, his tone full of guilt. "You know... that company jail. We went to look at it."

"Sure and didn't I tell yez both to stay away from there?" she said.

Lower lips quivered and two sets of eyes once more refused to meet hers.

"What did yez want there anyway? There ain't nothing there fer youngsters to play with and nothing ye'd want to see. I don't like them people down there."

Even Michael was wordless. He shrank down in his chair, for now content to be the baby and let his older brother produce the explanations.

"We weren't going to go there," Daniel finally said, "but Patrick and Bobby went and we went with them. Just to look... We're sorry, Mom... There was a big wagon come up from the train station with all kinds o' boxes and they was taking them in, so the doors was open and we just wanted to look, that's all. It was just for fun. We didn't do nothing. We just wanted to see. We wondered what they keep in there."

"That's right," his brother piped up, now that he could follow the other's lead. "We didn't do nothing and then this mean man with the gray beard comes out o' the door and tells us to get outta there. He said bad words, too. Then he threw the stick and we ran away. We didn't want to get put in the jail. Do you know what he called us? He said we were...."

"Never ye mind what he called ye. What's all this blather about a jail?"

"Everybody says it's a jail," Michael said. "Mr. Brogan says so... I mean he used to say that, before... before..." And the tears started. Their mother took them in her arms, her pain as great as theirs and the tears now back in her eyes, too.

"There, there now... No need to cry. I know ye miss him, but ye know that Mr. Brogan is all right now that he's gone to the good Lord. Why don't the two of yez go and play in the front room fer a while, while me and Mrs. Dougherty have our visit."

"I bet if Mr. Brogan was here he would'a done something to that man with the stick," sniffled the older. "He would'a taught him a thing or two."

"Mr. Brogan would'a told yez both to stay away from there," she said. "He wouldn't'a been hanging around with the kind that goes in and out o' that place."

"But I bet he wouldn't'a been scared. He'd'a scared them with his gun." Michael's voice began full of bravado, then slipped back to sadness as it hit him again that Brogan would no longer be around, with or without his gun. Jen felt so very sorry for them. Whoever had killed Brogan had brought all this other misery as well.

"He'd do no such thing," their mother said, with a sidelong glance at her visitor. "He wasn't the sorta man to go after people with a gun. Ye never seen him do such a thing."

"But he had a gun, Mom, you know he did, and that's what guns are for. I bet it's in that box you put in the cellar yesterday." Daniel's insistence did not please her at all, and Jen knew that her displeasure came in large part from the fact that he had said this in her hearing.

"Yez can both go and play now. We'll talk about everything later." She headed them toward the front room, then came back and refilled Jen's cup, offering no comment on what had just transpired. With the corner of her apron she dabbed at her eyes.

The uncomfortable silence lengthened. Jen had to make up her mind. She could simply ignore all that had been said; or she could take the plunge and see where it led. She had no desire to jeopardize their friendship, but she knew that ignoring what she had heard would serve no good purpose for either of them. She made the only sensible decision.

"Mrs. Corrigan, were you aware that Doctor Dougherty is conducting an examination into Mr. Brogan's death? In fact, that is what he is doing right now."

"The boys from the mine told me about it when they come fer the clothes. But it don't mean much, does it? It's too late fer a doctor. It's not that I don't appreciate his efforts but, if ye'll excuse me saying so, I don't see what earthly good he can do. It's not like Brogan can answer any questions, and it sure can't bring him back, can it?" Her voice cracked and she closed her eyes. Her tone was not belligerent, just dejected.

"I know it must seem hopeless. The whole thing is so dreadful. But my husband was specially trained in these matters and I know that he can help. But he will need all the information he can get, and some of that must come from those who knew Mr. Brogan. Can you help, do you think?"

She closed her eyes and put her hands to her face as if about to cry, but did not. Jen could see the internal struggle as she decided if she should tell what she knew, if indeed she knew anything worth telling. She sighed. She rolled a corner of her apron into a tight little tube and then unrolled it and flattened it carefully against her thigh with her palm. More than once she was about to speak then decided against it. Jen waited, hoping she had not made a mistake and pushed her too far.

"D' ye really think he can do anything at all?"

"He can try, but his efforts may be fruitless if people refuse to tell what they know."

"Truth to tell, there's precious little I can say. Maybe nothing at all."

"Did Mr. Brogan have enemies? Was he worried? Did he seem afraid of anyone?"

She considered that, saying nothing at first, but her silence was not the refusal to answer so much as the effort of intense concentration. The questions had sparked some memory. Jen did not push, just let her go at her own pace.

"When they said he was shot, I couldn't credit it, d'ye know? A mine accident? That could happen to anybody. But shot? Who'd want to hurt Charlie Brogan? But, ye know now that ye ask, I think there was something. Brogan was friendly enough and spoke when spoken to, but most o' the time he had something on his mind, like a weight he couldn't get rid of, if ye know what I mean. He'd say what was fitting to say and then he'd be gone back to thinking again."

"Did he give you any indication of what his problem was?"

"That he did not. I think it was something from the past, cause he never done nothing here that'd account fer it. The sight o' me two boys always perked him up, but even then it was never long till he'd be brooding again."

"And he never gave you any clue that he might have had enemies?"

"Not in so many words, but what the boy said was true. Charlie did have that gun. I found it yesterday with his things. But o' course, there ain't many as don't have one these days."

That was true, Jen thought. They were common enough, especially since the war. Even James had a gun that had been given him by his landlady in Philadelphia when he finished his medical studies and left for the army.

"You said he didn't like the gang that works down at the new building. Did he say why? Do you think he had some sort of quarrel with them?"

"Sure, he never said fer certain, but I ain't heard o' nothing like that. I'd say he felt like the rest of us — ye know what I mean... The new building is part o' the company and that bodes no good fer the likes of us. And ye've seen fer yerself the crew that's down there. A bunch o' toughs. City people from Philadelphia, I'd say. They're up to something and it ain't going to be fer our benefit in the end."

She was right. They were unsavory types. Their stares had made Jen uncomfortable more than once when she had passed by the place. She tried another tack.

"Did Brogan ever carry the gun with him, do you know, or did he simply keep it among his belongings?"

"He might'a took it with him, but I couldn't say fer sure. I never seen him with it."

"Do you know what was wrong with him these past few days?"

"No, not fer sure. He never had the runs, nor lost his meals. He just said he was too sick to work and stayed in his room. He come down fer meals, when the others wasn't here, but he didn't eat much. If it wasn't that he said he was so sick, I'd a taken it fer just plain worry. Besides, when he wasn't working he wasn't getting paid and nobody's likely to do that just cause they're worried about something, are they? He really musta been sick."

"How did he get along with the other boarders?"

"They all got along fine, I'd say. I don't tolerate no fighting nor bad language. They can come and go as they please, long as they're quiet about it and don't disturb the house. But they always eat together and there was never a sign o' them being at odds. Any arguing was always the good natured sort that had them all laughing in the end, don't ye know? Nothing mean."

"Was Mr. Brogan a special friend of any of them? Or did he show any special dissatisfaction with one of them?"

"Well, there was just Brogan and the three others and they all seemed to get on fine with one another. Two o' them sleep in the front room upstairs and one in the back. O' course there's room fer two in the back room easy, and that's where I'd'a put Brogan, but he didn't want to room with nobody, so he lived in the attic. It ain't so nice in a lot o' ways. Hotter in summer and colder in winter, not high enough fer somebody as tall as Brogan to stand up straight except at the roof's peak. There ain't hardly room fer nothing but a bed and a chair. But that's what he wanted, he said. I didn't argue the point and none o' the others begrudged it to him."

"Have the others lived here long?"

"Let's see... Frank McGehan's been here all o' three years now and Hugh Doyle — he rooms with him — come a year before that. Marty Carroll's been here six months. He's in the back room. Fer a while he roomed with another boyo, Eddie Malloy, but Eddie found himself a good girl, a skinny little thing name o' Celia Lawler, but pretty in her own way and a hard worker. They married and a cousin o' hers found Eddie a better job in Pottsville, so off they went. I ain't heard o' them since."

"But so far as you know, Mr. Brogan had no sort of falling out with McGehan, Doyle, or Carroll? And am I right in thinking that he never even met Malloy?"

"Just as ye say... no arguments and he never even laid eyes on young Eddie Malloy."

"When your boarders go out, where do they go?"

"Ye mean other than work or church? To the saloon more than likely, I never ask, but they don't come home stinking. Like I said, they're a good lot."

"Do they always go out together?"

"No, not always. They all have their own buddies."

"Did Brogan ever go with them?"

"Once or twice, I'd say, and even then he come back early and come out to the kitchen to talk and to play with the boys if they was still up and about, like he did most evenings. He was a good man."

Her eyes were brimming again. Jen wanted to put an arm around her, but knew if she did, they'd both end up in tears.

"What else can I tell ye?" she asked.

"What about the box the boys mentioned? Is there anything there to help us?"

Her reaction surprised Jen. She had expected either acquiescence or resistance, not this evident embarrassment. Mrs. Corrigan's cheeks colored and she averted her eyes. With only a moment's hesitation she stood up, lit a candle, and went to the cellar for the box. Jen heard sounds of objects being moved, as though the box were hidden behind other things. When she returned she had in one hand a cheap and well worn traveling case held closed by leather straps, a black bowler and the candle in the other.

She extinguished the candle and cleared a space on the kitchen table. There she placed the leather case, unbuckled the straps, and laid back the lid to reveal the contents. Together they removed the various items and arranged them in stacks.

There were clothes — a well worn jacket, trousers, shirts, stockings, and a few sets of unmentionables. Nothing was new, but all of it was clean and well cared for. Even the mending, where mending had been required, had been done with precision and care.

Beneath the clothing was the gun the children had spoken of. When Jen had heard mention of the gun, it had occurred to her that Brogan might well have been in a gunfight with someone and been killed in the process. But here it was, so he must have been unarmed when he was shot. The manufacturer's name was stamped into the barrel. Colt, Model 1862. It was similar to the pistol that James had, which she knew was a .36 caliber, but this was shorter barreled than his, easier to carry in a pocket or under a jacket. The stock was walnut, worn and polished by use, cracked on one side but not broken away. It would have held five shots, but was now empty.

Two things remained in the traveling kit: A packet of letters, neatly tied with a faded red ribbon, and a large brown envelope.

"Have you already looked at these?" Jen asked.

"I have not," she said. "I can read some, ye understand, and I can write me own name, but the handwriting ain't so easy fer me. Anyway, I considered them things private and I just put everything away in his kit cause I didn't want to leave nothing laying around where somebody might look at what Charlie didn't want seen. I didn't want nobody snoopin' into his business. Like I said, he was a man liked his privacy. But I guess now it don't much matter and looking might even help yer husband figure out what to do next. I don't like it, but let's look and get it over with."

There were ten letters in all. Jen looked at the first two or three. They began, "My dearest Charles," and ended, "Your loving Mary." No last name, no return address. They expressed Mary's love for Charlie Brogan. By their content, he must have answered her from wherever he had been and Mary longed for his return.

The brown envelope held a hodge-podge of documents, newspaper clippings, and handwritten notes, only one of them seemingly new. Whether they would tell what had happened to Charlie Brogan, she could not say, but the letters from Mary filled her with a sudden and dreadful sense of sadness.

"Mrs. Corrigan," she said, "may I take these things with me? I would like to show them to my husband. They may help us learn what happened to Mr. Brogan"

"Take them, please do. Ye'll take good care o' them, won't ye?"

"You may be sure that I will."

Mrs. Corrigan seemed satisfied and Jen had no way of knowing that her last vestige of uneasiness was due not so much to parting with the items in the box as it was to her guilt at what still remained in the cellar — something she alone knew about now that Brogan was gone.

Jen put all the papers, the letters included, into the large envelope, and took the gun for James to examine. She was glad she had come. It had turned out to be far more than a simple social call.

Chapter IV: To Wake the Dead

WĀKE, n. 3. The setting up of persons with a dead body, usually attended with drinking. *Ireland*.
   Noah Webster, LL.D. (1758-1843)
   An American Dictionary of the English Language (ed. 1852)

[Tuesday, January 9, 1866]

The snow intensified and windy gusts flung it in their faces. The horses forged ahead, yielding to their riders' will, even though, left on their own, they would have had the sense to find a sheltered spot and wait it out. As they neared town, they picked up speed, sensing the proximity of the stable with its warm stalls and abundant oats. It was not yet three o'clock, but the looming clouds and whirling snow created the illusion of already encroaching twilight.

"Do ye intend to wire a report to Mauch Chunk tonight, Major?" McBrien shouted over another of the windy blasts.

"I've been thinking of it, but I hesitate."

"Ye mean our friend Williams?"

"Precisely. I'll write the report and send it to Brodhead by rail."

"Ye realize, Major, ye'll never get it to him today then. The down train leaves at 3:20 and it'll take longer than that to do the writing."

"I'll wire him that we've done our task and that he can expect the report tomorrow. That will be soon enough."

What could he report? He had no clue to the killer's identity, even though he knew the bullet was not the cause of death. Brogan could have gone a long way with that bullet inside him, so he may not have been shot in the mine. That substantiated the claims of the men in the gangway that they had heard no shot and it cleared up the issue of how the killer could have taken aim in the mine's murky darkness. He hadn't. He had wounded Brogan, followed him to the mine, found his chance, and simply knocked out the supporting timber. Gravity did the rest. And the killer did it without a second thought for the other men in the mine.

Was it possible that one person had shot Brogan before he entered the mine and someone entirely different had killed him once he was inside? It was a theory, but it strained credulity. It would suppose either an organized conspiracy or the existence of two unrelated mortal enemies both hunting Brogan at the same time. Was that plausible for someone who had been in town so short a time as Brogan? It might have appealed to Edgar Allan Poe for one of his stories. It did not suit in the real world.

In the back of Dougherty's mind was a disquieting thought: In spite of what they had learned, it was all too likely that no real investigation would ever take place. There was no one in Penrose Valley, no resident representative of the sheriff and no police presence to undertake the task. Dougherty's own mandate was now fulfilled. No witnesses had come forth and none were likely to. That might end the matter, and the thought angered him.

It was a relief to arrive in town. They saw to the settling of the horses and then stopped at the telegraph office, where they burdened Owen Williams with an agony of indecision — caught between the Scylla of his usual desire to heap up obstacles in the path of whatever was wanted of him and the Charybdis of his endless appetite for knowledge of his neighbor's business. His eyes lit up when Dougherty mentioned a telegram to Brodhead and, rejecting the joys of obstructionism, he took up pad and pencil and waited hungrily for the message. The glow in his eyes flickered, faded, then failed altogether as he took down its contents: **TO ASSOC JUDGE A G BRODHEAD ESQ AUTOPSY COMPLETED STOP RESULTS TO BE SENT BY RAIL WEDNESDAY AM STOP DOUGHERTY.**

"Ye needn't thank us, Mr. Williams," McBrien said. "We know ye don't care about our doings, so we'd not have ye wearing yer poor fingers to the bone having to tap out a big long boring telegram on so bitter a day as this."

An obedient man, Owen Williams! He took McBrien at his word and didn't thank them at all, just sent the telegram and got back to whatever he had been doing, trying his best to pretend that any report of theirs really did mean nothing to him.

The lingering aroma of the morning's baking lent some cheer to Dougherty's homecoming, but there was no answer to his greeting.

The note on the kitchen table told him where Jen had gone. With nothing else to distract him, he went to his office, made a fire, lit the lamp, and got down to business. He put the tissue samples safely away and began the report.

It was well past four o'clock and he had almost finished the first copy when he heard the back door and Jen called his name. He looked up, surprised to see that it was dark as night outside. She came into the office still wearing her cloak, the snow on her shoulders so slight that it must have all but ceased. She kissed him, then handed him the large brown envelope.

"How is Mrs. Corrigan holding up?" he asked.

"It's hard on her and the boys. She was even more attached to Brogan than I'd realized. Did you know that he is to be waked at the boarding house this evening? Should we go?"

"I think so. McBrien will be going, too. We heard about the arrangements when she sent out the clothes for his burial."

He opened the envelope and spread its contents across the desk.

"These belonged to Brogan," she said. "We can examine them later, but I would like you to look at this first."

She shuffled through the pile and pulled out a folded sheet torn from a cheap writing tablet. Even at a cursory glance it was different from the rest. They were faded and worn frail from folding and unfolding, this was new, none of the tint that such cheap paper so soon acquires.

"Oh, there was this, too," she added.

From somewhere in the voluminous folds of her cloak she drew forth and set before him a .36 Colt Police Revolver. He had seen many of them in the war. They were popular with officers as personal sidearms. They were lighter than the official models — less than two pounds — but just as functional. This one was well cared for, even with its damaged butt. He smelled the barrel. It had not been recently fired.

He unfolded the paper. There were four lines of text, written in pencil, smudged, and bearing the marks of soiled fingers.

> I no all wat hapened in Philadelphia.
> I hav wat you want.
> Mete me at Brakker Noon — Mundy.
> P.S. — Miss this mete at yur perl!

It was in a hand as clumsy as that of a child — the work of someone unused to writing, or wishing to appear so.

"Who is Mundy?" he asked. "Can you think of anyone of that name?"

"I wondered that when I first read it, but I had time to think on the way home, and I've reconsidered. I think it means 'Monday,' not 'Mundy.' Yesterday. Couldn't this be from someone who wanted to get Brogan out to the breaker where he could kill him?"

"Of course," he said. "It must be."

"I wonder, then, why he went to the mine instead? Why was he shot there?"

"He probably wasn't," Dougherty said, and explained what they had learned about the cause of death.

"He could easily have been shot near the breaker," Dougherty said. "The report of a .22 revolver is not loud. It would have gone unnoticed. The steam engines and chain drives make a dreadful din, and even their sound is nothing compared to the grinding of the breaker."

Its roar is nearly unimaginable. Cars from the mine are dragged clanking to the top and their contents dumped down into the hopper of the crusher, the two enormous iron toothed cylinders that pulverize the coal into smaller pieces called chestnut and acorn and pea coal, from which the breaker boys pick out the slate and stone and scrap that eventually end up on the ever growing culm heap, the main source of the town's black dust.

"Then we are left with two questions. What happened in Philadelphia? And what did the letter writer have that he knew Brogan wanted?"

"We may find some answers in the rest of the papers you've got here," he said.

"So we may," she said, "but it's already late. We'd best eat supper and change if we're going to Brogan's wake. There's fresh bread and a bowl of beef stew in the pantry."

By the time they had finished eating, Dougherty would much have preferred to stay home. The beef stew was hot and savory, full of split peas and onions and potatoes. With the fresh bread it was just what the doctor ordered for a cold winter's night. The next step should have been to read or talk for a bit, damp down the fires, and retire to the comfort of their feathered bed. Alas! By 6:30 they were dressed in proper wake attire and on their way out.

It was still dreadfully cold, but the snow had practically ended and the wind was little more than an intermittent breeze, leaving behind a clearing sky with patchy clouds alternately revealing and concealing the rising half moon. From further up the hill came the sound of sleigh bells, a more pleasant pastime in the moonlight than walking to a wake. The belles and beaux, covered with lap robes and Afghans, loved to swing around the neighborhood to the jingling of bells and the crack of the whip.

The passage of earlier horses and pedestrians had worn a path in the street along which they walked, the moonlight reflected from the fresh, clean snow providing a soft illumination. There were plans afoot to place streetlights throughout the town, but thus far no light standards had sprouted on the corners. The only gas lights were still confined to the area of the Hazle Creek Bridge Station.

Mrs. Corrigan's house was alight and neighbors came and went. It was a small wake — not so much, Dougherty suspected, by reason of the bad weather as because so few in town knew Brogan. No keeners, no lamentation, but no less sad for all that.

McBrien was already there, but there was no time for conversation. Father McGuire was there, too, and he was ready to lead the rosary for the repose of Brogan's soul. They joined in the Our Fathers and Hail Marys and the telling of the Sorrowful Mysteries. Father McGuire's voice alternated with the responses, the rhythmic cadence and the steady, repetitive murmur offering a comfort beyond the power of mere words. It ended in silence and then, one by one, voices raised in whispers and then in normal conversation.

The coffin sat atop two sawhorses, its lid removed and set against the wall. Brogan's face was cleaned, his hair combed, and his hands crossed restfully across his chest. In the soft light of the whale oil lamps he lay quite at peace, without hint of bullet hole or the crudely sutured autopsy incisions hidden beneath the shirt and coat.

"Doctor Dougherty, how have you been? And Mrs. Dougherty? I am so pleased to see you. It is kind of you both to be here."

Father McGuire was short, less than five and a half feet tall, compensating for it in broadness of beam. He was in his mid-sixties and had come as pastor to Penrose Valley from Philadelphia some few years ago when the parish of Saint Margaret was founded. He was balding, with the remnants of his graying hair cropped shorter than was the fashion. The gold chain of his watch lay across the broad expanse of his clerical vest, the only decoration to relieve the somber black. From his pocket he withdrew a clean white handkerchief which he used to polish the lenses of the spectacles whose wire frames he had so carefully freed from behind his rather large ears. It was a habit, rather than the response to any real need to clean them. He drew Dougherty off to one side.

"I hear you've undertaken to investigate Brogan's death, Doctor," he said. "Have you learned anything?" His voice was strong — the result, Dougherty supposed, of years of preaching and because he was hard of hearing — so his words were audible to more than his intended audience.

"Very little, Father, apart from the cause of death. At this point anything else is pure conjecture. I performed an autopsy today, but that is as far as my brief extends, and that was only because I happened to be here. I expect that any real investigation after this will fall to the sheriff." He tried to keep his voice down by leaning a little closer to the priest but was not totally successful. Heads turned toward them and ears pricked up.

"Do you, now?" he said with the ghost of a smile, as he slipped the wire frames back onto his ears and settled the spectacles upon his nose. He refolded the handkerchief, smoothed its creases, and replaced it in his pocket. "It's my own opinion, Doctor Dougherty, that unless you interpret your authority somewhat more broadly and continue to work on this matter, the case will die as fast as Brogan did.

"Now I don't want you thinking the wrong thing," he went on, "It's not that I suspect some nefarious plot to avoid finding who did this. It is just that Charlie Brogan was a good man, but for many he'll be just one more dumb mick that got himself killed, no doubt by some other dumb mick. Aren't they always fighting anyway? Besides, Sheriff Reuben Ziegenfuss isn't here. He's in Mauch Chunk and there's no great likelihood he'll spend a lot of time on this."

"There is Doctor Longshore," Dougherty said, "and he no further away than Beaver Meadow."

Doctor John B. Longshore was well known to Dougherty, since Beaver Meadow is where he had been born and raised and where the rest of his family still lived. Longshore was the county coroner and Beaver Meadow was just over the mountain, less than three miles away. It was an arduous trek by carriage in bad weather, but it was only fifteen minutes by train.

"Doctor, wouldn't you agree that if you were to call upon Doctor Longshore for help, he'd tell you that you've already done all that he could have done? The autopsy is over and Brogan's ready for burial. Doctor Longshore is at the end of his term of office as coroner and I doubt he will get or want another. If you don't pursue this matter, who will?"

It occurred to Dougherty that Father McGuire was trying to persuade him to do what he already wanted to do in any case, what he probably would have tried to do even without anyone's insisting upon it. It was himself he was hoping to convince by getting Father McGuire to supply the reasons. And so he graciously yielded, knowing that McBrien and Jen would never let him live it down if he unintentionally proved his point so well that he relinquished the matter into the hands of someone else.

"I will contact Judge Barrett for authorization to continue the investigation beyond the stage of medical questions. I don't know if he will want to grant that."

"Perhaps you will allow me to see to that," Father McGuire said. "I will contact the Judge on your behalf. I am aware of your work with Doctor Brownson at the Jefferson Medical College. I've no doubt Judge Barrett will grant the authority."

They were both satisfied with the conversation, so when his driver appeared with his coat and hat and announced that his buggy was at the front door, Father McGuire said his goodbyes to Mrs. Corrigan, and Dougherty saw him out to his carriage.

When he returned, Jen was with Mrs. Corrigan and the other women. The two boys, all spick and span in their Sunday best, sat nearby whispering, unable completely to tear their eyes away for more than a moment from the body. The men had adjourned to the kitchen, so Dougherty followed them.

"Ah, there ye are, sir," said Sean McBrien, seated at the kitchen table next to Frank O'Laughlin. "Have a seat." He pulled another chair up to the table.

"Frank here was telling me just now how he was at Antietam, same as ourselves. He was in the 125th Pennsylvania—a sergeant. He seen action in the West Woods, down by the Dunkard Church."

So Dougherty had been right about O'Laughlin's air of authority.

"Ye'll take a drop with us in honor o' Brogan?" Frank asked.

"I will," Dougherty said and O'Laughlin poured him two inches of good Irish whiskey.

There were three men seated near the stove, deep in discussion, all of whom nodded and murmured a quiet, "Evening, Doctor," and went back to their talk. Three more were seated at the table with McBrien and O'Laughlin.

"I expect," said McBrien, "that ye may not yet be acquainted with these gentlemen." He named them as Frank McGehan, Hugh Doyle, and Marty Carroll — Mrs. Corrigan's three surviving boarders.

All three were dressed in their best, chins freshly shaved, shirt collars buttoned up tight, and looking uncomfortable, all — save for the youngest — puffing on their pipes. Dougherty withdrew a cigar from his inner pocket, clipped its end, and accepted McGehan's matches with a nod of thanks. He took his time lighting up, thinking how best to open the conversation. McGehan saved him the trouble.

"I hope ye'll not take it amiss or think me an interfering type," he began, "but I heard what Father McGuire said to ye after the rosary. Are ye gonna learn who killed Charlie, God rest him?"

McGehan was the oldest of the boarders, a short, stocky man with kindly blue eyes and a soft voice. He was most likely in his mid-fifties, but the years in the mines had taken their toll, and the incessant work in the cramped spaces of the low, narrow gangways had given his shoulders a permanent stoop.

"I don't know, Mr. McGehan. I will try. Do you think you can help?"

"Well, sure and I've no idea at all who might'a done such a thing, but I know something was eating at Brogan ever since he first come here. Wouldn't ye say so, Hughie?"

"As ye say... something was bothering him," Doyle agreed, "but I never thought it nothing to make him fear fer his life. It was just he was thoughtful like... always had his mind somewhere else." Then came the anger. "But it's too late to ask him and ye sure as hell ain't going to find out his secrets by slicing up the poor bugger like ye done. Ye'd no right to do that to the man."

He spoke without lifting his eyes, avoiding even a glance in Dougherty's direction, but the resentment was aimed at him. Doyle was in his early thirties, heavily muscled, with enormous, strong hands that gripped the edge of the kitchen table as he poured out his outrage at what Dougherty had done to his friend. He wondered if Doyle were about to hit him. Of course, McBrien would not allow that to happen. He sat, unmoving, seemingly unconcerned, his hands on the table, cupped around his glass; but Dougherty knew McBrien, whose eyes were focused on Doyle's hands, was ready to respond to the least threat.

"Oh, fer Heaven's sake, man, stop and think fer a minute will ye, before ye make a damned idiot o' yerself?" O'Laughlin's voice was quiet, conciliatory, but full of the authority Dougherty had noted the day before. "It ain't the doctor that's at fault here, is it? And it ain't him yer really mad at, is it? It's the bastard that done fer Brogan ye'd like to get yer claws on, ain't it? Well that's what the doctor's trying to do, too, and he knows how to go about it. So keep a civil tongue in yer head and try to do something that'll help."

There was no response, but the blood returned to Doyle's knuckles as he relaxed his grip. He still refused to look directly at Dougherty, just finished his whiskey and reached for the bottle, not answering O'Laughlin, but the worst was over.

Marty Carroll had sat in silence all this while, his eyes also downcast, due, Dougherty supposed, more to shyness than anger. He was no more than sixteen or seventeen — a spindly strip of a lad, redheaded, with a complexion pale and freckled. His hands were large, still out of proportion to the body which had yet to achieve full manhood. He looked too young to be on his own and Dougherty wondered where he had come from — surely not a native of Penrose Valley, else he would have been living with his own family.

"And you, Marty Carroll, what have you got to say?" O'Laughlin's question caught him by surprise.

"Uh... Well..." The words did not gush forth, but the redness flooded his cheeks, causing him further embarrassment. "We didn't much know him... But he was nice enough... He always had a kind word. I'll miss him."

Carroll's language had the touch of the Irish, but no strong brogue. His family, like Dougherty's own, must have been in America for at least a generation.

"He traveled, you know." Marty, now that his tongue had found its strength, was not ready to lapse into silence. "He was interesting to talk to. He'd gone places, Brogan had."

"Really?" Dougherty asked. "What places?"

"Just about everywhere, I guess," Marty said, "Philadelphia... New York... Washington City... lots of places... even Richmond!"

Not such a broad selection after all, but far more than Marty had ever seen. None were places where a miner would have found work, but then no one had mistaken Brogan for a miner. Richmond? Probably in the army, then, at the end of the war. The most immediate question was, What had brought Brogan to Penrose Valley?

"Was Brogan born in Ireland?" Dougherty asked.

They all looked at each other, each waiting for the others to say something until, at last, O'Laughlin broke the silence.

"So don't none o' yez know?"

"Charlie wasn't a great talker. Ye already know that." McGehan sounded surprised. "Still, ain't it funny a thing like that never come up? Ye almost always know where a man's from. But Brogan, now that I come to think of it, never said nothing about his family and never asked nobody else about theirs. It was just something he didn't talk about."

"How about you, O'Laughlin? Don't you know nothing? After all, he was yer partner underground, wasn't he?" It was Doyle's first contribution to the discussion since O'Laughlin had cooled him down earlier. Dougherty had been thinking that Shannon and O'Laughlin were partners since he had seen them together the night before — then he recalled that O'Donnell had mentioned the same thing in the shed.

"Sure he was me partner, but only fer the last three weeks — till he got sick and didn't show up Saturday. I never heard him say where he come from. By his speech, I'd'a said Ireland. But if ye was to press me on it, I couldn't be certain."

"Just how sick was Brogan?" Dougherty asked. Jen had already told him what Mrs. Corrigan had said to her.

"Sick enough that he couldn't get to work, and a man'd need to be sick to miss his pay for even a day." Young Marty was getting more loquacious. Or maybe his earlier reticence was because McBrien and Dougherty were strangers to him.

"That's generally true, to be sure," McGehan's mild voice broke in, "but there's times when something else might be reason enough."

"And do you think," Dougherty asked, "this was one of those times?"

"Might'a been, Doctor, just might'a been. He said he was sick and he could'a been, but if ye was to ask me what he had, I couldn't'a told ye, fer I saw no signs of it. He was fine when we come home Friday. Then at supper he said he was going to bed early. Felt poorly.

But I couldn't see it. Next morning when he heard me up and about he yelled down that he wasn't coming to work. Said he was sick. We didn't see him after that. Whether he come downstairs at all Saturday, I can't say, but he never did while we was home — not even Sunday, not even to go to Mass, and that wasn't like him."

"Did anything happen on Friday that was out of the ordinary?"

"Nothing that I seen."

"Just the message," Marty Carroll said.

"What message was that?" Dougherty asked.

"Mrs. Corrigan gave it to him at supper Friday. He opened the envelope and read the note, but didn't say a word about it. But it was after that he got sick. Till then he was his old self, enjoying his meal. After that he lost his appetite."

"Mr. O'Laughlin," Dougherty said, "where were you and Brogan working when you worked together? I mean, in what part of the mine?"

"Why, we was working right in the gangway where ye seen the roof caved in."

"Why weren't you working in there yesterday instead of O'Donnell and McGinley?"

"Because Brogan didn't come to work and Will Shannon's partner broke his leg last week, so Shannon was alone. The boss told me to team up with him and he sent O'Donnell and McGinley to work the gangway me and Charlie was working on Friday."

Had Brogan gone there looking for O'Laughlin, Dougherty wondered. And, if so, why? Or had he just gone there in the hope of escaping his assailant?

"Good evening, ma'am." Frank McGehan's gentle tones broke in as he rose to his feet. Dougherty turned around to see Jen and Mrs. Corrigan come into the kitchen, each carrying one of the boys, both fast asleep. Jen gave him a glance.

"Are you ready to leave?" he asked her.

"Yes, if you are," she said, "as soon as I help Mrs. Corrigan with the boys. They've had a long day."

They carried them to the room behind the kitchen where they lived with their mother. When they came back, Dougherty and Jen got their coats and Mrs. Corrigan walked with them to the front door, where they had a moment out of anyone's earshot.

"Mrs. Corrigan," Dougherty said, "On Friday at supper you gave Brogan a letter."

"That I did."

"Who brought it here?"

"Ye know, it's funny, but I've no idea. Somebody pushed it under the front door. Whoever it was didn't even knock, fer I was here the livelong day and not a single knock did I hear. I just come into the front room before supper and there it was right on the floor with Brogan's name on it."

"You have no idea what it was about? He said nothing of that?"

"Not a word. I give it to him and he opened it and read it and stuck it right in his coat pocket."

"You didn't see any of the letter, did you?"

"O' course not! What d' ye take me fer? I'd not look at what was his unless he asked me to!"

She was so indignant that Dougherty apologized, explaining that he hadn't meant that at all, but that sometimes we may see something without actually intending to do so.

"Well, I didn't," she said, somewhat mollified. "All I seen was a plain piece o' paper such as ye'd see in any schoolboy's tablet and with three or four lines o' writing."

"Do you know when Brogan left the house yesterday morning?"

"Sure and I don't. I never heard him at all. I called up to him about 8:00 o'clock to see if he'd be wanting some bit o' food, but no answer did I get."

"Just one more thing, Mrs. Corrigan," Dougherty said, "I thank you for giving us Brogan's belongings to examine. They may help. But could you tell me if there was anything else of his you may have forgotten to include?"

"There was not!" she said. What he had asked as a simple question had been answered as though it were an accusation and he wondered why.

"Once again, I thank you kindly," he said. "I am truly sorry about Mr. Brogan's death."

"Will ye catch whoever done it?"

"I can make no promises, Mrs. Corrigan, but I can truthfully say that I will do my best."

She patted his hand and then hugged Jen. As the door closed behind them, they saw the gleam of tears again in her eyes.

"Did you learn anything?" Jen asked as they walked home, the snow crunching under their feet at every step.

"Perhaps I did. For one thing, it is quite possible that Brogan went into the mine yesterday looking to find Frank O'Laughlin. I wonder why he would have done that?"

"I suppose, my dear, that a great deal would be far more evident to us if we could only know what was in Brogan's mind, but we may run into problems there, unless you can discover a way to wake the dead."

The Diarist

> February 20, 1861 — Was I too hasty? Should I have stayed where I was? For the past week I thought so, but now I think not. Life here is new, unfamiliar in many ways, but the advantages are incalculable. So many come and go, so many jammed into each neighborhood that it is the ideal place to be oneself and never be seen. The ideal place to begin anew.

The Diarist stopped writing and put everything away. That would not ordinarily have been the case, so engrossed would he become in his composition. But he simply had to get out in spite of the frigid weather. The wind whistled and there might even be snow in the offing, but he still had to get out. He bundled up and walked the stairs down to the front, seeing no one on the way but hearing voices from the other apartments.

It excited him more than he had thought possible. The crowds, the noise, the endless activity both day and night. He thought it must be like this to be abroad, to roam the continent of Europe, passing from country to country with endlessly varying languages, customs, costumes, foods, aromas. Here the changes were as rapid as a move from one block to the next. People poured in every day, all strangers to each other but soon enough finding their own kind — something that would never happen to him. There was no one like him, he was sure. They made their own little worlds, trying to recreate where they had come from. Why? Why leave in the first place if all you wanted was what you had already abandoned?

He walked, oblivious to the cold, until at last he came to an area he had not yet explored. He smelled the river, saw the furled sails on the masts of the ships as he looked down the side streets, heard the uproar of the saloons he passed by without entering. Saloons, warehouses, and cheap boarding houses constituted the bulk of the scenery, but he took it all in with the avidity of a tourist seeing for the first time the famed sites of some European capital. Everything interested him. He was glad he was here.

It was hard to remember that not so long ago, had he been asked, he would have said that he fully intended to spend his whole life in Philadelphia — that most unurban of all cities, that agglomeration of innumerable juxtaposed villages. A city in its expanse, a small town in its mentality. Now he was glad to be gone. Here was a city where a man could lose himself, could live life as he wished with no one the wiser, no one who really gave a damn.

The police had never guessed who had killed her. They had never even understood what to him had been so obvious in the way she died — had to die! He could have stayed there fully unsuspected, but he had chosen not to. Why test fate?

From the darkness ahead of him a couple emerged. A sailor, not falling down drunk, but wavering, mildly reeling, as though he were still on the deck of a moving ship. He laughed at something the woman said and leaned over to kiss her. Ta, ta! None of that! You're nice enough, but everybody pays for the privilege. It's not that far, be patient. Just ahead there. She steered him toward a house between two of the saloons, a house whose curtained windows showed a dull light, a light that beckoned.

Be patient, she'd said, and something within the Diarist came alive. As they drew nearer he noted beneath the hood of her cloak the dark hair that swept across her forehead, how her head barely came to the shoulder of the sailor. He was overcome with a thrill of anticipation and a sudden undercurrent of longing that surprised him by its intensity. He watched as they entered the house, marked its location, and turned to go back to his rooms.

Chapter V: Laid to Rest

> I pray you in your letters,
> When you shall these unlucky deeds relate,
> Speak of me as I am; nothing extenuate,
> Nor set down aught in malice...
> William Shakespeare (1564-1616)
> *Othello*, Act V, scene 2 (1604)

[Wednesday, January 10, 1866]

It was late when they left Mrs. Corrigan's, but they were in no especial hurry. Tonight's fresh, white sheet of snow would soon enough be tomorrow's dirty blanket, and it was simply too pleasant to abandon readily. They took a longer route home, holding hands, at first saying nothing, relishing the silence. Stars twinkled merrily, the breeze sped the clouds on their way, and the moon's reflected glow was bright beyond expectation. That was why, when he looked down, he could not miss the tears. He stopped.

"The boys?"

"Yes," she answered, the word catching in her throat and she said no more.

He drew her to him, letting her bury her face against his chest, heedless of what any passerby might think. Her eyes were tight shut, and still the tears coursed down her cheeks to be absorbed in the rough wool of his coat. And only that morning, she thought, she had written to her mother with such brave assurance that all was well.

"I ought to be ashamed of myself," she said. "She is such a good soul and she has had so much grief with the loss of her husband. And now Brogan. She takes such pride in the boys and wants only the best for them. And I am mean and envious enough to begrudge her the joy of her Michael and Daniel. It pains me when I see her with them. What sort of person am I?"

"Ah, Jen."

She heard the pain in his voice. He paused and she knew that it was to recollect himself so that his own struggle would not make hers the worse.

"You haven't a mean bone in your body, sweetheart. And you know that you begrudge Catherine Corrigan nothing at all. You spent a lot of time with the boys today and it was hard on you. You fear that we may never have what she has. But we will. I'm certain of it. We're young. We've not been married two years yet. It will all work out. You'll see."

She'd been in her sixth month in July and all was going so well. The baby was all they talked about. Would it be a boy or a girl? Which of them would it favor? What name should they choose? Would they make good parents? And then, with no warning, in the middle of the night, came the piercing pain. They both knew it was too soon, but they clung desperately to the illusion that it would be all right after all. It was not. When it ended in the early morning hours, their first child, their son, was a tiny, pathetic, bluish corpse just moments after birth.

Deep down she knew James was right. She harbored no ill will against Catherine Corrigan. But the sadness always took her by surprise, just when she was convinced it was finally coming to its end. That nagging mix of yearnings and longings and regrets. The self-recrimination, the fear that she might have done something to cause what had happened, even though she knew full well she hadn't. The empty dread that they might never have another chance, then the equally terrible fear that they might and that they would fail again. She felt ashamed of her aching envy of those who had not endured this cross, even though everyone — Catherine Corrigan included — had crosses of their own to bear.

James had assured her there was no evidence of permanent damage and that they would be able to have children in the future. He had arranged a consultation with a noted professor at the Jefferson Medical College, and he was equally reassuring. He found no reason to think that this would happen again. And she did believe him, but still she struggled to bring the agonies of the heart into subjection to what reason told her was true.

They stood there in the cold, saying nothing, together in pain and consolation. Then with his right arm around her shoulders and her left about his waist, like a pair of young lovers, they went slowly on their way. By the time they got home, she was at peace — knowing that this was bound to come and go until it had run its course, whenever that might be. Back in the kitchen the final tensions melted, but she was left exhausted, drained to her depths.

They were about to go upstairs when James groaned. He had yet to make his own copy of the autopsy report and there would be no time in the morning. He hated to leave her, but she knew that he should. The world has the nasty habit of going right on turning in spite of our troubles.

She was sound asleep when he came upstairs and he did not wake her. By seven the next morning they had eaten and he was off to the station to arrange with the conductor of the 8:10 to deliver the report to Associate Judge Brodhead. After that was the funeral, scheduled for nine o'clock. She was already dressed for it. She had nothing black that was suitable, but her darkest blue frock seemed properly somber and looked just fine with no additional adornment beyond the blue bonnet with its black ribbon, black kid gloves and the black shawl to wear beneath her cloak.

James had left his copy of the autopsy report on the desk in his office, not wanting to suggest it, but knowing she would read it if she wished to. When he had first known her, he had been hesitant about sharing such things with her, but he had long since realized that she was truly interested in what he did — and he had come to appreciate the insights she always had, so often seeing things that had escaped him.

She found the description of the body as intriguing as it was gruesome. The carefully written report with its technical language could not disguise the sadness of what had happened. A few items aroused her curiosity — the signs of earlier trauma, for example. They brought to mind a possibility, but she didn't know enough to be certain. She would have to ask James about it.

She replaced the report on the desk and looked again at the items in the envelope she had been given by Mrs. Corrigan.

She began with the two handbills. Their thick paper was so brittle and their folds so worn as to be on the verge of tearing. Both, to her surprise, were broadsides for a circus. They invited the public to performances in October of 1860 and May of 1861, both in Philadelphia. In spite of their claims of presenting "magnificent exhibitions of the most refined and instructive amusements," she could think of no reason why Brogan should have preserved them. She read through their descriptions of performers and attractions and found no familiar name, nothing to connect them with Brogan — but, then, she did not really know Brogan. Nor had she any reason to assume that the items in this stack of random materials had any connection with the person who had caused his death. Her efforts might be no more than a waste of time.

She set aside the letters tied with the red ribbon for a later reading and turned instead to the other handwritten documents. They were written on a variety of papers and in more than one hand. Some were dated; some were not. The earliest was written in 1860 and the latest just a few months ago, November of 1865. Perhaps with some astute reading they could use their contents to place even the undated ones into chronological order. There were no signatures. Some of the handwriting was careful; some, barely readable.

She turned to the newspaper clippings, of which there were thirty or more. The names of the newspapers were not on them, but each was marked with a handwritten date and the name of a city. That should be of some help. As she read the succession of headlines, she found herself aghast at what they proclaimed. These might indeed have something to do with Brogan's death; but just what, she could not say. Since there were dates on all of them, she set them in order and prepared to do her reading.

"Jen! Are you ready to go?"

She started, thoroughly engrossed in what she was doing. She looked up at the large clock on James's bookcase. How quickly time had passed! The clippings would have to wait. She put everything back into the envelope.

"Coming!" she said.

St. Margaret's church was less than six years old, but looked older. It was a plain wooden structure, no frills, its once white weather boards and brown shutters already aged by the steadily abrading coal dust into varying shades of the same dirty gray. The eight steep steps to the front door had been swept clean so that the coffin could be safely carried in for Mass.

It was a small congregation, mostly women and a few old men. Brogan was not well known; but, even had he been, not many of the men could have afforded to be there. Mrs. Corrigan sat in the front pew with her two boys, one on either side, cuddled up against her and sheltered within her arms, their eyes watery, their lips pouting to hold back the sorrow. The colorless winter sun shone through the plain glass windows, a square of it falling upon the three of them like the frame for a portrait of pain.

Father McGuire, flanked by two altar boys, came from the sacristy to stand at the sanctuary gate as the company store pine coffin was carried in by its rope handles and placed on the covered sawhorses at the head of the aisle. The pall bearers were Mrs. Corrigan's three boarders and Frank O'Laughlin.

The priest turned back to the foot of the altar, handed his biretta to the altar boy on his right, and, facing the altar, began the prayers. His somber tone suited the black vestments and some had tears in their eyes, but maybe from force of habit. These were the ones who made a practice of attending all the funerals. It was they who sang the mournful *Dies Irae* before Father McGuire read the gospel and preached a sermon — something he did not always do at a funeral.

Its content surprised them. He expressed his sympathy and spoke kindly of Brogan's time in Penrose Valley. But he soon turned to the evils of violence, implying that Brogan's death was no isolated incident. He saw it in the context of the strife that had marked the coal regions ever since the draft protests of 1862. No longer a message of sympathy or a paean to the hope of eternal salvation, his sermon became a warning against the use of force and the risk of association with those who did so.

James and Jen looked at each other, both wondering. Had Brogan's death been a single violent act? Or had it been part of a larger pattern? The answer to those questions made a considerable difference in how they would go about looking for the killer.

The Mass ended and Father McGuire came again to the head of the aisle with his two servers, one now carrying a thurible and incense, the other a bucket of holy water and the aspergil. He read the prayers and they heard Mrs. Corrigan's muffled sobs as he circled the coffin, raising up clouds of incense and staining the rough pine lid with drops of the holy water.

In spite of the weather, the grave had been dug, and they followed the procession out to the graveyard. They said the Our Fathers and Hail Marys and Father McGuire gave the coffin one last sprinkle.

"Anima ejus et animae omnium fidelium defunctorum per misericordiam Dei requiescant in pace. Amen."

It was over. The coffin was lowered on its ropes and the sexton began shoveling in the clods of frozen earth. Jen and James heard the hollow thuds as they paused at the tiny grave two rows over. It was terribly cold and she shivered as she took James's arm and they left for home. She hoped she wasn't catching something.

They warmed themselves with bowls of soup and had ham sandwiches on buttered slices of the bread she'd baked the day before. James had patients to see, first in his office and then two at their homes. The cold was so hard on the elderly and made no distinction between poor and rich. One of his patients lived down near the railroad station; the other, up on the hill. Both suffered chronic bronchitis and for both he had prescribed tincture of colchicum with spirits of nitric ether, three drops to be placed on sugar three times per day to alleviate the cough.

Jen changed back into her house dress and spent the afternoon on household chores she had not finished the day before. She fixed boiled mutton with carrots and potatoes and, for a special treat, miniature rice puddings — more than two of them. James always enjoyed one later in the evening. And so, her thoughts were all domestic and Brogan's murder was left to simmer at the back of her mind.

It was not until after supper that they finally got to the envelope and decided to examine the newspaper accounts in chronological order. The first six were all from Philadelphia, the oldest dated October 19, 1860.

DREADFUL CRIME IN CITY STREET — A heinous crime was yesterday discovered when John Ambrose, a dock worker at the Archer and Brand Shipping Company on Front Street, while on his way to work at 5:00 A.M., saw in the shadows of an alley what he took to be discarded clothing. Curious, he went closer and was horrified to discover the terribly mutilated body of a young woman whose identity has not yet been determined. She is described as between twenty and twenty-five years of age, with black hair, and somewhat full figure.

The medical examiner concludes that she had been dead for some hours prior to the discovery of the body. The precise cause of death is expected to emerge in the autopsy, but there can be no doubt that this is a case of murder. The victim's throat was slashed and there was considerable further stabbing, according to informations received by this reporter.

Whether the victim had been otherwise molested prior to death has not been learned. As further information becomes available, you may be sure that it will appear in these pages.

"Would October 19 be the date of publication?" Jen asked.

"Most likely," he answered. "If so, then Mr. Ambrose found the body on October 18, early in the morning. So if she died 'some hours prior' to that, she must have died very late on October 17 or just after midnight on October 18."

"I wonder what day of the week that was?"

"We can find out easily enough," he said and went to his office where he kept copies of the almanacs of previous years. He was back in a moment.

"Isn't that always the way?" he smiled. "The oldest we have is 1861. Well, we can use that to count back."

They calculated that October 17, 1860, was a Wednesday and that the article appeared on Friday — which told them nothing at all, but amassing details at least creates the illusion of having learned something.

"Weren't you in Philadelphia then?" she asked. "Did you ever hear of this murder?"

"I was there," he said, "but I didn't begin to work with Doctor Brownson until December and he never mentioned this case. He may not have been involved. I'm sure it was big news at the time, but I was in my first full month of medical studies in October and wasn't paying attention to anything else. If need be, we can find out. It may give us a good excuse to visit Doctor Brownson."

The next article was dated October 22, the following Monday. By then the murdered woman had been identified.

RESOLUTION OF MYSTERY IN SIGHT? MURDER VICTIM IDENTIFIED — Three days past we reported a young woman brutally dispatched in the prime of life. The public's dismay was augmented by the fact that the victim could not be identified.

The quality of her slashed clothing led detectives to conclude that she was of good family and not resident in the waterfront area where the body was discovered. Furthermore, despite extensive mutilation, the amount of blood at the scene was less than experienced observers should have expected at the murder site. Logic demands that she must have been killed elsewhere and her body transported to the place of discovery.

Accordingly, police extended their investigations and so identified her as Abiageal Conroy, 24 years of age, whose parents had reported her missing late on October 17. They reside on Twentieth Street, near Rittenhouse Square.

Miss Conroy had departed her parents' home early on Wednesday afternoon to walk to the home of a friend, where she was to remain for dinner. She never reached her destination. Her friends had not thought to inquire after her, since the invitation had been indefinite.

The police seek anyone who may have seen her that afternoon, about 2:00 o'clock or later. Miss Conroy was five feet six inches tall, about 145 pounds, with fair complexion, blue eyes, and very dark, curly hair. She wore a pale yellow gown, a brown silk shawl and gloves, and yellow bonnet with a brown ribbon. The police will welcome information.

The viciousness of the crime indicates the act of a deranged person. The police offer every assurance that they will apprehend this madman.

"This was written five days after the murder. The police claimed great progress in catching the killer. Do you think they meant it?" She sounded doubtful.

"They might have," James said. "They probably thought it had been done by someone in the family. That's where they would look first. But I'd have had some doubts. A body so mutilated points to more than a family argument. That might have resulted in a heavy blow or a gunshot wound or a stabbing, or even something that seemed accidental... a fall against a hard object... something of that sort. But none of those things fit this case."

"What does fit?"

"They say she had left her home and was expected by friends who lived nearby. It was in the afternoon, and the area around Rittenhouse Square is far from dangerous, so it was probably not a random attack. I would think that it was planned and that she was taken somewhere and killed. The body was later transported without anyone seeing anything. That sounds like neither family violence nor the act of a totally irrational madman. He was lucid enough to realize what he had done and clever enough to take steps to divert suspicion from himself. Yet the violence points to a terrible rage."

"What in the world could a young girl have done to provoke that?"

"I have no idea," James said. "Maybe she was mistaken for someone else. But, still, that seems unlikely."

The next article was dated October 26, rather brief.

POLICE PROGRESS IN MURDER — Police continue to investigate the murder of Miss Abiageal Conroy, only child of Mr. and Mrs. Peter Conroy of Twentieth Street, this city. The devastated parents can offer no reason why this should have happened. They describe her as a happy young lady engaged to be married next Spring and looking forward to connubial bliss.

The police reveal no details of their investigation, but insist they are about to apprehend a likely suspect. Our readers will be informed of all developments so that fears may be alleviated in knowing that this maniac has been taken and that the streets are again safe for the fairer sex.

"So they had a definite suspect after all," James said.

"Isn't it also possible," Jen suggested, "that they were trying to placate the public and avert panic?"

But four days later, on October 30, the paper reported that the police had made good on their promise.

MURDERER ARRESTED! POLICE SOLVE TRAGIC CRIME — Yesterday, at his home on Twentieth Street, police arrested Henry Carlton for the brutal murder of Abiageal Conroy, whose savaged body was discovered on the morning of October 18 just off Front Street.

Less than two weeks ago the police solicited the public's help in apprehending the fiend, and it was that which led to his capture.

A mother strolling with her infant son, remembered seeing Miss Conroy proceeding south on Twenty-first Street on the afternoon of October 17. Her attention was drawn to Miss Conroy by the fact that she too was dressed in yellow and the witness was surprised by the similarity of costumes. She saw a man "with a crazed look in his eye" approach Miss Conroy as though to ask directions.

She described him as near thirty years of age, quite tall, broad shouldered, strong looking. His hair was dark and fairly long, covered by a black bowler which he did not remove. The witness was across the street and heard nothing that was said.

The man wore a light colored shirt, dark cravat, brown Tweedside jacket with matching trousers, and dark green waistcoat. He was clean shaven.

Police conducted a canvass of the neighborhood and found their quarry a few blocks from the Conroy residence. He lives alone and it is reported that neighbors found him aloof, but had no reason to think him guilty of a crime.

Carlton is in custody and is expected to go to trial in the near future.

"And so the case was solved after all," Jen said, "and that quite quickly."

"There are two more articles," he said, and handed them to her. The first was from November 9, 1860.

PRISONER RELEASED, HIS INNOCENCE ESTABLISHED — Mr. Henry Carlton, the man accused of involvement in the tragic murder of Miss Abiageal Conroy, was today released from custody, the police having received reliable testimony to substantiate Mr. Carlton's claim that he was not in the city at the time of the murder, but had been in New York City on business. Associates there verified his claim.

The last article was dated December 12 and served no purpose but to indicate that the perpetrator of the crime still had not been found. Public interest was waning, as it always does, even with murder.

And so, in the end, Miss Abiageal Conroy was dead and the mystery of her murder unresolved. Why, they wondered, had Brogan collected these clippings?

That ended the first set, but there remained two more, one of articles from New York and the other from the city of Washington. James looked quickly through the headlines and saw that all had to do with the murders of women and all had occurred after the murder of Abiageal Conroy.

"Do you suppose," Jen asked, "that Brogan may have known this Abiageal Conroy?"

"He may have, but then what of all the others? Surely he could not have known every one of them. But just a moment... let me look at something."

Once more he went through the New York and Washington reports, this time looking at more than the headline. His expression became graver each time he set one aside and took up the next.

"We will have to examine all of these in detail," he said, "but I can say at least this: All of these murders are as gruesome as that of the Conroy girl, and all seem to have certain elements in common — more than can be explained by coincidence. My first impression is that all may well have been committed by the same person."

"Someone going from city to city murdering women?" she said. "I've never heard of such a thing. It makes no sense at all."

"But suppose that, for whatever reason, someone was doing exactly that and that Brogan somehow became aware of it and set out in pursuit?"

"And he was too successful," she said, "and got himself killed for his cleverness?"

James went back to the envelope and took out the handwritten note they had read earlier.

> I no all wat hapened in Philadelphia.
> I have wat you want.
> Mete me at Brakker Noon — Mundy.
> P.S. Miss this mete at yur perl!

"Look at this in the light of what we've just said. If Brogan was looking for information, this note was the perfect bait to get him out to the breaker. How could he refuse? And if it was the killer who wrote the note, then his trap succeeded, even though Brogan almost got away even after he was shot."

It made sense and Jen found herself cringing to think that this monster could be in Penrose Valley. Then her mind leapt to another possible conclusion. What if the articles were perverted souvenirs of Brogan's own actions? What if they expressed some insane pride in what he had done? And in that case, then who had sent the note? She explained her thoughts to James.

"And so," she said, "what if we read the note in that light? It becomes a threat to Brogan. A threat of exposure or of punishment. Perhaps sent by someone avenging one of the deaths."

"In which case," James said, "solving this murder may mean bringing to justice someone whose crime was to have killed a horribly vile killer."

"I know," she said, "but we have to do it, don't we? Like it or not, we have to go on."

"You're right," James said. "So shall we go on? Shall we look at the ones from New York? They start in April of 1861."

"Would you mind very much it we were to take the letters next instead?" she asked.

"I don't mind at all," he said. "They may be a relief from the horror for a while." He set the two stacks of clippings aside and reached for the letters.

There were ten of them, all written on plain white stationery, most two pages long, a few somewhat longer. He opened the first, looked at the salutation of "My dearest Charles" and the concluding "Your loving Mary," then examined its physical aspects — which they would soon learn were common to all. They were in black ink, the penmanship clear, small, precise. The lines of writing ran across the pages as evenly as if the paper had been ruled. Punctuation and spelling would have pleased Noah Webster himself. Whoever Mary was, she had been well educated and that was not always the case with women. It was one of the thing Jen had appreciated in what her own parents had given her.

"We may as well put them into order as you did the clippings," he said. "Too bad we have no return address and no idea where Brogan was when they were sent to him."

As he spoke, he unfolded the letters and put them in order. The next to the last was thicker than the rest, and as he unfolded it something fell out. It was a small photograph, a *carte de visite*, from which two faces stared with that solemnity of expression required whenever the photographer uncovers his lens and says, "Be still, please... one... two... three..."

"It's Brogan," James said, "younger, but not much changed for all that."

Brogan looked directly at the camera. His right hand was tucked Napoleon-like into the front of his vest, where two buttons had been undone. The left hand rested in rather a proprietorial fashion upon the back of the chair behind which he stood. In the background was a draped curtain looped back by a tasseled cord to reveal a rural scene, obviously painted on a wall size canvas. His hair was combed down flat, head held stiff above the high collar and wide tie. Even in the formality of the suit, his broad shoulders and muscular arms were impressive.

A woman, perhaps in her early twenties, posed, seated stiffly in the chair, making her height difficult to judge. The smallness of her clasped hands suggested a slight stature. Her hair was dark and thick, its curls rich, caught up in ringlets at both sides. Even the formal pose could not fully eradicate the impression of closeness between the two. She was quite pretty. Jen wondered who Mary was and where she was now. If they could find her, they might learn a great deal more about Brogan's end.

The back of the photograph was inscribed, "With love, Mary." Like any *carte de visite* it had probably once had a border, upon the lower portion of which would have been printed the name of the photographic studio where it was made. This one, however, had been trimmed and no border remained. But there was something else that got their attention immediately.

"Do you see it?" James asked.

"The resemblance, you mean?" It had struck her, too. "One might take them for the same person. Of course, once you examine the photograph, you see the differences as well."

"Could they be related, do you think?"

"It's not totally out of the question, I suppose, but Mary's style of dress puts her somewhere above Catherine Corrigan's social status."

"On the other hand, would you not have said that she seems beyond Brogan's social class as well? Yet, there he is in the photograph. And there is no mistaking him. It is our Charlie Brogan. And Mary is enough like Mrs. Corrigan to be her sister."

"Tomorrow," Jen said, "I will see Mrs. Corrigan and ask her about it."

The letters were dated, some with a full date and others only with month and year. The letter from which the picture had fallen was one of the earliest, written in April, 1860. In it Mary spoke fondly of their recent time together and her elation that her parents, with some reluctance, had finally agreed to their betrothal. She went on at length (it was the longest of the letters), full of hope and the assurance of a rosy future, the certitude of young love that has not yet realized the trials that even the most perduring of loves will inevitably experience. Jen was glad that Brogan had known such a love. The picture, Mary indicated, had been made when he last visited and he had been required to depart before it was ready. Departed for where? Unfortunately that was not revealed.

There was only one letter earlier than that. It was dated April 1, 1860, and so must have preceded the other April letter. Apparently this was the first one written to Brogan after his departure for whatever his destination had been. She spoke playfully of April

Fool's jokes that people had played, and wished that Brogan could have been there. She said that her parents were having serious reservations about the marriage, reservations that must have been resolved before the other letter with its indication of their reluctant agreement. Why were they so reluctant? What was the cause for their attitude? Again, nothing in the letter revealed where Mary lived or where Brogan had gone.

There was only one letter for May, possibly at the end of the month, since it referred to her pleasure at the fact that the June weather would so soon be upon them. However, she also referred to other letters that they had exchanged recently, leading them to believe that the letters they now possessed were not the full correspondence.

In the letter of June 10 they found the first clue to Mary's residence. She wrote of an excursion that she and her father had made to see the arrival of a most exotic delegation from the Orient.

> Although the hotel was closed to us, we joined the throng lining the streets all the way from the railroad depot. The delegation was a large one, between fifty and one-hundred people, I should say. Their costumes were such as I have never seen in all my life, most elaborate, all colors of the rainbow, all made of the finest silks. Many of the men carried hand fans. The Japanese must be a wealthy people. We remained for a long time, staring like curious children, until the doors of the Continental closed behind them.

"That leaves us in no doubt about where Mary was," James said. "In June of 1860, the Japanese delegation went to Philadelphia and stayed at the Continental Hotel. People still spoke of it when I was a student. So Mary is from Philadelphia. I wonder if she still lives there? And, if so, can we find her?"

The remaining letters were dated June, July 15, July, August, September, and October 1. In the last one she is filled with anticipation; Brogan is to come back to Philadelphia and she can hardly wait for the day. She is certain that her parents have now fully overcome their earlier reservations and that they will welcome Brogan with open arms. As Jen read it, she hoped that Mary had been right, and that her joy was not just wishful thinking. But there the correspondence ended with no inkling of the outcome, apart from the fact that Mary had not been with Brogan when he arrived in Penrose

Valley. Had they married? Was she still in Philadelphia waiting for him to return? Had her parents changed their minds and stopped the marriage? The letters had yielded that one concrete fact of her residence in Philadelphia, and then had raised even more questions to which they offered no answers. And those were the questions in which they had now become far more interested. Should they rejoice or commiserate with Brogan's loving Mary — although the outcome of Brogan's time in Penrose Valley made the rejoicing all but impossible. Was she even now waiting somewhere for a letter that would never come?

One more thing — was it possible that the same Brogan who had been so loved by Mary, the Brogan to whom Catherine Corrigan had been so strongly attracted, could have been an insane killer? Jen turned that over in her mind. She could not disprove it, of course, but everything within her rebelled at the very thought. If someone like Brogan could be so vicious, how could anyone ever be sure of anything or anyone else ever again?

It was late. They locked everything in James's office cabinet for safekeeping and went to bed. Her mind was so full of questions, that her earlier ones about the old traumas that James had discovered upon the body of Mr. Brogan had for the time being, like him, been laid to rest.

Chapter VI: The Truth

Soun ys noght but eyr ybroken,
And every speche that ys spoken,
Lowd or pryvee, foul or fair,
In his substaunce ys but eyr.
    Geoffrey Chaucer (c. 1343-1400)
    The House of Fame, Bk. II

[Friday, January 12, 1866]

    Father McGuire was a man of his word. But then, Dougherty thought, if he couldn't be trusted, we all may as well throw up our hands in despair. Father McGuire had telegraphed Judge Barrett first thing Wednesday and by 8:30 Thursday morning a boy was knocking at Dougherty's door with a telegram announcing that His Honor had appointed him to investigate the death of one Charles Brogan, and that the coroner and the sheriff had both concurred in this judgement. Written documentation, it said, would follow, and so it had with the arrival of the 12:50 P.M up train from Mauch Chunk. The Judge, too, was a man true to his word. The condition of the world was clearly improving.

    Jen visited Mrs. Corrigan that same morning and learned nothing at all. She had never heard of the Mary who had signed the letters and did not recognize the photograph. She saw the resemblance to herself as quickly as had Dougherty and Jen, but could offer no explanation for it. She was certain, however, that she and Mary could not possibly be related to each other. Their visit was friendly, as it always was, but when Jen left it was with a feeling of uneasiness. She had no inkling that anything Mrs. Corrigan had said to her was untrue. Still there was an underlying uneasiness, a feeling that there was something else that she was holding back; but what it was Jen could not imagine.

* * *

    The office was paneled in a close-grained wood, stained dark and buffed with beeswax to a rich, soft luster. Its somber tone was unrelieved by the colors in the now age-darkened portraits that hung upon it. The mahogany furniture was heavy and imposing. On the east side of the room, the two full length windows which might have let in the morning sunlight did not do so, being covered as they were by the forest green drapery that had been pulled tightly shut. Instead, a more muted light came through the windows on the adjacent wall, falling upon the thick carpet and the rich upholstery of the four chairs that had been drawn into a circle about a low table, as though ready for a meeting of some sort. The opulence of the room, as tastefully subdued as it was, still created the uneasily oppressive sense of a self-conscious wealth.

At present there were only two men in the room, neither of them seated in the circled chairs, the one clearly the superior of the other. He sat at the desk in a high-backed, leather upholstered chair, while the other faced him across the desk from a straight-backed, plain, wooden chair with a caned seat.

The man behind the desk was Beverley Arkwright. He had been born in England, but had come at the age of twelve to the United States with his parents some twenty or twenty-five years ago. He was now an American citizen, but still cultivated a British accent and mannerisms. It was his family's London connections which had gotten him his present position as local director, answerable to the Board of Directors in Philadelphia and, through them, to the London owners, who liked the idea of having a Brit in charge of their local interests, even if he was a transplanted one.

He was only in his thirties, but his dark hair had begun to gray at the temples, a feature he was pleased to accentuate, thinking it gave him an air of maturity appropriate to his position. His clothes were impeccably tailored by a venerable London firm and he had the resonant voice and frank manner of a man born and bred to lead. These qualities, together with his six foot height, had enabled him to dominate many a gathering. At the moment, he had no need to impress. The man who sat before him already knew who was in charge and was not the sort of person likely to forget it.

Captain Morgan Maddock had always been one to know his place and to exercise it to his own best advantage in relation to those both above and below him, making himself indispensable to the former and an object of a certain fear to the latter. He sat now as though at attention, his civilian attire unable to disguise the military experience as sergeant-major in the India forces of Queen Victoria and, more recently, as a captain in the Army of the Potomac. His posture made him seem taller than he was. Trim and muscular, he looked at the world through sharp, suspicious eyes, set deep in a countenance framed by a precisely trimmed beard and moustache, both streaked with gray, as was his full head of hair. When he moved, it was with the cockiness of the bantam asserting his station in the barnyard. He was giving his undivided attention to Mr. Arkwright, his most recent superior.

"Dunne's murder is just one more sign of the urgency of the whole affair," Albright said. "Deplorable as it may be, we must nonetheless take advantage of it. Would you not agree?"

"Deplorable is what it is," Maddox said, "but we'd be fools not to see that it can help." The Welsh accent came through, in spite of Maddock's effort to seem American. He was as intent on being American as Arkwright was on being British.

"The labor people seem determined to do themselves in, so I see no reason not to help them. The Pottsville part of it is already in process. There will be a protest meeting tomorrow night to get the citizens behind a plan to take steps to end the spate of violence that's plagued these upstate counties since before the war. Take a look at this."

He took a sheet of paper from the top drawer of the desk and handed it across. One passage had been underlined.

> The curse of Schuylkill County is miserable, inefficient officials, who are either afraid to or do not know how to discharge their duties. The fact is that we must turn from the imbeciles here to the state for protection from the bands of secret assassins that infest the County.

Maddock read it, then looked up as he handed it back.

"Bannan?"

"Who else?" Albright said with a smile. "It's an editorial that will appear tomorrow."

Benjamin Bannan, also of Welsh stock, was editor of the *Pottsville Miners Journal* and for the past ten years had been denouncing groups he identified as "Buckshots" or "Molly Maguires," trying to tie them to every crime committed in the coal region. He was a proponent of free labor, which for him meant that workers should bear their burdens in virtuous long-suffering and not harass the mine owners with their incessant demands for a living wage and improved working conditions. He styled himself a "nativist," distrustful of all immigrants who did not come from England, Scotland, or Wales.

"I see," said Maddock, "and we may have something similar here, you think? This Brogan killing?"

"Why not? Of course, it is not as direct an attack on the mine owners as was the murder of Dunne, but that doesn't mean that it's not part of the labor dispute. The Irish themselves are at odds on this, aren't they? Always fighting over who's in charge, who'll be the workingman's true friend? And that makes it our business."

"And it also means that if we can find who killed him, it will be just one more proof of the need for the Coal and Iron Police. It can show our ability and our necessity at the same time."

"Exactly," Arkwright said, "and that's why we can't afford to have Dougherty and McBrien work on this all on their own. In any case, the state will probably authorize the Coal and Iron Police within days, and the governor will sign the bill into law. But it's still to our advantage to be seen beyond all doubt as effective as well as legal."

"So we will have to be sure we keep both of them in tow, eh?" He smiled. "That shouldn't be too hard, should it?"

"We'll discover that soon enough."

* * *

"So, sir, d' ye have any idea whatsoever o' just who this Mary might be?"

As they drove up the hill, Dougherty had been describing what they had learned from the letters.

"None at all, and we don't even know where to look next, apart from the fact that any search may have to begin in Philadelphia."

Dougherty's buggy arrived at their destination, with both of them wondering why they were there. The day was not unpleasant and they could have walked, but that would have seemed less dignified and Beverley Arkwright put great stock in dignity — his own above all.

Dougherty pulled the carriage into the driveway and was immediately met by a servant to take charge of it, directing them straight to the house. Quite a house it was. The largest in town and in the most commanding position. It stood three stories high with a majestically designed façade, its woodwork newly painted, even though the height of the situation and its location west of the breaker allowed it to escape much of the coal dust that afflicted everyone else.

The door opened at their approach and a butler, as British in fact as Arkwright was in pretension, took their hats and overcoats, and led them past the grand curved staircase with its curving, highly polished banister, and along a corridor toward the rear of the house.

"Mr. Arkwright will greet you in his office, gentlemen." He opened the door and stood aside to allow them to enter.

"Doctor Dougherty! Mr. McBrien! How kind of you to come. I am honored. Seeing you reminds me again of how fortunate we of Penrose Valley are to have our health in such capable hands."

He had the hearty handshake of the born politician but, as McBrien had once said, when he let go you'd be wise to see if you still had your cuff links and all ten fingers. He turned to another man standing near the desk.

"Doctor Dougherty, Mr. McBrien, may I present Captain Morgan Maddock. Captain Maddock is to be head of our Penrose Valley Coal and Iron Police, the new force that is to be appointed for our protection."

Maddock made no move to extend his hand, just gave the least token of a nod and rose up slightly on the balls of his feet, as though about to click his heels like a visiting Prussian general. He stopped himself before the click, as though he'd thought better of it or had decided they did not merit it.

"The Penrose Valley Coal and Iron Police? And, sure now, just who might they be, sir? Never a thing have I heard o' them."

"Ah, but you shall Mr. McBrien, you certainly shall." Arkwright's lips held a smile; his voice did not. This was not a topic for humor. "The force is not yet formally established, but will be soon enough. Legislation is pending at Harrisburg and will pass this session for the mines just as it did last year for the railroads. It is merely a matter of time."

The railroad police had private police powers to arrest people for offenses along railroads or on railroad properties, and public authorities were required to lock up such offenders for prosecution. The mining companies now looked for the same sweeping authority.

"You'll have noticed our new building on Main Street?" Maddock asked, "That is where we will be headquartered. You must visit us when the office is completed."

"We've seen it," Dougherty said. "Quite substantial. It puts me in mind of a fortress."

There was a soft tap at the door and the butler entered. "Your coffee, sir," he said to Mr. Arkwright. Behind him was a pretty young maid with a tray and coffee service for four.

"Gentlemen, please be seated and refresh yourselves." Arkwright was the affable host, getting them situated in the circle of deep leather chairs, seeing to their comfort, and murmuring inconsequential pleasantries until the maid and butler had withdrawn. Then, properly creamed and sugared, he got to the point.

"As I was saying, gentlemen, we are about to have an efficient police force here in Penrose Valley — a much needed addition to our community. You must agree that it will benefit all of us."

"D' ye mean then, sir, there's been an outbreak o' crime here in our little patch and, due to our being s' busy, meself and the Doctor, we just completely missed it? What's been going on, Mr. Arkwright, sir, that ye think we ought to know about?"

"Not precisely an outbreak of crime, as you so picturesquely put it, Mr. McBrien," Arkwright said, choosing to ignore McBrien's tone and confirming Dougherty's suspicion that he wanted something from them and was willing to make certain small sacrifices — even of dignity! — to attain it. "But crime does occur in any village, no matter its size, even crimes as serious as murder. Indeed, Doctor, I understand that even now you are investigating the murder of a man — Brogan is it? — one of our miners. Is that not so?"

"You surprise me, sir. How did that come all the way to your attention?" Dougherty asked.

"It's a small town, Doctor. How can anyone keep a secret here?" He smiled, signaling that he had no desire to offend.

"Doctor, investigating a murder takes a special sort of knowledge... and a proper force of men. A police force. That's the ticket!" Maddock was anxious to get this conversation over with. He was not one likely to suffer fools gladly and he had already put them into that category.

"You may have a point," Dougherty said, "but it would be a point better taken if we actually had a police force. In fact, we do not."

"Besides, Captain Maddock, can it be that ye know nothing o' the Major's background in matters such as this? Sure and he's had his share o' schooling in the scientific investigation o' crime," McBrien said.

"That may be so, but schoolboy learning can never replace experience. I have five experienced men and it would be to your advantage to have their assistance in this matter." Maddock addressed himself to Dougherty, not even acknowledging that it was McBrien who had spoken.

"A generous offer, to be sure," Dougherty said, addressing Arkwright and ignoring Maddock, "but, unfortunately, the Captain and his men are not — at least for the present — a legally constituted body. It would be imprudent to act without legal sanction, especially in a case of murder. It would be all too easy to create a legal dilemma that could later damage even an otherwise strong case against a suspect. I know you would not want that."

"My dear Doctor, the legality should be no obstacle, should it? Were you not authorized by Brodhead to perform the autopsy? And were you not just yesterday authorized by Judge Barrett's telegram to proceed with a full investigation? There should be no difficulty in extending your authority to include the kind offer of Captain

Maddock and his capable men. I should think their help invaluable. It would be foolhardy to reject it."

Dougherty heard the scarcely veiled threat in the words. Why was Arkwright so interested in this case? Because it had occurred on company property? Or because Brogan had been a company employee? Dougherty thought not. His motive was much more transparent than that. It would not do if McBrien and Dougherty solved the case while Maddock and his cohorts twiddled their thumbs in ignorance and idleness. On the other hand, Arkwright's mention of the telegram was more informative than anything else he had said. Dougherty now knew where Arkwright's information came from. Owen Williams strikes again.

"It is a kind offer under those terms," Dougherty said. "Very generous of you to place Captain Maddock and his men under my command. On that ground, perhaps we can use them after all."

Arkwright and Maddock looked at each other, and McBrien took a sip of his now cold coffee to cover up the smile that he could not fully suppress.

"Apparently you fail to grasp the meaning of Mr. Arkwright's offer," Captain Maddock said through clenched teeth. Apparently he failed to grasp the humor of the situation. "I am sure he does not expect me to work for you." He looked to Arkwright.

"Of course not," Arkwright said. "After all, Captain Maddock and his men are the professionals here. His direction of your efforts, Doctor, would be of much help to you."

"I'm sure it would," Dougherty said, "if he had any legal standing. How truly unfortunate that he does not."

"Let me be frank with you," Arkwright began — the usual opening for someone who intends not to be. "You have heard of events in Schuylkill County two days ago, have you not?"

"No. I can't say that I have."

"A man was killed — a Mr. Henry Dunne. He was superintendent of the New York and Schuylkill Coal Company. A good man. Lived in Heckscherville. On his way home he was shot down and killed on the main road near Pottsville."

"He was robbed?" Dougherty asked.

"He was not," said Maddock. "It was more insidious than that."

"So it would seem," Arkwright said. "His money and his watch were never touched. The motive was something else entirely."

"Has this something to do with the death o' Charlie Brogan?" McBrien's eyebrows lifted incredulously.

"It very well may. Please permit Captain Maddock to explain."

"This was no robbery, as I've already said. This was cold blooded murder, plain and simple, and there's no doubt it was done by a gang of malcontents out to hurt the mine owners."

"What evidence have you for that accusation?" Dougherty asked, even as, in the back of his mind, he recalled Father McGuire's sermon aimed at senseless violence.

"The evidence of common sense! That and what's been happening right under your noses in this part of the state since before the rebellion." Maddock did not like being challenged.

"Witnesses saw five men, all strangers, headed out to where Dunne was killed." Arkwright tried to be conciliatory. "O.W. Davis, Dunne's employer, considers that it was an attack on the mining company itself."

"So he does," said Maddock, "and he's backed up his opinion with a reward of five-thousand dollars for information that leads to the capture of the murderers."

"So then, sir, do I read ye right?" McBrien said. "Are ye saying that Brogan, God be good to him, was done in by the Buckshots? Or by the Mollies? That he was the victim o' some great plot?"

"Why not?" Maddock snapped before Arkwright could speak. "You know as well as I that they're capable of it and it was a crime against the Penrose Valley Coal Mining Company as well."

"Was it indeed? Against the company was it? D' ye mean that his death done harm to the company? That the company couldn't afford to lose him? Or is it that the company's so fatherly to each of its employees that it takes the death of a mere laborer as a personal affront? I'd no idea their affection for the working man was so tender. Ain't it amazing how wrong ye can be at times?"

"Now, now, Mr. McBrien, I see your point." Arkwright was being heroically patient, determined to keep the peace. Control of this investigation was that important to him. "Brogan's death may or may not be the work of a secret society, but it can do no harm to pursue that line of inquiry, can it? We're all after the same thing: the simple truth. Even if that line of thought proves fruitless in the end, it would be foolish to ignore it, don't you think? Of course, there are differences — serious ones — between labor and management, but that does not make the company unfeeling about any death."

"To accuse the Molly Maguires of Brogan's death," Dougherty said, "makes little sense. If there is such a society, it's the mine owners they disagree with, not some newcomer who is a problem to no one. He wasn't even a threat to another man's job."

"Don't expect the actions of these people to make sense." Arkwright's veneer of patience was beginning to wear thin. "They're a depraved lot and don't see the consequences of their own actions. Their efforts to control the mine owners are pathetic. Working men simply cannot control mining operations. They've neither the intelligence nor the capital. Their efforts in this regard are nothing short of suicidal. Success on their part would mean driving the owners away, ending everybody's jobs and taking the bread out of the mouths of the very ones they pretend to help. They'd have their children starve to gain their own ends. Most people see that and do not support them in their foolishness. They have got to be stopped for all our sakes."

"Ah, sir, I'd beg to disagree with ye." McBrien spoke with a calm — the one that comes before the storm. "I can hardly imagine any group o' workmen who could actually exert sufficient pressure on the mine owners to make them abandon anything so lucrative as the anthracite business. Indeed, wouldn't it just make sense fer them same owners to want a little opposition? To just stir up enough of a fuss to get them that precious police force they're so set on having? Their motives ain't all lily white and they don't put quite enough food in people's mouths to make them fat and lazy, do they? I'd keep a close eye on both sides — present company excluded o' course, who're just trying to find out who killed Brogan. All of us after the simple truth, as ye so elegantly put it."

"Do you mean to imply, sir, that the mine owners themselves are committing these atrocities to achieve their own goals?" Maddock's face was scarlet and his voice shrill.

"Ah, Captain dear, not these particular atrocities, to be sure. Never would I think such a thought, and ye ought to be ashamed fer thinking it yerself. A slip o' the tongue, I've no doubt. Otherwise I know ye'd never even hint at such a thing. Ah, never!"

"Gentlemen, gentlemen... let us not be at odds with each other. After all, we are here in the interest of justice — to find out who did take Brogan's life and to follow the investigation to its conclusion, no matter where that takes us." Arkwright was again the voice of reason, his veneer now back in place, his appeal full of common sense.

McBrien smiled, still calm. Captain Maddock pushed back, red faced and fuming, his mouth tight shut, his hands gripping the arms of his chair.

"So, Doctor Dougherty, are we in agreement on cooperation in this investigation?"

"Why, Mr. Arkwright, I have no intention whatsoever of being uncooperative. The question is simply one of the kind and extent of the cooperation. If the investigation is to be effective, then it must also be fully legal, as I know you will agree."

"If it's legality you're concerned about," Maddock said, "then you can take my word. I've had the police experience to make decisions about that."

"I thank you, Captain, for your kind offer. But it was Judge Barrett who assigned me this task and it is Judge Barrett who must resolve the issue. I will contact him and, should he wish me to have you take part in the investigation, I shall be happy so to inform you."

And there it ended. The Captain acquiesced, but not nearly as gracefully as did Arkwright. Dougherty knew, of course, that this was merely the first step in the dance. There would be more to come. Even if Judge Barrett did not involve them, Arkwright and Maddock were bound to proceed on their own and try to prove what they had decided to prove — which might or might not be the truth.

The Diarist

July 30, 1861 — No one grasps the truth. No one sees the obvious. Their obtuseness is beyond me. They are like fools who see a great painting, a masterpiece, and discuss *ad nauseam* what it means and who could have painted it, while not one bothers to look at the signature so clearly painted in the corner. For all of their endless jabbering not one of them appreciates the obvious.

He stopped writing and turned again to the most recent article that he had so carefully clipped from that day's paper to add to his growing collection. Sometimes he wondered why he even bothered. It was becoming little more than an assemblage of their communal ignorance. They laid out the facts, but they comprehended nothing. He read it again.

VANDERVEER CORONER'S INQUEST HELD — Yesterday, Monday, a coroner's court was convened in the case of Miss Cornelia Vanderveer. It resulted in the expected verdict of criminal homicide by person or persons unknown.

Two boys who had discovered the body testified and were near tears as they told the court the horror of that moment. Their testimony was kept mercifully brief, to the relief of the onlookers whose natural sympathies went out to the them.

Police Constable Harold Watkins, first on the scene after the two boys, described in detail what he had found as he removed the wooden packing crate concealing the results of the heinous crime. Horrified gasps could be heard in the courtroom and one woman, near swooning, was assisted from the room. Constable Watkins testified that he had almost been overcome by the odor of putrefaction. The victim lay face down, her dark hair loosed and spread across her shoulders. Her arms lay straight at her sides with her nether limbs straight and close together. Her white dress was much soiled by the refuse in which she lay. Constable Watkins' first impression was that the body had been purposely arranged to create an impression almost military in its studied stiffness.

The fullest extent of the atrocity was discovered only when the body was returned to a supine position. It had been cruelly maimed. The dress was slashed and multiple stab wounds inflicted. The face was so disfigured as to horrify even that seasoned veteran of police work.

Doctor Giles Cranfeld, was called next. He testified that the victim had been strangulated with a cord or thin rope which had been taken away, but left bruises ringing the neck. It had been used with such force that the ligature had penetrated the flesh along the circumference of the neck. The lower abdomen had been stabbed some 25 or 30 times with a dreadful vehemence.

Both sides of the face had been cut, not with a mindless violence such as had been perpetrated upon the lower part of the body, but with what he described as "surgical precision." Each side of the face bore a single incision from the corner of the mouth backward and curving slightly upward almost as far as the ears. The madman had attempted to recreate on the face of this innocent the death's head smile of the naked skull. "Never in all my years," Doctor Cranfeld testified, "have I seen the like. It is the work of a monster." The courtroom was shrouded in silence as the horror sank in and naught was heard save sounds of indrawn breath and muffled sobs.

The police offer assurance that so deranged a lunatic cannot fail to be captured. His depravity will draw the notice of all decent persons and will bring him to the attention of the authorities. His capture is imminently expected. The parents offer a reward of $5,000.00 to whoever brings this killer to justice.

He dropped it in disgust and wiped the sweat from his brow. The heat was stifling. That alone was enough to give him pause about remaining here. Why not move on? But something held him back, a sense of a needed completion and that it would be some time before it could be accomplished. A vague notion, but it had taken hold of him two days ago when he had purchased the candy. He had a weakness for sweets, which he seldom indulged. Indulging weaknesses was not a good habit to cultivate. But habits of childhood are not so easily undone.

The candy had started it, but it was not the taste of the candy that lingered in his memory. It was the seller. She might merit further consideration.

To hell with them, he thought as he quenched the candle's flame and prepared to leave for his evening stroll. His stroll... one more habit it was becoming hard to change, but not so bad a habit after all.

To hell with them. If they were too obtuse to see the truth, there was little he could do to enlighten them.

Chapter VII: Begin the Chopping

The newspapers! Sir, they are the most
villainous — licentious — abominable —
infernal — Not that I ever read them —
no — I make it a rule never to look in a
newspaper.
    Richard Brinsley Sheridan (1751-1816)
    The Critic, Act I, sc. 1 (1779)

[Friday, January 12, 1866]

    Jen's morning had been taken up with chores, those rote actions so necessary to life yet so utterly mindless; but therein lies their redeeming grace, for one can derive from them a sense of useful accomplishment and all the while devote one's mind to things entirely different. Her attention that morning was not on doing the dishes, dusting the furniture, filling the coal bucket, or soaking the salt from the boxed codfish she would cream for supper. Her mind was on the murder, with one small corner devoted to curiosity about James's appointment with Mr. Arkwright, who would ordinarily have seen the Doughertys as minor satellites orbiting on the outermost perimeter of his private solar system, and Sean McBrien as another part of the galaxy entirely. It must have to do with Brogan's death, but why should a man like Arkwright care about the death of one laborer?

    She was eager to get back to the study of the remaining documents and newspaper accounts. She arranged everything in order on the kitchen table, hoping that they would not be long in returning. She was curious, too, to see what McBrien would make of everything.

    "We're home, Jen!" The back door opened and the chill entered with them. Without the wind of the past few days the temperature was more refreshing than bothersome; but they had just returned the horse and carriage and walked home in the cold from the livery stable, so they were happy for the pot of coffee she had on the stove.

    She laughed at some of McBrien's comments and was proud that James had resisted the effort to subject the whole matter to a still non-existent police authority. But she was uneasy as well. What were Arkwright and Maddock really up to? Perhaps it was nothing but the desire for final authority in the matter, but they were still not to be trusted. Besides, when McBrien mentioned Maddock's graying beard, she remembered the man who had thrown the stick at the Corrigan boys, and wondered just what sort of police force the town was about to acquire.

"I see you're ready to put us to work." James nodded toward the papers on the table as he refilled his cup. "Let's show McBrien what we've got."

McBrien read the letters from Mary and studied the Philadelphia articles. Like Dougherty, McBrien had also lived in Philadelphia before the war and could easily picture the areas where the events had occurred. Jen lacked that advantage, having been in Philadelphia only once, when she and James had visited his former landlady and his mentor from the medical school.

"What do you think?" she asked.

"The fact is, I remember well when this happened," he said. "As ye'd imagine, the city was in an uproar — women going about scared o' their own shadows and thinking it fatal to be out and about after dark — even though the poor girl'd been taken during the day, if the reports was true. Fer a while there, any man that looked suspicious ran the risk o' getting himself beat up or worse.

"I worked on the docks in them days and I know the place where the body was found. It's on Front Street, near where ye get the Knight's Point ferry. Ye'll recall where that is, Major?

"And I remember when they arrested the Carlton fellow. People talking about lynching him. Nothing come of it, and a good thing it didn't, fer the man was innocent. When the poor devil got outta jail, he found all his windows smashed and some o' the neighbors all sheepish looking. Anyway, ye know how it is... that was the middle of October and by the end o' November the whole city'd forgot it."

"Look at these," Dougherty said. He handed him two sheets of paper, each written in a different hand. They were neither dated nor signed. The first said:

> I have known Harry Carlton for twenty years and can not believe him guilty of any crime, and surely not of murder. He lives alone in the house left him by his parents. He was mortified at his treatment by the police. Some neighbors damaged his home when he was jailed and now they hold that against him too.

There was no indication of the writer's identity. The second sheet must have come from the woman, the young mother, mentioned in the newspaper on October 30. It read:

> I do not know Mr. H. Carlton but seen him many times, living not far. He is of simler size to man I saw with Miss Conry but not same man. The won with her ws drest in cloes of a kind to flash for him I'ud say. I don't think he done this. Police askt me to look at him and I told them it wasnt him but they took him anyway.

"So there ye have yer police tactics. Carlton wasn't their man. They knew it even before the word from New York. I'd guess they wanted to do something to look like they were hot on the trail."

"Could they really be so callous?" Jen asked.

"Ah, Mrs. Dougherty, ye've no idea what some o' them'll do. It was just such a type me and yer husband met this morning."

"Do you think they considered anyone else? I wondered if it might have been a robbery gone wrong, but then, course, the abduction makes no sense. Besides, what would a young woman on her way to visit a friend have that would be of any value?"

"I think you're right about that, Jen," James said. "This seems more the result of passion than avarice."

"I wonder, d' ye think they investigated the woman's intended? Or even her father? It's a dreadful thought, but who's to know what mightn't happen if there's bad blood and heated words? I seen enough idiotic arguments in the army that all of a sudden turned mean."

"I suppose," Jen said, "we could try to learn who was investigated, but that may be hard to do. I don't think the police will be eager to discuss it with us."

"Even then, Mrs. Dougherty, we don't know if that'd get us one whit closer to who killed Abiageal Conroy, let alone tell us who done in Brogan. Or did yez have something in mind that I'm missing?"

"No," she said, "We didn't. But no matter who killed Abiageal Conroy, why did Brogan collect all these papers? What was his interest? Is there a link with his death that we simply don't see?"

"That's a bothersome point," James said. "There was the note that Brogan received — the note that may have gotten him killed — and that note referred to something in Philadelphia. It may well have to do with the murder of Abiageal Conroy. Or it could have something to do with Mary, the woman in the photograph. Or it could be something else altogether. But there were more murders that caught Brogan's interest. Let's look at those."

They began with the New York clippings, the first of them dated April 25, 1861.

MURDER VICTIM DISCOVERED — Early yesterday morning the body of a young woman was discovered at the Harwood and Sampson Warehouse in lower Manhattan. The warehouse had been unused for some time and Mr. Oliver Harwood, the owner, had come to inspect the premises with a view to renovations.

The victim is Emeline Carding (sometimes calling herself Erma Carling), known also by the soubriquet of "Raven," a tribute to the tresses of which she was so proud. She was well known in the area. She was youthful in appearance, but of dubious reputation.

Her body was dreadfully mutilated and she was strangled with a cord or a thin rope. Its marks were pressed deep into her neck.

She was last seen one week ago yesterday by the other young women with whom she lived. Any relevant information should be given to the authorities.

"D'ye know anything at all about this Emeline Carding? Why in the name of all that's holy would Brogan be interested in her death?" They had no answer.

"When you first came to America," Jen said to McBrien, "you lived in New York City before you went off to the Mexican war. Do you know the place where the body was found? Does it suggest anything to you?"

"A warehouse in lower Manhattan? The waterfront, I'd say... no place fer high society. Emeline Carding was a local. And look here," he said pointing to the paper. "She's got a name of her own and another one she used and the nickname o' Raven. And it talks about the women she lived with. Now that's a polite way o' saying she was a... Well, ye might say... I mean, begging yer pardon, Mrs. Dougherty, but she was part o' what they sometimes call the *demimonde*, if ye know what I mean."

For all his bulk, McBrien was sensitive in his dealings with women. It was one of the things Jen so liked about him. Right now his face was as red as his beard, but his meaning was perfectly clear.

"Do you think the same person could have killed both Abiageal Conroy and Emeline Carding?" Dougherty asked. "Or is that a bit far fetched? What motive would account for two murders so far apart?"

"Far fetched? Maybe. But there's still the possibility, ain't there?"

"Both bodies were left near the waterfront," Jen said. "What could that mean?"

"Maybe just the obvious," McBrien said. "New York's like a lot o' cities. The waterfront's a tough place. He'd be less likely to be noticed there or to be questioned. O' course, a girl like Abiageal Conroy surely would'a been noticed in that part o' town, so he'd need some sort o' conveyance to get her there. But the Carding girl in New York? Who'd'a thought twice about seeing her with a man, no matter what he looked like? And there was the empty warehouse to take her to. Have ye any more information about her murder?"

"Almost nothing," said Dougherty, "We looked over the articles and her name comes up later on, but this is the only piece specifically about her, so there's really nothing to help us."

"I've been thinking," Jen said, "that there may be more than one reason for that. For one thing, Emeline Carding was a person of no consequence as far as most were concerned. The murder was brutal, but even then who would have pursued the matter? Unless there had been a reward, and who would have posted it? And another thing... that was April of 1861. That's when Fort Sumter fell and Virginia seceded, and war was on everybody's mind. What news could compete with that? The papers were full of nothing else."

"Ye mean it all ends right there? There's nothing else said of Emeline Carding?" McBrien asked.

"Oh, there's more," Dougherty said, "but only by implication, but it makes rather more than less of a mystery."

Jen had the next seven articles divided into two sets, one of four and the other of three. The first began with July 23, 1861.

DISTRAUGHT PARENTS SEEK MISSING DAUGHTER — Readers are called to come forward with information in reference to Miss Cornelia Vanderveer, who has been missing for six days.

She is the daughter of Mr. Dewitt Vanderveer and his grieving wife, the former Betje Lange, daughter of well known wool merchant, Mr. Devoss Lange, deceased.

Miss Vanderveer was last seen departing her home in Gramercy Park on the day of her disappearance to take a stroll about the neighborhood. The day was unseasonably fresh for July and was a great relief from the oppressive heat that had preceded. She had left her parents' residence at about one o'clock and was expected back within the hour. Her failure to return was not remarked until the dinner hour, when inquiry among acquaintances failed to discover her whereabouts.

The distraught parents enlisted the police in their search, but subsequent investigation failed to determine her whereabouts.

Miss Vanderveer is twenty-two years old, five feet five inches in height, about 140 pounds of weight, of fair complexion, with brown eyes and dark hair. She was last seen wearing a dress of white piqué sprigged with brown and pink, a bonnet trimmed in pink ribbon, and held a white parasol with pink fringe.

Readers may proffer all information to the police or directly to the offices of this newspaper.

"Now there's a disappearance to stir up some activity. Gramercy Park, is it?"

"What do you mean?" Jen asked.

"Sure now, Gramercy Park makes Rittenhouse Square look almost poor. It's at the top o' Broadway. Gramercy Farm it was once upon a time, but it ain't a farm now. It's a place where the riffraff ain't going to be found. That's why it ain't unusual fer a young woman to take a stroll there unattended. Only fifty or sixty families there and it's them alone has the use o' the park. Ye'd find more'n that in any tenement downtown. The Vanderveers ain't likely to be paupers, and the daughter's disappearance must'a been taken dead serious by the police."

"Then what happened next should most surely have been a source of consternation," she said.

McBrien read the next article as Jen watched his growing horror. At her own first reading she had cried to think of what this young woman must have suffered. The article was dated two days after the preceding one.

MISSING WOMAN MURDERED! — The startling discovery was early yesterday made of the ravaged remains of Miss Cornelia Vanderveer, whose disappearance had only two days ago been reported in these pages. The body might still have gone undiscovered but for the excessive heat of last week. The enervating temperatures gave rise to the olfactory evidence of decay that ended the search.

The body was found in an alley behind a dwelling on Orange Street in the Five Points, covered with the remnants of a damaged shipping crate. A stray dog uncovered the body and was promptly chased away by two youngsters who intelligently summoned the police.

The dead woman's clothing was much soiled and slashed, but was clearly that previously described in this newspaper. Family members performed the grim task of identification. Medical examination showed that the death was due to strangulation by a cord or rope. The body had been savagely slashed and stabbed numerous times. Thus far no witnesses have shed light upon this hideous crime.

The mystery is deepened by the fact that the location of the body of the deceased is so far from the place of her disappearance. Neither she nor her family are associated with the Five Points, nor had Miss Vanderveer any reason to have gone there.

It is speculated that she was abducted forcibly from near her home in Gramercy Park and then brought, either prior or subsequent to death, to the location at which she was found. How she was brought there remains a matter for conjecture.

He finished and closed his eyes. They did not hurry him. The description was overwhelming in its graphic horror. That any woman should end her life in such a way and in such squalor was more than one could contemplate.

"So she was found in Five Points," he said at last. "No wonder they say she was abducted. Never would she'a gone there freely — not by herself and not even with someone else. The place is a cesspool — saloons ye'd not enter without taking yer life in yer hands — opium dens — the poorest o' the poor — every tenement a brothel, begging yer pardon, Mrs. Dougherty. I'm not afraid o' much, but that's a place I always avoided like the plague."

"From the papers it appears she may have been dead since her disappearance. Is that possible? Could a decomposing body have lain in an alley that long unnoticed?"

"Major, sir, I have no doubt of it at all. The alleys there are garbage dumps. The streets ain't much better."

"And you see," Jen said, "that it is another strangulation and more slashing and stabbing. Don't you agree that it is the same killer?"

"I'll not deny what yer saying, Mrs. Dougerty, but it's still hard to see the connection with Abiageal Conroy in Philadelphia. And how does the whole thing get back to Brogan? Why did he collect all this stuff? And why the written statements about the Conroy girl's death? Does he have statements from New York, too?"

"He does," Dougherty said, "but we'll get to those after we finish the articles. The next one is dated four days later — July 30."

This one described in all its horror the testimony taken in the coroner's court, the apparent posing of the body, and the viciousness of the strangling itself. The detail of the disfigured face was worst of all. McBrien looked sick.

"Dear Mother o' God! I thought we'd seen all the suffering there was to see during the war, but all them things was done in the heat o' battle. This is madness! Ye wouldn't treat an animal the way this poor dead soul was treated. What does it all mean?"

Jen heard the anguish in his voice and wondered again if the girl's parents had read these words. In all likelihood, they had. They would have searched the reports, trying in vain to make some sense of it all. How their hearts must have broken all over again! The person who did this must lack all trace of human feeling — must be full of anger and rage and hatred, everything diabolical. That one human being could so treat another was more than terrifying. It raised the dreadful apprehension that so much evil might indeed lurk deep within any of us, all unbeknownst to ourselves. James, she thought, must have read her mind, for he reached over and took her hand in his, squeezing it to give her strength.

"There is no meaning," he said, "or at least no meaning that a sane person could decipher. If there is a logic, it is the logic of a madness I cannot begin to fathom."

"Maybe that's worst of all," Jen said, "that it does have a logic. The arranging of the body, the disfigurement of the face — almost like creating a scene or carving a countenance on the deceased — distorting a young woman into a caricature or a vision from a nightmare."

"It's more than the mind can grasp," McBrien said, "That he'd be so depraved. To think he's got some plan o' his own makes ye wonder what he'll do next, don't it?"

His brow furrowed as a question occurred to him.

"Tell me, Major," he said at last, "D' ye think it's true like the paper says? I mean, does a lunatic really look different? Can ye spot him so easy as they seem to be saying?"

"I doubt it," Dougherty said. "There have been theories, but experience doesn't support them. Some demented persons may look the part, but most don't. Of course, the phrenologists are convinced that the shape of the skull or its various bumps and lumps are surefire indications of dementia. But if you study Esquirol or Prichard or even Dunglison, they will soon convince you that external appearances generally tell you nothing."

"So, sir, ye think the paper's promises that the killer's looks'll give him away are a bit o' hogwash, do ye?"

"I'd say so. I suppose the people who said it may have believed it, but it's no more than whistling in the dark to give the public courage. I'd put more confidence in the promise of the substantial reward — provided someone knew who the killer was."

"Well, ye know how that is, sir. I've known some cops who'd not be above faking some evidence to collect the money — or handing over a nice safe dead villain."

"I suppose you're right," Dougherty said, "but, at least at first, that was not what happened. Things just quietly ended."

He handed McBrien the final report of the series, the one dated August 14, 1861.

HAS THE MONSTER DEPARTED? — It is a month since the murder of Miss Cornelia Vanderveer of Gramercy Park. The police guaranteed that the monster guilty of this crime could not fail of prompt apprehension.

Where then is this unnatural brute and why have we not heard of his arrest? One solution to this enigma is that, if he is not already dead by his own hand or that of another, then he must have fled the city and be no longer among us. In either case, the people of this city may breathe a sigh of relief. That the monster has indeed departed is a consummation devoutly to be wished. All evidence points that way.

"Those are all the reports we have on the Vanderveer murder," Jen said. "There may have been more, but those are the only ones Brogan had in his possession."

"And again," James added, "there are two written statements. One probably from a woman who lived with Emeline Carding and the other from a policeman who had seen the Vanderveer girl on the afternoon of her disappearance."

McBrien took the two sheets and examined their short accounts.

> Emmy was my frend she come her from Albany an she was a good girl no matter how she erned her keep. The coppers ast me to tel them if it was her an it was. I cried to see her so. She kared for her hair it was all spred out. Her dres was all bluddie in front her face was awfle cut across like a big mouth. I seen for days in my mind an my dreems I never seen nuthin like God help her poor thing. We work tagether I miss her she was fun.

"So! The same fiend done fer both Carding and Vanderveer. Ye'd both agree with that, wouldn't ye?" They did. He read on.

> I was on the beat in Gramercy the day the Vanderveer girl went missing. I saw her about one or one-thirty walking. She was across

> Twentieth Street going the opposite way from me. I turned down Third Avenue and didn't see her again. I saw a man beyond her on Twentieth Street further down. He was a big fellow, young I thought. He got out of a carriage. Never saw him before, but he was well dressed and looked like he belonged there and I thought nothing of it.

"Maybe something, maybe nothing. But it is a man and a carriage, ain't it? D' ye think it could'a been him?"

"We thought so," Jen said, "but that's only a hopeful guess. Even if it was him, we still don't know any more than we did."

"So it sounds like it come to an end. But it didn't, did it? There's a lot more clippings."

"A lot more," Jen said. "But if these clippings represent all the murders, then nothing happened for more than a year — not until September of 1862."

"Ye don't say! Sure, that was during the Maryland campaign... Antietam. And ye said that the Carding murder was during the month when Sumter fell. And July of 1861 was First Bull Run. Does that mean something, do ye think?"

Antietam... Just a few miles from her parents' home in Maryland, Jen thought. She had been nursing the wounded for the first time, nineteen years old and trying to be grown up and confident — and yet so happy that her mother was there with her. And in New York, she thought, some poor soul was being murdered by a madman. McBrien was right. Each death coincided with a great battle. What could that mean?

"The September killing was done by the same person? Where? New York again?"

"It was New York, all right," Dougherty said. "The first news was a little paragraph on September 18." He handed it to McBrien.

SPECIAL NOTICE!! — Early this morning just before this edition went to press, the discovery was made of the body of a young woman brutally murdered. The remains were found in an alley parallel to Howard Street between Braxton and Mulberry, in the Five Points. Details will follow.

"Five Points again. Was she abducted from somewhere else, Major?"

"Abducted indeed. She was from some place called Little Germany. Read what was written the next day, and tell us what you think."

HAS THE MONSTER RETURNED? — The mutilated body found yesterday in the Five Points was that of Miss Berdine Griswald, daughter of Mr. and Mrs. Albrecht Griswald of Rivington Street in Little Germany or, as our German neighbors call it, Kleindeutschland. She worked in her father's confectionary store on the ground floor of their residence.

This crime recalls the horrors of July last, when a woman was savagely murdered and her body left no more than two blocks from where Miss Griswald's body was discovered. Both victims were abducted from near their homes.

Miss Griswald was well liked by her neighbors, who describe her as pretty, cheerful, and popular with all who frequented her father's place of business. She was five feet four inches in height, fairly robust, with lovely black hair. She had left the store near 2:00 P.M. to make a delivery some five blocks away. When she did not return within the hour her father became apprehensive and sent her older brother, Franz, in search of her. Neighbors aided, but no trace was found. One woman recalled seeing her leave the shop, package in hand.

According to police, near 1:30 A.M. yesterday a woman resident in Howard Street, saw from her bedroom window a man place a large bundle in the alley. He looked upward upon hearing her window open, and ran off before he could be identified. He may have had a beard. The woman, in company with another of the same house, descended to the alley to investigate, both recoiling in horror as they gazed upon a woman's body.

The body lay prone, its hair spread out across the shoulders. It had not been placed haphazardly. Rather, it was in that attitude which military men describe as "at attention," with feet close together, legs straight and parallel, and arms stiff at the sides.

Upon turning her over, they found the abdomen violated with multiple stab wounds, and the face horribly slashed. Doctor Giles Cranfeld was summoned to the scene. He had last year given medical evidence in the case of Miss Cornelia Vanderveer. (The reader is directed to page 3 of this issue for a resumé of last year's reports.)

Miss Griswald's body was warm when found, from which

Cranfeld concludes that she had been dead for an hour or less when discovered.

Police seek information of anyone in possession of same. They have special interest in the acquaintance of anyone who recalls the man running away or other suspicious actions at about that same time. Thus have evaporated, as surely as the rains of summer, last year's hope that the madman had abandoned his onslaught upon the public of this city.

"Looks like the same reporter — or at least someone who remembered the headline o' the year before."

"What can you tell us of where the girl lived? Was the area poor? Wealthy? In between?"

"Little Germany? Well, Major, I told ye what sort o' place Gramercy Park is and Little Germany ain't far from there. Not above a mile and half, I'd say. But were ye to see the two places, ye'd think it another city all together — maybe even another country. Ye go from mansions in the one place to beer halls in the other and everybody speaks German. Rivington Street is poor, but it's a decent place. There's families and churches, but everybody's packed in tight. Then, ye go another half mile and ye're in Five Points and ye'd be happy to run right back to Rivington Street and spend yer life there rather than stay an hour in Five Points, given those as yer choices."

"The description of the body leaves no doubt that the killer is the same," Jen said, "Unless there is a second one doing the same things, and that is beyond belief, in my opinion."

"God help us, Mrs. Dougherty, I'd not want even to consider the possibility!"

"Do you think the man they saw over the body could have been the killer?" James asked.

"Could be. If the girl'd been dead longer, I'd'a said not a chance. Ye'd not expect him to stand there admiring his handiwork, would ye? But what if he'd just finished when she seen him? O' course, ye'd have to admit that anyone, killer or not, might just run away if somebody seen him there. Did they ever learn any more about him?"

Dougherty handed him the last of the seven articles, the one dated September 29.

MAD MURDERER KILLED! REIGN OF FEAR AT AN END! — Ten days ago the police issued a general call for information about the man seen near the murdered and maimed body of Miss Berdine Griswald. The mode of death, the placement of the body, and the peculiar surgical cutting of the young woman's face into what he described as "a ghastly smile" led Doctor Giles Cranfeld, medical examiner, to connect this crime with the earlier murder of Miss Cornelia Vanderveer, although subsequent inquiry revealed no other connection between the two.

Doctor Cranfeld holds that the same fiend may be responsible for the death of a poor *demimondaine* in April, 1861. That victim could not have had a connection with Misses Vanderveer and Griswald, but the method by which the victims were dispatched was the same, all three having been savagely strangled prior to further depredations.

The woman who witnessed a man standing over the body of Miss Griswald in the alley behind Howard Street could give only the barest of descriptions. Two men who were standing on Lafayette Street at the time saw a man emerge from the alley behind Howard Street. Upon ascertaining the presence of the two, he changed course and walked rapidly away, but not before they recognized him as a neighborhood "character" known as "Crazy Karl."

Police had more than once taken him into custody for drunkenness and being a public nuisance. He had been accused of petty theft, but never convicted. He had no known address, but slept in doorways or "five cent flops."

About 5:00 yesterday morning two police officers, Detective Michael Boland and Detective Sergeant Gerald Toolin, spotted Crazy Karl and gave chase. They took him into custody after a struggle in which he received bruises later noted by observers.

The suspect was questioned for some hours and finally admitted to the crime of murder. He wrote and signed a confession acknowledging that he had killed both Miss Vanderveer and Miss Griswald. The two officers left the room momentarily to report the confession to their superior, Captain Hartranft. Both officers testify that the door of the interrogation room was securely locked when they left, but the prisoner made his escape. He reached the street with the two officers in hot pursuit. Upon his refusal to stop after repeated warnings, the officers drew their weapons and fired, killing him instantly.

The man's identity remains unknown, although earlier records had used the name "Karl Schmidt" for the sake of filling in the required information, but of his guilt there can now be no doubt in view of the testimony of witnesses, the written confession, and the guilty attempt at flight. We can assure our readers that the mad murderer is now departed this city and this life. The police are to be congratulated. Both detectives are entitled to the reward which will now be theirs.

"There ye have it, sir. It took a year, but somebody got that reward and the culprit was safely dead. To be sure, they got a signed confession, but ye don't have to be guilty to be persuaded t' make yer mark, do ye? And he was kind enough t' throw in the Vanderveer case too, the one with the nice five-thousand dollar reward. That must'a given the detectives a moment o' pleasure."

"I expect this will come as no surprise to you, but there are three more statements. Take a look." James handed them over.

> This written accurately as dictated to me, the witness being unable to write: "The alley was dark. My eye ain't what they was but I thought he had a big package. He looked up when I opened the window and right away he run. Like I told the cops, it was a man and maybe had a beard. I don't know."

The second was from one of the men who had seen Crazy Karl come from the alley.

> It was maybe one thirty or two when we seen somebody come out a the alley onto Lafayette. We looked cause you got a be careful down there. It was about half moon, so there was some light. We seen it was only Crazy Karl. Soon as he seen us he took off the other way like he always done. We told the cops it was only him and we dint think they ud go after him cause he was crazy and never done no harm. But good thing they did cause Karl told them he done it. The dead girl I mean.

The last could have come from anyone in Five Points, someone who knew Karl.

> Karl never hurt nobody. He was always scared and ran away. I think it was because he did not speak English even after all the years here. He did not read or write not even his own name.

They spent the next hour discussing the clippings, then divided a sheet into four columns, one for each of the murders, and listed for each victim a summary of names, backgrounds, residences, locations of bodies, witnesses, manner of death, and whatever else they thought might be helpful. They also listed the battles and events of the war which had occupied the news on each occasion. And at the end, no clear line of thought had emerged, just more busy work, this time without even the illusion of accomplishing anything useful.

It was early afternoon when they ate a light lunch and decided to defer until later the last batch of reports and statements. Dougherty had office hours and some patients to see at home. McBrien had prescriptions to prepare and deliver. In any case, they all needed a respite.

Jen found herself alone in the kitchen with chores to perform until at last it was time to prepare supper. She peeled the potatoes and put them on to boil for mashing. The cod was properly desalted and ready to cook. She would make cream sauce and flavor it with butter and minced onions. She thought for an instant of how she had cried those months ago over their own sad loss. And she had cried over these dreadful murders. She got out the cutting board and the sharp knife and prepared to cry over the onions. It was time to begin the chopping.

Chapter VIII: Arkwright Was Right

I've a head like a concertina, I've a tongue like a button stick,
I've a mouth like an old potato, and I'm more than a little sick.
   Rudyard Kipling (1865-1936)
   Cells (1892)

[Friday, January 12, 1866]

Marty Carroll had gone to bed on Thursday with an aching head, a pain that seemed to pulse just behind his eyes, and the feeling that he could not stay awake for another minute. The others had noticed something wrong at supper, when his usually voracious appetite was seen to have left him entirely. He made the effort, but to no avail. Then, despite his exhaustion, having gone to bed he tossed and turned all night, feeling first too cold and then too warm, pulling the quilts up and pushing them back down, even though the temperature in the room followed its normal curve from evening cold to morning colder. When it came time to get up, it was all he could do to pull on his clothes and trudge behind the others out to the mine. By noon he was so sick and so oppressed by what had now become the first signs of a fever, that he reported to the foreman and was excused for the day.

He dragged himself back to the boarding house, embarrassed at his age to be wanting nothing more than to go to his own home and the tender ministrations of his mother — a wish impossible of fulfillment.

When he cleaned up at the frigid pump and entered the warmth of the kitchen, Catherine Corrigan took one look at him, sat him down for some soothing tea and a piece of toast (which he was unable to eat) and sent him off to his room to crawl back into bed, feeling like a whipped puppy.

She resolved to let him rest for a while, after which she would look in on him. Then, if he was no better, like it or not, he would be visited by the doctor. That was a visit that, like Marty but for reasons all her own, she was not eager to receive.

* * *

Dougherty wrote to Judge Barrett after lunch, and McBrien dropped the letter off at the station for the afternoon train. It was slower than the telegraph, but bypassed their inquisitive telegrapher. It seemed best to inform the Judge of Arkwright's attempt to control the investigation, and Dougherty volunteered to travel to Mauch Chunk at Barrett's convenience to discuss the matter. He expected Arkwright and Maddock to contact the Judge as well, but with some reserve since they could not afford to jeopardize Maddock's appointment to the new police force before it had even begun.

In any event, Judge George Rodden Barrett was a man not easily pushed. Appointed from Clearfield County in the center of the state to fill a vacancy on the bench in Mauch Chunk, he soon found himself treated as the outsider. That was in 1853, when he'd been opposed by the Democrats. Then, when they decided to change tactics and support him in 1855, he ignored them and got himself elected without campaigning or even visiting the district. He beat Thomas Bell, the Know-Nothing candidate, and did it through the support of the newspapers, so enthralled by his independence that they actively campaigned on his behalf. Maybe it also helped that he had been a newspaper editor himself and knew how to deal with them. He had held the judgeship ever since. By 1865 he was the candidate of both parties. Arkwright would think twice before testing Barrett's mettle.

Dougherty entered his office and opened the waiting room door for the first patient. Six pairs of eyes rose in perfect unison and lowered with equal precision, as though rehearsed in advance. All were silent, not a smile in the lot, all faced with the dilemma of which was worse — to bear the current ailment or to submit to the mystery of treatment.

The first six were replaced as fast as he tended them, and so it went for two more hours. As surely as spring showers bring summer flowers, the cold spell had produced the usual crop of sore throats and respiratory complaints. Snow and ice added a sprained wrist, a nastily twisted leg, and a broken finger.

Happily, none of his sore throat and respiratory patients yet exhibited the inflamed throat and fauces of more serious afflictions. In addition to warmth and rest, he prescribed liberal quantities of a cough elixir that he and McBrien had found useful when the Army of the Potomac had lain in winter encampment and hibernal ailments had run rampant. McBrien produced it in large quantities, dissolving over a fire a half pound each of balsam of tolu and gum Arabic in a gallon of good cider vinegar and a quart or two of honey. Once cooled, he completed it with eighteen fluid ounces of tincture of opium. It made a soothing remedy with a prescription of four or five teaspoons per day.

The last patient was Mrs. McGinty, a lovely old soul to whose house Dougherty would gladly have gone, but she would have none of it. "Sure, I'm not that old yet, that I'd be dragging the doctor out to me house when the exercise o' getting here does me the world o' good."

He hadn't the heart to argue with her; indeed, he stood in awe of her independence and hoped he would do as well at her age — whatever that age might be. He should have guessed the very late seventies, but only once had he made the mistake of asking.

"Me age is it, then, young man, that yer after?" she'd said, "Did yer mother never tell ye that's not a question to be asking a person? Tisn't a needful thing or I'd'a told ye without yer asking."

She was about to leave, when the outer door opened and he heard the hush of nervous whispering, the sound of children's voices. It was the two Corrigan boys he found in the waiting room, looking awkward and whispering to each other. Both mouths snapped shut as he appeared, and not a word was said until Mrs. McGinty had made her goodbyes.

"Good afternoon, boys. Are either of you sick?"

"Oh, no, Doctor, we ain't sick at all," said Daniel, the older of the two.

"My mom sent us," said little Michael.

"How can I help you?"

"It's Marty Carroll..."

"You're supposed to say 'Mr. Carroll,'" Michael said, "That's what mom said."

"Mr. Carroll's awful sick," Daniel said, yielding to Michael's sense of propriety, but favoring him with a dark look, "He come home from work early and took to his bed. Mom says would you look in on him."

"She said to say please, too." Michael was on his best behavior and was going to see that Daniel did the same.

"Please..."

"Do you know what was wrong with him?"

"He was coughing and sneezing and his face was all red."

"Mom said he has fever, too." Michael was the man for details.

"You can run home and tell your mother that I will come. I have a few other patients to visit first, but I'll be there within the hour."

There was a moment's hesitation, and Dougherty guessed why. In his office was a large jar that Jen kept filled with candies for just such occasions. They each got a handful and they were off. He let Jen know that he would be visiting patients and then he, too, was off.

It was past 5:00 when he finally knocked on Mrs. Corrigan's door, glad to get in out of the cold. Nothing would do her but that he have a cup of tea "fer the chill" and stop by the stove for a minute before he saw Marty Carroll, "fer otherwise he'll be catching the chill ye brung in with ye."

"The poor boy ain't good a' tall," she said. "He was coughing and hacking this morning when he left fer work, and, as ye'd guess, he wouldn't hear tell o' staying home. But he was so miserable by noon that his buddies made him knock off fer the day and get back here."

"How is he now?"

"The cough's worse and the fever, but I got him to take a sip o' tea. He's wrapped up in his blankets and dozing off and on. I'm worried fer him. Fer all his work, he's just a lad."

"Let's have a look," Dougherty said and she led the way up the narrow staircase, her candle casting long and wavering shadows on the wall.

At the top of the steps was a short corridor. The door nearest the stairwell led to Marty Carroll's room, the rear one over the kitchen.

Two other doors further front led to the room shared by Doyle and McGehan and to the attic stairs.

Marty's room was small, but clean and neat — a tribute to Mrs. Corrigan's housekeeping and Marty's upbringing. The room was warm, heated from the now opened floor register just above the kitchen stove. The single window's drapes were pulled shut and the close atmosphere emphasized the sick room odor — compounded of Marty Carroll's fevered perspiration and a not yet emptied chamber pot. Mrs. Corrigan tsk-tsk'd, took it from beneath the bed, put the lid on it, and set it out in the hall.

Marty had been in a fitful sleep when they entered, but either he heard them or the cooler air let in from the corridor told him they were there. He lifted his head, the quilt clutched up tight about his neck — the reflex of the feverish patient. He looked disoriented, then his eyes focused and he came to himself.

"Doctor, it's you, then. I thank you for coming." He was hoarse, his eyes bloodshot, and he had the faraway look of fever.

"What's wrong, Marty?"

"My throat hurts, doctor, and my head, and I can't say if I'm freezing or burning up."

"Let's have a look at you and we'll get you back to normal in no time."

His pulse was strong, a bit elevated — about 90 — some of that possibly an iatrogenic symptom. Forehead and cheeks were warm — perhaps 102°, but no worse. Thoracic percussion proved mostly clear, auscultation indicated a mainly dry rhoncus with some sibilance upon exhalation. An ordinary catarrh, Dougherty concluded. Marty was young and strong and should escape acute bronchitis. He recommended hot tea, warmth, bed rest, and gruel — no milk, no meat, some toast if his stomach stood it, and maybe a soft-boiled egg as the fever abated.

He also prescribed lozenges for day use and a mixture of mucilage of acacia, syrupus papaveris, and water, a tablespoon at bedtime and as needed during the night, mustard plasters to help allay the congestion, and soaking his feet in warm mustard water to help him overcome the chills.

He wrote the prescriptions and Mrs. Corrigan dispatched her boys to McBrien's pharmacy. Marty was ready to sleep and she promised to be back later with the medicine and a cup of tea.

"Doctor," she said, as he was donning his coat preparatory to taking his leave, "can ye spare me a minute? I've something to say and I'd prefer to do it while the two boys're out and the men ain't home."

"Of course." Her voice shook, and her eyes were downcast. What could be worrying her? "Has it to do with your health? I hope you're not coming down with something, too."

"Ach, it's nothing like that. It's a worry I've had and I need to say something about it. To get it off me mind, ye know. It's eating away at me, and I ain't sure what to do."

"You know I'll help if I can."

"Well, first of all... have ye learned anything more about who killed Brogan?"

"Not yet, I'm sorry to say. We're hoping that all the papers you gave us may set us in the right direction. But for now I cannot even speculate on the identity of the murderer."

"I have something else to say to ye then, and fer all I know it may tell ye nothing at all or it may tell ye a great deal. I've said not a word o' this to another soul, but I know it's something ye should be told about. I feel ashamed o' meself fer not saying it before. I had me chance twice when yer dear wife come here, yet I done nothing. I felt bad about that. She was so nice to me, and she left not even suspecting there was something I was hiding."

Not quite so, he thought, for Jen had already told him of her feeling that Mrs. Corrigan had something more to say; but he simply waited, not wanting to interrupt. Let her go at her own pace.

"Well, Brogan left something I never mentioned. It had me name on it, so I kept it, but it's been a misery to me thinking about it. I've no doubt he meant it as a kindness — but I've no idea why... I mean, why would he... I tell ye what... let me get it fer ye and then ye can tell me what I ought to do."

She went to her quarters off the kitchen and came back with a heavy little tin box, to which was affixed a piece of adhesive plaster bearing her name. Inside was a paper reading, "For the use of Mrs. Catherine Corrigan," and beneath it were coins — many coins — all, so far as he could see, ten dollar gold pieces, more, he was sure, than Mrs. Corrigan had ever seen in one place.

"That's over a thousand dollars in there," she said, "and I've no idea what to do with it. I feel awful keeping it, even though it was there with me name written right on it clear as day. But what if it has to do with his death? And what if it ain't honestly come by? But fer the sake o' me soul, I can't think bad o' Brogan. I'm sure he done no wrong. I hope ye believe me that I never stole it... Ye do believe that, don't ye?"

"I do indeed," he said. Catherine Corrigan was an honest, hard working woman, and he could not conceive of her stealing from anyone. But what did it mean? And where had it come from? Stolen? Gambling winnings? He could understand why her possession of it made her so uncomfortable.

"Thank you for telling me about it," he said, "but I don't know what it means. As to what to do with it... have you a safe place for it?"

"I have," she said, "Ye'd not easily find it were I not to show ye. D' ye want to see?"

"No," he said. "I suggest that you put it back there and hold it in safekeeping until we learn more. Tell no one else about it. He addressed the box to you and he said that its contents were for you, so I'm sure he had faith in what you would do with it. For now, just keep it safe and I'll see if we can find out where it came from."

She heaved a sigh of relief.

"It does suggest one thing," he said. "The fact that it was packed in a box already addressed to you may mean that Brogan was having some fears — that he may have thought himself in danger, perhaps even feared for his life."

At home he and Jen ate their creamed cod and he told her about the money. Then they set the mystery aside and talked about other things, including his concern for some of his patients. It was after 8:00 and they were once again in the kitchen when the knock sounded at the back door. It was McBrien.

* * *

After he saw the letter off to Mauch Chunk, McBrien walked back up Main Street to his pharmacy, glancing uneasily at the new police headquarters as he unlocked his door. He entered, as he always did, with a sense of pride at the well-stocked shop he had created from his army savings and the comfortable quarters above. He was grateful to Dougherty for the encouragement and for suggesting the move to Penrose Valley. It was good to be back in a small town — more like Ireland in the old days and better for him than Philadelphia had been.

Inside the door, on the floor beneath the letter slot, were the orders and prescriptions put there by customers who knew that everything would be sent to them before the end of the day. He packaged the orders, and then began compounding the prescriptions.

It was near 6:00 when he finished. He was about to close up and make himself some supper, when the little bell on the door tinkled and a head peeped around the edge. That was followed by another as the two Corrigan boys came in and shut the door behind them.

"Well, now, me fine young gentlemen, what can I be doing fer yez?"

"The doctor sent us," Michael said, sounding as serious as a soldier on a special mission.

"It's for Mr. Carroll," Daniel added, "He's awful sick."

They handed over the prescriptions. McBrien looked them over, said he would make them up, and sent them home to assure their mother that the medicines would be along shortly.

Of course, they could easily have waited and saved him the trip. The lozenges were already made up, being so useful at this time of year, and the other prescription was the work of only a few minutes. But he didn't want to be saved this trip. Making his own delivery would have the added benefit of visiting Catherine Corrigan. He decided to make the delivery first, before he fixed his supper, so Marty would have his medicine the sooner. Actually, had he been totally honest with himself, not having eaten might make it possible to accept if she should by any chance suggest that he eat with them.

The boys had not been gone more than fifteen minutes when he blew out the lamps, locked the door, and took the small packages to the boarding house. The boarders had finished eating and Catherine Corrigan and the boys were having their own meal in the kitchen when he arrived, apologizing profusely for the intrusion. After some protestations that he hoped would be unsuccessful, he was persuaded to have a bite with them. But it was after supper that he made the discovery he thought Dougherty would want to hear about, so instead of going home after he left, he decided to make one more stop.

* * *

"I hope I'm not disturbing ye then, Doctor... Mrs. Dougherty."

"Not at all," Jen said, "Come in and warm yourself. Won't you join us in some hot chocolate? We were just about to have some."

"With pleasure, ma'am."

Jen got out another cup and a plate of cookies, *ne potus noceat*, as the Latin adage has it.

"I seen yer light on me way home and thought I'd knock. Ye might be interested in what's just come to me attention.

"The Corrigan boys come by with young Marty's prescriptions just as I was in the middle o' some other things," he seemed to hesitate, then went on, "I told them I'd bring the medicines by, once I finished what I was doing."

That surprised Dougherty. It would have been more usual for McBrien to ask the boys to wait or to have them come back. But, then, he was a kindly man with always a soft spot for children. And then, he thought, there was Catherine Corrigan — petite, lively, younger than McBrien but not by so very much, and looking even younger than her years. The dark hair had not a strand of gray, her figure was full and youthful, her eyes twinkled with a quiet wit much like McBrien's own. Dougherty finally caught on to what Jen had seen almost at once. Well, he could do worse and not much better. McBrien was still explaining.

"Mrs. Corrigan was glad to have the medicine and nothing'd do her but that I sit meself down and take a bite with her and the boys. She took the lozenges and a pot o' tea up to the patient and, when she come back, she told me he'd asked to see me.

"When we were done eating, I went up, but he was asleep and I hadn't the heart to wake him, so I started to leave. He must'a heard me, fer just as I was about to close the door behind me, he said, 'Mr. McBrien? Is it you then?' So I went back to hear what he had to say. And I'm glad I did."

What McBrien learned told them a bit about Brogan's character, but not much. Like a dim light in a dark place, it hinted at new outlines but cast as many unwelcome shadows. Enough to make Dougherty wonder if Arkwright and Maddock had a point after all.

"Marty's a young fellow, ye know. Not been here that long. He's a good lad, but not yet sure of himself. He'd taken a shine to Brogan 'cause Brogan let him talk about things and took him serious, and didn't mind if he kept quiet to think before he spoke. He says when he does that with some people they ignore him. Anyway he was missing his parents. They're up near Ashland and he don't get to see them much. Brogan sort o' took him under his wing. And he did have some serious things to think about.

"He says he's being pushed by some o' the lads in the mine to join the A.O.H., and he ain't sure if he should. He was afraid it'd offend his parents — his dad makes a point o' not joining and Marty, no different than Brogan, is a regular churchgoer and don't know how joining would square with that."

"Just what is the A.O.H.?" Jen asked. "I've heard people mention it, but I've never asked about it. Why would it be a problem with the Church?"

"It's the Ancient Order of Hibernians," Dougherty explained. McBrien and he had been familiar with it for years, but Jen hadn't known it in Maryland. It had not yet gotten all the publicity it would in the next ten years.

"Just exactly what does it do?"

"Well, Mrs. Dougherty, that depends, I'd say, on just who ye're asking. If ye was to ask the people that belong to the Order, they'd like as not tell ye that it's a fraternal organization dedicated to mutual aid and works o' charity, formed to care fer its own, fer nobody else'll help them. And maybe that's the truth of it."

"Is that wrong?" she asked.

"Not at all," Dougherty said, "but that's only if you ask the members. You'll get a different response if you ask someone like Benjamin Bannan. He'd tell you that the A.O.H. is nothing but a bloodthirsty gang of Irish ruffians and drunkards, banded together to terrorize the weak and extort money from the rich by threats. And I've no doubt he'd also tell you that there is no least difference between them and the ones who resisted the draft in the war and caused the workers to strike against the mine owners. Besides, so far as he's concerned, the A.O.H. is Irish and Catholic and that's more than enough to condemn it right off. They're the ones he calls Buckshots and Molly Maguires.

"You'd get still another answer from Beverley Arkwright. He'd tell you the A.O.H. is a sham society formed to hide an illegal combination of workers, a union out to destroy the coal industry, the enemy even of the poor working man who might be put out of a job."

"And the Church?"

"Now there's still another point of view. During the war Archbishop Wood sent out a pastoral letter from Philadelphia and had it read at Sunday Mass in all the churches. He reminded people that the Church is opposed to secret societies. Nobody had a problem with that when he named the Masons and the Odd Fellows and some other Protestant groups. But in the same breath he named the Buckshots and the Molly Maguires, and that didn't sit well in the coal region. The parishioners took it a condemnation of the A.O.H."

"So ye see why poor Marty Carroll's in a state o' such confusion. He don't know what to make o' the whole thing. Is the A.O.H. a dark danger? Or is it just there to care fer the poor mick miners. That's what he talked to Brogan about."

"And what did Brogan advise?" Jen asked.

"He didn't exactly advise anything. He just told Marty not to jump in too fast, but he didn't come right out and say not to join. He just said to watch what ye get into, fer ye don't want to step in a hole before ye know how far down is the bottom."

"Was Brogan a member?" Dougherty asked.

"That he was not. And there's the heart o' Marty's problem now. He don't know just what to make o' Brogan's being killed like he was, and he's almost scared o' finding out who done it. According to Marty, Frank O'Laughlin is the man to know if ye want to get into the A.O.H. in this town. And he might be the man to know if ye had the mind to step into one o' the deeper holes, too. And it was Frank O'Laughlin talked the most to Marty about joining — just like it was O'Laughlin talked to Brogan. Him and Brogan worked together and had a lot o' arguments about it. Marty heard them at it more than once. Nor did Brogan like the way O'Laughlin was trying to recruit Marty Carroll. He told him to back off and let the youngster make up his own mind in his own time. O'Laughlin didn't like that."

"So there was bad blood between Brogan and O'Laughlin?" Jen asked.

"When ye come right down to it, ma'am, I think not. I put it to Marty, and he couldn't say. He thought Brogan and O'Laughlin was sometimes at odds, but that they respected each other — they hadn't quite come to bad blood, but it could'a happened in time."

It was late when McBrien left and they agreed to meet the next day. Dougherty had begun to like Frank O'Laughlin and the respect he got from the other men — not, it seemed, a respect inspired by fear. He hoped that he had nothing to do with Brogan's death. On the other hand, much as he hated the notion, Arkwright and Maddox had planted a new seed in his mind — a seed he hoped would not sprout as it seemed about to. He did not relish even the hint that Arkwright was right.

The Diarist

> November 4, 1862 — Were I foolish enough to believe in omens, I would say that my departure was foreordained. Death is the final departure and, if the newspapers are to be believed, then I died more than a month ago. I find myself losing confidence in their accuracy. However, it was time to depart and that is what I have done. Time for something new, something to ease the ennui. New people, new faces, new opportunities to continue my mission. The day is on the horizon, the day to purify, to purge, to bring happiness once more.

It was a time of unparalleled excitement and the Diarist was delighted to be at its hub, to be caught up in the great events of the day. New York was finally tiresome. He needed to move. He presented himself to a recruiter, spoke of his previous experience, and was directed to the means of acquiring the appropriate rank and assignment. He was now in uniform. Not a new experience, but a different sort of uniform than the one he had previously worn.

He still walked at night and Washington was even more interesting than New York. Just now, as he looked about he was delighted at the activity this late at night. Even in this misty drizzle. There were few street lamps in this area, and in warmer weather he knew that the stench of decay and corruption from alleys and canal would be all but unbearable. Yet it was a popular quarter, given what it had to offer for a price.

All around him were men in uniform, men looking for pleasure or trouble or just a means of escape from the humdrum of camp life. Women stood at their stoops, calling out to passers-by, ridiculing the shy, enticing those who showed the least spark of interest. A cacophany of laughter and music and incessant bickering and outbursts of violent fighting came from the establishments on all sides. This no more than a short stroll from the seat of government. A neighborhood of alleys, shadowy doorways, dirt smudged windows, stray cats and dogs. It was a place many would shun from fear. The Diarist was not a fearful man.

The uniform was a strange thing, he thought, a thing of contradiction. In one sense it immediately identified him, made him as visible as one could be. And at the same time it hid him more effectively than could any elaborate disguise. Here he was so much like the others, that his presence was scarcely noticed and would most certainly never be recalled. That was a gift.

It was here, in the place they call Murder Bay, that he saw her. Like the others, she was plying her trade, but unlike the others seemed attached to no particular house. He would not have noticed her, had she not noticed him first and called out to him. Even then he would have gone on his way, but in her effort to draw him she lifted her skirt: Not high, just enough to afford him a glimpse of well turned calf, togged out in cheap stockings striped vertically in red and black. He walked off into the mist, but not far. It was late, she would either find a customer or go home, so he waited. A light fog began to envelop the area and he thought he might lose her. Then he saw her emerging alone from the gloom and he followed, saw where she stayed and marked the place for the proper day.

Chapter IX: The Two Visitors

> Here are a few of the unpleasant'st words
> That ever blotted paper.
>   William Shakespeare (1564-1616)
>   *The Merchant of Venice*, Act II, sc. 2 (1597)

[Saturday, January 13, 1866]

Words. Black ink upon white paper. The illiterate may not grasp the power such markings have, the knowledge they communicate, the depth of emotion they evoke. Surprise, fright, terror, mystery, nostalgia, humor...

When the weekly *Carbon Democrat* came on Friday's evening train from Mauch Chunk, Jen did not know which emotion best suited one of its articles, the most recent in an intermittent series that had begun with the start of the cold weather. A handyman at the Mansion House Hotel in Mauch Chunk had gone out at night to fetch fire wood. Dogs were barking excitedly near a shed against the side of the mountain and, as the man drew near, one of them yelped in pain and a shadowy form bounded up the steep slope into the darkness. Its speed was described as spectacular, but witnesses claimed it was no less spectacular than the performance of the handyman as he returned to the safety of the hotel's kitchen door.

The mysterious beast was seen again, but always in the dark, and its species remained unidentified. Numerous cats and dogs disappeared without a trace, and one large dog was found half devoured, after barking furiously the night before.

Speculation was rife. A few adventuresome souls tried to track it, but their dogs had more sense than they and refused to go past the edge of town. It had been variously identified as a mountain lion, a catamount, a panther, a tiger, and even, of all things, a kangaroo. This week it had reappeared.

THE WILD ANIMAL ABOUT AGAIN — We thought, for the past month, that the animal which had committed such havoc in the dog tribe, had left us and gone to some more congenial locality, but we were mistaken. On Monday night about 11 o'clock it captured a pig on Broadway, above the Presbyterian Church, and amid a great deal of squealing carried his pig-ship back of Mr. Zellner's photography gallery; a woman hearing the noise proceeded near the spot and frightened the animal off; in the morning the pig was dead and partly devoured. On Wednesday morning about 3½ o'clock as the railroad watchman was going his rounds to awaken the conductor and train hands, he heard the caterwauling of a cat, as if in agony, in Broadway, near the willow tree, and discovered through the darkness that a large animal was devouring the cat. Not having any weapons he dared not attack the beast, and before he could call aid to his assistance, it was gone. He says it is about two feet high, but cannot, owing to the darkness, describe its color.

The writer found an element of the comical. Jen did not, especially with James intending to visit Judge Barrett in Mauch Chunk; but when she showed him the article, he smiled.

"What next?" he said.

It had not inspired in him the feelings it had in her. She told him it worried her. He hugged her and said he did not expect to be long in Mauch Chunk, and, anyway, it seemed to avoid human beings. Still she worried.

McBrien arrived early and they got back to the newspapers, this time from Washington City. Five murders from 1862 through 1865. The first was dated December 19, 1862.

MURDER! DISGRACE TO OUR CITY — Early yesterday, just after first light, a woman discovered near the back door of her residence the body of a young woman lying face down. Seeing no sign of violence and thinking it a local unfortunate under the effects of strong drink, the woman attempted to rouse her. She turned her over and found the front of her dress bloodied. Her scream attracted the other women of the residence near the intersection of C Street and Twelfth Street West.

Police determined the time of death to have been late on the preceding evening. No one had seen the commission of the crime, nor heard sounds of violence. Such general deafness and blindness is not uncommon in that section of the City, variously designated "Louse Alley" or "Murder Bay," a locale of ceaseless suspicious activity and terrified silence.

Therein lies our disgrace, that this area South of Pennsylvania

Avenue, running from our nation's capitol to the mansion of the Executive, should be the heart of corruption, rowdyism, saloons, gambling dens, and houses of assignation. The neighborhood is a magnet for the disreputable, a maelstrom of malice into which flow the worst elements of a society of indigent ex-slaves, wastrels and military deserters who escape detection through the cooperation of the area's denizens.

One expects in times of civil unrest to hear sad tales of violent death. Such horrors are part of the tragedy of war, rendered the worse when brother fights against brother, and hundreds — nay, thousands! — fall on fields of battle — husbands, fathers, sons, brothers, sweethearts — all mown down by the sweeping scythe of that black shrouded Reaper unleashed upon the world by man's failure to reconcile his differences without recourse to violence.

Yet there are horrors on a smaller scale, brought on by man's disregard for virtue, crimes no less horrible for their lack of militant magnitude. Such was yesterday's horror and therein is the disgrace of our city!

"Sounds to me like this reporter settled fer a good dose o' righteous indignation to fill up the holes in his information. There ain't even enough here to tell us if she was killed the same way as the others. I suppose there's more to come?"

"More indeed," Dougherty said. "The next report makes it all clear."

"A report dated December 22," Jen said. "What a horrible thing just days before Christmas! This account comes from a different newspaper — an obvious rival of the other."

INFORMATION SOUGHT ON RECENT CRIME — On Thursday last, a woman residing with Mrs. Maggie Walters on Twelfth Street West found in her back yard a person murdered the previous night.

While other reporters hasten to editorialize when information is unavailable, this reporter, adhering to the policy of this newspaper to seek out and report the truth, brings you a factual account of what happened.

The young woman, still unidentified, was strangled with particular vehemence by means of a cord or wire pulled so tightly about her neck as to have broken the flesh. The body seemed, at first, in repose rather than dead, even though face down in the mud. Miss

Sally Florin, who discovered the crime, described the body as "all orderly," hands at the sides, feet close together, dark hair covering any sight of face or neck until the body was rolled over. It was that which so horrified Miss Florin. The victims's abdomen was covered in partially dried blood. There were numerous wounds, the worst being to the dreadfully disfigured face.

The victim was less than five and one-half feet in height, of generous figure and youthful appearance, perhaps twenty-five years in age. She was clad in ordinary garments, indicating neither wealth nor poverty. Thus far, investigation suggests that she had come from elsewhere, since residents of the neighborhood cannot identify her, nor is anyone there reported missing.

"So it's the same killer, ain't it?" McBrien looked at Dougherty, whose constant watchword was to never to jump to conclusions. "Or do ye think, Major, I'd be best advised to suspend me judgement? Though I'm of the opinion that ignoring that conclusion'd stretch me judgemental suspenders to the breaking point."

Dougherty had to laugh. "No," he admitted, "even my suspenders couldn't bear that weight of coincidence."

"So he moved from New York to Washington. I guess that ain't much of a surprise, is it? It was the war years and lots o' people was moved to new places."

"I wondered," Jen, said. "if he could have been in the army or involved in government or was one of those who ran to Washington looking for army contracts."

"Sure, it could be any o' those reasons," McBrien said, "Or could it just be that New York was too hot fer him? Maybe he thought the cops were onto him? O' course, they claimed they had the killer, but they'd have to whistle a new tune if the killings started up again."

"That's true," Jen said, "so leaving New York made sense for him. It was the next articles that made really made me think he was in the army. You'll see what I mean. But there are loose ends. *If* there was a witness and *if* that witness saw someone in uniform and *if* that someone really was the killer... Well, *if* all those 'ifs' are true, then he may have been in the military and that means he couldn't have been too old to serve — perhaps in his early thirties at most." She turned to James. "I know I'm jumping to conclusions, but don't you think it's a reasonable jump?"

"Reasonable enough." he said, "There is still not enough evidence to put all our hopes into the one theory. But it won't hurt to keep it in mind."

"Well, let's give Mr. McBrien the opportunity to read the article that was printed the very next day in the first of the two papers," Jen said.

TRUTH ABOUT BRUTAL MURDER — Persons dwelling in vitreous abodes are well advised to avoid casting lithoid projectiles, as the sage reputedly said. That common sense adage might be profitably contemplated by a certain reporter who accuses others of error, then does not tell the whole story.

It has come to our attention that while police sources were deploring the dearth of witnesses to last week's brutal slaying on Twelfth Street West, witnesses there must have been. How else explain the unusual development that the investigation has been abruptly handed over to the office of the Provost Marshal? In fact, forcibly removed from the grasp of the civil police and put into the control of the military!

What can account for such an action but the totally logical surmise that the police and the Provost Marshal agree that there is a military connection? One can only conclude that someone did indeed see the killer — if not well enough to identify him, then at least well enough to establish that it was a man in uniform. As more is learned, it will appear in these pages.

If more ever appeared in the newspapers, they could not say, since these were the only reports preserved on that killing. In fact, Jen felt sure that no more articles had appeared. That was, after all, December of 1862 and everyone was thinking only of Fredericksburg's startling defeat and the rumors of General Burnside's imminent replacement. And the victim was, after all, a nameless prostitute — part of the flotsam of that all engulfing ocean which was the war.

There were handwritten addenda, their writers again unidentified. The first was probably written by an inhabitant of the Twelfth Street house where the body was discovered.

> I seen the body rite behint our house. I went out wen sally skremed. She found it. Them coppers wont do nuthing. They seen rite off jest like we done that she was in our line of werk an who give a dam fer us. They ast some questions but they wasnt given us no mind jest ast an looked an dint wrote nuthing down even. The one who kilt her was crazy i say. Her poor face i still see it wen Im goin ta slepe. We told them there was some sojers here that nite lots of sojers. That got the blubellys coming here they ast more questions but nuthing come of it. They don care neether.

"Sounds like cops everywhere, if ye ask me," McBrien said. "The extent o' their investigating depends on the status o' the victim, and this one didn't mean much."

"The next statement must be from a policeman," Dougherty said, "and he, at least, wasn't happy about not pursuing the investigation."

"That's true," Jen said, "but was that because he truly wanted to find the killer, or because he was insulted at the army's interference?"

> She was a prostitute but new to the area. Girls came and went. I had a beat in that area and I didn't know her. She was a pretty little thing, but not when I saw her. I seen cruelty before, but not like that. The face made me sick. The big gash. You could see all the teeth. Maybe we wouldn't have solved the crime, but we never had a chance. A witness said the area was full of soldiers that week, and all of a sudden the Provost Marshal's office was after us to hand them the case. Some bright young lieutenant looked into it. He was good willed I guess, but he never got anywhere. It didn't surprise me. That was after Fredericksburg and the desk boys in Washington were taken up with that. Why waste time on a prostitute? I still wonder why they got into it at all. It looked like they took it over just so they could bury it in the back of a drawer somewhere. What sense would that make?

The last sheet held just a few lines. Someone (Brogan?) had questioned the Provost Marshal's office and been rewarded with a succinct report.

> I spoke to the Provost Marshal's office about the Twelfth Street murder. I asked who had done the investigation. The answer was unambiguous. "Go to hell!"

"Well, at least that's a man easy to understand." McBrien said, "but I'd like to know why he felt that way. Was he sick o' the whole thing? Did he take a dislike to whoever asked the questions? Did he have something to hide?"

"Could be any or all of those reasons," Dougherty said, "but it seems a strong reaction if the only question was who conducted the investigation."

"Unless," Jen said, "the one answering the question was the investigator and had reasons of his own not to pursue the matter. But I suppose we'll never know. And we still can't say for certain that these murders from the past will tell us who killed Brogan in Penrose Valley. Are we wasting our time on something that doesn't really get us anywhere?"

"Possibly," said Dougherty, "but am I wrong in thinking that deep down your intuition tells you that these old murders hold the key to what happened this week?"

"Not wrong at all," she said. "And you think the same, don't you? So I suppose we ought to move on to the next one."

He smiled and took up the next four sheets of paper.

"This time," he said, "the interval between killings was six months. The first article is dated June 19, 1863."

VIOLENT DEATH ON ISLAND — Late last night the body of a young woman was discovered along the Island side of the Washington City canal, where it intersects with C Street South. The body was hidden by shrubbery and debris purposely placed to conceal it. Doctor Wilson Packett, the police surgeon, estimates the time of death at as much as twenty-four hours earlier.

The deceased was discovered by a couple who had taken advantage of the fine weather to stroll along the canal, whose usual pungency was alleviated when Thursday's thunderstorms broke the oppressive heat. The discovery of the body was fortuitous, There was no moon and the victim wore dark clothing. The couple, for reasons unexplained, had entered the bushes, where the young lady tripped over the feet of the corpse. Her screams drew the attention of a woman across the street at an establishment operated by a certain Mary Murrey. They summoned the police.

Police at first detained both the man and the woman. The man's conduct was suspicious, for upon hearing the screams of his companion, he had run off into the darkness. By chance the arriving policeman took the same route of access as the escaping witness had chosen for his egress. He refused to identify himself. The young woman is employed at an establishment situated on Third Street and identified herself as Carla Selener. Her companion finally identified himself as Sterling Ross, clerk at the War Department. He was released on condition of appearing to testify as required.

We have not learned the cause of death, but the police verify that it was violent. The identity of the victim remains a mystery.

"What do they mean by the island?" Jen asked.

"They call it that, Mrs. Dougherty, but it ain't really an island," McBrien said. "The City Canal cuts across to join two points at a bend o' the Potomac, so it forms a sort of island. That's another area ye'd not want to visit, not even in daylight."

"Even less," said Dougherty, "when there's no moon. I think our Mr. Sterling Ross was not there on an errand for the War Department."

"I wonder... Are you sure it could not have to do with the War Department? Perhaps spying of some sort?" But even as Jen said it, it seemed to her one complication too many. The more sordid side of that area sufficed to explain Ross's conduct. Either way, it said nothing good of his character: To leave a woman in the dark with a dead body while he ran home like a scared little boy. His sort prefer the office to the battlefield.

"No," she said, "forget that. I think we can safely set aside spying as an occupation for Mr. Sterling Ross."

"Do we know who the dead woman was?" McBrien asked.

James handed him the second of the four articles.

NEW YORK RESIDENT MURDERED IN WASHINGTON — The murdered woman found on June 18 was Miss Theodora Miles, daughter of Mr. and Mrs. Alexander Miles of New York City. The decedent was 27 years old, described by relatives as pretty, charming, of delightful disposition and endless good humor, in looks younger than her years.

Miss Miles had been visiting her uncle and aunt, Mr. and Mrs. Leon Shepherd of Georgetown, a visit that she made each year. Her visit had ended three days ago and she was to return home by train. Joseph Doiler, a servant of Mr. Shepherd, took Miss Miles to the B&O Station and, having seen to her luggage and tickets, accompanied her to the telegrapher to notify her parents that they might expect her by the next train. He then left her at the Station to await her departure which had been delayed and would occur in about one half hour.

The next morning Mr. Shepherd received from Mr. Miles a telegram informing him that the young lady had failed to arrive in New York City. Inquiries at the B&O Station proved fruitless. No one had seen her leave the station, nor could anyone verify that she had boarded the train, although her luggage had arrived in New York City. Police assistance was elicited, but without immediate result.

When the police discovered the body at the side of the City Canal, an officer was dispatched to summon Mr. Shepherd to the morgue. That gentleman was horrified to see that the victim was indeed his missing niece. He said that the girl had no enemies nor did she know anyone in the Washington area apart from a few acquaintances among their immediate Georgetown neighbors.

Police now seek witnesses who may have seen Miss Miles in the company of anyone in or about the area of the B&O Station on Wednesday afternoon. Miss Miles was dressed in brown garb, darker than seasonable, since she was still in mourning for her younger brother, slain in the famous cornfield at Antietam this September past. She was of slightly more than medium build, dark haired, fair of complexion, attractive in features with dark blue eyes and a ready smile. She was five feet six inches in height. Anyone with information is urged to contact the authorities.

The police are not at this juncture willing to supply further information about this crime, in spite of the fact that the native intellectual powers of even the least gifted among us would dictate as a course of practical action the open presentation of factual information that might lead citizens to be of help in the resolution of what is now a mystery. It is to be hoped that the hearing scheduled for Friday, June 26, will go a long way toward showing why and by whom this crime was committed.

"Major," McBrien said, "does any o' this make sense at all when ye really think it over? Don't it all seem just too strange to be real?"

"What do you mean? That it didn't really take place?"

"No, not that, to be sure. I've no doubt it happened. But things don't just happen fer no reason. Ye know full well when ye set out to catch a killer, ye ask yerself why he done it. Now here are six women murdered, if ye count Abiageal Conroy in Philadelphia. And I'm o' the mind to count her, as I think the both o' yez are as well. What in the name o' God could be the reason? Financial gain makes no sense. And I can't imagine all these women could'a been a threat to someone. Not even hatred fits the bill. How could one man hate so many women — all unknown to each other and from all sorts o' places and families? It just don't make one damn bit o' sense... begging yer pardon, ma'am."

"You may have hit on the heart of this question," Dougherty said. "Without a motive it is hard to make sense of murder. Still I have heard of motives that I would not have thought sufficient to warrant murder, but that made perfect sense to the killer. The trouble is that we may see the motive and never recognize it, since to our minds it does not suffice."

"And there is something else, James. What if the killer is truly mad? He could have a motive that makes no sense whatsoever to a sane person." The thought sent a chill up Jen's spine. "Is there a way to recognize madness? Can one at least tell that it is there?"

"I wish I could say so, but madness is not always evident. Its external signs may be so subtle as to go unnoticed."

"Is there nothing then to tell us why the man acts as he does? Is there no way to get at what's in his mind?"

"I'd not say that," Dougherty said. "We could try to find all the common elements of the various murders and see where that leads us. That might uncover something. What do we have to work with?"

"Some things are fairly obvious. Look at the descriptions of the victims. All of them were written by different reporters in different cities, but they all might as well be describing the same woman," Jen said as she leafed through the articles, pulling out those describing the victims' physical appearance. "Any one of them could be taken for any of the others: Fair of complexion, dark hair, pretty, youthful looking, full figured, about five and one-half feet or less in height. The eye color is not always the same, but apart from that they are in all basic respects the same type. That should tell us something, should it not?"

"I expect that it should, but what?" Dougherty was puzzled, as was she, but she could see that her words were setting him off on a new train of thought. "Surely he is not trying to rid the world of a type of woman that he does not like!"

"It don't seem likely, Major, but remember it's a madman we're trying to capture."

"Then on with our reading. See if the physical similarity continues to be borne out, and see what else emerges. The next report is dated June 27, 1863."

INQUEST RESULTS — Yesterday's inquest into the savage murder of Miss Theodora Miles was the occasion of revelations unprecedented in the annals of crime in our city. That a young woman of good family should be abducted in broad daylight in the shadow of this nation's capital is an evil not to be comprehended. That she should then be taken forcibly to a place of violent death and woefully abandoned in a low neighborhood, is utterly intolerable. Yet such, one must conclude, is precisely what did occur.

Doctor Wilson Packett, the police surgeon, testified to cause of death. The young woman was choked with a length of cord or thin rope, drawn tight with such barbaric force as to embed itself deep into the tender flesh, as though intended to decapitate her. The weapon was removed and has not been discovered.

Post mortem the body had been maimed in a depraved manner. The abdomen was stabbed more than twenty times, with such force that some blows had passed clean through the body, indicating the use of a long knife. The woman's thighs had been slashed after death. Doctor Packett described in technical terms another shocking mutilation. "The killer, possibly with a scalpel, had made bilateral incisions of the muscles of mastication, from the outer perimeters of the obicularis oris to the temporomandibular joint, just anterior to the ears."

He described how the body had been so arranged as to hide the extent of the wounds, laid face down, with arms and legs straight and parallel, the hair let down and fanned out to cover the shoulders. The skirt hid the nether limbs in a manner almost modest. The whole was concealed by bushes and debris found in the immediate vicinity.

Miss Carla Sclener, who discovered the body, had screamed in terror, although in the dark she had not seen the full extent of the atrocities. She testified, however, to the apparently peaceful position of the body when first found. Her erstwhile companion, War Department clerk Sterling Ross, took the required oath, but was less forthright, mumbling his responses and obviously embarrassed when pressed to explain his abrupt departure, which he attempted to justify on the plea of dashing off in the darkness to seek help.

Police Officer Samuel Culver, the first officer on the scene, examined the body by the light of a lantern and described his shock at the death's head smile of teeth fully bared from ear to ear.

The final witness was a woman of mature years, Mrs. Dorothea Waller. She was at the B&O Station to meet her daughter on the day Miss Miles disappeared. She recalled a woman of Miss Miles' description who was approached by a man in uniform who handed her a note, which she read and then, distraught, departed with him. Mrs. Waller was at a moderate distance from the two and without her spectacles. She was able to say little of the man in uniform, save that he was much taller than the young woman to whom he spoke and that he may have had a moustache.

"The manner of death is the same," Jen said, "but, if one can judge from newspapers, he grows more vicious with each killing."

"Yes," Dougherty said, "The stabbing now passes completely through the body. The strangulation is near decapitation. The thighs are slashed. What can it mean?"

"And what d' ye think o' the old lady? Too bad she didn't have her specs with her. A man in uniform she said? No doubt that'll get the attention o' the Provost Marshal?"

"That it did," James said. "Look at the report of June 29."

INVESTIGATION INTENSIFIES — The police today announced their satisfaction that the office of Provost Marshal will give full cooperation in the investigation of the murder of Miss Theodora Miles. This offer arose from the report that a woman resembling the victim had been seen in the company of a man in uniform on the day of the murder. The identification was not certain, so connection of this crime with any military person is at this point no more than vague suspicion. The office of the Provost Marshal stated that all personnel in the area had been fully accounted for and that the person in question may have been an imposter. City police are nonetheless pleased that the Provost Marshal is willing to enlist the vast resources of the army in their aid. Strenuous action and a speedy resolution are now not to be doubted.

"And there it ends," Jen said.

"Interesting, ain't it?" McBrien said. "When the military got involved the other time, a great silence come over the world and so it is again. But that time the cops hated it and now it's all of a sudden peaches and cream, if ye see what I mean."

He looked through the articles and pulled out the one on the December murder in which it was announced that the Provost Marshal had become involved.

"There it is. It says the case was 'forcibly removed from the grasp of the civil police,' and this time it's all 'Oh thank ye, kind sir, fer taking this nasty case off of our poor, helpless hands and giving us the use o' all yer fine resources.' I wonder what that's all about?"

"There is an explanation," Dougherty said, "but we mightn't have learned it without Brogan's papers. Look at this. It's another written testimony, taken down only six or seven months ago and from a newspaper man — maybe the reporter who wrote the June articles."

> I remember the affair. It was two years ago this month. I'm not proud of it, but it was wartime and the nation was in crisis. We had lost at Fredericksburg and Chancellorsville. McClellan was gone, Burnside was gone, and Hooker was in, but nobody with a brain in his head put much stock in him. Lee was across the Potomac and headed for Pennsylvania. We couldn't afford to undermine confidence in the army, especially with Hooker pulling troops away from Washington and everybody all nervous. The murder of Miss Miles was a pure horror and we wanted to report it, but the war filled the papers and the murder couldn't compete with the scare of invasion. So when I got the summons to 213 Pennsylvania Avenue, I knew what he wanted even before he told me. He had just been promoted from no rank at all up to colonel a month before the Miles murder. He had power before to clap people into jail on his own say so, without benefit of judge or jury. Now he had rank to go with it. I knew he wasn't part of the Provost Marshal's office. Baker and Patrick hated each other. But he knew how to investigate and he told me his own men would handle it. For reasons of national interest he wanted it to seem that the Provost had taken over. The Provost Marshal wasn't happy, but he had to go along, same as I did. If they ever caught the fellow, I couldn't say, but I do know there was never a public trial. That didn't surprise me. I supposed that when they did catch him, the trial would be done in the army and not announced in the papers. The investigator was some new lieutenant in Baker's detective bureau — Gardner, I think, was his name. I never met him.

"At least I see now why the Provost's man said, 'Go to hell,' when he was questioned in December. I'd be willing to bet Baker took over that one, too." Jen sat up straight at the anger in McBrien's voice.

"Who is Baker?" she asked.

"General Lafayette C. Baker," James said. "He was head of the National Detective Police, with headquarters at 213 Pennsylvania Avenue. It wasn't an official group, but he had almost unlimited authority. Nowadays he says he was head of the United States Secret Service, but he wasn't. Most of his secrets, I'd say, were shady ones. He made a lucrative living in the guise of doing his duty."

"And Patrick?"

"That was Provost Marshal General Marsena Patrick. He got that job after Antietam, when Pinkerton left. He had no time for Baker. He thought he was a cheap swindler."

"Did you remark the fact," Jen asked, "that none of the accounts in the papers drew a connection between the murder in June and the one in December?"

"I did," James said, "but I'd wager that was also due to Lafayette Baker. If he silenced one murder that reflected poorly on the army, he would do all in his power to suppress the notion of two done by the same man. And when Baker wanted something, he could be ruthless."

"Still, don't you think the public would have seen the stories of both killings and made the connection? The horror should have led to a public outcry."

"Under the circumstances, Jen, that may not have occurred. Remember how so many other events were buried under the avalanche of war news."

"And don't forget, "McBrien added, "how fickle is the public memory. Two killings six months apart, and the first victim a woman of ill repute? How many would'a said, 'A pity indeed! But she brung it on herself, wouldn't ye say?' And there'd be an end to it as far as that one was concerned."

Jen wished it were not so, but she knew that he was right. And the six months between killings made a difference. They saw the connection and a pattern now, only because of Brogan. He'd shown them everything at once with his clippings. Jen found herself asking again what she had asked earlier. Had Brogan been searching for an answer? Or were the articles a memoir of his own life and deeds? The thought appalled her, but it had to be considered.

"Ye said, Major, that there was five killings in Washington. Should we look at the next?"

"The last interval between killings was six months. This time it was eight months. The first report was on February 19, 1864."

ASSISTANCE SOUGHT IN POSSIBLE ABDUCTION — Two days ago in late afternoon Miss Isabelle Semple departed her home near the corner of Fifteenth and H Streets en route to the home of her cousin, Miss Clara Dale. She was expected there at 4:30 but failed to arrive. By 5:30 her cousin, alarmed at her absence, sent a servant to the Semple residence.

Inquiries were made among neighbors and one, Mrs. Nora Barlow, recollected seeing a young lady. She was not acquainted with Miss Semple, but had seen a person of her description and similarly garbed. Mrs. Barlow resides on the South side of H Street near Seventeenth and was there awaiting her carriage.

She saw the young lady across the street. The distance was not great, but the day was dark and wintry. The young woman was speaking to a man who may have given her a message, for she was holding a sheet of paper in her hand and he seemed to be explaining something. He then accompanied her toward a buggy and they drove off together. They passed in front of Mrs. Barlow just as her carriage arrived, blocking her view and preventing her from properly identifying either person.

Mrs. Barlow said of the man in the buggy that he was tall and wore a greatcoat, possibly dark blue, and a slouch hat of the type worn in the military. The hat was pulled low and he never removed it while speaking to the young lady.

Mrs. Barlow's driver, who was in the best position to see the occupants of the buggy, had his full attention on his own passenger and did not look in the other direction.

Miss Isabelle Semple is 24 years of age and five feet four inches in height. She weighs about 140 pounds. Her skin is fair, almost pale, and her eyes blue. Her hair is dark brown, nearly black in hue. She wore a visiting frock of violet silk trimmed in black and over all a winter cloak of deep maroon decorated in black fur. Miss Semple is the only daughter of Mr. and Mrs. Horace R. Semple. Mr. Semple is a purveyor of arms and well known in this city as a loyal son of the Union.

"There it is again," McBrien said, "the description that fits all the women."

"And something else," Jen said. "The tall military man delivering a message."

"What of the place where this occurred?" James asked, "If I remember correctly, that area of H Street is quite well-to-do."

"Indeed and it is that. That's where the swells live, ain't it? All o' them wanting to be near the President's mansion, I suppose. That's where McClellan lived — maybe so he'd be ready to move in if he could get Mr. Lincoln to move out. But what happened to Miss Semple?"

"The next two articles tell us that," Dougherty said, "on February 22 and February 29."

MISSING WOMAN STILL SOUGHT — As of this date, there is no word of Miss Isabelle Semple. Neither family nor friends can explain her disappearance. Testimony still unsubstantiated implies that she may have left willingly in the company of a man still unidentified. This has not been verified. That she should willingly have gone in the company of a person not previously known to her, her parents find unthinkable. That she went off with someone she knew seems equally untenable, since all of her acquaintance have been interrogated and none can offer any information.

"That last bit o' reasoning seems hazy, don't it? I mean the part about her not having gone off with an acquaintance. It's based on the fact that her acquaintances had no information to give. But, o' course, if one o' them was guilty, he'd not speak up, would he?"

"Then, too," Jen said, "we certainly can't rely on the fact that she would not have gone off with a stranger. She may well have done just that, if the stranger gave her a good enough reason."

Dougherty laughed. "In other words, they've learned nothing at all, have they? Let's go on to the next report."

BODY FOUND AT BEEF DEPOT — Yesterday was the occasion for a slaughter of cattle at the beef depot south of the City Canal. That depletion of the herd further diminished the area required for the remaining beeves, which were accordingly removed to smaller pens. In the emptied pen nearest the eastern boundary of the area, drovers found in the vacated space near the outside fence a human body, partially covered in mud and debris. They promptly closed off that pen and summoned the police. The remains have not yet been identified.

"Dear sweet Lord! The beef depot! Who'd put even a dead body in so damnable a place? The report don't say the body's Isabella Semple, or even that it's a woman. But it's her, ain't it?"

"Oh, yes, it surely is," Dougherty said, "and putting her body there is as much an act of hatred as was the murder itself."

Dougherty and McBrien had seen the beef depot during the war and described it for Jen. It lay beyond the canal and occupied the area all the way past the still incomplete monument to President Washington, which had been built up over a hundred feet, then work stopped and there it sat. So the army used the grounds for grazing cattle — thousands of them — and built a slaughterhouse and holding pens. The filth and stench were a daily part of life in the capital. The odor drifted over to the President's mansion when the wind was right, and discarded entrails sometimes lay feet thick waiting to be hauled away and burned. James was right, Jen thought, finding it hard even to imagine the squalor they had described. Putting her body there was a proclamation of the utmost hatred and contempt. But why?

The next article was dated March 3.

MURDERED WOMAN IDENTIFIED — The body discovered at the beef depot has been identified as that of Miss Isabelle Semple, who disappeared some two weeks ago from H Street near her home. The identity of the abductor remains a mystery. The body fit the description of the missing woman and so did the clothing, in spite of its deplorable state. Her father performed the painful task of identification.

Neither her parents nor her acquaintances have been able to offer a reason for this dreadful deed, nor can they suggest anyone who might have been her enemy. She was a young woman of quiet habits and well-liked by all who knew her.

"Don't seem like much, does it? I mean, ye'd expect a murder of a young woman to merit more notice in the papers, wouldn't ye?"

"Unless someone took care to see that it was kept quiet," Dougherty said, "and the final article, printed March 8, the following Tuesday, shows that."

INVESTIGATION PROGRESSES — The Provost Marshal's office has assigned its best investigators to pursue the vicious murder of Miss Isabelle Semple, whose body was found on Sunday at the military beef depot. There is no evidence of "military" crime, but the body was upon army property.

It appears the young woman was killed elsewhere and her body transported to its place of abandonment. The deceased had been placed inside the depot fence near Fifteenth Street, in a pen which had been in constant use until Sunday, when there was a large slaughter of cattle for immediate use by reinforcements recently arrived at fortifications around the city.

The body lay face down, covered with the dark cloak that the deceased had worn at the time of her abduction. Mud and snow had caused the body to remain hidden, and cattle milling about in the area had delayed its discovery.

The Provost Marshal's office assures us that progress has been made and that we may expect the murderer to be brought speedily to justice.

"But he wasn't, was he?" McBrien said, as he set down the paper.

"He wasn't. And the papers took no further notice of it," Jen said.

"No doubt due to Baker again," Dougherty said. "That's when the papers were full of Kilpatrick's insane raid into Richmond to free the prisoners — another fiasco. And that's when Grant came from the West and President Lincoln named him lieutenant general. Poor Isabelle Semple was lost in the shuffle — as I am sure Baker intended."

"But how do you imagine he kept the Semple family from raising a fuss?" Jen asked. "Surely Mr. Semple had influence and would have tried to get something done. I can hardly credit it that Baker could have stopped him."

"The extent of Baker's influence should not be underestimated. I don't know how he did it, but I am certain that he did. Perhaps an appeal to patriotism? Or specious reports of progress made privately to the family? Lafayette Baker was resourceful when it came to achieving his own purposes."

"Have ye no more information on this murder? Was there nothing else to go on?"

"There are two reports," Jen said, "one from Mrs. Nora Barlow's driver and the other from a doctor, most probably Doctor Wilson Packett, I should say."

The first was but a few sentences.

> I bin drivin Miz Nora a lot of yeres. Her site ant so good but she seen rite that day. The tall gent handed the smal ladie inta the carridge and went of with her. I seen it when I come around the corner. He had a slowch hat and long cote but I nevver see his face on count I was lookin at Miz Nora when I puled up to the howse.

The second was more interesting and more deplorable than even the newspaper accounts. It appeared to be a summary of a medical report, possibly somewhat less technical so as to suit the needs of the recipient. The killer must be the personification of evil, so far as Jen was concerned. Even to read of what he had done filled her with dread, and as McBrien read it aloud her eyes brimmed with tears.

> At 4:00 P.M. on February 28, 1864, I was summoned to the stockyard at the corner of Fifteenth Street West and B Street South. The pen had been emptied of cattle where a drover had found a body. He closed the pen and left the body *in situ*.
>
> The body was in an angle of the fence in such a position that, while it was hidden by the mud and muck at the base of the fence, it had not been trampled by the cattle. It appeared at first that the body had been pushed under the fence or dropped over it without the perpetrator's having to enter the enclosure. That impression was dispelled by a more careful examination. It had been put in its final position with great care and was, in my estimation, arranged in a manner most particular.
>
> The victim wore a dark maroon cloak with fur about the neck, but so soiled by the mud and manure that to the casual observer it was indistinguishable from its surroundings. The woman's body was face down with her mud stained hair spread across her shoulders. The arms were stiff and straight, parallel to the sides of the torso. The legs were perfectly straight, close together, the feet pronated, the toes pointing straight back.

Transfer of the body to the supine position revealed the full extent of injuries inflicted. The front of the dress was torn and cut in the general area of the lower abdomen. The face was covered in mud, but mutilation was visible as both sides of the face were cut. The state of the body led me to conclude that it had been dead for some days. No less than one week, no more than two.

The body was transported to my operating theater for the postmortem examinations. The body was cleaned, revealing the corpse of a young woman in her twenties, in generally good physical condition, 5 feet 4 ½ inches in height, estimated to have been between 140 and 145 pounds in weight during life, although that could only be estimated and not actually determined, in view of the sort of mutilation that had occurred. She was identified by her father as Miss Isabelle Semple.

The cause of death was strangulation, most probably with a strong cord or some type of garotte. It had been carried out with a force that suggested a cord fastened between two wooden handles for added leverage. The cord had dug deeply into the neck, breaking the skin and causing severe damage to the larynx. Strangulation was further verified by the presence of extensive *petechiae* in the eyeballs.

There was no evidence of illicit carnal knowledge. The face was grossly disfigured. Both cheeks were cut from the outer corners of the mouth to the region of the ears, creating the image of the death's head smile of the naked skull. The lower abdomen had been stabbed as many as twenty times with a sharp instrument, some of the strokes so forceful as to penetrate the lower body and emerge at the back. The upper thighs bore a series of downward slashes parallel to each other and to the median line of each leg. The same instrument was possibly used for both stabbing and slashing. The wounds suggested a weapon with a blade highly honed and a sharp point. I would suggest that it was perhaps 9 inches in length and perhaps 1 ½ inches at its widest part, something on the order of a surgeon's large amputating knife or catlin. The wounds were reminiscent of ones I had seen eight months earlier in the examination of a young woman named Theodora Miles, although Miss Miles had not been disemboweled.

Miss Semple's body bore a long incision, starting with a puncture wound in the area of the symphysis pubis and extending to the xiphoid process of the sternum. Through that incision, the internal organs had been removed. Some had been replaced haphazardly in the bodily cavity and fell out when the body was turned over by the police. The rest had been taken away by the killer. It seemed a reasonable conjecture that they had been disposed of by mingling them with the piles of animal entrails and ordure that were always to be found, sometimes two or three feet in depth, about the slaughtering pens.

It was and still remains to this day the most brutal conjunction of savage murders that I have ever seen, nor has any solution ever been proposed. There were later unconfirmed rumors that the culprit had been an army officer who was sentenced to death for desertion, thus bringing him to justice, although without publicizing his murderous activities. There were, after the killing of Miss Semple, two other murders done by the same person and prior to the death of the aforementioned officer. No motive, apart from utter insanity, has ever been advanced. No connection between the victims was ever brought to light to explain why they should all have been killed by the same person.

"This must for a certainty have come from Doctor Packett. Yet don't ye feel that it's still missing something? His full report must'a gone into more detail. It might'a told us more."

"I'm sure it would," Jen said, "but I don't know if I could have taken any more."

"It's worse with each murder," Dougherty said. "Why the disembowelment? It's as though each killing serves to fuel an even greater rage. It's never extinguished. It seems a force beyond his control."

"Just so, Major, but he's got control enough to be clever about hiding his tracks. The witnesses may'a seen him, but he knows how to be seen and stay hid at the same time. He ain't stupid and that makes him more of a problem."

"The deaths come at odd intervals. I wonder why."

"I'm sure there is a reason," Dougherty said, "but it may be unintelligible to a sane person. Once we've examined the next two murders, we can try to make sense of it."

The loud, authoritative knock at the front door brought them back to the present. Two sharp raps. A pause. Two more raps full of impatience. Jen glanced at the clock. It was almost 11:30. The morning had flown by.

She went to the door. Through the sheer curtain covering its glass pane she saw two silhouettes, both men.

She opened the door to face the impatient knocker who stood stiff and straight, his bearing clearly military. His heavy woolen coat was tailored to suit him, its generous collar turned up to shield him from the cold — a cold not nearly as severe as on preceding days, but still enough to vaporize the breath and make the ears and nose tip tingle. His polished boots gleamed, as though the snow and mud in the streets had received strict orders not to settle upon his person, lest they suffer dire consequences. He was not as tall as his companion, but force of personality supplied what he lacked in size. The perfectly groomed gray beard identified him for her. McBrien and James had described him perfectly.

"You will be so good as to tell your employer that Captain Morgan Maddock wishes to see him immediately." It was an order, not a request. He'd obviously seen the house dress and apron, and taken her for a domestic. She had to smile. Little did he know that he was confronting the whole staff.

"Which employer would that be?"

"Doctor Dougherty, of course!"

"Oh, you refer to my husband then. And by whom, sir, are you are employed?"

The cold had made his ears red. The rest of his face now followed.

"I am Captain Maddock of the Penrose Valley Coal and Iron Police. I beg your pardon for mistaking you for a servant, Mrs. Dougherty."

It was an apology, but without sincerity. On the other hand, the man with him enjoyed the exchange. He stood behind the Captain, out of his line of sight, and his lips had slipped into the start of a smile at Jen's comment and then were brought back under control. He was younger than the Captain, perhaps in his mid-thirties, clean shaven, dressed well, but without the militarily tailored bearing of the other. He had removed his hat when she had opened the door, and a momentary breeze ruffled his hair. He was really quite handsome. He was given no introduction, nor did he seem to expect one.

"If you gentlemen would care to come in, I will show you to the Doctor's office and perhaps he can make time to see you, even without an appointment."

They followed her, Maddock removing his hat and then not being sure what to do with it. Handing it to her would seem a repetition of his error about her status, and she was mischievous enough not to relieve him of his discomfort. Hat in hand, he entered the office with his companion. She closed the door on them and went to tell James of his visitors.

"How interesting," he said. "I wish I knew what Maddock is up to. I suppose the best way to find out is to let him talk. Come with me, McBrien. If he has reinforcements, so will I."

Interesting indeed. She had the feeling that whatever Maddock was after, it did not bode well for anyone but himself and Mr. Beverley Arkwright. She would wait patiently — or almost patiently — for James to return and let her know what this was all about. In the meantime she fixed lunch — lunch for three, since she did not expect James to invite his guests to share their meal. As she went about her tasks, her thoughts were not only on the past murders which had occupied them all morning long. They were now also full of curiosity about the two visitors.

Chapter X: One More Mystery Solved

He gazed at Allen in bewildered astonishment.
"By whose authority do you act?" he exclaimed.
"In the name of the great Jehovah and the
Continental Congress!" replied Allen.
    Washington Irving (1783-1859)
       of Ethan Allen, May 10, 1775
    Life of Washington, Vol. I, ch. 38 (1855-1859)

[Saturday, January 13, 1866]

Captain Maddock had begun the day, as he had every day for some time now, with his mind stuffed full of all the abundant details of the establishment of the Penrose Valley Coal and Iron Police. He had overseen the construction of its new headquarters and jail — weeks of prodding workmen prone to slack off when no one was looking, of urging suppliers to get materials and equipment without the string of delays that they seemed to manufacture just for their own convenience. And on top of all that, he had to keep Arkwright satisfied that all was well and completely on schedule. The plan was to have the forces in place, ready to appear in full uniform the very day that the politicians in Harrisburg decided to get off their duffs and make good on their promises. And that day was not far off.

The uniforms were on hand, even if they could not yet wear them. But that did not prevent Maddock from trying to exercise his authority, since its legality was now a foregone conclusion. Besides, Arkwright was already pressing him on the Brogan business. That was probably a waste, since there were no known witnesses and none was likely to come forward. But a solution to the murder wasn't essential. Perhaps not even desirable. What Arkwright wanted was to pin the thing on the labor agitators, even if specific persons could not be brought to trial. What was important was the spreading of a shroud of secrecy and uneasiness that would undermine the sway that these Buckshots and their ilk held over the micks. Divide and conquer. That's the ticket!

He hadn't much to work with. The men he's hired would all be imposing enough to keep things in line, all of them ready for a bit of head knocking as required, or even just as a reminder of their presence. But none of them were real policemen — with the one exception of Carter. Like Maddock, Carter had the military experience. But he also had a police background in Baltimore before the war, as his glowing letters of recommendation had established. He'd bear close watching. This might be someone Maddock could make use of, once he tested his intelligence and his loyalty. He wanted a decent amount of the former and all of the latter.

Yesterday he had sent Carter into the mine to see the scene of the crime and to talk to the people there. He'd come back with a clear report. He knew what to look for and seemed adept enough at judging character. He might just do for the things Maddock needed in an assistant. That was why he'd decided to take him along when he went to see Dougherty — the doctor, the major, the investigator. And under it all just one more damned Hibernian.

* * *

He now sat poker-straight as if called to attention, his hat on his lap, one hand either side of it on his knees, his spine not touching the back of the chair, his feet flat upon the floor. Nor did he change position so much as a fraction of an inch when McBrien and Dougherty crossed the threshold. The narrow lips had no curve of smile or frown, merely a tight, straight line. He made no move to rise, as though this were his office and Dougherty the humble suppliant come to seek his favor. Only the eyes gave anything away, for they narrowed at the sight of McBrien — making Dougherty all the more pleased he had invited him. Angry people often say more than they intend and he had already seen McBrien's capacity to add a little steam to Captain Maddock's boiler.

His cohort stood with his back to them, hat in hand, seemingly lost in a perusal of the titles in Dougherty's still modest medical and surgical library. The sound of the door caused him to turn around, his posture easy, quite unselfconscious. His facial expression was neutral — none of Maddock's stoical pretense, no effort to reclaim control, nothing but placid attentiveness to the situation.

"Captain Maddock, welcome," Dougherty said, extending his hand but not advancing more than a single step into the room. One could almost read the Captain's mind — the need not to offend without reason fighting the desire to dominate. Domination lost. He rose and came forward to shake Dougherty's hand, his heels came together, his feet at the proper parade ground angle of 45 degrees. He stepped back to his chair without greeting McBrien, but did not sit as he realized that Dougherty had not moved and was looking at Maddock's companion. Like it or not, Maddock was forced to take the next step and introduce him. As McBrien later put it, a few more sessions such as this and they might acquaint Captain Maddock with the niceties of civilian etiquette.

"Officer Steven Carter," he said, his eyes never moving in the man's direction, as though the mere acknowledgment of his presence was hardly worth the effort.

"I am pleased to meet you, Doctor," Carter said and came forward to shake his hand with a warmth and spontaneity that Maddock could never have mustered. "I have heard much about you and I look forward to our opportunity to work together. And I suppose this is Mr. McBrien, our pharmacist?" and he shook his hand as well. How long, Dougherty wondered, could so polite a man endure Maddock? And how long would he last in the Penrose Valley Coal and Iron Police? And what made him think they would be working together?

He was older than Dougherty by a few years, but still wide-eyed and enthusiastic. He had a straight nose, slightly thick brows above alert dark eyes, strong jaw, every appearance of a pleasant forthrightness. He was an inch or two taller than Dougherty and more muscular. To be a colleague of Maddock, he must have the strength of personality, the simple toughness, required in a policeman, but there was none of the grating forcefulness that marked the character of his superior. Yet it was surely by his own choice that he worked with Maddock, and Dougherty wondered why. His bearing suggested an effective investigator, perhaps a formidable detective. Would that be an asset or a liability in a police force whose purpose was more the suppression of opposition than the welfare of the public? He decided he would reserve judgement, but found himself liking him — something he had not felt toward Maddock.

"Please, be seated," he said, pointing to the chair next to the Captain's. He settled himself at the desk, McBrien just to his right. Maddock tapped the arm of his chair with the fingers of his right hand, fed up with these time wasting social amenities. Dougherty waited for him to begin.

"Since last we spoke," he said, "you will have had time to reflect upon our conversation. You will agree that Mr. Arkwright demonstrated the advantages of cooperation. My men are best suited to take over and pursue this matter of the Brogan fellow's murder. He suggested that I speak to you once more and explain more clearly our position."

He paused, as though the need even to mouth the words had displeased him, but he had his orders. The phraseology was civil, the tone clipped, sharp, peremptory, no least expectation of demurrer. The father instructing his recalcitrant offspring. The sergeant major training the naïve recruit.

"A fine idea, Captain sir, very kind o' ye," said McBrien, "fer ye made not a whole lot o' sense the last time we spoke and yer further efforts at explanation will surely be welcome."

No more tapping fingers, Dougherty noticed. The steam was beginning to rise. Still, he remained in control of his temper, his tension contained in the now clenched fist pressed tight against his leg.

"The question, Doctor, is one of legitimate authority. There is no denying that your own authority has been confirmed by Judge Barrett. I'll not contest that, nor does Mr. Arkwright, and so neither does the Penrose Valley Coal Mining Company. We were in error if we gave you the impression that we did contest it." He could have choked on the words. "But there remains the question of the ability to bring this matter to conclusion. That creates the dilemma, don't you see? The time will come when the Coal and Iron Police will be a reality — of that you need harbor no doubt. But you were partly right at our last meeting. As of this moment, I lack the authority that has been granted you by the Judge. He may choose, upon reflection, to transfer that authority to me; but until he does, the dilemma remains. You have the authority, but lack the means. I have the resources to be effective, but lack the legal authority. I am willing to share my resources with you in the person of Officer Carter here, who will in turn act upon your authority."

Dougherty's mind was racing. Maddock was worried about any appearance of illegality, but why was he so intent on having to be the one to find Brogan's killer? Was he convinced that the Molly Maguires or the Buckshots were at the heart of the matter? If he could prove that, then his employers could not fail to be impressed. Maybe he hoped to prove it, true or not, and produce the same result; but either way he needed to know what evidence Dougherty had uncovered. Or was there something of which Dougherty had not thought? Did Maddock know something more about Brogan? Mrs. Corrigan had told Jen of Brogan's antipathy toward the new police. Had it been something more than the distaste most people felt?

"Precisely how do you and Officer Carter propose to assist us?" Dougherty asked.

"You need an experienced investigator. Everyone on my force has had police experience."

"And yerself, Captain sir, what experience have ye had, if ye'd not think me too bold fer daring to ask?" McBrien's tone was polite — which Dougherty was sure did not fool Maddock any more than it did him, but it was a reasonable question and it would be foolish not to answer it. "Were ye with the police in New York or was it in Philadelphia?"

"Neither," he said. "My experience was gained in the army."

"Ah, the army is it then, sir? Well no doubt that'd give ye the best o' training fer putting down riots and suchlike, but it don't offer so much in the way o' finding criminals does it? Nor investigating a murder? Ye might gain something after all from working with Major Dougherty, fer he's had grand learning in all such matters. Sure, yer never too old to learn, are ye?"

"It relieves me to know that," the Captain said, trying hardly at all to hide the contempt in his voice. "However, my experience in Her Majesty's service included the investigation of crime. I was assigned to the office of the Provost. And you will be reassured to know that I served with the Provost Marshal in Washington during the recent war. Shall we agree that we are all qualified and capable of conducting an investigation?" He waited for a challenge, but they offered none. "Let us then move on to what I wish to suggest."

Wonderful, Dougherty thought, they had progressed from demands to suggestions.

"That will simplify things," he said, "Please do proceed."

"Yesterday I sent Officer Carter to the mine to examine the scene of the murder and to speak to those who had been there. He can tell you what he learned."

Carter took a notebook from the inside pocket of his jacket. He leafed through it, collecting his thoughts, and then spoke.

"My investigation, you will understand, was unofficial, but I found that those interviewed were cooperative and willing to talk about what had happened. As instructed, I entered the mine and was taken to the scene of the accident. This was on Friday morning about 9:00 A.M."

That was while Dougherty and McBrien had been meeting with Arkwright and Maddock to listen to their plea for acceptance of what they presented as merely the *intention* to investigate. He was sure Carter would hear about letting that time slip.

"The accident scene is much altered. The rubble was removed and new timbers installed, although drilling and blasting at the breast will not begin until Monday. I spoke to..." He consulted his notes. "...Manus O'Donnell, one of the two caught in the fall. The other... Edward McGinley... is still at home, not having the full use of his arm. O'Donnell's recollection was clear enough. He heard a rumble and saw the ceiling start to crumble. He saw Brogan in the shadows just before everything came down. Beyond that he knows nothing, except that Brogan was not supposed to have been there at all."

Interesting... On Monday O'Donnell was unequivocal in his certitude that Brogan had *not* been there; now he recalled him. Memory, Dougherty thought, tends to "improve" upon reflection. He was glad he had done his questioning and made his notes immediately after the accident, and that McBrien had arrived in time for McGinley and O'Donnell to repeat their stories for his benefit — before O'Donnell's miraculous recovery of memory.

"I spoke to William Shannon and Francis O'Laughlin. They dug out McGinley and O'Donnell. O'Laughlin described how you, Doctor Dougherty, set McGinley's arm and how you discovered Brogan's body. He was impressed."

There was no hint of sarcasm or approbation either real or feigned, simply a statement of fact. Officer Carter would make a good witness in a courtroom, Dougherty thought. An asset for an officer of the law.

"Those I interviewed told me that Brogan had been killed by a bullet in the back. O'Donnell said that neither he nor McGinley ever heard a shot, but he was of the opinion that the sound of the shot must have been covered over by the roar of the cave-in."

O'Donnell kept improving as a witness, but fact and fiction were starting to overlap.

"I was of the opinion," Carter said, almost as though reading Dougherty's mind, "that O'Donnell wanted to help, but — shall I say — a little too much? The more he thinks, the more helpful he may want to be. Of all those I met, O'Laughlin seemed the most accurate. He told me about the gash in the timber and why he thought that the cave-in was no accident. He put the timber aside in a safe place — on your orders, he says, Doctor — in the event that it were needed for evidence. Is that so?"

"Of course," Dougherty said.

"Then why did you not tell us of this yesterday," Maddock snapped, as though Dougherty had been caught in a fatal slip and he was about to take full advantage of it.

"That is no mystery," Dougherty said. "I have no desire to offend, but to put it bluntly, it was none of your business, was it? You may have been a policeman in the past. You may be a policeman again in the future. At present you are merely a private citizen, albeit interested, and I am the judicially authorized investigator in the matter. It would be irresponsible of me to discuss these matters with you or with anyone else who was not actively involved in assisting me. I have no doubt that in my position you would do the same. Nor do I doubt that, in the same position, you would not condone a private citizen — such as yourself or Mr. Carter — interfering in an investigation."

Carter sat there perfectly at his ease. In fact — if Dougherty's instincts did not fail him — he was enjoying this. Maddock was not. His ears were red enough to burst.

"You are seriously mistaken, Doctor. There are things you do not understand. I am convinced that this Brogan's death is the result of a conspiracy. You Irish pretend that the Molly Maguires are non-existent and that the A.O.H. is nothing but a benevolent association. You are wrong — or you are hiding the truth." He must have noted the anger in McBrien's countenance as well as in Dougherty's. He modified his statement. "I do not refer to you in particular, Doctor, but to those who hide behind a secret society in order to frighten their own people into submission for their own ends. You asked yesterday why the Mollies would kill one of their own, an Irishman like themselves. Did it never occur to you that the only Irishmen they care about are the ones who submit to them? What if Brogan did not do that? What if he advised others not to give in to them? What if he simply would not join? Would he still be 'one of their own'?"

Dougherty thought of the advice Brogan had given to Marty Carroll and wondered what Maddock would make of that. It would surely support his theory.

"Have you evidence of this conspiracy?" Dougherty asked. "Evidence that Brogan was at odds with some secret society? If you do have such evidence, then present it here and now. I can assure you that I will act upon it, no matter where it leads."

"Look about you, Doctor. The workers are not to be trusted. They were rebellious during the war. They took every opportunity to evade the draft and refuse their service. They are the same now. They fail to support the country that took them in and now they try to bite the hand that feeds them. I am making you an offer of help. Do not turn it down."

"I take that to mean that, in fact, you do not have such evidence. On the other hand, I never turn down help given in good faith,

Captain, and I'll not turn it down now. But I will not accept it without first consulting with Judge Barrett."

"Then speak with the Judge when you meet him on Wednesday evening and I am sure that he will advise you to accept the services of Officer Carter."

On Wednesday? Dougherty had not heard from Judge Barrett, and here was Maddock telling him when they would meet. Was Maddock in contact with him? Or was Arkwright? Dougherty did not think so. Judge Barrett was an independent man and it was hard to imagine him taking his lead from Arkwright and certainly not from Maddock.

"As matters stand," Dougherty said, "you have a theory about the Molly Maguires or the Buckshots, but no evidence to support it. I am willing to pursue that line of thought, but not at the neglect of others. I will not bend evidence to suit one theory over another." Maddock bristled. "Relax, Captain, I am not accusing you of that. I merely admonish against the tendency in general, for it can create blindness."

"May I ask a question?" Carter's voice was calm. Dougherty had all but forgotten his presence, so still had he sat through all of this.

"Surely," he said.

"One thing did not make sense to me. What was the cause of Brogan's death?"

"The immediate cause of death was suffocation due to the cave-in," Dougherty said, "What leads you to ask?"

Maddock's expression said this was all a surprise to him.

"The bullet in Brogan shows he was the target of a killer, but I thought it possible that the shot was not fatal. O'Laughlin's remarks led me to conclude that the killer had started the cave-in, and the only reason for that would be that the bullet hadn't already killed Brogan. Of course, he might have done it to hide the body. But in the mine that would be senseless. The cave-in would be cleaned up immediately to avoid loss of profits. So why hide what will be found immediately in any case? I can't prove it, but it would not surprise me to learn that Brogan had been shot elsewhere and then sought refuge in the mine and was killed there."

"I cannot disagree with you," Dougherty said, "Your reasoning is sound."

This man was a talented detective. He had reasoned to this without having had the opportunity to examine the body or the scene in its original condition, yet had suspected that the shot might not have been fatal. Had he not been Maddock's man, Dougherty might have enlisted his help right then and there.

"That's fine," Maddock said, "but does it bring us any nearer to the real point of the exercise? Who killed Brogan?"

"That is precisely what I am charged with finding out," Dougherty said. "Have you anything further to say on the subject? If not, then I would not wish to detain you any longer."

"I expect to see you after you consult with the Judge," Maddock said. "And I hope the meeting will resolve any remaining problems with authority."

"Ah, Captain sir, I'm sure ye need have no fear o' the Major's concept of authority. He's a great respecter o' his superiors, is *Major* Dougherty — and even o' the lowliest of his inferiors — lieutenants and captains and such. Each gets just the measure o' respect he deserves, and so o' course will yer Honor."

Dougherty rose and bade them farewell. Maddock was no happier than when he had arrived, but Carter seemed perfectly content with the visit.

They gave Jen a full report over lunch, and she had a bit of news for them. A telegram had come while they were entertaining their visitors. Judge Barrett would meet with them at the courthouse in Mauch Chunk on Wednesday evening. Captain Maddock had been right. Mr. Owen Williams must have made a report to his friends at the police station even before he had sent the boy out to their home with the message. One more mystery solved.

Chapter XI: The Butcher Strikes Again

Our meddling intellect
Mis-shapes the beauteous forms of things;—
We murder to dissect.
    William Wordsworth (1770-1850)
    "The Tables Turned" (1798)

[Saturday, January 13, 1866]

It occurred to Jen how fickle human beings can be — to spend the morning contemplating vicious murder, stop for a pleasant luncheon, and then go back again to horror. Or, perhaps only thus can one deal with what must otherwise overwhelm and bring life to a halt. Vacillation may be, after all, among the more important virtues. She decided to think some more about it — but not now; she had other things to think about.

Papers again covered the kitchen table. She put on a fresh pot of coffee and they were ready to proceed. There were two more sets of reports before they could try to make sense of it all. If nothing else, perhaps they could find a pattern to the killings — a commonality of victims or backgrounds, although they had so little to go on. The newspaper accounts spoke sparsely of the victims' families, but Jen doubted that their family backgrounds would help. There was too great diversity — some of considerable wealth, some of middling, some working class immigrants, the unfortunates of the *demimonde*. One could hardly find a more divergent group.

The penultimate murder was in Washington in 1864, first reported on August 18.

YOUNG MOTHER REPORTED MISSING — The search is underway for a young woman gone missing as of yesterday afternoon. She is Mrs. Olivia Wharton, wife of Mr. Andrew Wharton, and mother of two children, Lucinda, two years old, and Walter, three.

Mrs. Wharton went to visit her seamstress, Mme. Jeanne Marie Fouchet at her studio on New Jersey Avenue. Her driver, James Kohl, deposited her at her destination shortly after 2:00 P.M. with instructions to return in two hours to take her home. When Mrs. Wharton had not emerged from the studio by 4:15 P.M., Kohl took the courageous step of seeking admission into that realm reserved by propriety to the fairer sex.

To his consternation, Mme. Fouchet greeted him with expressions of concern that nothing untoward had befallen the Wharton family. Her question created a look of such evident mystification upon Kohl's visage, that she felt compelled to explain. Mrs. Wharton had departed an hour earlier upon receipt of a message delivered by a youngster of about ten years of age. Mrs. Wharton read the note he handed to her, placed it in her reticule, and declared that she must take her leave, since her presence was urgently required at home. Mme. Fouchet described Mrs. Wharton as "agitated."

Mr. Kohl drove to the Wharton abode to find that Mrs. Wharton had not arrived there. When she had still not made her appearance by 6:00 P.M., her husband notified the police who promptly undertook a search.

Mrs. Wharton, the former Olivia Curtis, is 26 years of age, living on Seventeenth Street just north of H. She has dark brown hair, fine arched brows, brown eyes, and a very fair complexion. She is 5 feet 5 inches of height and of lively and pleasant disposition. When last seen, she wore a rose colored dress, its bodice closed in front with a row of small buttons covered in the same fabric. The skirt is box pleated with slight hemline flounces in a darker shade of the same color. She wore a white bonnet of straw decorated in rose silk and carried a carriage parasol of similar color and decoration.

Mrs. Wharton's family anxiously await her return and seek the help of anyone who may have seen her. Mr. Andrew Wharton, known for his service in the U.S. Cavalry, was honorably discharged after a wound at Gettysburg. His father, Mr. Arlington Wharton, is in the employ of the War Department, in a position of great responsibility in aid of Secretary Stanton.

"Look at that, would ye? I'd been thinking he only went after unmarried women, but that ain't the case, is it? Or do ye think he maybe didn't know she was married?"

"Oh, I think he knew full well," James said. "He sent her a note to entice her to go with him, so he must have known who she was."

"Yer right, Major. And in other killings there was mention that he was delivering a message o' some sort."

"And that tells us even more," Jen said. "If he can write a note to overcome their fear of going off with a stranger, then he must know something about them. He must use care in preparing his abductions. They are not a matter of chance."

"I wonder how he picks his victims in the first place," James said. "How does he get to the point of such rage at a stranger that he kills her?"

"Are we so sure, James, that he was a stranger to all these women?" Jen asked.

"I should think so," he said, "It's unlikely he could have been equally well known to so many women, all of different classes and living in so many places."

They moved on to the article dated August 20.

MRS. WHARTON STILL MISSING — Mrs. Olivia Wharton, whose disappearance was reported two days ago, has not yet been heard from. The only additional elucidation in the matter came of a further police interview with Mme. Fouchet, the dressmaker from whose studio Mrs. Wharton was abducted. Mme. Fouchet saw her off at the door and recalls that she was approached by a man who spoke to her and then walked with her toward a carriage which stood a short way down the street. It was a plain black buggy, dusty as are all conveyances in this summer weather, with its hood turned up as a protection from the sun. She was unable to describe the man apart from the most general impressions. He wore a darkish colored suit of clothes, possibly brown, and a hat of the "slouch" variety, which seemed somewhat out of keeping with the rest of his attire. She could not say if he was young or old, although his movements seemed those of a younger man. He was taller than Mrs. Wharton.

By August 22 the status of the case had changed, and what had been thought an abduction was now known to be a murder.

DREADFUL MURDER! MISSING WOMAN FOUND! MAD KILLER SOUGHT! — Early Sunday morning the Sabbath rest was rudely violated when police were summoned to Saint Patrick's Catholic Church at the corner of Tenth and F Streets. The pastor, Reverend Jacob Walter, had sent for them at the behest of a parishioner, Mrs. Daniel Flynn, whose husband serves in the United States Infantry. She lives near the Church and was preparing to attend

Mass at 8:00 A.M. Her boys, aged 8 and 9, had gone outside. Contrary to maternal injunctions to preserve the appearance of their Sunday attire, the boys passed through the loose boards of an intervening fence and found, between the fence and the shrubbery at the back of the church property, the body of a woman. Their mother verified their report and went to the manse in search of the pastor.

The clothing led police to suspect that the body was that of Mrs. Olivia Wharton, the woman whose description has been so widely reported these past few days. Mr. Andrew Wharton, spouse of the deceased, identified the remains.

The victim had been horribly mutilated. Police surgeon, Doctor Marcus Calder, spoke to this reporter at length about the discovery of the body and the mode of death. The deceased lay face down behind a thick row of shrubbery. The hot, humid weather had ensured that the grass in the area was tall enough to disguise the presence of the deplorable sight. An odor had been noted as early as Friday, but had been attributed to the southerly breeze that so often wafts upon its currents the olfactory evidence of the military cattle depot beyond the mansion of the Executive.

The fully clothed woman had been placed face down in a stiff form of repose. Her dark hair was unbound and fanned across her shoulders.

Death was accomplished by strangulation with a cord cinched so tightly about the neck so as to have left a permanent imprint even after the fiend had withdrawn it. The lower abdomen had been stabbed numerous times and the thighs cut longitudinally with a sharp instrument such as a scalpel or a razor. A single slash had also been made from the lower abdomen up to the base of the breastbone, and through that opening internal organs had been removed. The face was deplorably disfigured.

Police found at the site nothing to identify the perpetrator of this abominable deed.

No suspicious activity had been noted near the church prior to the discovery of the body. The situation of the body is not overlooked by the windows of any house in the area, nor is that portion of the property much used. Police estimate that the corpse had been in the place of discovery since the night of the woman's disappearance.

The police are making every effort to apprehend this inhuman butcher. The fear caused by this event may soon surpass even that of last month when General Jubal Early's army of rebels encamped on the very threshold of this city. In that instance the sense of terror came from without and was clearly perceived. In this instance it emerges from within and comes in a guise of which we yet remain ignorant, casting suspicion on all sides.

"I'd imagine the next thing," McBrien said, "is to discover that Lafayette Baker's got his ladle in the stew?"

"So we thought," Jen said, "but apparently not this time. Take a look."

This account was dated August 24."

THE BUTCHER'S HAND? — Late on the evening of August 22, Mr. Jonathan Wilding, an employee of the Treasury Department, while on his way home noticed a light colored object behind a barrel set close upon the front of an unused building. He withdrew the object, a parasol, light pink in hue, fitting the description he had read in the pages of this newspaper in the woeful case of Mrs. Olivia Wharton. In the barrel were a white straw bonnet and a reticule to match the parasol. The reticule held a small amount of coin, and a letter. Having read the letter, Mr. Wilding went forthwith in search of a guardian of the law.

The contents of the letter were as follows: "My dear Olivia — Something has occurred which requires your immediate presence at home. The gentleman who brings you this note, Mr. Grantham, will be pleased to accompany you. Please do not delay. — Your husband, Andrew"

This is, one can scarcely doubt, the letter which Mme. Jeanne Marie Fouchet saw a young lad hand to Mrs. Wharton, causing her to depart in haste and without explanation.

Police interviewed Mr. Andrew Wharton at length and examined exemplars of his writing. There were similarities to the retrieved letter, but experts agreed Mr. Wharton was not the writer. Neither was Mr. Wharton able to identify any of his acquaintance who bore the name of Grantham.

That the letter was not written by Mr. Wharton does not decrease its significance. The logical conclusion is that the police now possess writing in the butcher's own hand. Nor is that all.

The unused edifice before which the parasol and reticule were discarded was searched. Its location has not been made public, but we have learned that the police discovered therein evidence of such a nature as to make it all but certain that the abducted woman had been taken to that place and there had met her end.

The net draws tighter and we are confident that the killer will be imminently in custody. The Butcher will soon have the honor of making the acquaintance of the Hangman. We hope that meeting will not be long deferred.

"And nothing from Baker's boyos? I don't believe it."

"That surprised me, too," James said. "But then I realized that this time there was nothing to cast suspicion on the military."

"Do you not find it most curious," Jen said, "that the reporters make so little of the obvious connection of this murder with the others that took place in Washington?"

"Aha! Mightn't it be, Mrs. Dougherty, that ye've just yerself pointed out Baker's signature? Sure and yer right — the reporters must'a seen the connection. But I'd be not the least surprised were ye to tell me that Baker suppressed that sort o' speculation. And he could'a done it easy enough. He'd'a pointed out the need to have no public uproar over the army just when the southern wolf was at the door, so to speak. He could say that the police were well on their way to the solution, what with the letter and the discovery of the murder site, so they needn't worry about the other killings, since bringing them into this matter served no useful purpose."

"I think you've got it," James said. "That must be what happened."

"So Baker achieved his ends," Jen said, "but the murderer was still out there. Maybe he would have gotten away in any case, but I wonder what would have happened if the police had pursued the matter with full vigor? Did Brogan think the same? Was he trying to rectify things? And, if so, why? What was his interest? And was that interest the reason for his death?"

"I wish we could answer that," James said. "Unfortunately, none of the remaining notices tells us anything beyond the fact that the police got nowhere in the end, and the press lost interest. By then it was caught up in the desperate struggles at the war's end."

The last articles were dated August 30, September 7, and September 15. But none was as newsworthy as Grant at Petersburg or the fighting in the Shenandoah or the race between McClellan and Lincoln for the presidency. The last two articles said nothing beyond the fact that the police continued their fruitless search. The article of August 30 was the only one to suggest productive activity.

BUTCHER CLOSER TO APPREHENSION — The police have been seeking persons named Grantham, the name in the letter used as a ruse in the abduction and brutal murder of Mrs. Olivia Wharton *née* Curtis, wife of Mr. Andrew Wharton and mother of two young children. It now appears that all persons of that cognomen resident in this city have been accounted for, and none is any longer under suspicion. According to police that was always the most likely outcome, since it would be foolish to think that the killer would have used his own name.

The true purpose of this investigation had been to seek information about any of their acquaintance whose actions or attitudes may have been suspect or unusual in any manner and who may have used the name to divert suspicion from himself.

Secretary of War Stanton, at the behest of Mr. Arlington Wharton, father-in-law of the victim, has volunteered military personnel to work with the police of the city insofar as legally allowable. With both civil and military police in full cooperation, it is to be expected that the so-called Butcher, will not long escape apprehension.

"And then, like the last rose of summer, the whole thing fades and is gone. The other two articles bemoan the lack of suspects and offer only the vain hope that the Butcher had gone away or died. It angers me!"

"Ah, Mrs. Dougherty, ye've got to keep in mind that they didn't have us to help them, did they? And, sure, we've just begun. It's too early to be letting it get us down, ain't it? Was there nothing else? No other documents?"

"Just one," James said, "probably from Doctor Marcus Calder." He handed it to McBrien.

> On August 22, shortly after dark, I was summoned to an unoccupied house on Second Street just above D Street. I was surprised to find that I had not been called to a murder, but the matter became clear when I saw what had been discovered. There were numerous internal organs placed in a heap in the center of the floor of an otherwise empty room at the front of the house, all in a state of decay due to the heat and the maggots. The organs were all lower abdominal in origin, nothing pertaining to the area above the diaphragm. Decomposition was not so far advanced as to render the remains unidentifiable.

Intestines were present, as were portions of the kidneys and almost the whole of the uterus, thus establishing the humanity and the sex of the victim. There were also torn and bloodied articles of female apparel, primarily undergarments. It was difficult to estimate the age of the organs, but I was fairly certain that they had been excised possibly from one to two weeks prior to their discovery. Everything suggested that these were the remains of Mrs. Olivia Wharton. That was subsequently verified, when her maid was called upon to identify the undergarments. Nothing suggested the identity of the killer. There was much dust throughout the residence, but it had been swept clean in areas in which one might have expected to discover footprints or handprints so as to estimate the size of the killer. There was much blood soaked into the wood of the floor. It had been my duty to examine Mrs. Wharton's body when it had first been discovered and the cause of death was almost certainly strangulation, with the dissecting having been performed *post mortem*. The large amount of blood on the floor thus led me to conclude that dissection had been accomplished almost immediately after death when the blood was yet in liquid state in the vessels and able to flow freely, even though the heart had ceased to beat.

He set down the paper without a word and went to the stove for a cup of coffee. Holding up the pot toward Jen and James, he raised an inquiring eyebrow. Both nodded, so he refilled their cups and all three sat in silence, stirring in their cream and sugar, all wondering where this was leading. There was one more murder to examine, and then what could they do?

"Shall we get back to it?" James asked.

The delay between murders this time was nine months. The war was over, Lincoln was dead, Jefferson Davis was in prison. They all recalled those days — the relief that the fighting had ended, the worry about what would come next, the fear that the nation might never reunite. That was when the Butcher struck again. It was reported on May 19, 1865.

MYSTERIOUS DEATH! BODY DISCOVERED AT OLD CAPITOL PRISON! — Early yesterday morning a body was discovered near the Old Capitol Prison. Police, civil and military, were summoned to the site shortly after earliest dawn, when a sentry found the corpus of a young woman near the southmost corner of the main prison building, tucked into an angle formed by the side of that edifice and the First Street wall of the exercise yard. Although the location is near the street, the body had not been seen earlier, due to the darkness after the evening's heavy thunderstorms. Furthermore, the body was under a dark brown cloak, probably the property of the woman herself.

Captain Wilbur Thomas of the city police described the victim as a young woman of about twenty-five years of age. The area where the victim was discovered is patrolled at regular intervals day and night by sentries. The body was not there at sunset the previous evening, nor has anyone been found who had witnessed it being placed there during the night.

There has been much coming and going in and about the prison these several weeks, due to matters related to the recent cessation of hostilities and the signing of the instruments of surrender at Appomattox Courthouse. The Old Capitol Prison has not yet ceased to play the part that began with the war and caused it to serve as home at times to such notables as Mrs. Rose Greenhow and the daring Miss Belle Boyd. As a result, sentries have grown accustomed to seeing police wagons, civil and military, picking up and discharging passengers near the front of the prison at all hours of the day and night. It is conjectured that the killer took advantage of that fact to make use of a police wagon or a conveyance disguised as such, and to await the opportunity to dispose of his gruesome cargo. It would have demanded a level of daring and patience, but it could have been thus done.

Captain Thomas assures us that more information is forthcoming, as well as a description of the victim, which should lead to the speedy identification and apprehension of her killer.

"Well, don't that beat all? It ain't bad enough he done the murder. Now he spits in their faces! He's out to make the cops a bunch o' fools. He drops the poor soul on their doorstep and thumbs his nose at them and marches away pretty as ye please. It's like he's saying, 'Yez thought yez'r getting close? Let me show yez how close I can get.' He's saying it's his game, his rules."

"It's horrifying," Jen said, "Is that what this is? A game? And the women he kills? They mean nothing at all? Why does he do it? And how did he put the body where it was found? The prison was surrounded by sentries. Why did no one see him?"

"That is probably not difficult to explain," James said. "Only once did I see the prison, but I recall it as a large structure. It was built for a capitol when the British burned the city in the War of 1812 and in this war it was a prison. All the buildings around it were part of it. Sentries patrolled the full length of the properties and back again. Anyone in a wagon could easily wait until the sentry went by and then do as he pleased and be off before the sentry came back. In the night he would not be seen, nor would the body if it was covered over with something dark — as indeed it was."

"This may be a foolish question and I'll likely kick meself fer wasting time in the asking of it, but was this definitely a killing by the same person? No doubt on that score?"

"None at all, I should say. This report appeared the very next day." Jen handed it to him.

THE BUTCHER IS BACK! — Our readers will recall last August's dreadful murder of Mrs. Olivia Wharton, wife of Mr. Andrew Wharton, and mother of two. The sanguinary cruelty of the slayer led to his being dubbed "The Butcher." Any hope that the Butcher had fled this area has now been destroyed. The murder discovered two days since at the Old Capitol Prison proves, upon investigation, to have been committed by that same fiend

Police surgeon, Doctor Marcus Calder, examined the body and confirms that this death and that of Mrs. Olivia Wharton are alike in more particulars than may be reasonably explained as coincidence. Both bodies had been abandoned in locations where they could be hidden for sufficient time to allow the escape of the murderer, but would nonetheless remain not long concealed. Both had been strangled with an especial violence, then further maimed by stabbings and slashings about the lower abdomen and upper portions of the thighs. Both were partially disemboweled with certain organs missing. Both had been disfigured with identical cuts about the face. They are also, in the opinion of this reporter, reminiscent of a number of earlier murders at the height of the war, often timed to coincide with moments of national crisis.

The most recent victim was found in a pose identical to that of Mrs. Wharton. It lay face down, feet together, legs straight, arms at the sides. The long brown hair had been laid out in fanlike fashion to form a cover for the shoulders.

The recent body has yet to be identified, so we publish herewith a description supplied to us by Doctor Calder. The body was that of a woman in her mid-twenties, less than five and one-half feet in height, of a little more than medium figure, perhaps of 140-145 pounds in weight. She had brown — almost black — hair, brown eyes, very light complexion. She wore clothes of good quality. The gown was brown with green vertical stripes, trimmed at collar and cuffs with white lace, and overall a brown cloak. All information will be welcomed by the police or by this newspaper.

"Interesting, ain't it? Not only do they have no hesitation in pointing to the Wharton murder, but they even bring up the earlier killings. What d' ye suppose accounts fer the change?"

"I'd wager that Baker no longer cared. He had bigger fish to fry. By then he was promoting himself as the mastermind behind the capture of John Wilkes Booth — building the myth of Lafayette C. Baker, righter of wrongs and protector of the nation."

"Why, Major sir, do I detect a semblance of a hint that in yer opinion the great General Baker might not be all that he claimed?"

Dougherty's anger gave way to a smile. "Am I so unsubtle?"

"I am sure you've both noted the physical description of the woman," Jen said. "It would have fit any of them. Why must his victims all look the same? If we knew that, I think we would be well on our way to a solution."

"I'm certain of it," James said, "but I am afraid we won't find that answer until the killer is captured and tells us. For the moment all we have is the newspaper accounts. The next is dated May 24."

MURDERED WOMAN IDENTIFIED — It is now one week since the inhuman murder of the young woman whose body was so callously discarded at the Old Capitol Prison. Yesterday the mystery of her identity was resolved, when Miss Ludmilla Kowalski told police that she might be of assistance.

Any hope she had of being wrong was shattered once Miss Kowalski was shown the photographs made by order of Doctor Marcus Calder.

The victim was Miss Edna Krantz of Chicago, whose father owns a number of dry goods stores. Miss Krantz was one of seven children. She has four sisters, all younger than she. Her older brother died in the war; her younger brother, held prisoner in the South, was recently returned to his home in Chicago — the destination to which Miss Krantz was bound in order to celebrate their reunion. She had departed Wednesday to return to Chicago. When she did not arrive as scheduled, her family at first awaited word from her. Finally, they telegraphed her Washington address. Miss Kowalski, with whom Miss Krantz shared lodgings near the Treasury Department, their place of employment as clerks, took the liberty of opening the message. Its contents alarmed her, since Miss Krantz had gone to the B&O Station as scheduled and was assumed to have left without incident.

Miss Kowalski had heard of the murder, but had not read the news accounts of the description of the victim's clothing, which she would have recognized. Furthermore, she thought her friend by then well on her way to Chicago. She had accompanied her to the depot and had left her there little more than a half hour prior to the train's scheduled departure. During that half hour she was lured to her death, for the train that day left promptly at 11:45 A.M. and Miss Krantz was not aboard. Neither has anyone found the brightly flowered carpet bag that she was carrying when last seen by Miss Kowalski. The police can find no one who remembers seeing Miss Krantz that day.

The remainder of the article was a repetition of the description of the victim and her clothing and the (by now hollow sounding) assurance that the police were doing all they could, that they were questioning people in all quarters, and that the Butcher would soon be taken in, and on, and on, and on. None of it any consolation in view of the previous murders and the abysmal failure to find even a clue to their perpetrator. There was one flicker of hope, on May 27.

BUTCHER CAPTURED? SUSPECT TAKEN INTO CUSTODY! — Police Captain Wilbur Thomas yesterday announced that police are holding a man in the case of Miss Edna Krantz.

Mr. Nicholas Porter, with business interests in Baltimore, Philadelphia, and New York City, keeps abreast of the news by regular reading of this newspaper. Last week, when Miss Edna Krantz was abducted, Mr. Porter was at the B&O Station. Only yesterday did he return home and read the back issues of this newspaper.

Mr. Porter had seen at the B&O Station a young woman answering the description of the victim. She was seated upon a bench and had the brown cloak and the brightly colored carpetbag she was known to have been carrying. Mr. Porter was at a distance of perhaps ten yards, when he saw a disheveled man speak to her. Mr. Porter saw her face for a moment, a countenance which corresponded to the description of Miss Krantz. She responded to the man and handed him something.

At that moment Mr. Porter heard his own name called, and turned to see a business acquaintance who was also awaiting the arrival of a train. They spoke for a few minutes, but when he turned back toward the bench, the young woman and the disheveled man were nowhere to be seen.

Mr. Porter was sure that he had seen this same man about the B&O Station on other occasions and could recognize him again. He accompanied police to the station and, within the half hour, was able to point to the very man, whom they promptly took into custody.

Captain Thomas has issued no report on the results of the interrogation of the prisoner, nor has his name been made public.

"It's like New York all over again, ain't it? They pull in some poor devil — begging yer pardon, ma'am — that hung around the depot asking fer a handout. Like as not some soldier got hurt and don't have enough to live on. What next? They solve the case by shooting him?"

"McBrien, you must have gypsy blood in your veins. If people stop using medicine, you can turn your hand to telling fortunes. You've got it right, except for the shooting. It may well be that the Washington police are of better quality than their counterparts in New York; but more likely they didn't think they could saddle this one with the blame and make it stick."

"I should think that was exactly it," Jen said. "They may not have been aware of the murders in Philadelphia or New York City, but they knew there had been five in Washington. If they convicted a man and then the murders continued, they would make absolute fools of themselves."

"Look at the next article of May 29, and you'll see just how quick they were to avoid holding the wrong man."

SUSPECT RELEASED — Captain Wilbur Thomas late last night released from custody Mr. Jonathan Jakes. Mr. Jakes had been questioned in regard to the killing of Miss Edna Krantz, the young woman whose body had been discovered more than a week ago near the Old Capitol Prison. Captain Thomas emphasized that Mr. Jakes was released because a careful investigation has established beyond doubt that Mr. Jakes could not have been guilty of this crime.

Investigation continues and our readers will be kept informed of its progress.

"That was nearly the end of it," James said. "There was but one more article, on June 6."

BUTCHER STILL AT LARGE — As of this date, no arrests have been made in the case of Miss Edna Krantz, brutally murdered less than one month ago. Her slaying is but one that may be the work of the same crazed beast the past three years.

We note that the killings may have coincided with great battles or points of crisis in the course of the war. It may be, as some conjecture, that the killer was made mad by the stress of the war, and its cessation may have brought him back to his senses. We pray that be not in vain. Police continue to search and are open to all additional information.

"All that's left," Jen said "is another unsigned account and after that nothing. It may have come from Doctor Calder or from one of the policemen."

> Jonathan Jakes was never a serious suspect. He talked to Edna Krantz just as Porter said, but he talks to everybody at the B&O Station and is there every day. He received a head wound at Chancellorsville and has not been right since. He said that he asked Miss Krantz if she had something for a needy soldier and that she was very nice to him. Jakes is harmless. No one has ever complained about him. He was held by the police because they hoped he may have seen someone approach Miss Krantz. He saw no one. Porter's story about meeting an acquaintance was also verified, but he was at first reluctant to mention the man's name. He finally admitted that he and his friend had a half hour until Porter's train and went for a drink. Porter did not get back until just before the train pulled into the station. He insists that the girl was not there then. His initial reluctance to admit to the drink was because his companion was a gentleman of whom Porter's wife has a low opinion and she does not approve of drinking, especially during the day. I met her, and I must say that I would not want to cross her. So Porter's testimony came to nothing, except to establish that Miss Krantz had been there before the train pulled in, but was not there when it actually arrived.

"That's everything," Jen said. "If there were other murders, we are ignorant of them. Still, I think that if there had been others, Brogan would have included them."

"Ye're right, in all likelihood, Mrs. Dougherty, but I'm wondering why Brogan come here to Penrose Valley a' tall. What was his reason?"

"Two possible reasons, I would say. Either he came to hide or he came to search. The newspaper cuttings may be a record of someone else's actions or of his own. Either he came looking for the Butcher, or he was the Butcher and someone else came here looking for him."

"And in either case, ye'd be saying, he got himself killed fer his trouble?"

"Exactly."

"I tend to think it was Brogan who was after the Butcher," James said. "If all he had were the newspaper articles, I would say it could be either. But he had all the handwritten documents as well, and I truly doubt that the murderer would have been so foolhardy as to get that close to people who might have somehow identified him."

"I hope you're right," Jen said. "As hard as Charlie Brogan's death has been on Mrs. Corrigan, it would be infinitely worse for her to learn that he was a brutal killer."

"Here's something else to consider. In view o' what happened to Brogan, don't ye think we'd best watch our step, too?"

"I'm sure we need have no fear in that regard," James said. But he said it too quickly, Jen thought, and she knew that his words were intended to allay her own fears.

"Well, we do have something to our advantage, Major. S' far as we can tell, the Butcher ain't got a hint o' what we know. I'd be willing to bet just now he's feeling pretty clever. As far as he's concerned, we've no notion o' why he killed Brogan. He must think he's off scot free."

"Then I'd suggest that we say nothing to anyone about what we've found," Jen said. "Mrs. Corrigan has read none of it, and I'll ask her to mention the papers to no one else — although I don't imagine she will tell anyone in any case. The question is, I suppose, where to go from here."

"Supposing we do know the motive for Brogan's murder," James said, "Then what of all the rest? What could these killings have in common?"

"Don't ye think, sir, the looks o' the women mean something? We've all noted that the one description could do fer the whole lot."

On a sheet of paper they wrote all the descriptions in columns. In each case, except that of Emeline Carding, their height was given. The tallest was five feet six inches, the shortest five feet four inches. A limited range, but probably matching a sizeable majority of all women. The hair color of the anonymous Washington victim was not mentioned, but all the rest were given as dark brown or black.

Six of the nine were of fair or light complexion. In every instance, save that of Olivia Wharton, the victim was described as full-figured or robust or in the area of 140 pounds. Most had brown eyes, most were described as young or as looking younger than their years.

"Look at the 'sameness' of the crimes," James said. "Details are repeated. The women are strangled and mutilated, all in the same manner. They are disposed of in the most deplorable places. It is utter madness."

"And why are the bodies placed just so? Face to the ground, hair spread out, straight posture? And d' ye take note, the mutilation is to the front o' the body and then it's all covered by hair and clothing."

"It puts me in mind of a child who does something wrong and then tries to cover it up before he can be punished," Jen said. "As though he is ashamed of his cruelty and yet wants it seen, so he puts the bodies where they are sure to be found. And what of the death's head smile? I must say, it all turns my stomach even to think of it."

"Ye'll realize, too, that he's getting worse? He choked and cut. Then he stabbed clear through the body. Then he strangled with force enough to cut into the neck. Then he started pulling out the innards and taking parts with him. God help us! It's like nothing I've ever heard of!"

"I am amazed," Jen said, "that, in the course of nine murders, this man was seen as many as six times. Was that accidental? Or does he simply not care?"

"And often as he was seen," James said, "there was no useful description. In Philadelphia he was broad shouldered, dark haired, clean shaven, well dressed. His face was partly hidden by his hat brim, yet the woman witness said that he had 'a crazy look.'"

"Ye'll also recall, sir, she was at some distance. And how tall was he? After all, she was comparing him to the Conroy woman, and she was only five and a half feet. And that 'crazy look'? Was it more imagination than memory?"

"You're probably right on all counts," James said. "We may accept the general descriptions, but we'd best be wary of details. And it's second hand information, colored by reporters telling a good story."

"In Gramercy Park," Jen said, "the constable saw a young man, well-dressed, tall, and in possession of a carriage. In the case of Berdine Griswald in New York, a man, possibly the killer, *may* have had a beard. That tells us little, except that if this was the same man who killed Abiageal Conroy, then *maybe* he had grown a beard in the intervening months."

"Beards, I fear," James said, "are of little help. They are easily shaved or retrimmed, or may even be false."

"Right ye are, sir, and ye'll notice that with Miss Theodora Miles, the old lady at the station said he had only a moustache, but the old girl was at a distance and without her specs."

"But she did see the man hand Miss Miles what may have been a message," Jen said, "and that tends to verify what Mrs. Baker saw — a man apparently giving a message to Isabelle Semple. And he did send a message to Olivia Wharton, so at least we know something about how he gets the victims to go with him. And he uses a conveyance of some sort to move them about. That comes up time and again. Then, too, he makes himself seem quite ordinary. He has a knack for fitting in, for drawing no attention to himself."

"There's something that bothers me yet," McBrien said. "The first one, Abiageal Conroy... The others were strangled, but her throat was cut. There's mention o' further stabbing, but nothing at all about the face being cut. Was it the same killer?"

James and Jen had the same reservation; and James still had in mind to consult with Doctor Brownson in Philadelphia, but for now they would treat her as a victim of the same killer.

"What is he trying to accomplish?" Jen asked. "If we knew that, then we might have an idea what he will do next."

"And where? He began in Philadelphia," James said, "but he has killed in New York and in Washington, too. For all we know, he could strike anywhere."

"What about the number of killings each year?" Jen asked.

There had been one in 1860, two in 1861, two in 1862, one in 1863, two in 1864, and one in 1865. They saw no pattern.

"How about the the spacing between the murders?" McBrien asked. "Does that tell us anything?"

James started with Abiageal Conroy in October of 1860. There were spans of six months to April of 1861, three to July of 1861, fourteen to September of 1862, three to December of 1862, six to June of 1863, eight to February of 1864, six to August of 1864, and nine to May of 1865. Again, no pattern. That was when James slapped his hand on the table so hard that McBrien and Jen almost leapt from their chairs.

"Sorry," he said, "but I think I've got it. At least, to the extent of hazarding a guess that there will be another murder within three weeks. I have no idea at all where it will occur, but if the Butcher is in this area, then I think it will happen not so very far from here. Do you see it?"

They didn't, but, as with many a puzzle, they felt almost disappointed when he explained it — it was so simple.

"Look at when the killings took place," he said. "There were murders in October, April, July, September, December, June, February, August, and May. Nine murders in nine different months, leaving January, March, and November with no murders. I think he is committing one murder for each month of the year — either in no order or in an order of his own devising — but he has three more to go. If our information is correct, then it is eight months since he last killed. This is a guess, but I think he looks forward to killing and may not wish to wait any longer. He will kill before the end of this month. Within the next eighteen days."

"But he has killed in January," Jen said. "He killed Brogan."

"So he did," James answered, "but I don't think the Butcher will count that one. Brogan was likely killed out of expedience. That won't satisfy the Butcher's appetite for a woman."

Jen's stomach clenched in terror, but James was right. They knew it, but they could identify neither killer, victim, time, nor place. They knew enough to say that disaster was imminent, but not enough to avert it. They sat in silence, lost in thought, all thinking the same thing. Could they possibly be so close and still be constrained to do nothing until the Butcher strikes again?

Chapter XII: Someone Else Entirely

As someday it may happen that a victim must be found,
I've got a little list — I've got a little list.
Of society offenders who might well be underground,
And who never would be missed — who never would be missed.
    Sir William S. Gilbert (1836-1911)
    The Mikado, (1885) Act I

[Saturday, January 13, 1866]

"If ye don't mind me sayin' so, Doctor, he don't give a damn who done Brogan in. Fer him the question is how to make sure the Penrose Valley Coal Mining Company comes out ahead — and himself along with it. I don't trust him as far as I can spit."

Frank O'Laughlin's face was red in the glow of the lamp's glass shade and his voice was full of anger, yet its volume never increased. That was his way, and more effective than any amount of bluster. His control was an asset in the present situation, since Mrs. Catherine Corrigan and her two boys were but a few feet away in the kitchen and Dougherty would not have wanted them upset. She had allowed them the use of her parlor, and he did not wish to mar her kindness by having the boys scared by an argument — or what they would have taken for an argument, although he and O'Laughlin were not really in disagreement.

              * * *

Dougherty's conversation with O'Laughlin had come about almost by accident, but it was a necessary conversation and Dougherty was glad it had occurred.

Earlier that day, when they had finished the newspaper accounts and the other documents, there had been but three patients in Dougherty's office — more coughs and sneezes and catarrhs, all needing prescriptions of cough elixir and the suggestion of warmth and rest — the latter harder to come by for working people. Still, none was serious enough for concern and he expected all to recover easily.

He'd visited the homebound patients and, as on the day before, finished his rounds with Marty Carroll. Marty was young and strong and would recover from his current illness with no repercussions, so a visit was not urgent. Still, he had been feverish and Dougherty wanted to see if it had broken. He was also curious about what Carroll had told McBrien — about the A.O.H. and the disagreement between Brogan and O'Laughlin.

The day had been snowless, but the temperature held well below thirty, and every puff of wind had sent a shiver up his spine. By the time he'd entered the Corrigan kitchen, the tip of his nose was numb and the edges of his ears so cold that they stung in the big stove's warmth as the blood returned to them. He was glad to accept the cup of hot tea she held out to him.

Besides, Marty had a visitor who had just arrived, so he sipped his tea slowly to allow him time. The man performing this corporal work of mercy was none other than Frank O'Laughlin and Dougherty wanted him to have the opportunity to speak to Marty. He hoped that O'Laughlin might bring up the A.O.H., and he was curious to see how Marty would react and whether he would talk about it. He also intended to ask Frank O'Laughlin if they could speak after he'd seen the patient.

"Marty's better today," Mrs. Corrigan said. "He ain't in the mood yet to eat nothing heavy, but the toast and tea are staying down, knock on wood. I'm thinking maybe he can try a boiled egg with his toast later. What d' ye think, Doctor?"

"He may enjoy it and it can't hurt him. Did he sleep well last night?"

"He said he did, but I think not. I heard him moving around during the night. But today, just about every time I went up to see him, he was sleeping peaceful as a babe. O' course, I never woke him up, but a few times when he woke on his own, that fevered look was gone from his eyes. I felt s' sorry fer the poor lad yesterday, but I'm sure he'll be up by tomorrow — he always goes to church of a Sunday — but I'll not let him out if it's cold as it is now."

Marty should count his blessings, Dougherty thought. Many a landlady would have been far less solicitous.

"And did ye learn any more about what we talked about yesterday?" She glanced at the boys who were sitting on the rug in front of the stove. They were fully absorbed in some game of their own invention and ignored the adults. "I mean what I showed ye?"

"Nothing," he said. "It may take a while. We're at the very beginning of the investigation. It takes patience. In the meantime, keep it in a safe place as you've been doing."

A door upstairs opened, voices exchanged goodbyes, a pair of heavy shoes clumped down the stairs. O'Laughlin entered the kitchen, with a look of surprise at finding the doctor there, but no least trace of alarm so far as Dougherty could see. He shook his hand.

"A pleasure to see ye, Doctor, to be sure," he said. "Ye'll be happy at how yer patient's coming along. Whatever ye give him, it done him the world o' good. He's talking about work on Monday and I think he's ready fer a bit o' nourishment — but, that's up to yer own judgement once ye've seen him."

"I'll do that now," Dougherty said, "and I wondered if I might have a moment of your time when I'm done?"

"Why, that ye could. I'd be honored. The fact is, I was thinking o' coming to see ye anyway. It seemed to me time we had a little talk."

"Frank," Mrs. Corrigan said, "why don't ye just sit yerself down and take a sip o' tea against the cold? Then, when the Doctor's done upstairs, yez can have the use o' me parlor. It'll give yez some privacy, and ye'll not have to rush out into the cold."

That settled, Dougherty took his bag and went upstairs. Carroll was sitting up in bed, still not back to full health, but far better than he had been. His color was near normal even in the light of the tallow lamp, and the last evening's exhausted, sweaty look had yielded to a normal tiredness.

"Ah, it's you, Doctor! I thought it was Mrs. Corrigan with my tea and toast."

"I'm sorry to disappoint you," Dougherty said, "Shall I leave and ask her to come up instead?"

"Oh, I didn't mean it like that, sir! I'm not disappointed at all — I'm happy that it's you... Well, I don't mean that I don't want to see Mrs. Corrigan. I mean to say..." His cheeks grew red, but this time not from fever, Dougherty was pleased to see. It was just his youth, and he smiled as he realized he was being teased.

"How are you?" Dougherty asked as he checked his pulse and felt the healthy coolness of his cheeks and forehead. He could hear that the congestion had much abated.

"I'm tired, but I feel good. Not like yesterday. By morning I hope I'll be up and about."

"It wouldn't surprise me," Dougherty said, "but be glad that tomorrow is Sunday. Make it a day of rest and stay in out of the cold. You should be able to go back to work on Monday."

"That's a relief, Doctor. I can use the money, and I already missed today and most of yesterday. I like to send something to my parents, so I can't afford to lose any more days."

"I can understand that," Dougherty said. "It's little enough they pay you."

He had meant nothing by the comment, apart from its obvious import. Marty Carroll took it to mean something more.

"Can I ask you something, Doctor?"

"Surely."

Still he hesitated, long enough that Dougherty decided he must have thought better of it and would drop the matter. Instead, he forged ahead.

"Are you familiar then with the Ancient Order of Hibernians?"

"I know who they are," Dougherty said, "but I've never had any association with them. Why do you ask?"

"I talked to Mr. McBrien about them and he told me maybe I ought to speak to you."

"What got you interested in the A.O.H. to begin with? Do you intend to join them?"

"That's what I don't know," he said. "I know my dad don't want me to. At least, I don't think he would... I didn't ask him, but I heard him talk about it often enough, and I know that he wouldn't join."

"Did he say why?"

"He did. The way he explained it, it's a secret society, and he don't know how an honest man can get himself into something like that. He says that you have to promise to keep secrets, but you have to make the promise before you have any idea what the secrets are — so you don't really know what you're being asked to keep quiet about. You don't know if it's good or bad, so how can you make a promise like that?"

"That makes sense," Dougherty said. "Why should you find it hard not to join? Does someone insist that you must?"

"I wouldn't say insist, but when he talks to me about it, I get to thinking that it might be a mistake not to join. It really ain't what you'd call a secret society. That's to say, it don't do evil things or nothing like that. There's just some things are private, you might say — not any kind of dark secret — just things like special words or handshakes for knowing whether a man's your friend or not, things like that. I know the Church don't like us joining, but maybe that's because the priests and bishop don't always understand the whole thing."

"Maybe that worries your dad, too," Dougherty said. "You're a young man, Marty. There's no hurry to join. Take your time and think some more."

"I've been thinking," he said, "and the reasons he gives make a lot of sense — but so does the things my dad says. It ain't easy to know what to do."

"What reasons does this friend of yours give?"

"Well, I ain't all that good at talking about it, but I guess it comes down to how we need to stick together. If you're Irish and Catholic, that's two marks against you right off. We need to stick together and the A.O.H. is a way to do that. It's what they call a 'benevolent association.' When a man's a member and comes on hard times, the A.O.H.'ll give a hand where it's needed. There's something else, too.

If the owners ever hear of a workers' union, they do everything to bring it down. But there's still strength in numbers, and maybe the A.O.H. can at least give us that. I'll tell you what... why don't you talk to Frank O'Laughlin about it? He's the one's been talking to me. He's better at explaining it and he won't mind talking to you about it. He respects you after what you done down in the mine and for how you're trying to do something about Brogan's murder, God rest him."

For a while they sat in silence, Dougherty rearranging things in his medical bag so as not to stare and make Marty nervous, and Marty struggling with whatever it was that he still had to say and wasn't sure if he should.

"You know," he said, "sometimes you can be in a good thing and maybe just go too far."

Again he stopped.

"Well, what bothers me," he finally said, "is that Brogan was the kind of man people take to, if you know what I mean. But he said what he thought too, and I know he was asked to join the A.O.H. and maybe some other things as well, and he wouldn't have a thing to do with it. That could have made him some enemies."

Marty's shyness seemed to have left him and he rushed right on.

"His mind was all on business of his own. I don't know what it was, but it worried him. He'd no time for other things. I never knew for sure and certain, but I got the idea like he was looking for something or hiding from something. It was the way he had of looking at people or listening to them. Like he looked for more than what they were willing to show, if you know what I mean.

"Some people thought he was stand-offish and they maybe didn't like him for it. Not like he ever done nothing to them. Just that he wouldn't do what they wanted. It's odd. Hard to explain. They liked him and then, when he didn't do what they thought, they didn't like him. Some people are that way."

"Are you afraid that may be what got him killed? That he didn't take to what people wanted him to do? That he advised you or others not to do what somebody wanted you to do? Like join the A.O.H.? Or maybe join... something else?"

"When you say it right out like that, it don't make a lot of sense, does it? But there's always some people have hot heads and do dumb things. Like I said, maybe Frank O'Laughlin could tell it better — even though I'm sure he don't think that's why Brogan got killed."

And that was how Dougherty got to talk to O'Laughlin. He found him at the kitchen table, sipping his tea, and playing a guessing game with the boys, who were both caught up in a fit of the giggles. They refilled their cups and took them into the parlor. O'Laughlin lost no time getting to the point.

"I bin told that Arkwright sent fer ye and that he had Maddock there to talk to ye — to you and Mr. McBrien. I ain't asking ye to tell me nothing that ain't me business, fer I'd not expect ye'd do that to me and I extend to you the same courtesy. But I'd be awful surprised if he didn't try to convince ye that the murderer o' Charlie Brogan was just some hot headed Irishman or else it was part o' some plot by a secret gang — the Buckshots or the Molly Maguires that the papers like to use fer their whipping boy fer everything that happens in the coal regions. To be sure, they usually do that fer acts against mine owners and ticket bosses and such, but they're not above trying to pin this on the same scapegoats. Why not get people thinking the Irish'll do in anybody, even one o' their own?"

"I'll not deny your logic," Dougherty said, "but are you certain that Arkwright is wrong?"

"Am I certain? Well, I'd say as sure as ye can be of anything in a world prone to sin. It makes no sense at all to think o' some secret group dedicated to the welfare o' the working man and the upset o' the capitalists, and then going around killing the working man they're supposed to be helping. And it's even more unlikely, wouldn't ye say, when there ain't no such vicious conspiracy in the first place!"

"Why do you think Arkwright has chosen to get into this matter at all? He may be wrong in what he sees as the solution, but at least he is concerned about who killed Brogan."

"If ye don't mind me saying so, Doctor, he don't give a damn who done Brogan in. Fer him the question is how to make sure the Penrose Valley Mining Company comes out ahead — and himself along with it. I don't trust him as far as I can spit."

"And what about Captain Morgan Maddock?"

"Arkwright's trained monkey, d' ye mean? He'll do what he's told and he'll dance to whatever tune his organ grinder plays. Given a free hand, I'd guess he's no better and no worse than many another copper. But, if Arkwright tells him ahead o' time who's to be found guilty, you can bet that's where the evidence'll lead, even if it has to be twisted to get there."

"Had Brogan made any enemies since he came here?"

"He wasn't here long enough to make real enemies. At least not the kind to kill him. Nor, fer that matter, was he here long enough to make real friends neither. Still, I'd say he was liked more than disliked."

"Somebody disliked him enough to put a bullet in him and then bring down a mine on his head — even at risk of killing two other men along with him."

"Yer right about that. Somebody didn't like him a' tall. But that don't mean the reason fer the dislike is here in the valley. Me own opinion, now I've thought about it, is he brung his trouble along with him from wherever he come from. Or else his trouble come here first and he followed it. And I ain't got a clue what it was. He was a decent man who done his work and kept mostly to himself. We had our points o' difference, as I'm sure young Marty must'a mentioned to ye, but I liked Brogan and I'd say he liked me."

"Have you any evidence that Brogan's problems started before he came here?"

"No. But it stands to reason, don't it?"

"You may be right. How do you think Arkwright and Maddock would respond if I found such evidence?"

"I don't think they'd give a damn. They'd want to get rid o' whatever ye come up with that didn't fit their theory, or else they'd find a way to make ye seem the fool fer even bringing it up. They'd be a lot better pleased to have ye prove that an Irishman done it — best of all a mine worker. There's loads of us down in the hole to choose from. Pick any mick in the mines. Who'll miss one when ye got a list o' workers longer than the list o' jobs to go round? Ye sacrifice one and scare the rest enough and that's the end o' the labor movement. Who'd support a bunch o' murderous riffraff full o' complaints against the kind-hearted mine owners who give them jobs? And ye can bet yer bottom dollar that any evidence they dig up will just happen to point directly at somebody involved in the labor movement — somebody in the Workingmen's Benevolent Association or the A.O.H. or, even better, a member o' both. Take me word fer it."

His ideas were food for thought. Dougherty was doubly glad he had not spoken to Arkwright or Maddock about the Butcher. If what O'Laughlin said was true, they might well cover up that part of the investigation and look for a scapegoat much nearer to hand. They'd been ready to join right in with Benjamin Bannan's notion of Buckshots or Molly Maguires as the killers of Henry Dunne — and were content that the same group had killed Brogan, even though there was no evidence whatsoever to support that.

O'Laughlin was perfectly correct: Under certain circumstances they might not want to catch the killer at all! They might prefer to keep alive the fear of conspiracy. The lasting suspicion would be more to their advantage than was the relief of an arrest and a hanging.

Dougherty thought of Steven Carter, a clever and competent detective. Would he, too, fall in with whatever became the official line of the mining company? Or would he actually seek the truth? That remained to be seen. In the meantime, Dougherty could not afford to let Carter know what they had learned or suspected. And that was too bad — his help could have been valuable.

"I hope ye'll not mind a word of advice," he said.

"Not at all." Dougherty meant what he said. O'Laughlin's words thus far had proven interesting, not at all threatening in even a veiled manner, but there was no missing his contempt for Arkwright and Maddock and their ilk.

"Don't let them take ye in," he said. "They've already got their hands into a couple o' cases, and they'd love to get one right here."

"You mean like Henry Dunne?"

"That'd be one o' them," he said. "The word's already being spread by Bannan and his pals that the killers was all Irish. And maybe it's so. I couldn't say fer sure. But that don't mean what Bannan wants it to mean. It don't mean that they killed him *because* they was Irish, nor *because* they was Catholic, nor *because* he was Protestant. They didn't rob him, so they must'a had some other reason — revenge or whatever. Anyway, it don't matter as far as Bannan's concerned. He'll make it all part o' some grand scheme on the part o' the Irish to get rid o' the Protestants. That's the way he wants it to be. Or to pit the Irish against the Welsh or against the English. Not that they ain't already pitted against each other, but he'd like it thought that every complaint an Irish miner makes is nothing more than one more sign o' the Irish trying to get rid o' everyone else. That way their real complaints don't count fer nothing. Do ye recall the murder o' David Muir in Schuylkill County last August?"

Dougherty recalled it well. Muir was a mine superintendent, born in Scotland. He was shot in Foster Township in broad daylight not far from his office, and no one had identified the killers or even admitted seeing them. Neither had anyone offered a motive that made sense — although some thought it could be traced back to problems with the draft resistance during the war.

"Take a look at this," he said, withdrawing from the inside pocket of his sack coat a folded copy of the *Miners' Journal*, Benjamin Bannan's Pottsville newspaper. It was that very day's issue. "It come in on this afternoon's train. Ye'll see that Bannan, as usual, makes up what he don't know fer sure."

This was the issue that contained Bannan's editorial denouncing the murderers of Henry Dunne, and Bannan had lost no time stating (or manufacturing) a link with Muir's murder. He had no idea who had killed Muir, but he twisted his lack of knowledge into an explanation of sorts, stating that Muir's "murderers — in consequence of the efficiency of the secret, oath bound organization that exists in this County — remain to this day undetected." The man was amazing in making uncertainty sound like proof and ignorance a virtue. Any killer who is unknown must therefore be Irish.

"So ye see, then, what Arkwright would dearly love to produce right here in his own backyard — his local branch o' the Molly

Maguires to take the blame fer all crime and so to keep us micks all in line and groveling in fear o' losing our jobs."

"Losing your jobs?"

"Why, o' course. I've no doubt but he'll soon take up Bannan's other favorite theme. He wants a blacklist circulated among all the owners with the names o' whoever was a 'troublemaker' (according to the owners' definition). Anybody on that list can just kiss his job goodbye, and he ain't gonna get another anywhere in the region. So everybody can just live scared o' being listed and behave like a good little mick. And do ye know what's worst of all? Even if there ain't a secret society, people like Arkwright and Bannan will damn soon push people into forming one."

Sad to say, Dougherty thought, he was probably right; only time would tell. But would time also tell who had killed Brogan? Was it the Molly Maguires? Was it the Butcher? Or was it someone else entirely?

The Diarist

> January 8, 1866 — He came and he died. He wanted the meeting. He wanted information. He came too close for his own good. Even at the end he was clever enough to come within a hair of escaping, but the mine didn't save him. Did he tell anyone what he knew? I doubt it. He worked alone. I will find out more once I see how this investigation is conducted. If there is an investigation.

It was almost a week since the Diarist had made that entry and still no one had referred to him or to his previous activities. An almost certain sign that his pursuer had taken no one into his confidence. As he had expected, the inquiry was a farce. A doctor and a pharmacist, indeed! If they had any notion of the truth, things would be different. He was certain that the pursuit was over and that he could get back to a pursuit of his own.

He had been busy preparing, and it was a relief not to have to keep looking over his shoulder. The choice had been difficult this time and he felt the pressure of his self-imposed schedule. Self-imposed, yes, but not for that reason subject to change; pride in his work would not allow him to change it. In the past he had known well ahead of time who it was that would be chosen. This time was different. But he had found her at last, and it was all the more exciting for the wait. He had seen her yesterday, and all was right on schedule.

He must be especially careful this time. This was no big city depot, no haven of anonymity. But that did not frighten him. It was all a matter of fate. He sat on Sunday afternoon in the rented room with its dingy walls and musty curtains, watching her as she walked toward the depot. For a moment his vision wavered, then he realized the tremor was in his hands, in their over-tight grasp of the field glasses. He breathed slowly, consciously relaxing. He looked again. She was so close that he wanted to reach out and touch her.

The time was so short. The train arrived, blocking his view and when, no more than three minutes later, the train pulled out, she was no longer there. But he was certain she would be back at the proper time. Three days. He did not at all doubt that she would be there.

There could be no setback in his plans. He had never failed before and he would not now.

Chapter XIII: Such Kindly Eyes

Beginning of the teaching for life,
The instructions for well-being—
Knowing how to answer one who speaks,
To reply to one who sends a message.
> Amenomope (XI Century B.C.)
> *The Instruction of Amenomope*, Prologue

[Wednesday, January 17, 1866]

It was near 1:30, the time for departure. McBrien was to meet them there, and he and James would be in Mauch Chunk before 4:30. Jen wanted to see them off. Their meeting with Judge Barrett was scheduled for 7:00 that evening in his office at the courthouse. James had finished his report just before the noon meal — he composing and Jen copying each page as he finished it.

The report was lengthy. They had included the autopsy notes and what they had learned of Brogan — which, in fact, was next to nothing. They did not mention the money now in possession of Mrs. Corrigan. The bulk of the report dealt with the earlier murders. Their summary gave sources of information, a catalogue of salient features of each of the crimes and victims, and presented in clear and cogent manner their theories of the past killings and their premonitions of the next.

"Is there anything else to pack?" she asked. They were in the bedroom, and she had laid out upon the bed his clothes, his shaving implements, and other needful articles. The report was in a large folder. Everything would fit easily into his traveling bag. He expected to be back on the early Thursday train.

"No," he said, "You've thought of everything, as always."

She brushed some all but invisible specks of lint from his best black frock coat one final time. He put it on, straightened its line, smoothed the lapels, took a last look in the mirror at the state of his tie, and checked that his watch chain lay properly in place across the front of his waistcoat. Jen smiled. He was so handsome, she thought, as distinguished as a judge himself. With his right hand he stroked the neatly trimmed beard. It was a gesture he had acquired in the first days of their acquaintance, when he had grown the beard to cover the scar where the bullet had pierced his neck and come within a hair of killing him. Each time she saw that unthinking gesture, Jen thanked God for the poor aim that had left no worse a wound, but had given her the chance to nurse him back to health.

"Do you think Judge Barrett will accept our ideas on the reason for Brogan's death?" she asked.

"That may depend on more than logic," he said, "I'm sure Arkwright will want to reach the Judge before we do. I don't know Barrett well enough to predict his response, but we've done our best to make the case. The trouble is we have no proof that this Butcher is here. The killer may be someone else entirely, and we must realize that. But I hope, at least, that the Judge will see that the investigation cannot be locked into one narrow line of thought. If he hands it over to Arkwright's workhorses, they'll look only with the blinkers he wants them to wear."

Jen applauded. "Bravo! Encore!" and he laughed along with her. He'd been talking as though she were a public assembly. But with good reason. It was a rehearsal for what he must present to Judge Barrett that evening and it worried him.

"Have you any more thoughts on Frank O'Laughlin?" he asked.

They had learned a lot. O'Laughlin had been in Penrose Valley ever since his discharge from the army in June of the preceding year. He had served first with the 125th Pennsylvania Infantry Volunteers and, when that regiment was mustered out in 1863 after Chancellorsville, he joined the 61st Pennsylvania and stayed in until the end. For a time he was in the Northern Defense of Washington and was there in 1864 when Jubal Early and his rebs made their failed attempt on the capital.

James had learned this after their discussion of Brogan's death and the A.O.H., when they sat and exchanged war stories. And he found out that O'Laughlin had worked on the New York docks before he joined the 125th.

"I still don't know what to think," she said. "When O'Laughlin spoke to you, it seemed no more than idle conversation and coincidence. After all, how many men from Ireland land in New York every day of the week, live there for a while, and then go off to greener pastures? And the places he went during the war? Those places in and around Washington? They were not in the least unusual for anyone in the Army of the Potomac... On the other hand, if he was trying to press to see what you know, what better way to test your reaction? I can't hazard a guess as to which he was doing. Not very helpful, am I?"

"I think, my dear, that you have the soul of a philosopher," he said, smiling as he put his arm around her and drew her to himself. "But I have the same problem, so you're not alone. What of Carter's ideas? What do you make of them?"

* * *

From the first, Steven Carter had not much liked Captain Morgan Maddock. His reputation for harshness in the military was well deserved, and he carried that with him into the the Penrose Valley Coal and Iron Police. His ruthlessness was advantageous in hunting down his quarry, and that gave him an impressive record for getting the job done. But that same ruthlessness was indiscriminate and could as easily be directed against those who worked for him or anyone who displeased him. Carter thought of the stick the Captain had thrown at some curious children just a few days ago. Carter despised that sort of violence. It was useless and destructive and produced no gain, no answers to the questions they should be concerned with. The fact was that, without the uniform, Maddock could as easily have been a criminal.

He found Dougherty and McBrien more to his liking. But Maddock was his superior and it was to him that he must answer. Carter had carried out his preliminary interrogations as ordered. When, at Maddock's command, he made his report to Dougherty, he could see that Dougherty was impressed. At the same time, the doctor gave away so little of what he had learned — possibly because he had learned so little. As to physical evidence, beyond the bullet and the scarred support beam, what was there? Carter's instincts told him that this case must depend on other testimony — background, conflicts, relationships — and he was surprised that Dougherty had so far done so little along those lines. That made him curious, because he did not think it was due to incompetence on Dougherty's part. But to make that judgement, he would have to wait and see.

It was only when they first visited Dougherty that Carter learned he was expected to work with him. Maddock may have made the decision on the spot. Even if he hadn't, it was like him not to have told Carter earlier. It was clearly not acceptable to Dougherty, in spite of the fact that Maddock thought his word was law. Nor had Carter heard anything further from Dougherty or McBrien after that meeting. They were not eager to accept his help. That was no surprise. In their minds he was an extension of Maddock. So he decided to take matters into his own hands, do his own investigation, then go back to Dougherty and see what information they could exchange.

On Monday, when Dougherty finished with his last patient, Carter was there in the waiting room, impeccably dressed as always and perfectly at his ease. He sat, right leg crossed over left, hat on the floor next to him, reading a book (he almost always carried one in his pocket, it relaxed him at odd moments), knowing that Dougherty would be willing to see him, if only to find out what he'd been up to. He was not mistaken.

"Mr. Carter," Dougherty said, "Can I help you? It's not your health, is it?"

"No, sir. In fact the cold weather agrees with me. I prefer this to the summer's heat. I just thought it was time I spoke to you about what I've been doing."

His report did interest the doctor. Carter had interviewed a number of people, and was developing a line of inquiry that he saw did not please Dougherty. For that matter, it did not truly please him either, but he considered it necessary. The object of his concern was Frank O'Laughlin. Much as Dougherty might have preferred to think him innocent, Carter's work was beginning to create doubts. He had learned a good deal.

"You already knew," he began, "that Brogan and O'Laughlin worked together, and that Brogan's sickness had changed that temporarily. I thought it was possible that Brogan did not know what change had been made, and he may have gone into the mine thinking he would find O'Laughlin at his usual post.

"Meantime, O'Laughlin was working with Will Shannon in a gangway twenty or thirty yards deeper in the mine.

"Just as McGinley and O'Donnell were able vouch for each other, Shannon and O'Laughlin did the same. Or at least it seemed so. But the more I looked at details, the more I had my doubts. The fact is that when the cave-in occurred, Shannon only *thought* he could vouch for O'Laughlin. In fact, he couldn't. Shannon was prying out the blasted blocks of coal from inside the breast, and O'Laughlin had gone out, dragging a loaded sledge to fill the empty car in the main tunnel. When he was pressed about it, Shannon had to admit that he'd have a hard time saying just how long they had been separated.

"I tried my best to pin it down, but the fact is that Shannon wasn't paying much attention to the time. His mind was on what he was doing. I learned that you have to be careful what you dig out of the breast. You have to get the cars loaded as fast as you can, and once they get to the breaker the ticket boss pulls your ticket from the car, estimates how much is slate or refuse, and deducts that from your tally. So you dig and load and you don't track the time until the whistle blows for the shift. The fact is that O'Laughlin could have been gone long enough to do the mischief and Shannon could never had said one way or the other."

He could almost see Dougherty readjusting his thoughts. At least some of this must be new to him, and Carter was pleased at that. He went on.

"What really seems to have happened is this: Shannon was in the gangway and O'Laughlin was in the main tunnel when the cave-in happened. O'Laughlin came running into the gangway, out of breath, and told Shannon to drop what he was doing and come help. They went down to the gangway where you found the body. Shannon said there was a great hubbub about the men trapped inside, so they got right to work. O'Laughlin sent the boy to get you, and all the rest you know, because you were there."

Dougherty was interested and he was impressed. Again he found himself wishing he and Carter could work together, but that couldn't be, not in present circumstances.

"What's your impression of O'Laughlin?" Dougherty asked.

"He's a likeable sort," Carter answered, "and I found it hard to think that he could have committed this crime. But then I added motive to circumstance, and I had misgivings. I'd heard more than one say that Brogan and O'Laughlin argued a lot. To hear O'Laughlin tell it, it was all friendly bickering, nothing serious. But some others — young Carroll, for example — took it more seriously. In my opinion, we need to know a lot more about those arguments, but for now I suspect they were not the insignificant disagreements O'Laughlin would have us believe."

* * *

"I seem," Jen said, "to be singularly unhelpful today. I've thought about what Mr. Carter told you, and I'm afraid it opens up some new lines of thought, but without closing any of the old ones. Could O'Laughlin be guilty?"

"I hope not," he said, "but, truth to tell, it begins to look bad."

His voice reflected his misgivings. He liked O'Laughlin and wanted him to be what he seemed — a good man, honest, full of the dignity and natural authority he'd seen when they first met. It was unthinkable that he had within him the deep darkness of the Butcher.

But for now it was time to go. The day was so beautiful that Jen knew she would enjoy the walk to the station and back. But that wasn't the real reason for seeing them off. The truth was that she was going to miss James. She knew it was silly. After all, he would be away only overnight; but, even if it seemed overly sentimental, she hoped it was a sentiment she would never lose.

When she was decked out in her almost best coat and bonnet, James took his bag in hand, offered her his arm, and they were on their way. The temperature was in the lower forties, totally unlike the freeze of the week before. The bright afternoon sun cast shadows as clear and crisp as if put into place by a painstaking artist. The sky was a startling blue. The gentle breeze that rose and fell, as it had done for the past two days, had dried the road and walkways. Jen drew a deep breath and smiled. Only then did she realize just how thoroughly her mind had been immersed in the murderous world of those newspaper articles. James must have been feeling the same, she thought, for she looked up at him only to find that he was looking down at her with a gaze of such gentle affection that she felt her eyes mist over for a moment from sheer happiness.

There were more people in the streets than they should have expected, probably brought out as much by the beauty of the day as by any pressing need. It was one of those times when people look for reasons to be out and about, full of a *joie de vivre* that needs only the flimsiest of excuses to bubble up to the surface and overflow into the friendly greetings that they exchanged as they went their way.

The Hazle Creek Bridge Station stood at the far end of Main Street. When they had first come here, Jen had wondered why it was not not called the Penrose Valley Railroad Station. Would that all mysteries were as easily resolved! The railroad bridge across Hazle Creek antedated the presence of the town, and so did the station, built for the convenience of the people from Buck Mountain and Hazleton, whose railroad lines converged here with the Beaver Meadow branch of the Lehigh Valley Railroad. It was a lovely little building with a cone shaped top on the turret that rose so modestly above the gray slate roof that also extended out over the platform. Before long a larger building would no doubt be needed to cater to the increased traffic, and she already felt a sense of loss.

Across from the station, Owen Williams' telegraph office was a reminder of the care they must take in what they did. They passed Captain Maddock's new office, but saw neither him nor his men anywhere about. The depot door opened and Sean McBrien stepped out, traveling bag in hand. At the platform the train waited, emitting its random puffs and sighs and bursts of hissing steam, like an elderly dragon working up the energy to take flight. McBrien waved and they went to meet him.

"Major... Mrs. Dougherty... Welcome to ye! I suppose we're all ready to go then, are we? And ye've got the report finished as well?"

"That we do," James said. "Have you got our tickets?"

"Right here." He held them up. "And the train's about ready to pull out."

"I suppose we'd better get aboard, then," James said. He set his bag on the platform and turned to take her in his arms, placing upon her forehead a kiss as gentle as the brush of a butterfly's wingtip. She was more moved than she should have expected and wondered why. One would have thought this a leave taking of greater consequence than a separation of less than twenty-four hours. For a moment she was conscious only of him, without a thought for McBrien or for the other eight or nine people now moving toward the train or even for the jangling harness and squeaking wheels of the buggy coming to a stop almost alongside them. She hugged him tightly for a moment, then stepped back and smiled, rather self-conscious at the sudden depth of feeling.

Then it came to her — the source of the strong emotion and of her fearfulness of parting from James. It was the fear of what they thought would happen within the next few weeks. The dread that some innocent victim, some totally unsuspecting young woman, would have her life brutally carved out, unless they could prevent it. And they had no notion how to do that!

"Have a good trip," she said. "Persuade Judge Barrett, as I know you will. And do be careful. Remember what we saw in last week's paper. That wild animal is still on the loose and if it's daring enough to come into town and kill a pig, then it cannot be safe to be about town at night."

"I will do my best to carry out all your parting admonitions," he said, "and I'll see you tomorrow." He smiled as they got on the train.

From the corner of her eye she saw a man emerge from the buggy and enter the station, but her real attention was on the conductor as he pulled in the bench-step and closed the doors of the passenger car. From the window James waved, as the dragon came to life, gave a loud hiss, a puff of smoke, and two toots of its whistle to signal "brakes off." Then they were gone and she turned to go home, realizing that her momentary fear was nothing but a passing fancy, and that the beauty of the day would restore her fully by the time she reached their front door. Perhaps she would even stop for a cup of tea with Mrs. Corrigan on the way. And she knew she would enjoy seeing the boys.

The station door opened and the man from the buggy emerged. He was tall, well dressed, formal in bearing, yet the sort of man you might well see and never notice. One of the invisibles. He looked about and spied a lad of ten or eleven years of age, a child Jen had seen about town but whose name she did not know. They spoke and then both turned in her direction. He placed in the child's hand a card or a small envelope and waited as the lad came toward her.

"Beg pardon, lady, but ain't you Mrs. Dougherty? The Doctor's wife?"

"I am."

"That gent over there asked me to give ye this and says could he talk to ye?"

He put into her hand a calling card and skipped off as she looked over at the man who had sent him. Where had she seen him before? And she was fairly certain that she had. He was one of those persons you may pass in the street day after day without even seeing, and then something happens to push him into your conscious thought and you are puzzled at his familiarity. He had about him a commonality, the look of everyman. The sort who is seen and not seen, visible and invisible. Yet now that she actually looked directly at him, he was quite pleasant, with his tentative smile, that look of doubt about whether she would or would not know him. There was something so pleasant about him. He tipped his broad-brimmed hat. He had such kindly eyes.

The Diarist

> January 17, 1866 — It is over. She was at the terminal, as fate decreed. I see it again in my mind's eye. The look of curiosity. Do I... know you? The hesitance to speak to a stranger weighed against the fear of snubbing a half forgotten acquaintance. But she knew. She accepted the pain. She had to be cleansed. She knew that I loved her. Make mommy smile.

Then he, too, smiled. He set aside the pen, corked the inkwell, gently breathed upon the page until the ink was dry. He closed the diary and put it into his pocket, put the pen and ink in their little tin box. He looked again at how she slumped so lifelike in the carriage, as though napping. He blew out the light, plunging the whole area into darkness. He opened the door, mounted the carriage, took the reins in his capable hands, and clucked at the horse, skittish because of the odor of blood, to get it moving out into the darkness. He stopped and went back to close the door, then remounted next to his smiling passenger. It was time to show the others what he had done, to offer them one more chance to learn.

Chapter XIV: He Could Not Flee

The door flew open, in he ran.
The great, long, red-legged scissor-man.
> Heinrich Hoffmann (1809-1894)
> *Struwwelpeter* (1848), "The Little Suck-a-Thumb"

[Thursday, January 18, 1866]

The tapping had begun gently, but now was loud, insistent. A voice said, "Doctor... Doctor....," in that whispered shout one uses in the vain hope of waking the inhabitant of one room while allowing others nearby to remain peacefully asleep. It never works. He heard the stirring and grumbling in the rooms on either side as he opened his eyes.

"Yes? Who is it?"

"It's me, Al, from the desk downstairs. I have a message for you, Doctor."

"One moment, please."

He pulled on his robe and opened the door. In the dimmed gaslight of the corridor was the night clerk, a thin man, stoop-shouldered, with a fringe of gray hair edging his otherwise bald head, a pair of jug-handle ears, and spectacles perched on the tip of a long, thin nose, beneath which sprouted a magnificent gray moustache.

"Doctor, I'm sorry to disturb you, but there's a young fellow just came from the courthouse with this message for you. He's in the lobby waiting for your answer."

Dougherty took the envelope and opened it. Al turned up the hall light next to the door to make the reading easier.

> Doctor Dougherty,
>
> I am informed of a death about which it is imperative that I speak to you. Notwithstanding the early hour, may I prevail upon the kindness of you and Mr. McBrien to come to my chambers upon receipt of this message? Please acknowledge.
>
> Yr. Obdt. Servant,

Geo. R. Barrett
Presiding Judge

"Thank you, Al. Would you please tell the lad who delivered this to inform Judge Barrett that I will be along presently? And please be so good as to wake Mr. McBrien and ask him to do me the kindness of meeting me in the lobby as soon as possible."

He left. Dougherty lighted the lamp in his room. His watch said 5:20. It was still dark, the fire in the grate was almost out, and the room was cold. Who had died? Why was Judge Barrett in his office at this hour? Speculation is interesting (sometimes more so than facts), but it couldn't supply one iota of the information he would acquire by simply getting dressed and going to the judge's office.

* * *

James had experienced an unwonted sense of reluctance in parting from Jen. Something was bothering her. She'd done her best not to show it, but they knew each other too well for that. As the train pulled out and he leaned from the window to wave one last time, he saw the concern in her eyes and the almost little girl hesitance in her wave. Even in her winter coat, she looked so thin, so small, so vulnerable.

The train had gathered speed as it pulled out and then almost immediately slowed again as they prepared to pull into Weatherly. A few passengers on, a few off, and they were on their way. The windows were shut against the cold, so they had not to contend with sparks or ashes blowing in upon them. But neither did they have the lush green of the forests. Still, there was a beauty even to these winter trees, so stark against the snow on the slope of Broad Mountain — but their naked branches could not disguise the damage the mines had done. Their voracious tunnels devoured an endless diet of timbers, and the hills around every town in the region were stripped bare to satisfy that insatiable appetite. It was one of the reasons Dougherty so liked the stretch of track from Penn Haven to Mauch Chunk. The river gorge made logging difficult, less profitable, allowing it to retain the look that all the forests of the region must once have had.

When they sighted their destination, it was with the abruptness that always surprised him. The train curved along the Lehigh, crossed over at Coalport, and there ahead of them was Mauch Chunk, the county seat, nestled in the narrow ravine between the steep ridges of the surrounding mountains — ridges that were another source of the town's prosperity. The gravity-operated switchback railroad had once brought the coal down to the barges of the canal which ran along the river. It now did the same for the railroad cars which followed the same route. And as the coal gravitated here, so too did the money.

Directly across the river from the Lehigh Valley Railroad Station was the Mansion House Hotel — the scene of the first appearance of that wildcat which so worried Jen. It was an impressive sight, its five stories rising against the backdrop of the mountain whose face rose almost straight up just yards behind the building. It loomed above them as they stepped from the bridge, admiring the expanse of windows and balcony. They turned right and went the length of the street to the less expensive Central Hotel, at the corner of Susquehanna and Broadway, near the courthouse.

"Do ye think he'll let us go on as we been doing?" McBrien asked over supper. They had decided to take their meal in the dining room of the American Hotel.

"I don't think he will prohibit us from following any line of inquiry," Dougherty said, "provided I remain in charge of the investigation. My greatest concern is that he might yield to Arkwright's importuning and remove us. After all, we are simply private citizens dealing with this matter by dint of previous experience."

"I see what ye're getting at," he said. "Arkwright can just as easy argue that Maddock's men've got police experience — at least Maddock and Carter do. I know nothing o' the rest o' them."

"Nor do I," Dougherty said, "but it wouldn't surprise me if all their investigative skills came down to a night stick as an *aide memoire* for the suspect. I'm hoping the Judge will realize that the Coal and Iron Police are far more likely than are we to get caught up in conflicting interests."

"Well, let us hope that he will."

There was nothing else to be said, so they talked about anything but the case, as the minutes dragged by and the chef's good food was wasted upon their inattentive palates. Dougherty's mind, and, he was sure, McBrien's as well, kept returning to the large brown envelope which lay on the empty chair next to him. At last it was time to go.

It had turned so cold since sundown that they turned up their collars and pulled on their gloves even for that short walk. The street was busy, unlike the same hour in Penrose Valley. The gas lamps enhanced the dignity of the courthouse's brick façade and its four stone columns, tall and straight, their Ionic capitals two stories above the street. But it was not actually to the courthouse that they were going. The Judge was to meet them in the county office building, the Row Office. It was behind the courthouse, so they turned left onto Susquehanna Street, their eyes drawn up toward the brightly lighted mansions on the hill just past their destination. There was no one else on Susquehanna Street, with the exception of the grayish bearded man just leaving the Row Office. He glared at them, then turned, crossed the street, and set off toward the river.

The door to the office building was unlocked, so they went in. Dougherty was wondering where to go, when a voice called to them to come up.

Judge Barrett stood at the top of the stairs. He was then fifty years of age and had held the office of judge for ten years. He was no taller than Dougherty, but his position at the top of the stairs and his rigidly upright posture gave him the look of authority that he must have intended. The high forehead, the deep-set eyes, the first touches of gray in the hair, and the carefully tailored suit all proclaimed him the learned, serious, and fair-minded person who deserved to be a judge.

"Welcome, Doctor. Please accept my thanks for your willingness to visit me at this hour. At least I hope that this will allow you to be free to go home on the early train tomorrow. And this, I presume, is Mr. McBrien?"

They had not met before, so Dougherty performed the honors. They followed the Judge to his chambers. He sat at the dark rosewood desk, covered with neatly arranged stacks of folders, envelopes, and papers, all awaiting his attention. He gestured them to the two comfortable leather chairs before the desk. The room was, in fact, spacious enough, but felt closed in — the effect of the rows of books that lined the walls.

"I suppose you saw Captain Maddock departing as you arrived?"

"I did, Your Honor," Dougherty said, "but we hadn't the opportunity to greet him. He seemed in a hurry... no time for conversation."

"Perhaps not," he answered, "or perhaps just not the inclination. He does not seem one to pass time in idle chat. Well, that's neither here nor there, I suppose. Why don't we get to the matter at hand?"

And so they did. He accepted the report and Dougherty gave him a *précis* of its contents and what he hoped was a persuasive argument for continuing their investigation. As he spoke, Barrett followed along, flipping through the report, interrupting now and again with a question or a comment, none of them hostile. He sat in silent thought before he spoke.

"Your theory of the crime is far different from that of Captain Maddock. He is convinced that the whole affair revolves around discontent among the mine workers, a rough and lawless element, who in this instance had a falling out among themselves. He made no reference to this mysterious 'Butcher,' although he said he had spoken with you about the crime." He asked no question, simply waited for Dougherty's comment.

"There is good reason for that, Your Honor," he said. "First of all, we are not certain of the Butcher's involvement in this crime, although we lean strongly in that direction. Then, too, Captain Maddock is, at this point, a civilian, and it did not seem a good idea to take him into our confidence just yet. We told him nothing of the Butcher. And there was an even more pressing reason... One that is most sensitive... If the Butcher did kill Brogan, he has no idea that we are onto him. His ignorance may work to our advantage. Should he become aware of what we suspect, he may simply leave the area and begin again somewhere else. Or he may stay here, but be far more careful. As long as he is unaware of our knowledge, he may give himself away."

"And then, Yer Honor, there's the problem o' knowing who we can trust. The Butcher killed in Philadelphia and New York and

Washington, so it ain't likely he's a native o' the coal region. Most likely he just come there since last summer — but so did Maddock and his men. O' course, they ain't the only ones. There's men back from the army and there's men coming and going from one mine to the next looking fer work, and he could be any one o' them, or almost any one, but it still don't make sense to use the Coal and Iron Police, does it?"

"Under those conditions, no, it doesn't. I shall have to think about this. I am not dismissing your ideas, but I do need to consider everything. Captain Maddock, after all, has had police experience, as he says. He brought his credentials with him, and he told me about those of his men. I'm well aware that you, Doctor Dougherty, and you also, Mr. McBrien, have dealt with cases of murder before, so I have confidence in your abilities. But I must weigh the various factors before I decide. I have not told Captain Maddock that I was accepting his arguments, either. I told him just what I am telling you. I shall read your report carefully tonight and will speak to you early tomorrow in plenty of time for you to make your train back to Penrose Valley."

"There is one more thing," Dougherty said. "It is not in the written report. I omitted it because it is too uncertain, too conjectural, but I think I should mention it to you."

He told him what they had concluded about the pattern of the killings and of their fear that another was about to occur.

"Truly worrisome," he said, his incredulity not well disguised. "Does your investigation predict when or where this murder will occur? Or the name of the victim?"

"It does not."

"A dreadful thought. Horrible to contemplate. I will take it into account."

He stood and they realized that the discussion was over. He shook their hands and walked with them to the head of the stairs, then went back to his office. Dougherty hoped it was to read the report.

"What did ye think, Major?"

"I don't know. It encourages me that he will examine the report before he does anything further. I suppose there is nothing to do but wait. Why don't we go back to the American Hotel and have a glass of brandy and a cigar before we turn in for the night?"

* * *

McBrien was leaving his room as Dougherty emerged from his, so they walked down together and out into the crisp morning air, full of questions and not an answer between them. Judge Barrett was in his office, and so was someone Dougherty had never seen before, a young man, much on edge, anxious to get on about his business.

"Gentlemen, good morning." His Honor's tone was most serious. "I regret having to disturb you at this hour, but I had no other choice. There has been a death and your medical expertise is required."

Why mine? Dougherty wondered. He should have expected him to turn to the doctor who had been in Mauch Chunk for some years now, Doctor Rensselaer Leonard, who just two years ago had been county coroner. As though reading Dougherty's mind, he answered the unspoken question.

"I suppose I should have notified Doctor Leonard, but he has been quite ill these past few days, and it didn't seem right to disturb him. I know that he has full confidence in you. I consulted him when Father McGuire wrote to me on your behalf last week and he told me of your background."

Dougherty was sorry to hear of his illness. He had intended to pay his respects to Doctor Leonard before leaving town. Now he would make a point of it. He had been five years old when Doctor Leonard came to Beaver Meadow. As a youngster he had done odd jobs for him and the doctor had taken an interest in his education. Years later, when he moved to Mauch Chunk, he had sent for Dougherty and taken him on as an apprentice, making it possible for him to undertake his education at the Jefferson Medical College in Philadelphia.

"How can I help?" Dougherty asked.

"You've heard of the wild animal that has plagued Mauch Chunk these past weeks?"

"I saw the notice of its killing a pig up near the Presbyterian Church last week."

"Yes," he said, "In fact, almost directly in front of Doctor Leonard's office. It's been seen often enough, but only in the dark. The tracks indicate a wildcat, but until now it has been more of a joke than a threat. I am afraid that is no longer so. Deputy Klein can tell you about what happened this night."

He looked to the nervous young man, who was holding his hat by its brim and twisting it round and round in his large hands, his eyes cast down toward it as though what he was doing with it was of the utmost importance. At the mention of his name he gave a start, then looked at them, his pale cheeks suddenly scarlet. His Adam's apple bobbed up and down as he summoned the courage to speak. Deputy Klein was clearly new to all of this and was as uneasy as had been Dougherty at his own first investigation of a violent death.

"It's a dead person," he said, and then stopped — either for dramatic effect or because he thought that should have been enough for them or (most likely) to swallow and lick his lips, which had gone suddenly dry.

"It's a woman," he went on. "Little Bobby McFadden found her. He works down at the livery stable and he was headed there about an hour and a half ago to tend the horses."

The livery stable was not two blocks from where they were. It occupied the space between Susquehanna Street and the tracks of the Jersey Central Railroad, just at the foot of Race Street. It consisted of two large stables positioned in the form of an L, and an office on the opposite side of the exercise yard bounded by the stables.

"She was laying there in the yard," he continued, "and Bobby tripped over her in the dark. He run and got me 'cause I live right nearby. I went over to look and I sent Bobby to fetch Sheriff Ziegenfuss. I found her where he said, a young woman and she was dead for sure. I waited for the Sheriff and he told me to find Judge Barrett. The Sheriff brung a lantern, and that's how we seen she was tore up by that wildcat. The Sheriff's there now and he don't want to move her till the Judge says so."

"And there you have it gentlemen," Judge Barrett said. "I think that you should examine the scene and the body most carefully. If nothing else, it may at least give us enough information to determine what this animal is. I will arrange a place for you to work in the basement of this building and I will send to Doctor Leonard for the autopsy tools. Will you see to it? I want this done expeditiously, before anyone stirs up the town with a mad fear of wild animals and we have an army of men with rifles wandering about town in the dark and shooting all the dogs and cats."

Deputy Klein, happy at last to be on his way, set off at a brisk pace. He was probably too young to have served in the war, but Dougherty thought he would have been one of its marching champions. The sky was pre-dawn gray; before long the sun would dispel the patchy fog that lay close to the ground this near the river. Even at this early hour a small crowd had gathered, kept out of the yard by orders of the Sheriff but still gawking in the chill at the canvas covered body, inspired, Dougherty imagined, by the chance of seeing something when it came time to move the corpse. He greeted the Sheriff and introduced McBrien. Deputy Klein was visibly relieved to turn them over to his superior.

"Do you know who she is?" Dougherty asked.

"Not yet we don't," the Sheriff said, "but don't worry, we will."

He spoke with great assurance, a business-like officer of the law. He was shorter than Dougherty, ramrod straight, neatly dressed in a long, dark overcoat and black bowler. He left no doubt that he was in charge, although he treated them with perfect courtesy.

"Klein, you stay here and don't let anybody come in, you hear? Doctor Dougherty and Mr. McBrien, why don't you come and see what we've got here?" To a young lad standing with the spectators, he said, "Bobby, you stay here for a bit with Deputy Klein."

He led them to the object which lay near the corner of the two stables and handed Dougherty the lantern. He lifted the canvas, but so that it blocked the view of the onlookers. She lay on her back, her exophthalmic eyes staring straight up into the sky. This was not the work of a wildcat. Her neck bore the mark of a cord or wire, pressed so hard into her flesh that it had drawn blood at front and sides. Her mouth was a grotesque slash, revealing her teeth from ear to ear. The front of the dress was much cut and sliced and marked with blood. Dougherty looked at the Sheriff.

"Yes. I've noticed," he said. "That isn't the work of an animal the way Klein said. But I didn't tell him that. He's a good lad but he talks a little too much, so I thought it was better if he talked about that animal and didn't start telling the world that we may have a madman in our midst. They'll find out soon enough. You ever seen anything like this?"

"Never," Dougherty said.

He lifted each of the hands and looked carefully, palms and backs. They were clean, no blood or flesh beneath the nails. No cuts from fending off a knife. The fingers were stiff. He touched the neck and the face, finding stiffening there also. The arms moved with some small degree of difficulty. The flesh was cold to the touch but not yet clammy. It had been a cold night. He judged the temperature at 25 to 30 degrees, sufficient to slow down the process of *rigor mortis* and many of the other changes that occur as the body decomposes. She may have been dead for as many as twelve hours, maybe since five or six o'clock the previous evening. Once they took the body inside, the changes would accelerate.

"Was the body like this when it was found?" Dougherty asked. "I mean, in precisely this position?"

"Deputy Klein," the Sheriff called over his shoulder, "why don't you come over here a minute?"

He came, but not with alacrity, and he stood in a position from which he would not have to look at the body. Dougherty couldn't blame him. He had never seen anything so horrible. He asked him about the state of the body when it was discovered.

"Well, it was right where it is now, just about... I turned her over to see if she was dead."

"Could you describe just what you saw when you first looked. Exactly how was the body placed? Was there anything else nearby? Were there any marks at all?"

"It was dark, like I said, when Bobby McFadden brung me here. He said he tripped over her, but that he never touched her apart from that. When I come, I brung a lantern. I rolled her over to see if she was dead, but I didn't have much doubt even before I looked."

"Tell me exactly how she looked when you first saw her."

"She was flat on her face right on that frozen mud." He pointed to a spot a foot or two to the left of where the body now lay. "If it wasn't that it was so cold, I'd'a thought she was asleep. I didn't see the claw marks till I rolled her on her back. When I first looked she was laying there all straight. Her hands was right by her sides and her feet was together, like she'd been standing straight up and just leaned over and went smack down on her face."

"What did her hair look like?" She had long black hair.

"I didn't notice nothing much about it," he said. "It was just there, just laying straight out so I couldn't see her face at all. It covered her right down to the shoulders."

"Thank you," Dougherty said, "you can go if the Sheriff is finished with you here."

Ziegenfuss motioned with his head in the direction of the crowd, and Klein took off, happy to be away from there, Dougherty thought.

"So, Doctor, just what is it that we aren't talking about? How is it you just got here and you know what questions to ask before we finish telling you what we've seen?" The Sheriff was suspicious. Dougherty could hardly blame him.

"Sheriff, I won't keep things from you, but I think it better if we talk elsewhere. For now let's look around, and then have the body moved to where we can have privacy."

They covered her again, then took the lantern and made a careful examination of the spot where the body had been lying prone before Klein turned it over.

"No marks," McBrien said. "The ground was frozen solid when he put her here, wouldn't ye say? Ye'll recollect it was just getting down to freezing when we come out o' supper to go meet His Honor. If ye was to ask me, I'd say the body wasn't put here until maybe an hour or two ago. What do ye think, Major?"

"It makes sense," Dougherty said. "What do you say Sheriff?"

"I agree." He stooped down and rubbed his fingertips across the earth then looked at them carefully. He brought the lantern closer and moved it back and forth over the spot where the body had been. "Did you take a close look at the front of the clothing? It was bloody, wasn't it? But not nearly as much blood as you might expect."

"Killed somewhere else and then brought here," McBrien said.

"I'd say so."

"Sheriff," Dougherty said, "Is there a place not far away where she might have been taken and kept out of sight while the killer did this? An abandoned house, perhaps?"

"A house? No. I don't know any," he said. "I tell you what though, there's a few stables haven't been used in a while — one at the far end of Broadway and another over on Race Street. Could be one of them. If it isn't, then we can start looking outside of town."

"I think they may be the places to begin," Dougherty said. "Can you have some of your men do the searching? They should look for blood and even for bodily organs. If they find anything, warn them to touch nothing. Just make sure that the building is closed and that no one else enters until we examine it."

"We can do that," he said, "but I need to have that talk you mentioned. Bodily organs you're saying now? You're seeing a lot more here than I can, and it's not because there's anything wrong with my eyes. I'd say you came here knowing a lot more about this than you've explained so far. That doesn't make me feel good."

"Let's have the body taken to the basement of the Row Office for the autopsy, and we can go together to Judge Barrett and discuss the whole matter. I think we can answer your questions, but we can't do it here. I'd also suggest that you have someone question the people who live above the stores on the other side of Susquehanna Street and find out if they heard or saw anything during the night. Perhaps a wagon or a carriage? Something that may have been used to transport the body."

He wasn't pleased, and Dougherty couldn't blame him, but he accepted the wisdom of not discussing the matter where they were.

He sent Klein for a few more men to help — men who had worked for him before and could be trusted to do as ordered and do it carefully. He told the crowd to get on about their business, to go home or to work or to wherever they had been going when they had stopped to stare. He was going to stay and guard the scene until his men came to remove the deceased. It was also growing rapidly light and he intended to examine the area once more just to be certain they had missed nothing in the dark.

The last thing they did was talk to Bobby McFadden. He was eleven years old and worked at the livery stable — cleaning stalls and sometimes exercising the horses. He could tell them nothing. He had been headed for the stable when he tripped over the body, not seeing it in the dark, due to her dark coat and hair. When he recognized what it was, he headed as fast as his legs could carry him to find Deputy Klein. He was just now beginning to calm down and starting to be impressed at being the center of attention. They thanked him and left for the office building.

Judge Barrett had acted quickly. In the basement were two tables: One to receive the body and a smaller one with the implements for the autopsy and two canvas aprons. Doctor Leonard had been generous with his help.

It was another half hour until two deputies came with the stretcher and helped them position the body on the table. Neither showed any desire to take part in the remainder of the proceedings. Ashen faced, they withdrew as quickly as they could. Their earlier curiosity had been sated beyond all expectation.

Before starting the autopsy, they went to Judge Barrett's office, where Sheriff Ziegenfuss had just arrived. His search of the site had been fruitless. He had no idea who the dead girl was, nor had his deputies. His conclusion was that either she was just arrived in town on one of yesterday's trains, or she was someone who had only recently come to live in the area. He knew generally which families were new in and around town, and there were not many. He would visit them. If she had simply come on the train to visit, that might prove a little more difficult, at least until someone realized she was missing and came looking for her. He would have a photographer to take a picture of her. The Sheriff was losing no time.

"And now, Doctor," he said, "why don't you just tell me what was so blasted important that we couldn't talk about it before."

Judge Barrett looked increasingly puzzled, and Dougherty realized that he had not yet been told that this death had nothing to do with wildcats. They described what they had found in the livery stable yard.

"Good Lord," he said, "so it seems that you were right after all! I was afraid you might be, but it still seemed too far fetched to be true. So it was the Butcher who killed Brogan after all!"

"The Butcher? Brogan? What the hell is all this about? Does everybody but me know what's going on here?" Sheriff Ziegenfuss glared at the three of them, as angry as he was curious.

And so they explained the whole thing, including their prediction of a January murder, and he sat and listened without a single question until they had finished.

"You had an idea that this killing would occur, and you did nothing about it?" The Sheriff was not pleased.

"Sheriff, what could they have done? The evidence was tenuous. They could not have predicted the identity of the victim, nor the time or place. And let me ask you this: Had they come to you with what they suspected, what would you have done? Would you have believed them? They spoke to me about it last night, and I thought it as unlikely as I am sure you would have before the fact." Judge Barrett made their apologia better than they could have done themselves.

"Yes... I apologize, gentlemen. His Honor is right. I'm sure you are as disturbed about this as I am and just as determined to catch this fiend."

"There is one question, Doctor," Judge Barrett said, "Since your prediction of this murder was accurate, when will the next occur?"

"If we are correct," Dougherty said, "the next two should occur in March and November."

"You mean another murder like this one in two months!" The Sheriff was horrified.

"Ah, Sheriff Ziegenfuss, it's worse than that," McBrien said, "March and November may well be the proper months. It's the damn year we ain't so sure of."

"Where do we go from here?" The Sheriff's dismay was obvious.

"I don't know," Dougherty said, "but there is another matter to discuss. First of all, do you both agree that whoever murdered this girl must be the same Butcher who committed the other atrocities?" They did. "In that case, do you also agree that it might be prudent for us not to publicize our awareness of the previous crimes? I fear that announcing what we know may make the killer more careful and prevent our ever finding him." Again they agreed.

"Yer Honor," McBrien said, "sure, I've no desire to be pushing ye, and I hope ye'll not take it so, but from the way we're talking it seems to me that yer intending the Major here to continue to run his investigation o' Brogan's death. Is that right?"

"It is," he said, "I will see Captain Maddock this morning and let him know my decision. I doubt he will be happy, but I do not think that he should take over."

"One final point," Dougherty said. "I've learned that telegrams received in Penrose Valley go to Captain Maddock before they reach their intended recipients. I suggest sending nothing by that route unless we wish its content known."

There was nothing else to say and much to do. Sheriff Ziegenfuss had families to visit and deputies to consult. Judge Barrett had a court session to conduct. Dougherty intended to send a telegram to Jen letting her know that he would not be home until Friday and (following his own advice) to say nothing but that until he saw her. And then there was the autopsy.

McBrien took notes as Dougherty dictated. The woman was young, mid-twenties, full-figured, five feet four inches in height, in weight about 145 pounds. Her skin was fair, eyes deep blue, hair dark brown rather than the black it had seemed in the pre-dawn light. In spite of the mutilation, one could see that she had been pretty.

Her coat was dark blue wool of exceptional quality, well tailored to her figure. Beneath was a frock of yellow silk with matching fichu, all skillfully sewn and surely expensive. It was a costume meant for day wear, perhaps for traveling.

They removed the unbuttoned coat. The top of the skirt and waist area were marked with blood — patches of it rather than a large amount. There were as many as 25 or 30 cuts in the dress, not long slashes so much as slits produced by repeated stabbings, probably with a blade a little over an inch wide. They turned her partly over and saw in the back four places where the stabs had passed completely through the body. The blade must have been eight or nine inches in length, Dougherty thought.

They removed the clothes. The petticoats and the lower portion of the chemise showed the same stab wounds as had the dress. The underdrawers, on the other hand, were not cut at all, although stained with blood. Some of the body's stab wounds were within the area covered by the drawers — showing that they had been removed prior to the stabbing and then been replaced. Their replacement may have been done hurriedly, for they were on backwards. The drawstring (which was not tied) was at the front instead of at the back as it should have been. She wore shoes, but her stockings had been removed. Why? Dougherty thought. Perhaps they would discover them if ever they found the actual site of the killing.

They now saw the full extent of the mutilation — so vicious that one could credit it only to a human being. Animals kill quickly and efficiently and only because they seek food. This was the product of an insane rage, a bloodlust that could be nothing but human.

Dougherty began with the face. As with the earlier victims of whom they had read, the sides of the face were not ripped; they had been sliced by a blade sharp as a scalpel, a single careful cut on each side beginning at the corner of the orbicularis oris, along the length of the risorius, and across the breadth of the masseter, thus laying bare all the teeth clear to the back of the mouth, leaving behind the same death's head smile that all the newspaper reports had indicated.

There was little doubt about strangulation as the cause of death. The face was livid and swollen. There were *petechiae* in the bulging eyes. There were ligature impressions about the neck, so impressed into the skin that one could make out the twist of the cord that had been used. It was composed of three thinner cords, its marks forming a circle about the lower part of the neck. It had been pulled so tight as to break the skin and draw blood, damaging the trachea and its adnexa. With a rope so thin, the killer would likely have wounded his hands unless he had worn gloves or attached handles to the rope in the manner of a garotte. Dougherty suspected the latter as more likely for so experienced a killer.

The abdomen had been stabbed repeatedly (they counted 28 wounds). An incision had been made from the symphysis pubis to the lowest point of the sternum, jagged at the point of entry and then one smooth incision to the top. There was no corresponding mark in the clothing.

There remained the final mutilation which had begun to appear on the bodies of the Butcher's later victims. The thighs were slashed, but not as Dougherty had imagined when he had read about it. He had pictured vicious, deep cuts. Not so. The cuts were shallow, delicate, running the length of the thigh. They were parallel, about an inch apart, evenly spaced around the whole upper leg, both right and left, as though the Butcher had been attempting to simulate the appearance of vertically striped stockings. This attention to detail made it all the more grotesque. There was scant blood, indicating cuts made after death. Dougherty wondered if the Butcher wanted to recreate a picture, perhaps a figment of his imagination, perhaps some particular scene which held meaning for him and which might help to identify him, if only they could decipher the clues.

When they combined all these items, they had a picture of what had probably happened. The woman had been strangled. That was the cause of death. Her underdrawers had been removed either before or after the strangulation, but before any of the other atrocities were carried out. After strangulation her dress and chemise had been pushed up or removed and the long abdominal incision had been made. The stockings were removed. The legs were cut, the dress put back in place, and then the repeated stabbings had occurred. Finally, the drawers had been replaced, but backwards.

He began the internal examination. Through the incision already there, he removed a number of the internal organs and placed them in a basin for examination individually. They were also marked with the puncture wounds and some had been cut into when the abdominal incision had been made. But some were not there at all. Missing were the kidneys, possibly portions of the small intestine, and most of the uterus, which had been excised with one clean cut across the lowest part of the cervix.

The organs above the diaphragm had been left *in situ*, nor had they been stabbed. The insane rage of the murderer was directed specifically at the young woman's femininity.

It was only after they had removed all the organs and were examining the inside of the lower portion of the cavity, that portion where the stab wounds had penetrated, that they found the one item that the murderer had left behind. Supposing that the crime had occurred at night, and possibly in the dark, he may well have left the scene without ever realizing that he had left a potential clue to his identity. A tiny piece of metal was imbedded into the lowest lumbar vertebra. Dougherty used a strong forceps to work it loose. It was the tip of a blade, perhaps a quarter of an inch in length, most likely broken off in the killer's frenzy. They sealed it in an envelope and marked the contents on the front.

It was just past noon when they finished. Dougherty had sewn up the incisions, including those on the face, and prepared the body for identification. The horror and pain of the victim were just the beginning. The evil would spread like a plague among her family and friends, turning their joy into sadness and their love into dust and ashes, and there was nothing anyone could do to camouflage the agony that had been hers at the moment of death. The only trace of consolation Dougherty could offer was that he had found no evidence that she had been sexually assaulted.

This crime, even more than others he had investigated, brought home the devastation that evil produces. Dougherty was not by nature a violent man. Really rather the opposite. But if this Butcher had been before him at that moment he might have shot him to death with not a moment's hesitation nor a speck of contrition. How easy, he thought, for one to become the very thing he sets out to combat.

* * *

Neither McBrien nor Dougherty had eaten since their early morning rising, so they went to the American Hotel in search of sustenance. They were eating hearty ham sandwiches, drinking steaming hot coffee, and eyeing the slices of apple pie the waiter had just brought, when Sheriff Ziegenfuss walked in, looked around, and headed directly for their table. He sat and waited while the waiter brought a cup and poured him some coffee.

"Judge Barrett'll be done in court by three. He wants to see us then. What have you learned?"

They gave him a sketch of the report they intended to complete before the day was done. He suggested that Dougherty take custody of the knife point and the tissue samples and keep them with the evidence from Brogan's case, since there seemed no doubt now that both crimes were the work of the same person.

"I have two more families to visit," Ziegenfuss said, "and I'll be doing that shortly... In fact, before the Judge is ready to see us. But there's something else I wanted to tell you.

"Yesterday Rupert Calvin, the ticket seller over at the Jersey Central Station, sent word to me that someone had stolen a buggy from in front of the station. It was there just before the train got in from Easton, and when the owner went out to get it, it was gone. We looked for it, but with no luck. This morning, when we found the body, it never occurred to me that there was any connection between the two. Then about 11:00, Rupert sent word to me to stop looking. Said the buggy was back were it belonged. He had no idea when it was brought back or who'd done it. Says it could have been any time, he just hadn't noticed. Seemed mighty odd, so I went over to take a look. I was glad I did. On the seat I found some spots that looked like blood. They were down in the joint where the back meets the seat. If there was any blood out in the open, it'd been wiped clean. And there was this stuck in there, too."

From his pocket he took a piece of paper and unfolded it to reveal a few threads of dark blue wool. Dougherty had no doubt that they had once been part of the victim's coat. Dougherty had the waiter get an envelope, sealed the blue threads inside it, and had the Sheriff write his signature, the date, and a statement of the contents across the flap.

"So now we know how he moved the body," Dougherty said, "and, if his method was the same as before, then I think he must have met her at the station and gotten her to go with him. He took her somewhere and killed her and then took his time doing what he wanted to her body. When he was done with the buggy, he just put it back and walked away. He must be extraordinarily phlegmatic."

* * *

It was nearer four than three o'clock when Judge Barrett was ready for them, and by that time there were new developments. Deputy Klein had come to get them at the American Hotel just minutes after Sheriff Ziegenfuss had left.

"We got something, Doctor," he said, obviously pleased with himself. "Didn't think we could do it, but we did. We looked at the stables, the one on Race and the one on Broadway, but didn't find nothing. Just doing them two took a lot of time, because it ain't easy to tell if anybody's been in a stable or not without checking on just about every nook and cranny. We found nothing. Then I remembered that the Brandt family out past the end of town ain't been home for the last two weeks. They're gone to visit their daughter in Bethlehem. She's... Well, I mean it's the time for... She's about to have a child, is what I mean."

He blushed. Deputy Klein was a very young man.

"They boarded their horse at the livery stable while they're away and that left their house and stable empty, and the property stands all alone outside town near Hackelbernia."

Hackelbernia was a tiny patch just west of Mauch Chunk.

"We looked in the stable, and we found the place where he done it. At least I think it was. Do you want to come and look? I got a fella guarding the place and nobody's touched a thing, just like you said. I got a buggy right outside."

When they got there he showed them the barn, set back from the road, far enough so that no passerby could have seen or heard anything that went on in or around it. Inside a space had been cleared on the floor in front of the stalls, a circle of six or seven feet in diameter, all swept clean. At least it had been clean. Now it bore stains that were almost certainly blood. But there was something else: A pair of women's stockings, plain white, now stained with blood and the dirt that over the years had been ground into the wood of the floor and had not yielded to the sweeping that had made the circle. And something worse: Bloody bits of tissue. They sent Deputy Klein to get a container, and he came back with a large glass jar that he had found on the back porch of the Brandt house and had cleaned with water from their pump. Dougherty identified a length of human intestine and a kidney cut in half. They would add them to the evidence. Nothing else was to be found, nothing that could have belonged to the killer.

When they finally got to see the Judge, Sheriff Ziegenfuss had just returned from his visitations and had found someone who might be able to identify the deceased. McBrien and Dougherty went to the basement first to make sure that the body was presentable, covered with a clean sheet which revealed only her face. That sad face... The Sheriff entered the room with an older gentleman, white-haired, hat in hand, and an expression of mingled hope and fear. Even as he approached the table, Dougherty saw the hope die and the tears begin to flow from the corners of the pale blue eyes. It was all he could do not to look away from this moment that was too personal to be subject to the scrutiny of anyone, but from which he could not flee.

Chapter XV: Beware the Ides of March

And there he plays extravagant matches
In fitless finger stalls
On a cloth untrue
With a twisted cue
And elliptical billiard balls.
    W.S. Gilbert (1836-1911)
    The Mikado (1885) Act II

[Friday, January 19, 1866]

Evodia Zellner was the daughter of Milton and Florence Zellner. She was twenty-three years old, engaged to be married in June to a young man in her home town of Easton. A few months ago her uncle and aunt, Mr. and Mrs. Amos Zellner, after thinking about it for some time, had moved from Easton to Mauch Chunk. The Zellner's had come originally from Switzerland to America and settled in Easton when Amos was but twelve years of age. Milton was born a few years later. The family had prospered and both brothers, although not enormously wealthy, were well off. Amos, now seventy-one years old, decided to move to Mauch Chunk. It put him in mind of his youth. The mountains of Pennsylvania could not really compare with the Alps, but he was happy.

Amos and his wife, Tullia, had never had children of their own, but had grown especially close to their nieces and nephews. Evodia had been coming to visit a few days at a time to help her aunt and uncle settle into their new home. She had fallen into the pattern of coming by train from Easton on a Wednesday or a Thursday and returning on either Saturday or Sunday, just as she had this week. Upon arrival at the depot she would hire a carriage to take her across the river to East Mauch Chunk. When she did not arrive on Wednesday, it had raised no alarm. They presumed that she would be coming on Thursday. They described her as a young person of especially sweet disposition and a delight to have in their home.

Sheriff Ziegenfuss had dealt with bad news on many occasions, but this moved him more than he had thought possible. When he had come to their door, they were not overly disturbed; but as he described the deceased and her clothing, they were uneasy and then frightened — particularly when he spoke of the victim's coat, for they had at Christmas given their niece a garment of precisely that description. Mr. Zellner, therefore, went with the Sheriff and, as soon as he entered the room and caught his first glimpse of the young woman's face, all his fears were justified; it was his niece.

In an instant this kindly, dignified, old gentleman had been oppressed by the burden of his years in a manner he had never before experienced. He nodded to signify his recognition of the dead woman and attempted to speak, but no words came forth, only tears. There were no sobs, no moans, no groans of anguish, no sound at all, just great and grave silence as the tears streamed steadily from the sad gray eyes and rolled down cheeks still rosy from the crisp outside air; and the once happy face, like a suddenly shattered piece of pottery, caved in upon itself.

Jen had not witnessed these events; but as James recounted them her eyes filled in pity for this sad old couple, who were not only grieving their loss, but must also be blaming themselves for not having met their niece at the station or even for changing their place of residence to begin with. They would have no more happiness in Mauch Chunk. None of it, of course, was their fault, but they would bear the agony. They and Evodia's parents were now further victims left in the wake of this madman's murderous progress. Jen felt no satisfaction that their prediction had come to pass. It simply amplified the fear of what was yet to come if their thoughts about March were true — futile emptiness bordering on despair. The evil grew.

"The Butcher must have planned this carefully," James said. "I cannot think it a chance occurrence."

James and McBrien had arrived from Mauch Chunk on the 12:50 train and had come straight to Dougherty's home. They had spent the next hour having lunch while they told Jen all that had happened.

"Hardly a matter o' chance," McBrien said. "He'd planned it all out, o' course. He must'a known the train times — which was no trouble at all. That's the purpose o' the schedule, after all, fer people to see it, ain't it? But this young woman wasn't just anybody. She was exactly the type he always goes fer. If ye was to describe her to someone who'd never seen her, ye'd use all the same words ye'd'a used in describing any o' the others."

"He must have been at the station before," Jen said. "He knew he could count on finding an unattended carriage or two while their owners were in the station or at the courthouse or at one of the hotels."

"And there's the strongest point of all — he knew just where to take her to do his work. He must'a known the Brandts was away from home."

"He is most meticulous," Jen said. "That has been the case in all of the killings. He must watch his victims. I wonder if any ever saw him without realizing that she was being studied?"

"When we spoke with Mr. Zellner," James said, "I asked if Evodia had shown concern or curiosity about anyone who seemed overly interested in her. He said not. The killer must be adept at not drawing attention to himself."

"Don't it seem strange to ye that he's so clever at getting these women to go with him? I'd wonder they'd even talk to the fellow if he's a stranger. And he must be a stranger to them. Otherwise, he'd'a surely turned up in the course o' one or another o' the investigations. Somebody would'a noticed that the same fellow was always in the wrong place. So how do ye think he gets them to do what he wants?"

Jen could not help but smile. She had not yet told James of her encounter at the railroad station, just after he and McBrien had left for Mauch Chunk.

"It may not be so very difficult to explain, after all," she said. "On Wednesday, just after your train had pulled out, I was approached by someone right there on the platform."

She described to them the circumstances, the calling card presented by the boy, and the kindly expression of the man who so patiently awaited her reply.

"Good Lord, Jen, you didn't actually talk to him after all we'd learned! I cannot believe you would do such a thing!" James sounded angry, but it was fright and concern more than anger.

"I almost did something else," she said. "The stories in the papers had made me well aware of what might happen, and we already suspected that the Butcher must be somewhere in the area. When the child gave me the card and I saw the kindly look on the man's face, my first thought was to scream loudly enough to get the attention of the station master and of everyone up and down the street. I had already drawn a deep breath before I realized who he was."

"You knew him?" James asked.

"I did. Do you remember Mr. Michael Appelby?" He looked puzzled at first, then he began to smile, and she knew he was thinking just what she had thought at the station.

"Mr. Appelby? The salesman from Tiemann?"

"The very one. And you know how it would have affected him had I actually let out the blood curdling scream that was within a breath of being unleashed on the public. We might be now attending his funeral or preparing his body for shipment to his family in New York. I think he would have curled up and expired on the spot."

Mr. Appelby was a traveling representative of the George Tiemann company in New York, a purveyor of the finest surgical instruments. He made his regular rounds, visiting clients and potential clients, in the hope of selling them supplies for their practices. When they had first come to Penrose Valley, Mr. Appelby was one of their first visitors, always ready to attend the needs of the budding physician. He was a meek, mild, soft spoken man, without the brashness of the typical traveling salesman. Jen was sure that he would at the very least have fainted dead away had she actually screamed. She was glad she had recognized him in time, but she did not regret the instinct that made her ready to scream. She assured James that he need not worry that she would be taking up with any strangers, no matter how meek and mild they appeared.

"Mr. Appelby asked me to say that he was sorry he missed you. He had been in this area for the past week or so, and had driven over the mountain from Beaver Meadow in a rented buggy. I was surprised that the road was even open after all the snow of the past week. He went looking for you at our house and someone told him we had left a few minutes earlier and were headed toward the station — it made me realize how hard it is to do anything in a small town without being noticed! I'm glad we lead a respectable life. He followed after us and the station master sent him out onto the platform, but your train had just pulled out. When he heard you were away, he decided to go that afternoon on a later train to Mauch Chunk, but I didn't mention that you were staying there that night. I was sure you would be too busy with the judge. Anyway, he left you a catalogue and said he'd be back to see you in a few months."

"I am grateful, at least," James said, his momentary anger now gone, "that you didn't cause his early demise."

"The encounter with Mr. Appelby made me think," she said. "What if I had never heard of the Butcher? What might have been my response to a stranger? It would not have been to scream or to do anything else to draw attention to myself. Nor would I have wished to seem impolite. I suppose I would have listened to what he had to say and then gotten away as politely as possible. But what if he had some plausible story to tell, some seemingly good reason to cause me to go with him? What then? I can readily understand how the Butcher gets these women to do what he wants."

"You're absolutely right," James said. "He plans in great detail I would say, and I am sure that includes knowing enough about his victim to be able to offer her some reasonable enticement. He knows how to use curiosity to his advantage. We've seen that."

He went to his office and was back in a moment with the folder of clippings and documents that had been Brogan's.

"Look at the note to Brogan."

I no all wat hapened in Philadelphia.
I hav wat you want.
Mete me at Brakker Noon — Mundy.
P.S. — Miss this mete at yur perl!

"This was Brogan's summons to his execution, but how could he refuse to go? He could not afford to."

What he said made perfect sense.

"You know," Jen said to McBrien, "you said that it was as though the Butcher is killing the same woman over and over again. Do you really think that's true?"

At first he said nothing, his face all concentration.

"To tell the truth, I said it as a matter o' conversation, but now that ye put it to me, I'd say yes, I do think so. It's crazy, ain't it? But then we've agreed that he's crazy, so maybe this all makes some kind o' sense in his mind."

"That's our problem," James said. "We agree that he must be insane, and then we try to make sense."

"We need another point of view," Jen said. "It's as though this man sees the same world we see, but through a pair of spectacles that make curved lines straight and turn cubes into spheres and he follows paths that for us are aimless but for him lead to some end — an end we do not understand. We must learn to think askew if we hope to figure this out."

"Suppose," James said, "that Sean has hit upon the real reason for what this Butcher is doing — that he kills over and over again in the delusion that it is always the same person who dies. When next he sees a woman who reminds him of the first one he killed, then he is moved to do it again."

"Do ye think, Major, that it's possible he's generally sane until some kind o' fit comes over him and that's when he kills?"

"That may be part of it," James said, "but if they are fits, they are more than momentary. He takes his time. He studies his victims and plans his crime. As Jen said, he is meticulous. What he does is insane, but once he sets his goal, his path to it is not at all insane."

"I cannot imagine," Jen said, "that he sets out to kill all women who fit some particular description. Surely there must be more than that. He must see many women who look alike but he can't kill all of them. How does he choose? There must be something more than looks. Is it the place? Or the time? Up to now he has never killed twice in the same month. Now that he's killed in January, there are two more months left. But why? It means something to him that we simply don't understand."

"And what if he is killing the same person over and over again?" James paused, thinking. "Who was the first? Was it Abiageal Conroy in Philadelphia? Did the police ever find a motive for her killing? What did they learn that was never mentioned in the papers? There must have been much that they never revealed to the public. We might start there. And I fear we have no time to lose. March is not far off."

"Then I think we should contact Doctor Brownson," Jen said.

"Even better than that," James said, "I think we should visit him. Let him look at our evidence, and see what he knows of that first murder. I can telegraph to see if he can receive us."

"Good," Jen said, "but be careful what you send. We don't want to reveal anything to Maddock and his crew."

"Especially now," McBrien said, "fer, as ye'll recall, Major, Maddock was in Mauch Chunk when the last killing occurred. We've less reason than ever to put our trust in him."

They had seen him on Wednesday evening. The following day, after the Judge had told him his decision, he had taken the next train to Penrose Valley. In between he had not been seen at all. They learned that he had stayed at the American Hotel. They made some discreet inquiries, but no one could say when he had come in that night, or even if he had come in at all. And he had been in Washington during the war. But so had many others. And, as distasteful as Captain Maddock may have been, he seemed far from insane.

It was time to learn what they could in Philadelphia, and to heed Spurinna's advice to Caesar: "Beware the Ides of March."

Chapter XVI: Another Adventure

In Boston they ask, How much does he know?
In New York, How much is he worth?
In Philadelphia, Who were his parents?
    Mark Twain (1835-1910)
    What Paul Bourget Thinks of Us (1899)

[Monday, January 22-Tuesday, January 23, 1866]

One fairly small bag and a dispatch case to hold the documentary evidence and written reports. That will suffice, Dougherty thought. Which, he later concluded, just goes to show how different are a man and a woman. Jen spent Saturday evening and a good portion of Sunday deciding what clothing to take and finding that it required far more than one fairly small bag.

Dougherty did not mind one bit. In the past two weeks he had seen something happen. For months Jen had struggled to pull herself out of the doldrums of their baby's death, trying to hide her anguish. He loved her for her bravery, but, precisely because he loved her he could not fail to see her pain. But for two weeks now her mind had been focused on this case. It took her outside herself, caught up in someone else's sorrows instead. Her flurry of packing was but one more sign of her renewed interest in life, and, so far as Dougherty was concerned, she could do all the packing she wanted and he would enjoy every moment of it. Her sharpness of mind and wit were back, not because she had to make a conscious effort to exercise them, but because they were simply part of her, part of the wonderful woman he had married, and they had again been given their freedom. The weight of the bags could not begin to compare to the other weight that had for now been lifted.

The trip was long. It was 8:10 in the morning when they left Penrose Valley, past noon when they arrived almost a half hour late at Allentown, and after four o'clock when they came at last to Philadelphia. In a hired carriage, surrounded by bags and boxes, they reached their final destination, the home of Doctor and Mrs. Carl

Gustavus Brownson. Six years earlier Dougherty had arrived at this same house, eighteen years old, bag in hand, on foot in the unfamiliar streets, staring with all the wonder of a hick on his first trip to the big city. But, then, that was what he had been.

Even before they were out of the carriage at the top of Dock Street, the door of the house burst open and Doctor and Mrs. Brownson were greeting them. The hugging and handshaking were accomplished midst clouds of vaporous breath, for the mild weather was gone, the cold had settled in again, and it was nearly dark.

For Dougherty this trip was a coming home. He had lived here for his two years at Jefferson. Mrs. Brownson had then been the widowed Mrs. Martha Kiley. Doctor Brownson, the confirmed bachelor, was his teacher at the college and his mentor in the study of forensic medicine. Dougherty boarded with Mrs. Kiley, who was shocked to learn of the work he was doing with Doctor Brownson and his various cadavers, but her natural curiosity inspired all sorts of questions that soon gave birth to a genuine interest in the whole field. It was Dougherty who introduced the two and was delighted when, in 1864, they wrote to tell him of their intent to wed.

"Well, young Dougherty, your letter sparked some memories."

Brownson and Dougherty were in the parlor and Jen had gone with Mrs. Brownson to the kitchen to help with the last minute preparations for the meal whose aroma already filled the house. Dougherty had to smile. Brownson had addressed him as "young Dougherty" ever since they had met, and Dougherty supposed that it would always be thus. Brownson was now in his sixty-sixth year, his energy unabated. In spite of the gray in the bushy hair and side whiskers, the full eyebrows remained black. He continued to favor black suits, baggy-kneed trousers, sleeves marked with chalk dust, and a vest front decorated with cigar ash. Neither dust nor ash were so abundant as in former days — a sure sign of Mrs. Brownson's sartorial inroads.

Dougherty had telegraphed on Friday to see if Brownson were free to receive them. That same day he had his answer, an invitation to spend a few days. By train Dougherty sent him a letter on Saturday, warning him about not trusting the telegraph, and asking if they might discuss the Conroy case and meet with some of the participants in it. He did not attempt to explain about the other cases, preferring to do that in person.

"So you do recall something of the Conroy murder?"

"I recall it all too well," Brownson said. "Horrible! That poor young woman and not enough evidence for even a reasonable suspicion. None of it made sense. The vehemence pointed to an unimaginable hatred, but she'd done nothing to inspire that in even the most overly sensitive of enemies. And there were no enemies. No one who knew her could conceive of any reason for what had happened."

"I never heard you speak of it," Dougherty said.

"No, I don't suppose you did. By the time you began working with me, the whole case had grown cold. The police overcame their usual lethargy and made a concerted effort to question everyone involved — and it led nowhere. I never dealt with a case like it. It was as though the killer came out of thin air, destroyed a woman chosen at random, and was gone. There were no witnesses, apart from the one young woman who may or may not have seen the killer. In the end, her intentions were good, but she couldn't help. The friends and family were above suspicion. They either had strong alibis or had no conceivable reason for doing her any harm. That was a major part of our problem: No one had any reason to do such a thing. No witnesses, no clues, no motive. And so the case died as abruptly as it had been born."

"At work so soon? What will we do with you?" Mrs. Brownson shook her head in mock despair as she and Jen came into the room, thick as thieves and clearly enjoying each other's company. "Why not wait until after dinner? Everything is ready."

Mrs. Brownson was five or six years younger than her husband, but where his hair was graying hers was already pure white and had been ever since Dougherty had known her. She was a diminutive bundle of energy, cheerful, full of life, with sparkling eyes and glowing cheeks, full of curiosity about the world around her and rejoicing to uncover solutions to its mysteries. And she was a wonderful cook.

For the next few hours they talked and laughed and laid to rest a quantity of food that Dougherty would have thought beyond their capacity under ordinary circumstances. There was ox-tail soup, roast beef, Yorkshire pudding, broccoli, and mashed potatoes. Then, to tide them over until breakfast, they ended with apple tart and cheese. It was past eight o'clock when Doctor Brownson and Dougherty finished their cigars, drank the last few drops of their brandy, and the four of them sat down in the parlor and turned to the dispatch case of evidence.

"Now, young Dougherty, perhaps you will explain to me what has created this great interest in the Conroy murder?"

"It all began," he said, "with the death of a man named Charlie Brogan, a rather recent arrival in Penrose Valley."

He described the death, their investigation, and the finding of the papers Brogan had left behind. He placed upon the small table next to his chair the articles that dealt with the murder of Abiageal Conroy. Next to them he put the folded circus posters and the packet of letters tied in red ribbon, with the picture of Brogan and the mysterious Mary tucked inside.

"I have just this moment recalled something," Jen said to James. "When I saw the circus posters two weeks ago and read the results of Brogan's autopsy, I had an idea, but there were so many things at the time that it slipped my mind. You described his strong musculature and the marks on the body — the scars, the broken nose and the damaged ear. Isn't that what they call a 'cauliflower' ear? And then there were his hands. They had soft palms, but were rough and hard about the knuckles. Is it possible that Charlie Brogan may have been a prize fighter?"

"Charlie Brogan? Are you certain that Brogan was his name?" Doctor Brownson had sat up straight in his chair as Jen began recounting the facts of the autopsy and now leaned forward, waiting for their response. "Can you describe him?"

"We can do better than that," Dougherty said. "I have a photograph of him together with a woman we know only as Mary — but in looks she could be the twin sister of a Mrs. Corrigan who lives in Penrose Valley. Brogan boarded in her house."

He untied the packet of letters and flipped through them to find the picture, which he withdrew and handed to Brownson.

"Dear Lord!" Brownson said. "It's them! Charlie Brady and Mary Conroy!"

"Brady?" Jen and Dougherty said in unison.

"His name was not Brogan?" Dougherty asked.

"No. His name was Brady. Charlie Brady. The prize fighting afficionados called him 'Bruiser' Brady, but he preferred his friends to call him Charlie. He was engaged to marry Mary Conroy. He intended to quit the prize fighting. He thought it was no game for a married man. He'd been good at it and had made a fair amount of money... money that he intended to use to start a business once they were married. That's why Mary's parents finally gave their approval. He was a decent man. He'd come from good parents — not wealthy, but good, and they liked him. It was the fighting they didn't like."

"Who is Mary Conroy?" Jen asked. "Is she Abiageal's sister? Did they marry?"

"Ah, of course you've no way of knowing, have you? Mary is the girl who was murdered. There were no sisters. She was an only child."

Dougherty recalled seeing that in one of the news reports. Doctor Brownson had paused, lost in thought, and Dougherty suspected that in his mind's eye he was looking again at the girl's pathetic corpse.

"Her full name was Abiageal Mary Conroy. Her parents called her Abiageal and that's how she was named in the papers. But she preferred Mary. That's what her friends called her."

"Charlie Brady and Mary Conroy... What were they like?" Jen asked.

"I never knew Mary Conroy," the Doctor answered, "but friends and relatives had not a bad word to say of her. I realize that many have good things to say of the dead, even when the day before they might have had a list of complaints. This was different. People were genuinely grieved and no one could imagine why anyone should have wished her dead.

"I did get to know Charlie Brady. He wasn't here when Mary was killed, but he was called back to the city for the funeral. A more woebegone and heartbroken young man you could not have imagined. He spoke to me any number of times, always hoping that there might be some further evidence. There never was. He went the same rounds the police had and found nothing.

"I liked him. He was a good man. He'd have been a good husband and father. He was around for a few months, but I saw him less and less as time went on. I heard that he joined the army in early '62, and then I lost track of him."

"Can you answer some questions, sir? When she was murdered, was her face mutilated? The newspapers said that her throat had been cut. Was that true? Or was she really strangled?"

"Dougherty, you amaze me! Yes, she was strangled, although the papers got that detail wrong and I never corrected them. I saw no reason to do so. Some reporter who saw the body took note of the blood at her neck where the cord had cut in and described it as a slashed throat. And there was bodily and facial mutilation. It was never reported in the papers beyond a very general statement that the body had been mutilated. May I ask you, exactly what sort of mutilation have you in mind?"

"Repeated stabbing of the lower torso. The cutting of the sides of the face from the corners of the mouth back to the ears."

"For Heaven's sake, young Dougherty, where did you come by all of this? What you say is true, but how could you have inferred it from what the papers printed? Please explain!"

That was when Dougherty told him of the other killings, concluding with the most recent in Mauch Chunk. It was a far from complete review, but enough to give him the sequence of events. The details he would reserve until Brownson could read the articles and their notes for himself. Dougherty looked forward to hearing his conclusions.

"It occurred to us that the murders were somehow all the same." Dougherty turned to some of the sheets of their own notes. "As you will see, the victims all resemble each other physically. The method of killing and maiming is consistent in every instance, but becomes gradually worse in its violence."

"We think that it must be a deep hatred that inspires these killings," Jen said, "but not hatred of the individual victims. It is as though he kills the same victim over and over again. That's why we thought to look more carefully into the first murder and, so far as we know, that was the murder of Mary Conroy."

"Do you think that she could have been so totally despised by anyone?" Mrs. Brownson asked. "From what you said of her and Brogan, and to judge by what Carl learned, she seems incapable of inspiring such hatred."

"I think you are right, my dear," Doctor Brownson said, "and it seems all but impossible that Mary Conroy could have been the cause of this string of killings. But I do subscribe to young Dougherty's theory that the first killing is the crucial one and is in some insane manner being repeated. But, in that case, I don't think Mary Conroy's murder was the first. There must be at least one more of which we are ignorant."

They talked for another hour, but between the train ride and the pleasant lethargy that follows a good meal, Jen and James were ready to sleep. They retired to their room, the same homely quarters that had been his when he boarded there as a student. They fell asleep with Jen's head on his shoulder and his arm encircling her. As he drew her to himself, he felt in her none of the tension that she had for so long shed only with great effort at the end of each day. He sank into a deep sleep, smiling to himself in the silent darkness.

* * *

The work day in Penrose Valley, especially in mid-winter, began well before daylight. So, too, in the city, but here it made considerably more noise. Jen had grown used to the sound of people walking to work and the breaker's vast steam engines and the blast of its whistle; but, loud as they were, they remained at a comfortable distance. Not so on Dock Street. There were not only people on foot. There were also enormous draft horses with iron shod hooves and large, heavy laden wagons rumbling up the cobblestone incline from the waterfront to the stalls of Market Street, there to unburden themselves, reverse course, and rattle lickety-split back to the docks for more.

None of it disturbed James. She listened to his peaceful breathing and felt the steady rise and fall of his chest beneath her hand. She wondered if the sounds, once so familiar to him, penetrated his slumber and took his dreams back to his school days. She quietly raised herself up on one elbow and looked at him. In the faint pre-dawn gray she rejoiced that they had found each other in the midst of the late, great war. Then she lay down again, nestled up against him and, in spite of the sounds, sank gradually into a deep sleep.

When next she opened her eyes it was light. James was awake and it was time to start the day. Doctor and Mrs. Brownson were waiting for them in the kitchen with fresh coffee brewed and the griddle on the stove. A young woman, introduced as Gisela Braun, was stirring a bowl of pancake batter and had a basket of eggs waiting to be cracked and fried. This was the woman Mrs. Brownson had mentioned to Jen the night before, when they were in the kitchen seeing to the final touches of her wonderful dinner. She had been marveling at the fact that she could let the dishes go until morning and enjoy the evening's conversation. Her husband had insisted that they hire someone for part of each day, something she was still growing used to. It made her embarrassed and proud at the same time — embarrassed at its newness, but proud that the Doctor was so solicitous of her welfare. She was no further past the newlywed stage than was Jen.

Fortified by Gisela's cooking, they decided how to spend the day, and it fell to Mrs. Brownson and Jen to make two visits, both of them interesting and both stirring up a little apprehension as well.

"I think," said Doctor Brownson, "that a visit by the two of you might prove far more profitable than one by me or young Dougherty here. The woman's touch, you know. Another point of view. I questioned these people back when the murder took place. I fear that I would do little but cover the same ground and produce the same results. They deserve a fresh look."

"Do you think they will be willing to see us?" Jen asked.

"They are. When I got your letter on Saturday, I sent a messenger. I wanted to be sure that they were at the same addresses, and I asked if they would meet with you. I would not have been surprised had they refused. An interview will probably revive frightful memories that they must want to put well behind them. But both sent back messages to say that you would be welcome. They still want to see this murder resolved."

They would visit Mr. and Mrs. Peter Conroy, Mary's parents, and Mrs. Sally Condren. She was the young mother who had seen Mary Conroy with her killer. James and Doctor Brownson intended to spend the morning reviewing the documentation and the afternoon meeting with some of the police who had conducted the investigation.

There was a distinct chill in the air as they descended the front steps to the carriage which had just pulled up before the house. James had hailed a young lad in the street and given him a few pennies to fetch one of the conveyances for hire that plied their trade along Market Street. The boy was on the seat with the driver and hopped down as soon as he saw them, taking off his cap and opening the carriage door with a flourish.

"Here's yer coach, missus," he said, addressing Mrs. Brownson as the older and so due the greater respect, but his eye was fixed on James, who had reached into his pocket for another penny.

James gave the driver Mrs. Sally Condren's address on Van Pelt Street, just off Spruce, and instructed him to remain with them until their visits were completed.

"Have you met Mrs. Condren or the Conroys before?" Jen asked Mrs. Brownson.

"No, my dear, I never have. Nor have I ever before played so active a role in one of Carl's investigations. We've discussed them at length, but I've never joined in one. I must admit that I am apprehensive, but I would not miss it for the world. Have you done this before?"

"I've helped James on a few occasions during the war, but never in a matter of such enormity."

"I thank God that not many would be. It is unthinkable that this man has killed ten young women. Did he know them? Did they mean anything to him, apart from the fact that he wanted to kill them? It terrifies me even to think of it! And Brady, too. Eleven deaths! And possibly more that we don't know of."

The driver had turned his carriage around and they were trotting west along Walnut Street. Jen felt as though everyone on the street should have been aware of the import of their errand, but they all went calmly about their business, ignoring the carriage, never suspecting that a killer may have once transported Mary Conroy — or her mutilated body — along this very street.

Buildings towered four and five stories on either side of the street, blocking out much of the day's brightness. Jen leaned out and looked ahead at the tall, leafless trees that marked the location of Independence Square. Traffic was heavy and progress went in fits and starts. The walkways were slippery in places, but most of the ice on the street was worn away by the constant passage of wagons and carriages.

"Where shall we begin with Mrs. Condren?" Mrs. Brownson asked. "Are there specific questions to ask?"

"The questions tend to come all by themselves," Jen said. "At least that has generally been my experience. If one starts with a given list of questions, it is all too easy to cause the answers to fall into a limited range predetermined by the questioner. And, as one might expect, the answers are to the questions asked and not necessarily to the questions one should have asked. It is usually better to get the person talking about what happened and ask questions as they arise spontaneously, and only then ask the ones you have already thought of, if they've not already been answered."

Their driver edged his way past a slow moving full trolley. Its large draft horses plodded along, treating their heavy load as no more significant to them than was their small carriage to its single horse. Once past, their driver moved to the center of the street, following the well used and therefore quite dry line of the tracks. The buildings on either side were no longer the business establishments that had marked their earlier progress. They were now west of Broad Street, among the brick and limestone façades of mansions lining the street from here to Rittenhouse Square, their wealth increasing with each block. Through the Square's now barren trees, Jen saw Holy Trinity Church's high, square tower, its flat top set off by the smaller, finial-like spires at each corner.

"What do you know of Mrs. Condren?" Mrs. Brownson asked.

"Almost nothing," Jen said. "She was referred to in the newspapers at the time of the murder, but they said little, beyond the fact that she was a young mother who happened to be strolling the neighborhood with her infant. They never even printed her name. There was also among Brogan's — that is to say, Brady's — papers, an unsigned statement that must certainly have come from her."

"Did it tell you anything at all about her?"

"It was just the one short paragraph, but the writing style and spelling led me to think her not highly educated."

"And you say she was out walking with her child? That would mean that she belonged in the neighborhood. Have you looked at the houses in this area?" She waved her hand in a sweeping gesture.

"Indeed I have and I was wondering about that. Perhaps Mrs. Condren is someone who came from poorer circumstances and married into a family more well-to-do." Even as she said it, she thought it not likely. In spite of all America's claims to democracy and egalitarianism, it remains a divided society, with money as effective a divider as is birth elsewhere.

Their carriage turned left onto Twenty-first Street — a street wide and carefully tended, where well dressed people passed to and fro. Nowhere was there so much as a hint of what had occurred here that bright October day six years ago, a day pleasant enough to bring out Mrs. Condren to show off her small child to her neighbors. The people they saw were not poor. They strode along full of the rightful assurance that they walked this street in safety, able to greet friends and acquaintances without fear that their lives were at risk. No one was suspect, no one threatening, just normal men, women, and children paying scant attention to each other. Mary Conroy must have felt equally safe on that, her final day on this earth. And her killer must, Jen realized, have seemed as normal as the rest!

"It may have been near here that Sally Condren saw Mary Conroy accosted by her killer," she said. "She described him as a man of perhaps thirty years of age, with dark hair. He wore a brown Tweedside jacket and green waistcoat. She said that his eyes seemed 'crazed.'"

"Do you think that she was accurate in her description? What was it that attracted her attention?"

"The article said that Mary Conroy wore a yellow dress and Mrs. Condren's attention was drawn to her because she was wearing the same color. They were on opposite sides of the street."

Mrs. Brownson looked out the windows, back and forth from one side to the other. Her eyes caught Jen's.

"I know," Jen said. "The street is wide."

"Precisely what I was thinking. Would she have been able to tell with certainty that he had a 'crazed' expression in his eyes? I don't know."

"Why do you think she would have said it?"

"Oh, I don't think she was lying. At least, I doubt she had any intention to do so. How did she happen to come to the police with her information?"

"Because of the newspapers," Jen explained. "They described Miss Conroy's clothing, the time of day when she would have been on the street, and they asked readers to come forth if they had any information to offer."

"That would explain it. In all probability Mrs. Condren did see Mary Conroy and this man in conversation, but her later testimony was colored by all she had by then read of the murder. And I am willing to accept that he was the murderer, although Carl would probably demand stronger evidence before accepting that hypothesis."

Jen laughed, and Mrs. Brownson looked at her in puzzlement.

"I am laughing simply because Carl sounds so much like James with his insistence on clarity and logic. Of course, they are right when it comes to real proof that will stand up in a court of law. But

I think that in the investigative process there is room for a good deal of intuition if we are to link together the bits of proof that fall our way."

"My dear, we are of one mind. How fortunate they are to have the benefit of our insight! — even though they do not always realize it."

"In that case, allow me to offer one other bit of intuition. If that man was the murderer, then Miss Conroy was much closer to him than was Mrs. Condren. I think, in view of that, he could not have seemed so very 'crazed.' He was able to persuade Miss Conroy to go with him, and I doubt that she would have gone willingly with someone who seemed dangerous."

"That makes it all the more terrifying, doesn't it?" She shuddered.

They had gone no more than two blocks on Twenty-first Street when the driver turned again, this time to the right. Less than half a block later he brought the carriage to a halt, jumped down and opened the door on Jen's side.

"We are here," he said, "This is Van Pelt Street." He pointed to an opening that seemed little more than an alley leading off Spruce, parallel to Twenty-First. "That there's the house the gentleman said you was to be brung to. Are you sure this is what you want? If it is, I can park here till you're done."

The house was a short way down Van Pelt, on the left. Jen revised her opinion of the status of Mrs. Sally Condren. It was a nice home, but could not have competed with the houses that lined the main streets in this part of the city. It was a simple structure of wood, the home of someone who worked for the owners of the mansions in the area, not of someone who owned one. The driver handed them down to the sidewalk, whose bricks had been swept clean of the snow. They entered the still slushy alley, paying close attention to where they stepped, and went to the door of the house. They looked at each other, then Jen took a deep breath and knocked.

* * *

Doctor Brownson used a room on the first floor of their home as an office and there, on a table, they had spread out the newspaper accounts and other documents in stacks arranged according to victims. He had spent the last few hours reading everything, making notes, and, from time to time, asking Dougherty to explain something or to elaborate on his opinions of certain facets of the cases.

"So, young Dougherty, where do we go from here? Are you satisfied that all these murders were done by the same person?"

"Yes, but I always have some reservations about what I read in the newspapers. There were times during the war when I read accounts of battles in which I took part and hardly recognized the written version of what had happened right before my own eyes. That was one of the reasons I wanted to speak to you about the Conroy murder. It was the one that didn't seem to fit the pattern, but you've cleared that up. As to the others — they already fit, even though in Washington either the Provost's office or Lafayette Baker did their best to stifle reports.

"There was also that first murder in New York — the one in April of 1861. It merited almost no attention from the newspapers, because the victim was a prostitute. On the other hand, Brady took it as one of the same killings, as did Doctor Cranfeld, the medical examiner. In September of 1862 he spoke to reporters of a link between the killing of Emeline Carding, the prostitute, and those of Cornelia Vanderveer and Berdine Griswald, both of which were certainly the work of the Butcher."

"I've no argument with your reasoning," he said.

"Sir, did you ever before hear of any of those murders, apart from that of Mary Conroy?"

"No, young Dougherty, I never did. But, like so many things these last five years, I suppose we may attribute that to the war. It took first place in all the newspapers. And remember, these killings were spread out over a long period of time, a span of five years, and in different cities. And some of the Washington ones were purposely kept quiet. Had it not been for the war, I think the Butcher might not have lasted as long. At least, I hope not. But I must admit that he seems capable of taking great risks and still escaping."

Even as Dougherty listened, another notion occurred to him.

"Do you think, sir," he asked, "that his bravado is itself part of the pattern? What I mean is that he gives every appearance of taunting the authorities. He tends to take his victims in broad daylight, in public places. He actually sends for them, just as he did for Olivia Wharton when she was at her dressmaker's establishment. He contacts them and persuades them to go with him. He must realize that he is bound to be seen by others, but that does not deter him in the least."

"I think you may have hit upon something," Doctor Brownson said. "Look at his placing of the body of Edna Krantz outside the walls of the Old Capitol Prison, right under the noses of the police. He might as well have been daring them to find him, taunting them, proclaiming his intelligence in the face of their ineptitude. Even the location of his most recent victim fits that pattern. She was left almost across the street from the courthouse. And he took her from the railroad station, but this time it was not a crowded station in a busy city; it was in Mauch Chunk. It may be the largest town in Carbon County, but it is hardly a metropolis. He took the greatest risk of being recognized, and he got away with it! I think he enjoys this. He makes his victims come to him. He discards them as ostentatiously as he can. In my opinion, he wants to show that he is in charge."

They sat and thought. Doctor Brownson broke the silence.

"Do you think this killer knows you're aware of all these murders?"

"I very much doubt it," Dougherty said. "Jen and McBrien and I have spoken of it only among ourselves. Apart from Judge Barrett and Sheriff Ziegenfuss, we've never mentioned it to anyone else. We knew that in telling others we might be unwittingly telling the Butcher himself."

"Do you think that the Butcher was aware of the information Brady had gathered?"

"He must have known that he had something," Dougherty said, "since he was so hot on his trail. Close enough that the Butcher felt compelled to kill him. But now that Brady is dead, I imagine he feels safe again. Otherwise, I doubt that he would have killed Evodia

Zellner when and where he did. He must have been reasonably certain that we did not yet suspect him."

"That makes sense," he said, "unless there was some reason that made it imperative for him to kill her then and there. But I cannot imagine what such a reason might be."

"That has been the problem all along. We try to find reasons that make sense, and we forget that we are dealing with a madman — not a raving lunatic, but someone whose reasons make sense to him and may mean nothing to us."

"Why does he move from place to place?"

"I am not sure," Dougherty said. "The most obvious answer is that he pushes his luck to the limit and then moves on. He taunts, but he does not go past a certain limit."

"I agree with you," Doctor Brownson said. "In the large cities like New York and Washington, he can risk killing in various parts of the city and disposing of the bodies in any number of places. In fact, the same is true of Philadelphia, but he seems to have killed here only that one time. I don't know why that was. He may have had some other reason for leaving here. Or perhaps he didn't yet realize how easy it was to get away with it. But now he's in a different situation. If he is in Penrose Valley, then he has fewer options open to him. He has done his deed in Mauch Chunk. He has nowhere larger than that in the rest of Carbon County. He has the train to take him from place to place, but even then his choices are severely limited."

Dougherty wondered where this was leading. Brownson spoke slowly, pausing to think, and Dougherty knew that he was working out something in his mind. His conclusion, when it came, was deeply disturbing.

"Judging from all that we now know," he said, "it seems to me that his next murder may very well take place in Penrose Valley itself. I think he would love the thrill of it, to act directly under the noses of the people in so small a town and get away with it. Does he know that you have been given the charge of investigating the murder of Edna Krantz in addition to that of Charlie Brady?"

"I have no idea," Dougherty said, "but if he does not already know it, I am sure that the news will be out soon enough. It always is in small towns. He may not know that we have any inkling of the connection between the murders of Charlie Brady and Edna Krantz, but that may make no difference to him."

"Then, young Dougherty, I suggest that you prepare to do your best to capture him and to prevent another murder. I feel certain that he intends to perform this murder in Penrose Valley and then move away. My guess is that he won't move immediately after the killing. He is too clever for that. It would give him away. No... he'll stay until things die down first, and then he'll move as though it is the natural thing to do."

"And so we must find him before March," Dougherty said, "if our timetable is accurate. And, if your notion is correct — and I fear that it is — this may be our last chance before he leaves Carbon County and begins again somewhere else."

In the back of his mind was another half-formed thought. Since he was investigating the two most recent murders, would it give the Butcher some special pleasure to kill in such a way as to act right under his nose and make a fool of him specifically? He did not find the notion pleasing.

* * *

Through the two small, blue tinted glass panes in the upper panel of the front door, they saw coming toward them the silhouette of a woman carrying a child. The door opened a crack and a brown eye peered out. Its owner must have been satisfied, for she opened the door the rest of the way and invited them in.

She was a pretty woman in her mid-thirties, with light brown hair and fair complexion. She wore a simple dress, quite becoming and of better quality than one would expect for doing the household chores. She had dressed specially for their visit. The child in her arms was about a year old. Seeing two new faces, the baby leaned back against its mother, took one more quick look at the two of them, and, with a barely audible pout, twisted around, buried its curly head against her shoulder and held on tightly with its little arms wrapped about her neck. The woman's face lit up and she laughed. In a gentle, circular motion she rubbed the baby's back.

"There, there, Daniel. No need to be scared, is there? The ladies are just come to visit. Show them what a nice smile you have."

She tried to turn him back toward them, but he was having none of it. He squirmed away from them and held on tighter than ever to his mother.

"Don't mind him," she said, "He don't mean nothing by it. He's not used to strangers, is all. Won't you sit down?" She led them into a small parlor, a room obviously seldom used, set aside for the reception of visitors. Its furniture was not new, but was well cared for. On the mantle was a framed photograph of a Union infantryman. She saw Jen glance toward it.

"My husband," she said, "Sergeant Condren, when he was in the war. It's too bad he's at work right now or you could meet him. He's a wonderful man. Thank God, he's home now, safe and sound." Her voice was full of pride and relief.

"I'm so glad for that," Jen said. "So is my own husband."

Two small heads popped around the edge of the parlor doorframe and quick as a wink pulled back out of sight again, followed by the sound of giggles.

"All right," Mrs. Condren said, "you can come in and say hello, but then it's back out to the kitchen with you and you can play until we're done talking."

The heads reappeared, this time followed by the two bodies as well. The boy was about six or seven years of age and the girl about four. Their names, their mother said, were Tommy and Sarah. They were lovely children who, now that they had succeeded in getting in to see the visitors, were overcome with shyness and voiced a barely whispered hello before they gathered close to their mother's skirts.

"Is it time, mama?" the little girl asked. "Is it time for the tea and cake?"

"Sarah! For goodness' sake!" but she laughed as she said it. "All right, then. We will have tea and cake. You and Tommy will have yours in the kitchen while mama speaks with the ladies. Mrs. Brownson and Mrs. Dougherty, would you excuse me a minute?"

"Do you think that Daniel might come to me now?" Jen asked as Mrs. Condren got up to leave with the children. He was no longer hiding his face and was full of curiosity about the two visitors. His mother looked at him uncertainly, then held him toward Jen. With what was but a *pro forma* show of hesitation, he held out his arms and came to her. By the time Mrs. Condren returned to the parlor with the tray full of refreshments, he was busy grabbing at Jen's hair and pulling at the buttons on the front of her dress.

She placed the tray on the table and poured each of them a steaming cup of tea — just what they needed after the chill of the carriage ride. She served them pound cake on dishes with a pleasant floral design — surely her Sunday best. The cake was delicious, and young Daniel shared Jen's with enthusiasm.

"You've come to talk about what happened all those years ago?" she asked.

"We have," Mrs. Brownson answered, "and we hope that the memory of it will not be overly disturbing to you. We know so little about what you witnessed that day, apart from what appeared in the newspapers, and that was only a few sentences. We are sure that you would tell it better than would the reporters. Would you mind?"

"I told the police all about it," she said. "When the papers asked for people to come forward, I thought I should. At first I wasn't certain it was the Conroy girl I seen. It was only a minute or two, you know. I was out walking with Tommy. He was just a babe in arms then, smaller than Daniel is now. It was such a nice day, I remember. I wanted to give him some air." She smiled. "Well, to tell the truth, he was my first and I enjoyed taking him out for his walk. So many people smiled to see him or stopped to admire him, and it just made me feel so good."

"How did you happen to notice her?" Jen asked.

"She was across the street. I was on Twenty-first, headed up towards Rittenhouse Square and that was when I seen her. Her yellow dress caught my eye. I had the same color. Of course, hers was silk and mine wasn't, but it was the color, you see. I thought it so cheerful on a sunny day. Well, anyway, she was on the other side of the street and there was this man, don't you know. He was a lot taller than her and he wasn't with her... I don't think he was. She was on her way down toward Spruce and he was going up in the same direction I was going. At least that was how it seemed."

"Had you noticed all of that before you looked more closely?" Mrs. Brownson asked.

"Well, I suppose not. I mean, it wasn't like I was looking that careful or anything. It was just the flash of yellow that got my attention at first. And that was when he touched the brim of his bowler like he was saying hello to her. He didn't take it off, just touched the brim. She was surprised, I'd say, like it caught her off guard that he'd spoke to her. I remember thinking that maybe he was lost and wanted directions, but why he'd ask a strange woman and not look for a man to talk to instead, I couldn't say."

"Do you recall what he looked like?" Mrs. Brownson said.

"Well, he was dressed nice, I'll say that for him. He had one of them Tweedside jackets, with just the top button buttoned like is fashionable. He looked respectable, so I guess I didn't think all that much that he spoke to her. But it was the expression on her face made me think maybe she didn't know him. Not like she looked scared. Just that she had a sort of question in her expression, you know, like she was thinking, 'Now who could this be? Do I know him?' I can't tell you much about his looks. He was neat and respectable. He had no beard, but whether he had a moustache, I just couldn't say. He was turning away from me, I'd say, just as I caught sight of him, and I could see the line of his jaw, but not his full face."

"One of the newspapers said that you thought he had a crazed look," Jen said. "Is that correct?"

"No. I never said that. I remember, when I saw it in the papers, it annoyed me they said that. The reporter come to the house to ask what I said to the police, and I never said that. He asked if I thought the man looked like a crazed killer, and I said I couldn't say. And then he said, 'So maybe he might have? You couldn't say he didn't have such a look?' And I said that of course I couldn't, since I hadn't been able to see. And then he put in the paper just what he wanted, even if I never said it."

"Is there anything else you remember?" Mrs. Brownson asked.

"No," she said. "It all happened so fast, you see, and I only saw them for a matter of seconds before the carriage blocked my view."

"What carriage?" Jen asked, and they both perked up their ears. This might be something new.

"Oh, there was a carriage parked there, right near them. It was just standing there. I didn't think anything of it, except that it stopped me from seeing any more."

"Do you think that the carriage belonged to the man who was speaking to her?" Jen asked.

"I really couldn't say," she said, "but, now that you ask the question, maybe it did. There was no driver and I don't know if anybody was inside. I couldn't see anybody. Maybe he was driving and got out to look for directions. But if he was the killer, then I guess that wouldn't be right, would it? He wouldn't be asking for directions at all. If it was his carriage, then maybe he was trying to get her to go with him. But I don't know why she would if she didn't know him. That wouldn't make sense, would it?"

"Was there anything distinctive or unusual about the carriage," Jen asked, "anything that might make it different from others."

"No. It was just an ordinary buggy. Black. But then so are most, I suppose. It did have its roof up even on so nice a day. That might be unusual, but maybe not."

"Mrs. Condren," Mrs. Brownson said, "later on the police arrested a man by the name of Henry Carlton. Did they do so on the basis of the description you gave them?"

"I hope not," she said. "They made me come to the station to see him and I told them he wasn't the one. I never knew Mr. Carlton by name before they took me to the station to see him, but I knew what he looked like because I seen him before, walking up around Rittenhouse Square. I think he used to stroll there in the nice weather. It wasn't him, but they arrested him anyway and then let him go. If they'd listened to me, they wouldn't have arrested him in the first place. Poor man. It must have been a terrible thing to go through."

Apart from that, she had nothing further to tell them. They chatted, enjoying the tea and cake and the antics of little Daniel, who was by now perfectly at peace in Jen's arms, and then they took their leave, eager to get to their next destination.

"I just hope," Mrs. Condren said, "that some of what I say may help catch the man who did something so terrible." But her voice conveyed no assurance that the investigation, in her estimate, would go any further than had that of the police six years earlier.

Their driver was waiting for them, just as he had said. Jen had worried about him, standing out in the cold while they were inside, but she need not have. His breath bore witness to sufficient liquid sustenance to stave off the chill, but not enough to interfere with his day's employment, so they retraced their path to Rittenhouse Square, then north two blocks on Twentieth.

"This is it, ladies," he said, as he opened the door to hand them down. "I'll wait here."

They were in front of a three story house, narrower than its neighbors, which were pressed up tight against it on both sides, as were all the houses in that block. Whenever Jen saw houses like this, even houses of the wealthy, she was glad that she had always lived in a small town, where there was room for a garden and where neighbors were close, but not nearly so close as this. It was of a whitish brick rather than the red of those around it. Two pillars and an arch framed the front door. It was attractive, obviously the house of people with a more than moderate income. They climbed the five stone steps and tapped the knocker.

A servant girl in black dress and white apron and cap opened the door.

"Would yez be Mrs. Brownson and Mrs. Dougherty? Mr. and Mrs. Conroy are expecting yez. Won't yez come in? They're waiting in the drawing room."

She led them along the corridor to a door, tapped on it, and entered. She announced them, then stood aside to let them in.

"Welcome to our home. I am Peter Conroy and this is my wife, Elizabeth," he said as he came toward them. He was a tall man, with thinning gray hair and a sparse moustache of the same color. His dark eyes protruded, as though he were perpetually surprised. He was quiet, quite refined in speech, with just a trace of a soft Irish brogue. He might have been a rather comic figure, had he not had about him such an aura of sadness. Jen placed him at about sixty.

His wife was small, even as her daughter had been. Her hair, still dark at her age (which Jen guessed as about that of her husband) was pulled back in a severe style that accentuated the structure of the fine-boned face, with its clear blue eyes and dark brows. In her youth she must have been quite attractive, the image of her now dead daughter. She was dressed in black, perhaps still in mourning for Abiageal. She stood just behind her husband, as though seeking protection from whatever these visitors were about to bring into their home.

"Have ye learned something, then? Is that why ye've come?"

Her brogue was more pronounced than that of her husband. The way she asked the question was disconcerting, as though they had come with news, perhaps that Abiageal was not dead after all.

"Why don't we all sit and discuss the whole matter," her husband said.

"O' course. Ye'll excuse me? It's just that yer coming today must be because o' something ye've learned recently. What could it be?" She sat and pointed them to their chairs. There was no time for idle chit-chat.

"Oh, my dear," said Mrs. Brownson, "we are, I fear, the bearers of bad tidings. We are here because of something that happened a few weeks ago in Carbon County. It is our sad duty to tell you that Mr. Charles Brady is deceased. We are so very sorry."

At first they said nothing. Mr. Conroy swallowed and made a visible effort to keep his emotions in check. His wife's hand flew to her mouth as she gasped and then to her eyes as she began to cry. It was the husband who first spoke.

"Charlie? Dead? What happened to him?"

"He was killed in a mine cave-in." Jen said.

"A mine cave-in? It was an accident, then?" he asked.

"No," Jen said. "The cave-in, we think, was purposely caused."

"You're certain it was the same Charlie Brady? It just doesn't seem possible. Charlie was no miner. I can think of no reason why he should have been in Carbon County. I doubt he knew anyone there. I'm sure it must be a matter of mistaken identity."

"I wish it were," Jen said, "but there is no doubt. He was going by the name of Charlie Brogan, but among his possessions was a photograph of himself and a young woman identified only as 'Mary.' We have since learned that it was a picture of Charlie Brady and your own dear daughter, Abiageal. It pains me to say it, but there is no mistake."

"Then why was he there? And who would have wanted to kill him?" His face was all confusion and pain.

As best she could, Jen explained about his death and about James's involvement in the investigation. She told them of the documents Charlie had collected and of the most recent murder. Mrs. Conroy's tears continued to flow and Jen's heart ached for the poor woman, but she knew it was best to have all this out in the open before they did anything else, much as she dreaded the task.

"And so you think that Charlie might have been close to finding the man who murdered our daughter?" Mr. Conroy asked.

"We think so, but we have no idea how he came to his conclusions or how he decided that the murderer might be in Penrose Valley. We wondered if you had heard from him."

"Not for a few years now," he said. "He used to keep in contact with us after Abiageal's death. For a time he stayed here in Philadelphia. He kept after the police to see what they were doing, but eventually he came to the conclusion that there was simply no evidence. He was so downcast, I began to fear that he might do himself harm. Then he joined the army early in 1862 and for a while we heard from him, but we haven't had a word since late in 1864."

He paused, as though deciding whether or not to add something else to what he had said and finally decided to say it.

"When he went into the army, I thought it was with the intention of ending his life by giving it for his country. Truth to tell, I always expected to hear that he had been killed in a battle somewhere. But his last letter was from a hospital in Washington where he was recuperating. Not from a wound. He'd broken his leg in building earthworks. In the letter he said that he had just heard something of interest to us, but would tell us more about it when he was able to learn more. That was his last letter, and we never did hear of him again until today."

"We were certain," Mrs. Conroy said, "that he'd learned something that had to do with Abiageal's death, but what it was we hadn't a notion. And now ye say he's dead. Ye know, when first Abiageal told us she wanted to marry Charlie, we were none too pleased. All we knew o' the man was that he was a prize fighter and neither of us saw that as any recommendation to marriage. We looked into the matter, o' course, and found that his parents had been decent people. They were both dead by then. Abiageal insisted we meet him, and he turned out to be a pleasant, responsible man after all. He'd done the prize fighting to earn a living, and he'd saved his earnings with every intention o' getting out o' the fights as soon as he could."

She stifled a sob and they waited as she composed herself. Finally she went on.

"When Abiageal died that October, he was already on his way back here from wherever he'd been, and it was his last trip, he said. He used to follow after a circus, ye know. He wasn't a part of it, but the fighters sort o' tagged along and did their own bit o' business nearby. It'd get the men coming to see the fights and making bets, and Charlie always had somebody betting something on himself. And he won almost all the time. And just when he was ready to quit and settle down, that's when Abiageal was killed. It broke our hearts."

The tears flowed as she spoke, tears both for Abiageal and for Charlie Brady, for it was obvious as she talked about him that her attitude toward him had at some point changed from distaste at his occupation to a sort of pride in the fact that he did it so well and for such a good intention.

"But you have no idea what he learned in Washington? What he referred to in the letter?" Mrs. Brownson asked.

"None at all," Mr. Conroy said. "How I wish we had! I can only hope that your husband's investigation will lead to the conclusion that Charlie didn't live to see."

"Is there no one you can think of who can give us any information at all?" Jen asked.

"No one," he said.

"How about his aunt?" Mrs. Conroy asked. She was hesitant, almost, Jen thought, fearful of speaking.

"His aunt? I doubt she could be of any assistance. You know how she is." His tone was surprisingly stern. Clearly this was a topic he had no wish to address, a matter on which they disagreed.

"He had an aunt?" Mrs. Brownson asked. "Of course, we don't know her and you do, so we will defer to your judgement about her ability to be of assistance, but I do think we should find her and let her know about Charlie's death."

Mrs. Conroy said nothing. Mr. Conroy looked as though he wanted to say nothing, but he could hardly refuse to tell them about her if what they wanted was to convey the news of her nephew's demise. He relented and told them that her name was Maura Brady, the widow of Charlie Brady's Uncle John. Having told them that much, he told them a little more.

"Charlie's Uncle John spent most of his life in Brazil, in the coffee trade. Charlie hadn't seen him in years, until they came back here to live. Charlie used to see them when he was in town. His uncle died three years ago. His aunt — no real relation of Charlie's, you understand, just by marriage, not by blood — now lives by herself. She's a rather odd person in some ways, so, as I said, you'll find her not very helpful, but I suppose you should let her know about Charlie's death."

He gave them her address, which was nearer the waterfront. They had learned as much as they were to learn that day and were soon back in the carriage on their way to Dock Street.

"I think I could come to like this questioning of people," Mrs. Brownson said. "It's more fun than gossip, but has such a respectable air about it. What do we do about Maura Brady? Do you think that we should see her?"

"By all means," Jen said. "Does Doctor Brownson know her, do you think? Perhaps he can tell us something about this 'oddity' that so bothers Mr. Conroy and seems no problem at all to his wife. And I suppose we should send her a messenger to let her know we are coming before we actually show up on her doorstep."

They arrived at the house just as James and Doctor Brownson came down the hill from Chestnut Street. James paid the carriage driver and they went into the house together.

"We got no help from the police," Doctor Brownson said. "They had nothing in their records that I did not already know. All they could offer was the name of a detective, a man called Samuel Gardner. I'd never met him, although he was here back in the days of the Conroy investigation. It seems that he kept on the case after everyone else gave up, always hoping to find something everyone else had overlooked. Gardner left Philadelphia some time after the murder and took with him whatever notes he had on the case."

"Did they tell you anything about him or where we could find him now?" Jen asked.

"They have no idea where he is now," James said. "When he left here it was to go to New York to join the police force there. He may be there still, but they have no other information."

"Did they think that he learned anything at all?" Mrs. Brownson asked.

"They didn't know," her husband responded, "but they did think that if anyone had gotten anywhere at all with the matter, it could have been Detective Gardner. He was apparently a sharp customer. Kept an open eye and was always good at knowing what questions to ask. I'll send a telegram to a certain police captain I know in New York City and see what else he can tell us."

There seemed little else to do, then, until they received an answer to that inquiry. Jen and Mrs. Brownson told them what they had learned — about the carriage at the scene of the abduction and about Mrs. Maura Brady. Doctor Brownson did not know her, but promptly sent a messenger to her house asking if Jen and Mrs. Brownson could visit. They had no idea what they could learn from her, but Mrs. Brownson was delighted at the thought of another adventure.

Chapter XVII: No Choice but to Wait

I'm Charley's aunt from Brazil—
where the nuts come from.
    Brandon Thomas (1856-1914)
    Charley's Aunt (1892) Act I

[Thursday, January 25, 1866]

Tuesday was the day of promise. The day the veil might be lifted from the Butcher's career. Doctor Brownson's telegram to his police captain friend in New York should lead to whatever Detective Samuel Gardner had discovered of Mary Conroy's murder. Perhaps more of those apparently inconsequential details that, when taken together with other equally random facts, create a picture that might otherwise have remained invisible. He may even have been involved in the investigations of the murders in New York, and could reveal what the newspapers had omitted or garbled.

Mrs. Brownson and Jen planned to call upon Mrs. Maura Brady. They realized that she was elderly and that her nephew may not have confided in her in the matter of such gruesome crimes, but perhaps some gentle questioning could spark the old lady's memory — provided that her mind was clear. They were not sure just what to expect in light of Mr. Conroy's attitude toward her. He acted as though she were not quite "right." Most troubling of all was the fact that she would not yet have heard of events in Penrose Valley, and it would fall to them to inform her of Charlie Brady's death. Jen shrank from the thought of it.

Doctor Brownson's Tuesday message to Mrs. Brady brought quick results — within the hour by the hand of the same messenger. He brought a cream colored envelope of high quality, containing a matching sheet of stationery imprinted at its head with the words "Maura Antonia Brady" — no title, no address. In a clear, attractive, and old-fashioned, hand was a brief message.

Dear Doctor Brownson,

It would give me the greatest pleasure to meet with Mrs. Brownson and Mrs. Dougherty. Unfortunately, I am unavailable tomorrow because of target shooting practice in the morning and I shall be further occupied with meetings throughout the day. However, Thursday the 25th *inst.* would be agreeable and I shall be most pleased to welcome the ladies to visit with me at my home at half-past three o'clock post meridiem for tea and refreshments, at which time we shall have the leisure to speak of the momentous matters indicated in your kind note. I look forward to our time together with great interest. I remain,

                Most sincerely yours,
                Maura Antonia Brady

Target shooting practice? More than ever Jen and Mrs. Brownson wanted to meet this woman, even if it meant waiting another day. They sent a message accepting her invitation and thanking her for honoring their request. But still they thought, Target shooting practice?

It was mid-morning Wednesday when the telegram came from Captain Crowley in New York. They were gathered in the parlor and that was where Doctor Brownson opened and read it.

> REGRET CANNOT HELP. GARDNER NOT IN NEW YORK. LEFT LATE 1862 FOR ARMY OF POTOMAC. NEVER SPOKE OF CONROY CASE. WAS NOT INVOLVED IN NEW YORK CASES YOU MENTIONED. PERHAPS RETURNED NEW YORK AFTER WAR BUT NO CONTACT WITH ME. WILL TELEGRAPH IF LEARN MORE. CROWLEY

And so Wednesday became their day of frustration, with no progress in the case and nothing to do beyond discussing and reexamining all the facts accumulated to date. But for Jen it was a day she was never to forget — a day of unexpected blessing.

Since there was so little to do, James and Doctor Brownson took advantage of the time to go to Jefferson Medical College so that James could visit with some of his former professors. Mrs. Brownson set Gisela to the dusting and mopping of the second floor, while she and Jen prepared a special supper in celebration of nothing in particular, apart from the pleasure of these days together. And so, as they worked in the kitchen they talked. Jen would always wonder if, after all, that was what Mrs. Brownson had had in mind when she made her suggestion. They did prepare a wonderful meal, but it was the conversation which meant so much to Jen. And from that day on, even though James and Doctor Brownson still addressed each other as "young Dougherty" and "sir," and would always do so, the two of them were Martha and Jen rather than Mrs. Brownson and Mrs. Dougherty.

Martha began with Mrs. Condren's lovely children, and especially little Daniel and how he had taken to Jen. Then one thing simply led to another. How foolish she had been, Jen thought, to imagine that she could teach Martha Brownson anything about the gentle art of interrogation! Before she knew it, she was pouring out all that she had been feeling for the previous months — much of it what she had already told her mother. But Martha Brownson, motherly as she was, was also an equal, a friend, and that was just what Jen needed. They sat in the kitchen and, full of patience, she allowed Jen to unburden herself of all that had so plagued her. She did not say, "There, there, it will be all right," or, "You mustn't even think such thoughts." She simply allowed her to say aloud what she had kept locked so tightly inside, thinking herself the only one who had ever felt as she had — all the blame that she had clasped so fiercely to herself when it was not hers to hold; all the disappointment that she thought she had caused James, when he had never given her the least reason to think so; all the confusions of hope and fear about what might happen should she discover herself with child in the future, her unreasonable dread of the very thing that she desired beyond measure. And when they were through and her tears were dried, she knew that she had crossed some invisible frontier and was ready to go forward. And so from then on they were, Martha and Jen. They had their supper and enjoyed it more than Jen could have ever hoped and that night, in bed, she told James what had happened and knew that he smiled in the dark; but she felt the dampness on his cheek as he kissed her and she knew that he truly understood.

Much as her conversation with Martha had helped, she soon learned that it had not increased her patience. Thursday progressed at a snail's pace. They had no sooner finished their breakfast than Jen found herself with an eye on the clock which, like any well bred member of the clock family, when repeatedly stared at, purposely slowed down so that she might study it the more easily. By half-past one o'clock she had finished the last touches to her hair, she had donned her visiting frock, and she was only prevented from putting on her coat and bonnet by the fact that it would have been uncomfortably warm in the house and rather foolish to have waited outside. Then, after all the fretting, three o'clock arrived precisely on time and so, too, did their carriage, with the same driver who had driven them Tuesday.

This trip was shorter. They went west along Walnut Street, turned left onto Sixth, passed along Washington Square, and continued southward for some blocks. Martha said they were in Society Hill — not that its residents had any particular pretensions of grandeur; it was named after a stock company, the Free Society of Traders, to whom the land had long ago been deeded by William Penn himself. But it did house a number of the city's affluent, and Jen thought that Mrs. Maura Antonia Brady's husband must have done well in the coffee trade.

They were almost at South Street when the carriage came to a halt, lurching slightly as one of the wheels struck an icy patch. The driver opened the door, tipped his hat, and said, "That's it, ladies," pointing to a house in the middle of a tightly packed row.

They were, Jen realized, just at the edge of affluence — the lower edge. The two story house in which Mrs. Brady lived was small, only the width of one fairly ornate door and a nicely designed parlor window. It stood timidly in its place, like a little brother sandwiched between two protective taller ones to its right and left. Some of what had once been fashionable residences nearby were now converted into businesses of various sorts, one of the early signs that a neighborhood is on its way to losing its residential status and is starting to deteriorate. The decline had begun some years ago, and Jen hoped that its completion would outlast Mrs. Brady, and so spare her the pain of witnessing it.

They climbed the steps and used the ornate brass knocker. The door was opened at once, and there stood Charlie Brady's aunt. She was a tall, almost painfully thin woman, with a face of the sort often described as horsey: Long and narrow, with large eyes, a thin nose, and slightly protruding teeth. She was not, never had been, a beauty, yet there was something striking about her. She was, Jen guessed, eighty or more years of age, but she radiated an aura of efficiency and intelligence that many must find disconcerting. The bright green eyes ranged expertly over them and, Jen was sure, missed not a thing. Fortunately, what she saw seemed not to displease her.

Her hair was done in the style of years ago, parted in the center, flat against the top of the head, and puffed out at the sides to cover the ears like a pair of outsized earmuffs. It was primarily white, with hints of its original red. But it was her costume that stole their attention. She wore a high necked blue, almost black, frock coat — military in style, buttoned to the chin, its lower part fuller than the frock coat of a man, much like the cut of an ordinary female skirt but with large pockets and ending at the level of the knee. Below that were visible the legs of a pair of trousers, sky blue with a yellow stripe down the sides.

"Mrs. Brady?" Jen asked.

"Who else, indeed?" she responded, "And you must be Mrs. Dougherty and Mrs. Brownson. Can you tell me which is which?"

This was not the voice of a feeble, old lady. It was loud and clear, her pronunciation crisp and precise. If she was this strong at eighty, Jen hesitated to imagine what she must have been in her prime.

"I am Mrs. Dougherty and this is Mrs. Brownson. We thank you for meeting with us at such short notice. As we indicated, it is on a matter of some importance both to us and to you."

"Well, it's nice to have visitors. Come in, won't you? No need to stand out here and freeze."

She led them into the parlor, whose lone window faced onto the street, with a chair near it convenient for reading and for looking out at the day's activities. The mantel and other surfaces were pleasantly cluttered with life's odds and ends, memorabilia of friends and family, artifacts whose value is sentimental more than monetary. And there were photographs — some of her in her younger days in the company of a man whose resemblance to Charlie Brady was striking and who, Jen was sure, must be his Uncle John. There was a photograph of Charlie in uniform, with an expression even more serious than the one usually required by the photographer. Three comfortable chairs had been placed around a low table upon which were a tea service and a plate of sandwiches and small cakes. She took their coats, went back into the hall with them, and then returned.

"Please be seated. And I suppose before anything else I should explain to you the meaning of what you may take to be an unusual form of garb. I find that if I don't say something about it right off, visitors think of nothing else and serious conversation is hampered by distraction. Did either of you ever subscribe to *Lily*?"

They both shook their heads.

"Well, it's been off the market for a decade or more now, more's the pity, but I was always an admirer of its foundress, Amelia Bloomer. I'm sure you've heard of her?"

They both nodded.

"A woman ahead of her time, in my estimation, far ahead of her time. I wish her well in her endeavors. Anyway, she designed a costume to give women greater freedom. If you lack the freedom to move, what other freedoms will you ever secure? Never really caught on, but it will some day. What I wear is a style based upon her design, but modified by Doctor Mary Walker during the recent war. I had copies made for myself. She wore it as she treated the wounded, and I think it a great improvement over bloomers. More businesslike. More professional. I decided that if it was good enough for a woman who had been awarded Congress's Medal of Honor, it is certainly good enough for me. So there you have it. You may think me sensible or you may think me a little crazy, and in both opinions you would be fully justified, but at least that's out of the way and now we can relax and have a nice visit."

Martha and Jen glanced at each other and knew they were of one mind in their immediate affection for Maura Brady. It was no mystery that Elizabeth Conroy had taken a liking to her and her husband had not, and why he was content to dismiss her as nothing more than an eccentric, when she was, in fact, a bright, intelligent, and strongly opinionated woman. Jen regretted that James was not with them, he would have found her a delight. Still, it was as well that he was not, for they had some highly distressing news to impart, and it might be easier for her in the company of women. They knew it could not be deferred.

"Mrs. Brady, when Doctor Brownson wrote to you, he said that we wished to discuss a matter of some moment." Jen paused, allowing her a chance to adjust to the seriousness of what was about to come. "It is about your nephew, Charlie Brady."

"Charlie? Do you know him then?"

"Mrs. Brady, I so regret being the bearer of sad tidings, but something dreadful has occurred. Your nephew, Charlie, has passed away."

The effect upon her was instantaneous and painful to behold. Those strong features, a moment ago so full of self-assurance, simply crumbled. Her eyes filled with moisture, then overflowed into tears. Her lower lip trembled, her mouth slowly opened into a small circle, and from it there issued the saddest, most plaintive moan Jen had ever heard. It went straight to her heart and it was all she could do not to burst into tears.

Martha reached over and took Mrs. Brady's hand, a gesture that Jen feared she might reject, but she did not. Instead, she clasped that outstretched hand as if it were a lifeline tossed to a drowning woman. She sobbed deeply, and Martha said nothing, simply waited for it to pass. And it did. After some minutes she brought herself under control again with a great act of the will, sat firmly upright against the back of the chair, and let go Martha's hand, simply patting it in wordless appreciation. Martha poured a cup of the strong tea and handed it to her. She sipped at it, giving herself time to recover, then set the cup back on its saucer at the edge of the table.

"Charlie is dead. Dear God, I can hardly believe it, even though I was so afraid that it might happen. Am I right that this was no natural death?"

"He was killed by someone," Jen said, "although we do not yet know the identity of his killer. That's what we're trying to find out."

"And just how will you go about that?" she asked.

Jen explained to her how she had become involved and told her of the previous investigations James and Doctor Brownson had conducted, wishing her to know that this was no foolish whim on the part of some interfering busybodies whose efforts were as likely to hinder as help in a serious investigation.

"Was he properly buried?" she asked.

Jen told her about the wake and the funeral Mass, and how his nearest friends had missed work to be there. She told her about Mrs. Corrigan and her children and their affection for Charlie, and his for them. And she spoke of the respect in which he had been held by the other miners, especially the men who boarded with him, and all that she said rang true because it was true, and Mrs. Brady took considerable consolation from it. At her insistence, Jen also told her how he was killed. At last, she was ready to turn to finding out who had killed him.

"Mrs. Brady," Martha said, "can you tell us what Charlie was doing? Have you any idea what might have led to his death?"

"I do indeed," she said, "and I have the notion that you do, too. If you're seeking the cause here in Philadelphia, then you must have heard about the murder of Mary Conroy. Am I correct?"

Jen told her of Doctor Brownson's part in the initial investigation of Mary's death. Then she thought it was time to broach the subject of the other killings and wondered how much of a shock it would be to Mrs. Brady.

"Did Charlie speak to you of any other murders?" Jen asked.

"Ah! So you've found his papers, then? You know of his search for the Butcher? He told me all about it. He always liked to talk things over with me when he was here." Her pride in that was evident. "He was here a few months back and stayed for a week. He had just returned from New York and said that he had good reason to believe that the man he was after had come to Pennsylvania and might well have gone to the coal regions." They leaned forward and she held up a hand to forestall what seemed their obvious question. "Before you ask, I can assure you that he did not tell me who the man was. Charlie himself didn't yet know, but he was beginning to have suspicions about a few people and wanted to watch them and see what he could learn."

"Can you tell us how he got on the trail of this killer?" Jen asked. "I realize that Mary Conroy's death must have been where he began, but how did he put that together with events in New York and Washington?"

"Of course, it began with Mary's death," she said. "They were so in love and so full of joy when her parents gave their consent to the marriage. I take it you have met the Conroys? Then you have already formed your own judgement of them. Mine is that Elizabeth is a lovely person, devastated at her daughter's death, and sorry the marriage never took place, because she had taken quite a liking to dear Charlie after she got to know him. Peter Conroy is another type entirely. He's pompous and difficult to deal with. He loved his daughter and still suffers horribly from her death, but he found it hard to accept Charlie. In the end, Mary and Elizabeth won him over. I think he had serious reservations about any such marriage. Charlie was a prize fighter and he considered him beneath them, even though Peter Conroy is not above attending the matches. And I am afraid that I was also one of the obstacles. Elizabeth and I had no trouble liking each other. Peter still does not know what to make of me, which I quite understand, even though I have no intention of remaking myself to suit someone else's notion of who and what I ought to be. Eventually, he got past that hurdle too, deciding to consider me no more than an eccentric related merely by marriage to Charlie. If that satisfied him, then it satisfied me. Mary and Charlie were disturbed and embarrassed at his attitude, but there was nothing to be done about it, and, quite honestly I didn't much care, since I got along so wonderfully well with the two of them."

Her eyes began again to tear up and she stopped to replenish her tea and to pour cups for her guests. They waited, knowing that she needed this distraction to regain her composure. At last she was ready to go on.

"Charlie wasn't in Philadelphia when Mary was murdered and when he came back for the funeral he was a different man. He'd always been on the serious side about his responsibilities, but full of good humor with it all. When he came home that time, he was so full of sadness I began to wonder if he would ever pull himself out of it. For a time he stayed here and spent his days tracking down everyone he thought could offer even a hint to who had done this. He got nowhere. In the end, he went back to the prize fighting. He'd already made up his mind to take his savings and get out, but after the murder he no longer had any reason to do so. He fought just for something to do. For a time I heard almost nothing from him, then in 1862 he joined the army and went to war.

"That was when he began to write to me regularly again. He was no happier than he had been when he left here, but he seemed in need of someone to write to, and I was his only relative, even if it was just by marriage."

She smiled at that.

"Charlie and I hit it off the very first time we met. That was after John and I left Brazil and came here. Charlie was like a son to us, especially after my John died and I was left alone in this house. John had seen to it financially that I would have no trouble staying here and no difficulty supporting myself, provided I exercise a little care. I guess he'd put up with me all his life and he knew how independent I was, and he saw to it that I stayed that way. Or maybe he was just too kind-hearted to let me inflict myself upon some other man after his death."

Again she stopped, a small smile on her lips as she thought of the days of her marriage, which must have been a happy one, and then she was back with them again.

"Where was I? Oh, yes! Charlie went into the army. He wrote to me about his life there and about the battles he was in and I began to fear that he was running risks, just waiting for a rebel bullet to bring his pain to an end. It never happened. Then he fell and broke his leg — which he could have done perfectly well right here in Philadelphia. It was a clean fracture, no breaking of the skin, and the surgeon who set it for him knew what he was doing, because he had no problems with it. But for a time it took him out of the action and left him in a hospital bed in Washington. That was where he was in August of 1864, when he read in the newspapers about the murder of a woman named Olivia Wharton. The details of what had happened to her convinced him that she had been killed by the same man who had killed his beloved Mary.

"Once he was up on crutches, he began to spend his days hobbling around the city, speaking to people who had been involved in the life and death of Olivia Wharton. That was how he came to learn about the other murders and how the army police had prevented their investigation — at least that was how Charlie saw things. He'd gotten that notion from a Doctor Calder who worked for the police in Washington. But he learned something else, too. In the hospital he got to know a lot of the other boys, and one was from New York City. When Charlie was reading about the Wharton murder, this New Yorker — he never told me his name — saw what he was reading and said that he'd heard of a murder just like that in New York back near the beginning of the war. He had no details, but he remembered how the killer had cut up some young woman.

"Charlie was put back on duty in the defenses of Washington as soon as he was off the crutches, but he tried every chance he got to learn more about the murders. In the end, it wasn't much, but he was still in Washington when there was another murder, a girl from Chicago, and her body was discarded like a sack of rubbish near a prison.

"By that time all the men in the army were going home, and Charlie got out and came here to visit. That was when he told me all about this. He'd decided that whoever was doing the killings was somehow involved with the army. He was convinced that the killer mustered out at the end of the war and left Washington. That's when he decided to go to New York to see what he could learn about the killings there. He also had a suspicion that the killer may have been working for the Provost or for the Secret Service. He wasn't certain of it, but he didn't go along with the idea that the investigations had been kept secret just because of the fear of panic among the citizenry. After all, there were killings all the time in Washington, and the rest of them were investigated. He decided that this Butcher must have been in a position to convince the people in the military to keep the thing quiet. God knows what reasons he would have given. Charlie tried to find out more, but he got no cooperation whatsoever from either the Provost or the Secret Service."

"Was that everything that he told you?" Jen asked.

"I think so, except for his last visit."

"When was that?"

"About four months ago. Charlie came back from New York with a list of murders from the early days of the war. He'd narrowed down his investigations to just a few men, all of whom had been in the army and in Washington at the right times and had been in New York early in the war. He planned to check on them one by one, and the first on his list was supposed to have gone to the coal regions in Pennsylvania, so he was headed there. He promised to write, but he hadn't so far, so I don't know whom he was following, or even if the man had actually gone there. But with Charlie murdered, I can now hardly doubt that he was following the right person."

"There is really no doubt at all," Martha said, and she told her about the most recent murder in Mauch Chunk.

They stayed with her for a while, eating the refreshments and sipping the tea even though neither their hearts nor their appetites were in it. But the conversation was helping Mrs. Brady and so they listened to her fond reminiscences of Charlie — stories she had probably not told in years and that now were so important to her and demanded to be told, so as to give life to his memory.

"I will visit her again in a few days," Martha told Jen on the way home, "and I hope she will accept an invitation to dine with us. I know Carl will enjoy her company. Even someone so independent needs friends."

There the investigation in Philadelphia came to its end. They were scheduled to depart for Mauch Chunk the following morning. When the four of them gathered that evening after supper to discuss the matter, they realized that there was little to do now except to wait and watch. James would speak to Judge Barrett and have him see to it that the newspapers in the county, especially in their March issues, carried continued warnings against women having anything to do with strangers. He would ask Sheriff Ziegenfuss to have his deputies keep a close watch on the railroad station and other public places from which this killer would be likely to abduct someone. They would look into the backgrounds of some of the people in Penrose Valley and hope that they could eliminate at least some as suspects.

They left the next morning under a nacreous winter sky, in a chill made even more penetrating by the rising breeze. In the West were hints of darker clouds to come and they knew that there would be more snow. Jen hoped it would not arrive until they were safe at home. Doctor Brownson and Martha had come with them to the depot. It was a normal railway depot, a site that had always been for Jen a scene of excitement and nostalgia, of comings and goings, of loving greetings and fond farewells. But as she looked about her now, she sensed danger as well and realized how little she knew of the people all about them or their reasons for being there. How she wished that they could bring this matter to its end! Yet there was no choice but to wait.

The Diarist

> January 25, 1866 —There is a certain satisfaction in being known, but there is no one who could bear the knowing. I must be content that *they* knew. After all, they were most important, they were the ones who smiled and departed. I long for the next, but this is not the time. Plan carefully. Patience, Sammy. Patience.

Already he knew who she was to be and had begun the long watch. It tormented him, this waiting. Yet it did have its own strange joy. Like the sweet agony of the child counting the days until Christmas. The longing only served to amplify the fulfillment.

He saw her now almost every day, even if only a glimpse, only at a distance, as she ran her errands and did her shopping and spoke to friends and neighbors in the street. Sometimes he felt an almost overpowering urgency to be done, to call her now, to finish it and so give her the gift that only he could give. But it was not time. Would not be time for many a day to come. He knew full well that he must wait, but, Oh!... the agony of that long delay. He had never before been in such repeated and prolonged contact with one of his special ones.

He looked up and there she was. She saw him and she didn't see him. He was simply there... part of the daily routine, part of the normal landscape. He was like a piece of furniture one walks around time and again and never adverts to. And even that was the source of some comfort to him, some inner satisfaction. That and the unending, tedious, careful, meticulous planning, so that when the time came it would be as though the final act were the incarnation of what he had already lived time and again in the depths of his soul. It would be his ultimate act of creation.

He turned aside in the most natural manner, glanced into a shop window as though that were his real interest, and then went his way. He knew he could wait. In delicious agony.

PART II
OCTOBER, 1866

Chapter XVIII: How Stupid They Were!

It is a capital mistake to theorize
before you have all the evidence.
It biases the judgement.
    Sir Arthur Conan Doyle (1859-1930)
    A Study in Scarlet (1888) ch. 3

[Friday, October 12, 1866]

"I hope the rain holds off for another few hours," Jen said.

"I know," James answered. "I'd hate to see the children disappointed."

They sat on the hard bench at the plank table, drinking coffee and enjoying food freshly made by the ladies of a local social club to raise money for charitable projects. The crowds were smaller than anticipated, but the fund raising efforts were not going to waste. It was not yet nine o'clock in the morning and the day was overcast and cool, but that encouraged others, just as it had Jen and James, to partake of something warming. The fair's promoters had hoped for a record breaking crowd this year. The weather had not cooperated, but it was at least the equal of other years.

Dougherty did not often get to Lehighton, but this was the final day of the Carbon County Agricultural Society's ninth annual fair and they were enjoying themselves. Yesterday might have been better for the weather, but this was the day of the trotting and pacing races, and the boys had their hearts set on them. The first was scheduled for ten o'clock and the second an hour later, but both would probably be delayed, as they usually were. It didn't really matter. If it didn't rain, they were in no hurry.

They had come to Lehighton the evening before, invited by McBrien to spend the night as guests of some friends of his. He knew they would enjoy the outing, but the invitation was as much due to his sense of propriety as it was to his concern for their pleasure. Jen and James were amused to be chaperoning Sean McBrien, who had surely not felt the need of a chaperone since before the Mexican War, if even then. But this was different.

He came toward them, a small boy grasping each of his large hands, both chattering and laughing with him and each other after their trip to the animal pens and the exhibition building.

"Sure, yez'll wear the poor man out, the two of yez!" Catherine Corrigan said to them, but they took her words as lightly as she'd intended them. She was as excited as they were, dressed in her finest, and the smile she cast on McBrien made her look like a girl in her twenties. She had been having a cup of tea with James and Jen, awaiting the boy's return.

"Ah, they're fine, and that's the truth of it," he said. "They're just having themselves a bit o' fun. But I was wondering if there's anybody within the sound o' me voice who's hungry? Or thirsty?"

Two simultaneous shouts of, "I am," solved that problem, and McBrien went to see what he could find. There was plenty to choose from. The women who'd done the cooking and baking for competition had made enough to sell at the stands.

"We saw the draft horses, the giant ones," they said, "and the hogs, too!"

"They're big as ponies, really big fat ones," little Michael said, "but they stink." And they both held their noses and made faces to suit.

"Now, ye needn't be describing it all in such detail. Mrs. Dougherty and the Doctor can go see fer themselves later, if they've the mind," Mrs. Corrigan said, but they still gave a full report. Even shy Daniel couldn't contain his excitement, and she hadn't the heart to make them stop. Besides, the Doughertys were enjoying it.

Sean McBrien's visit to Mrs. Corrigan's boarding house that bleak January day to deliver Marty Carroll's medicine had opened new horizons — to the thorough delight of Jen and James. Sean and Catherine made a handsome couple, and the two boys could not have been happier.

Now, nine months later, March was long gone, and, in spite of all their fears, nothing had happened. There had been no murder.

Ghoulish as it seemed, they had been disappointed — not that a young woman had failed to die, but that there had been not even an attempt. Had there been, they might have caught the Butcher; but either he was too cautious or too clever, or their schedule had simply not been his.

They'd taken precautions — even more than Dougherty had anticipated. Sheriff Ziegenfuss had seen to it in Mauch Chunk the whole month long and had notified authorities in every town along the railroad from Hazleton to Allentown to be on the lookout. It was all under the auspices of Judge Barrett, who did it without revealing what they knew of the Butcher's earlier crimes. He simply let it be known that the murder of Evodia Zellner had been investigated along all reasonable lines of inquiry, but all without result, leading to the conclusion that it had been perpetrated by some crazed person still on the loose, and that vigilance must be all the greater. Since she had been abducted from a railway depot, all depots merited special concern.

He had done one thing that made Dougherty uneasy. He had employed a number of unofficial guardians of the law, including Maddock and his men in Penrose Valley, telling them to be on the lookout throughout the month for suspicious persons, especially in the vicinity of the railroad station. Still, he had not hinted at their awareness of the Butcher, keeping his communications within the limits of what they knew of the death of Evodia Zellner and only that. Neither did he imply a connection between this request and the death of the man that everyone in Penrose Valley still knew as Charlie Brogan. He simply did not mention it. Dougherty continued to hope that, even if the Butcher got wind of what they were doing, he would still have no reason to believe that they knew about him nor that they suspected a link between Charlie Brogan and Evodia Zellner.

Nothing happened. And Dougherty had a growing doubt about further cooperation from Judge Barrett and Sheriff Ziegenfuss. They never said so, but he sensed their waning enthusiasm. He explained again that his theory about March or November had been verified by the killing in January. They half-heartedly agreed, but without their former ardor, and that distressed him. How willing would they be to take precautions again in November? They knew there had been no guarantee that the killer would strike in March, even if Dougherty's conclusions were true. It could be March of the following year, or even later. Dougherty felt certain of the months, but there was something else that moved this madman, and that remained to be discovered. His ignorance on that point did not inspire the continued confidence of either the Judge or the Sheriff.

The immediate crisis ended on March 31. The very next day — a wonderfully apt date so far as many were concerned — the Commonwealth of Pennsylvania expanded its Railroad Police Act. The formation of new bodies of police became legal. The authorization extended to "all corporations, firms, or individuals owning, leasing, or being in possession of any colliery, furnace, or rolling mill within this commonwealth." That very day, before the official papers were even drawn up, the Penrose Valley Coal Mining Company Coal and Iron Police had appeared in town, dressed in new uniforms, with both office and jail open for business.

* * *

The Coal and Iron Police had not been in existence even two weeks, when McBrien and Dougherty were summoned into the presence of Mr. Beverley Arkwright, this time not at his home, but at the office of the Penrose Valley Coal Mining Company on Main Street. It was to be no social call.

They were shown to his second floor office by a young clerk — polite, but nervous and obviously happy to knock on the door, announce them, and get out as fast possible.

It was a large corner office, with side windows facing west toward Arkwright's house on the hill. At the front, overlooking Main Street, it had a clear view of the new police station across the way. The room was spacious, well appointed, and designed to impress mere mortals with Mr. Beverley Arkwright's theurgic qualities. He sat at his oversized desk, not bothering to rise as they entered, feigning full absorption in the paper he held in his right hand. So, Dougherty thought, time for intimidation. No more sweet talk.

Maddock was there in full uniform, the long blue coat brushed free of lint, the boots and black belt and holster all perfectly polished, the badge and brass buttons shined to brightness. For additional effect, his hat sat firmly on his head, its black leather brim level with his eyebrows, and he posed just behind Arkwright, feet slightly spread, hands firmly clasped behind his back, his face devoid of any expression save the basilisk stare of the eternally vigilant guardian of the law.

Arkwright very deliberately set aside the paper and pointed to two straight-backed wooden chairs set before his desk, like front-row schoolroom desks where the teacher could keep an eye on the troublemakers. Neither of them sat, allowing his pointing finger to dangle foolishly in the air and leaving him with the disadvantage of having to stand or to lean back and look up at them as he spoke. He chose to look up.

"Good day, gentlemen. It is some while since we've had the pleasure, and I thought it time we spoke again. Are you still engaged in learning who killed Brogan?"

"We are," Dougherty said.

"Really? And have you made any progress?"

"Very little, I regret to say."

"How unfortunate. I am sure that you intend to continue your... investigation." The last word came out as a sneer. "You are free to do so."

"Mr. Arkwright, sir," said McBrien, "sure it's kind of ye indeed to take the time and trouble, yours as well as ours, to tell us what we already know. Comes as a sort o' consolation to the inner man, don't ye see, to think that ye'd want to confirm us in our rightful authority, just to be sure we ain't having any doubts about what we can or cannot do. No doubt ye've taken as much time to tell yer own police force just what they can do with their authority, too?"

"You were offered the assistance of Captain Maddock's police when the murder occurred, and you rejected it. You may continue to investigate to your heart's content, but be assured that the Coal and Iron Police will also be investigating and will require your full cooperation. When they contact you, it will be in pursuance of their official duties and you will act in accord with their legally appointed authority. Do I make myself clear?"

"I am quite clear about the extent of their powers," Dougherty replied. "They extend to any crime within the mines or upon the property of the mining company, and I will certainly not stand in their way."

"That's the ticket! And you'll also remember that the property of the Penrose Valley Coal Mining Company takes in all you see through those windows," Maddock said, breaking his silence. "There's nowhere out there you can plant your foot without having it fall upon that property. The company owns the mine and the town and the mountains around the town, above ground and below. So don't think to hide from my jurisdiction — not in this valley."

"It sounds as extensive," Dougherty said, "as the limit of the authority I have been given to investigate Brogan's death. I hope that we will not find ourselves in contention. But, provided that we are both in search of the truth, why should we be at odds?"

"You'll be visited by one of my men," Maddock went on, "who will question you about that murder and possibly about other matters as well."

"Sure and we'll welcome them, one and all," McBrien said, "these guardians o' the law. We'll be happy to answer all their questions, fer we consider it our Christian duty, don't ye see, Captain dear, to instruct the ignorant, even those unaware o' their own ignorance."

"You will receive whomever I send, and you will cooperate fully."

"Have I ever done otherwise? And isn't that what Mr. McBrien just explained?" Dougherty said and smiled a winning smile. He got none in return. They left.

The rest of April overflowed with events that Maddock interpreted as signs of the need for his special police and opportunities to make his authority felt and feared, if not respected. Those events had begun before their meeting with Arkwright. The day after the legalization of the police force, April 2, an incident in Mahanoy City provided a perfect excuse for detaining and questioning anyone who may have been connected with that town and even many who weren't.

The incident took place at Cole's Colliery. Two strangers came to the mine and fired a shot at a Mr. Lewis, the mining boss, who was at the time outdoors, in conversation with the mine owner's son and the outside boss. The ball hit Lewis's face, entering the right cheek and exiting the left. The three men wrestled the shooter to the ground, while his partner ran off. Two more shots were fired in the brawl, but without hitting anyone. Lewis, weakened by his wound, relaxed his grip on the captured man, who promptly leapt up and made a dash for freedom. He'd lost his gun in the scuffle, and the outside boss fired its three remaining shots at him, but missed. He was chased by others, one of whom shot him in the head and killed him. They also captured his partner, armed with a hatchet. Lewis recovered, but the incident became a pretense for questioning anyone with a reputation for the least connection with any union activity. Maddock used this to make his own authority felt, and he detained Frank O'Laughlin for "questioning." He was released a few days later, bruised and battered, but unwilling to press charges of his own and having given no information to Maddock.

Then, within a few miles of Penrose Valley, came a rumbling of discontent. In Audenried and Yorktown the miners' wage was reduced by twenty-five cents per car, a significant loss. Similar changes in Buck Mountain and Jeansville led to strikes and the mine owners had a hard time filling the places of the strikers, since there was a flurry of new railroad construction going on just then, so the striking miners got other jobs with ease. This was new to the owners, who usually had more laborers than they had positions to fill.

To head off the same at Penrose Valley, Maddock brought in "supplementary" forces in the person of a gang of toughs from the Philadelphia docks, outfitted in Coal and Iron Police uniforms, and kept on highly visible patrol in the streets of town and the areas of the mine and breaker for a few weeks, until the risk of "trouble" had ended. Again he hauled in Frank O'Laughlin and some others, and again he released them a few days later. Whether he had real suspicions or not, it was a warning to anyone thinking of crossing the owners.

Then, closer to home, came news of an assault in Beaver Meadow. Constable John B. Thomas, on his way to arrest a man named Joyce, was attacked by a group, one of whom he shot and killed, a man named Charlie Gallagher, and another he wounded. He then escaped by train to Mauch Chunk to get the sheriff's protection. Whether or not it had anything to do with the mines, it was another excuse for scrutiny on the part of the police.

The end result was that the murder of Evodia Zellner faded into the background, just as Charlie Brogan's had done. All attention was focused on the conflicts, both real and imagined, between miners and owners, which was just what Maddock had been hired to accomplish.

Dougherty's attention was caught by something else as well. The local paper carried a short notice of a vicious murder in Philadelphia. The first account was sketchy. A woman had been brutally killed and mutilated. Could they have been wrong, after all? Was the Butcher back in Philadelphia, killing on some other schedule? But the next issue changed Dougherty's mind. The killing had been not of a woman alone, but of a whole family: A man named Dearing, along with his wife, four children, a niece, and a hired boy, were horribly chopped with an axe. A month later the killer, Antoine Probst, confessed and in June was executed. He was a recent arrival from Europe, and could not possibly have been their Butcher.

Maddock kept his word about looking into the murder of Charlie Brogan (by which name he was still known). Officer Steven Carter, one afternoon shortly after the interview with Arkwright and Maddock, came again to Dougherty's office, where he appeared as before, reading a book in the waiting room after the last patient had left. This time he was in uniform. He slipped the book into his coat pocket.

"It has been a long time since I last spoke to you, Doctor. How have you been?"

"Fine," Dougherty said, inviting him into the office and offering him a seat. He was, as always, quiet and polite, but he was also, Dougherty thought, rather ill at ease. The reason was soon apparent.

"I have been ordered to ask you some questions and to deliver a message. Perhaps I had better do that first. I was told to say: 'Captain Maddock wishes you to know that you are *commanded* to respond to all questions put to you by myself or by any other officer, and that your failure to do so will be taken as a refusal to comply with the law and will be treated accordingly.'"

"May I ask, Mr. Carter, to precisely which law is the Captain referring?"

"An astute question, sir. The Captain did not indicate the answer to that." To Dougherty's surprise, he smiled. "I suppose I may assume that whatever answer you give will be in accord with whatever law you think is applicable. That should satisfy all conditions. The Captain is a forceful person, but he does not always explain himself fully."

"Quite satisfactory," Dougherty said, and relaxed a little. "How may I help you?"

They went over Brogan's death again, and again Dougherty said nothing of the Butcher. Carter had got no further than had they, but he was prone to find the solution in a miners' dispute and still suspected O'Laughlin. Originally he thought that Brogan had been shot outside the mine, found his way in, and died in an intentional cave-in — the same theory as Dougherty's, based on the fact that no one in the mine had heard a gunshot. He had now changed his mind, based on an experiment he said he had conducted.

"I went into the mine," he said, "during working hours, dressed as a miner. No one paid me the least attention, not even when I fired a shot in an empty gangway. It seemed loud enough to me, but for everyone else it was lost in the general work noises. The fact is, I fired my .38. It's a lot louder than a .22, and even then no one reacted to it. That gave me a new idea."

As he explained what he had in mind, Dougherty realized how much sense it made.

"O'Laughlin seems to me a real possibility as Brogan's killer. He and Brogan were at odds, for whatever reason. He was outside the gangway and wasn't observed by Shannon. He may have known Brogan would be there or he may have come upon him by chance. In any case, he took his opportunity and shot him. But Brogan ran and O'Laughlin went after him and caused the cave-in. Then he went back to get Shannon and reappeared as savior of the two who were trapped.

The problem was, Carter could prove none of this. It might have made perfect sense, had Dougherty not known about the Butcher. If

O'Laughlin was Brogan's killer, then either he must be the Butcher, or else Brogan was being hunted by two killers, and O'Laughlin was the one who got to him first. But what then about the note summoning Brogan to the breaker? Unfortunately, Dougherty could not tell Carter about that, since he knew that it would go right back to Maddock.

"Have you anything else that you can add, Doctor?" Carter asked.

"I can tell you nothing that I did not already tell you before," he said, a perfectly truthful statement veiled in mental reservation.

Carter did not challenge Dougherty, just sat with eyes downcast, the notebook in his left hand and the pencil in his right. Finally he looked up.

"I thank you," he said. "I will be on my way. If I can be of assistance, let me know."

"Do you expect that Captain Maddock will make things difficult for you, since you are returning to him with no additional information?"

"To tell the truth, Doctor, in my judgement Captain Maddock is not overly concerned with solving Brogan's murder, unless its solution involves a plot against the mine owners. Other than that, I doubt he gives a damn who killed Brogan. He'll keep after it though: He's afraid that you will solve it before he does, and that would make him look bad. Not a very worthy motive, but at least it keeps the case open. And that is just fine with me, because, like you I want to know who did this, no matter who it is, and right now Captain Maddock intends me to keep after it. That, at least, is real police work, and I am happy to do it."

"But surely it will do you no good with the Captain if you find a solution not to his liking."

"I am not overly concerned about that, Doctor. I may not work with Captain Maddock much longer. I am thinking of moving to a larger city and joining a police force there."

"Mr. Carter, you surprise me. Is this position not to your liking then?"

"You might say that," he answered. "When I came I thought it would be interesting, to work on a small force in an area in need of law enforcement. I did not expect my duties to be limited to enforcing company policy and trying to prove manufactured conclusions. That may appeal to Captain Maddock; it does not to me."

He tapped the pencil on the notebook cover, thinking again. He came to a decision, put the notebook and pencil into his pocket, and finished what he wanted to say.

"I hope this will go no further, but, if I were you, Doctor, I would not place great confidence in the Captain. The man has a cruel streak. It makes it difficult to work with him. I will be loyal to him so long as I am employed by the Coal and Iron Police. He can count on that. But I think I will be happy to part company when the time comes."

"Surely the Captain is a capable law officer," Dougherty said, "much as one may deplore his tactics. Perhaps your presence can temper some of what he does."

As much as the Coal and Iron Police were disliked, and Maddock in particular, Officer Carter was perceived by most as fair and reasonable.

"I doubt it," he said. "The Captain is what you might call a self-centered man. What you or I think of as 'tempering,' he would see as simple interference. He despises any intrusion into his affairs. Besides, his cruelty is not just a matter of doing his job too... enthusiastically? Too harshly? It is more than that. He enjoys it. But forgive me. I overstep myself, and I ask you to disregard that remark. It is merely personal opinion, and that is not always reliable, as you well know, no matter how strongly felt."

Dougherty made so bold as to suggest that, if he stayed on, he might some day replace Maddock and change things.

"What makes you think he will leave his present position?" Carter asked.

"Well, I should think his age would be a consideration, wouldn't you? He shouldn't be here so very many years more, I should think."

"His age? Don't let the gray beard deceive you, Doctor. He likes that. He thinks it gives him an air of distinction, but he is not so old as he may appear. He's not much older than I. In his office is his photograph with a group of Provost officers in Washington, when he was still beardless. He looks like a different person. Much younger looking — and that picture is no more than a year and a half old. No. I'm sure I will leave before he is old enough to quit."

There remained one more item which concerned Dougherty, and he decided now was the time to ask about it.

"Mr. Carter, perhaps you can help me with something?"

Dougherty felt a pang of guilt. He offered Carter nothing in response to his questions, and now he was about to prevail upon his goodness to learn something from him — something his superior would not wish Dougherty to know.

"It has come to my attention," he said, "that recently Captain Maddock has taken an interest in the activities of Mrs. Catherine Corrigan. I believe you know her. She runs a boarding house."

"Yes, I know who she is."

"Captain Maddock has been seen frequently in the vicinity of her home, and it makes her uneasy. Can you tell me what he is doing there?"

Catherine had told this to Jen. Often in the evenings, Maddock would pass by the house, apparently taking a stroll, but never failing to look at her house as he passed and sometimes slowing down or pausing, before he went on his way, only to come back again later.

"I'm not sure I should tell you," he said, "but perhaps it is best if I do. It's not Mrs. Corrigan he is watching. It is one of her boarders. Marty Carroll."

"Marty Carroll?" That surprised Dougherty. "Why Marty Carroll?"

"Because of the company he keeps. Captain Maddock is not especially concerned with Marty Carroll, but Carroll has become a great friend of O'Laughlin and that is important. I've no doubt that if the Captain knew I was telling you this, I would be out of his employ this very day, but I feel sorry for Carroll. He's just a babe in the woods, but he's going to get into trouble deeper than he can imagine.

He'd do himself a favor if he just backed off from O'Laughlin. The problem is that I'm not the one to tell him so. Maybe you can."

Dougherty had not spoken to Carter since, except to greet him in passing; but he was still in town and still in uniform. He did try to speak to Marty Carroll, but made little impression, and Mrs. Corrigan said that she continued to see Maddock near her house far too often.

* * *

Mrs. Corrigan and Jen had decided to walk through the exhibition hall to see the clothes and household items on display for judging — and, Dougherty suspected, to give equal attention to those that were on sale. When the boys heard that there were also drawings, toys, and photographs to be viewed with a stereopticon, they made up their minds to go along with them, leaving McBrien and Dougherty to finish another cup of coffee.

"Do ye still think," McBrien asked, "that the Butcher'll make his appearance next month?"

It was on his mind, just as it had been on Dougherty's, in spite of the holiday atmosphere of the fair.

"I think so," Dougherty said. "If he doesn't, then I don't know what our next step will be. I can think of no way to track him down apart from catching him in the act. There is no other solution without a great deal more evidence than we have now."

"I saw O'Laughlin a few days back," he said. "There's an angry man, if ever I seen one. O' course, who could blame him? He's put up with a lot since Maddock come on the scene, being picked up every time something bothers the Captain."

"What brings O'Laughlin to mind?" Dougherty asked.

"I'm sorry to say it, but it was talking about the Butcher. I like O'Laughlin, but since ye told me Carter's ideas about him killing Brady, I find meself wondering. I know it don't seem likely, but, like ye've always said yerself, ye can't just set something aside because it don't happen to appeal to ye as an answer."

McBrien, Dougherty noticed, had a tendency to quote him back to himself whenever he was not paying close enough attention to one of his own "maxims." Could O'Laughlin be involved in any of this?

How odd, Dougherty thought almost immediately. Why was he so reluctant to consider O'Laughlin a suspect? He disliked the very thought, but could he discount it completely? Could he prove that O'Laughlin was beyond doubt *not* the Butcher? Was there anything they knew with certitude that could clearly exclude him?

And then it came to him. In fact, it should have been obvious. The night of Brady's wake when they had sat at Mrs. Corrigan's kitchen table, sipping the good Irish whiskey, McBrien had mentioned that O'Laughlin had seen action at the Dunkard Church in the battle of Antietam, the first battle in which Dougherty had ever taken part, the same day on which McBrien and he actually began to be friends. Wednesday, September 17, 1862.

That was also when young Berdine Griswald had been abducted and murdered in New York City, so O'Laughlin could not possibly be her killer. Which meant that he was not the killer of all the other women either. He could not be the Butcher. Nor was he likely to have killed Charlie Brady.

Wednesday, September 17... How odd... Evodia Zellner had died on January 17, which happened also to be a Wednesday. Dougherty's recollections were hazy after all these months, but he went back in his mind to the first newspaper accounts they had read, those papers preserved so carefully by Charlie Brady. He remembered how Jen and he had puzzled over the accounts, and how, in his passion for detail, he had wondered on just what day of the week Abiegeal Conroy had died. He could not find the almanac for 1860, so they had figured out that October 17 six years ago next week, when she had died so gruesomely, had been a Wednesday. Wednesday, October 17.

Three murders committed on a Wednesday which happened also to be the seventeenth day of the month? Dougherty wished he had immediate access to the notes they had made, but they were all in his office in Penrose Valley. He could not think of the dates of all the news reports, but, unless he was mistaken, there was not a single murder that had not occurred in the middle of a month, and he was suddenly willing to wager anything that every one of them had occurred on the seventeenth, and that the seventeenth had been, in every instance, a Wednesday.

Why the Butcher should have chosen to kill on that particular date, Dougherty could not begin to conjecture, but that explained it — why there had been no murder in March. For March 17 had not fallen on a Wednesday. It was a Thursday. He remembered it well. The Feast of Saint Patrick, and Jen had made a special meal in celebration. If he killed *only* on Wednesday the seventeenth of the month, then did he *always* kill on that date? Dougherty couldn't answer that without examining the calendars of the past few years. And if he did kill on that date — only and always on that date — then when would the seventeenth again fall on a Wednesday? His stomach churned and he felt ill. Next Wednesday would be October seventeenth!

"What's wrong, sir?" McBrien was alarmed, and Dougherty knew why. The blood had drained from his face. "Ye look like ye've seen a ghost."

He explained and McBrien had no trouble whatsoever agreeing with his theory. His new theory. This time he hoped that it was a theory that took into account all the necessary information — information in their possession the whole time. All of their deep concentration had been expended upon the items that had seemed most significant, and it was this minor factor, this most obvious factor, that they had overlooked. Not "they," he thought. He! *He had overlooked it.* He, who prided himself on his attention to detail. He must verify the dates to be certain, but in his heart he knew that he was right. And they had only five days left. He knew that the Butcher would kill again, and he was certain that he would try to do so in a way that would show them just how stupid they were!

The Diarist

October 10, 1866 — One week. I burn within, but the time is at hand. I must give full attention to the preparations. One pleasure at a time. Little boys must not be greedy, Sammy. Patience.

Chapter XIX: Eyes Now Permanently Closed

> O, that it were possible,
> We might but hold some two days' conference
> With the dead!
> John Webster (1580-1625)
> *The Duchess of Malfi* (1623) Act 4, sc. 2

[Friday, October 12, 1866]

It was near ten when Jen and Catherine Corrigan left the exhibition hall. They had promised each of the boys they could buy a toy, but they would do that later. Right now their minds were on something else entirely. All week long they had talked of little but the pacing and trotting races, and the first was scheduled to begin momentarily. They would be brokenhearted if they missed it.

It was as James had predicted, Jen thought. Delays and more delays, until it was half past ten before the first race got under way. By then her excitement at cheering for the favorite had been tempered by what she had just learned. As soon as they found them, Jen saw that both James and Sean McBrien were preoccupied and she wondered what had happened. At first neither said anything and she did not ask, but on their way to the track James told her.

"Jen, I truly apologize, but I must leave early. In fact, on the next train." He took his watch from his pocket. "Less than two hours from now."

"Oh, James, the boys will be so disappointed! You know how they've been looking forward to this... and Catherine Corrigan, too."

"Oh, no," he said, "they won't have to leave, nor will you. In fact, it would be best if they stayed here for the day and if you could stay with them. Sean will be here to escort you, and I'll join you on the way home."

The others were ahead of them, Sean McBrien and Mrs. Corrigan walking with their heads together in conversation, the two boys scampering along, their spirits bubbling as they alternately ran ahead then turned back to be sure the rest were following. Jen didn't think she had ever seen them so excited. And what was more, she was also enjoying every minute of it. No tears, no regrets!

"I must go to Mauch Chunk to see Judge Barrett."

"You mean today? Is he expecting you? You'd never mentioned anything about it."

"I hadn't intended to see him," he said. "He has no idea that I'm coming. But I must see him today, as soon as possible. I may not be able to contact him on Saturday or Sunday, and Monday may be too late to do what needs to be done."

She heard the urgency in his voice and, once he told her what he and McBrien had discussed, she agreed completely. This simply could not wait. There were only two passenger trains available, and the first left at 11:55. That would have him in Mauch Chunk within ten minutes, making it possible to catch Judge Barrett at his luncheon, which he often took at the American Hotel. If he missed that train, there would be no other until the 5:39, the one by which they had planned to return to Penrose Valley. That might be too late to find Judge Barrett, and, in any case, even if they found him that late, they would be stuck in Mauch Chunk for the night.

"Are you certain," she asked, "that all of the killings occurred on the seventeenth of the month? And that the day was always a Wednesday?"

"I'll have to go through all the reports and compare the dates with the calendars for those years; but I can't afford to do that first, before I see the Judge. I must act now. I'm certain that the courthouse will have copies of the almanacs for all the years. I can at least assure myself that every murder occurred in a month in which the seventeenth was a Wednesday. If so, then it is too much to attribute to coincidence. When we get home this evening, we can look through the newspaper accounts and determine the exact dates of each murder — at least, I hope that we can."

She sensed his remaining hesitance, but she agreed with him that he had to act, and he had to convince Judge Barrett to act.

"What I'll do is this," he said, "I'll arrange things with Judge Barrett as though they were all committed on the same date and day. When we get home, I'll determine the exact dates, and early tomorrow morning I can telegraph the results to the Judge."

"Telegraph? Is that a good idea? What about Owen Williams? Telling him anything is the same as telling the Captain. Do you want him to be aware of this?"

"No," he said, "not a good idea at all. I am acutely uncomfortable when it comes to trusting Captain Maddock, and, with the possible exception of Carter, I have no faith in the rest of his crowd. I will send the Judge a coded message. Owen Williams will be none the wiser, and, even if he reports to Captain Maddock, it will give him no information."

"I wish you could be with us for the day," she said, "but I know you're right. You must see him today. Would you like me to come with you?"

"I don't think so. I may spend most of the afternoon cooling my heels waiting to see the Judge, or I may see him as soon as I get there. In either case, the rest of the time is likely to be spent looking at almanacs and planning what to do next. That may take some time and you'd end up bored to tears."

"I'm glad at least that we took our bags to the station this morning," she said, "That will save us the inconvenience of having to pack."

"I'll take care of them," he said. "When I get to the station, I'll have them put on the early train for Hazle Creek Station. They'll be there when we get home. I'll be at the Mauch Chunk depot when you get there this evening and we can go home together."

He stayed for only one race, then hired a conveyance to the station. Mrs. Corrigan was surprised at his departure, but asked no explanation when Jen told her that a matter of some urgency had arisen and that he must go to Mauch Chunk and would meet them there later. Jen trusted Catherine fully, but they had told not even her about the Butcher.

Jen enjoyed the day, even though her mind kept going back to the coming Wednesday. She thought that Catherine Corrigan must be wondering if there was something wrong with her hearing, because more than once she caught Catherine looking at her quizzically, awaiting a response, and Jen had to ask her to repeat what she had just said.

Their train pulled into Mauch Chunk on time and there was James on the platform. Jen waved to him to let him know their carriage and he waved back. The train rolled to a stop, the steps were put down, and the reveling Chunkers from the fair alighted, talking, laughing, and carrying the things they had bought. A moment later, James was aboard, along with a few other passengers headed for points up the line, and had taken his seat with them.

"Did you have a good time?" he asked, and the next fifteen minutes or so were taken up with the boys' recounting of all they had seen and heard and eaten, but the steady clack-clack-clack and the rocking motion of the train soon lulled them into quiet and then into the lowering of eyelids and finally into a contented sleep.

"How did things go?" Jen asked.

"Quite well," he said. "We have some work to do this evening, but things went quite well indeed."

They talked no more about it for the rest of the ride. James held her hand, Sean McBrien and Catherine Corrigan talked quietly together, and the boys slept. All the stops along the way were quick ones, passengers transferred in and out at each depot, and it was 6:55 on the dot when the conductor called the stop for Hazle Creek Station and they were home. The days had been growing shorter, and it was dark when they claimed their luggage and found a boy to bring everything to their various homes on a pushcart while they walked. Sean and Catherine had their arms full, each of them carrying one of the boys, both of whom, Jen was sure, would wake up in their beds tomorrow and wonder how they had gotten there.

They entered the house through the back door, so it was not until Jen finally went into James's office to collect the articles and other documents that she noticed, lying on the floor inside the front door, a white envelope addressed to James. It had been mailed from

Philadelphia and slipped under the door during their absence. There was no return address. Jen's first thought was that it was from Doctor Brownson, but it wasn't. James read it and laughed.

"Take a look," he said. "I wonder when the poor man ever gets home. He has been traveling the east coast since before the war. It must be a lonely occupation, going from town to town all the way from Boston to Washington and back again, staying in hotels, accumulating armies of acquaintances, but never having time to find real friends." He gave her the letter.

> Dear Doctor Dougherty,
>
> It is with pleasure that I write to inform you that I expect to be in your area during the week of the 15th inst. and would be honored should you be able to receive me at some time during my stay in Penrose Valley. It was with regret that the last time I had not the opportunity to renew our acquaintance and inform you of the latest surgical implements of the Tiemann Company. All are, as your previous experience will have confirmed, of the highest quality and workmanship and therefore of the greatest utility to the physician and the greatest benefit to his patients.
>
> I am, as is so often the case, in transit, and, therefore, can offer you no address at which to respond, but I hope that you will be available during my stay. It is with sentiments of esteem that I sign myself
>
> > Yr. Obedient servant,
> > Michael Appelby
> > Sales Representative
> > Tiemann Company

She knew what James meant, but she had to smile, too. Poor Mr. Appelby had the worst luck in timing his visits to Penrose Valley. Even if he succeeded in visiting James, he would find him with his mind on things other than the purchase of surgical implements.

It was an hour before they were unpacked and Sean McBrien was at the door, ready to hear what Judge Barrett had said and to help figure out the precise days on which each murder had taken place.

"The Judge had some reservations," James said, "but not enough to prevent his going along with our concerns. He wants me to let him know by tomorrow whether murders took place in every instance when Wednesday fell on the seventeenth and only in those instances. If so, he is ready to act."

"And, providing it's true, then what does he propose to do about it? Had he a plan?"

"Little enough, I fear," James said. "He will send out warnings about the possibility of a new crime and make sure that steps are taken to increase vigilance all along the line from Hazleton to Allentown. I explained Doctor Brownson's concern that the murderer is likely to strike in Penrose Valley, just to show his cleverness, but none of us thought it prudent to focus our attention here alone. We agreed that he will likely strike somewhere along the rail line, but no stop can be ignored."

"I know," Jen said, "but the more I think about it, the more I am convinced that Doctor Brownson is right. This murderer is terribly sure of himself, and he wants us to know that. He wants to rub our noses in it."

So they settled down at the kitchen table with a pot of coffee to keep them awake and the added stimulus of being finally hot on the trail of the truth. They set aside the murders of Abiageal Conroy and Evodia Zellner, since they were certain of those. October 17, 1860, and January 17, 1866, were both Wednesdays.

James had been almost certain that the murder of Berdine Griswald in New York City in 1862 had been on September 17, which they knew with certitude had been a Wednesday. From the papers they learned that Berdine Griswald's body had been discovered, still warm, just an hour or so after midnight on September 18, proving that she had died on September 17.

Emeline Carding, the New York prostitute killed in April of 1861, merited almost no attention in the press, but even that little proved enough. The lone article was dated April 25, 1861, and said that Miss Carding had been "last seen one week ago yesterday," making the day of her disappearance April 17 — which was a Wednesday.

In 1861, on July 23, the newspapers reported the disappearance of Miss Cornelia Vandeveer, "who as of today has been missing for six days." July 17. Another Wednesday.

The victim of December, 1862, the first to die in Washington, was never identified; but the report appeared in the press on December 19 and stated that her body had been found early the day before. The time of death was determined to have been sometime on the evening preceding the body's discovery — Wednesday, December 17.

Miss Theodora Miles' body was found late on June 18, 1863, and the police surgeon placed the time of her death at about twenty-four hours prior to that, on Wednesday, June 17.

Miss Isabelle Semple's body was found at the beef depot on February 28, 1864, so decomposed as to make it all but impossible to approximate the time of her death. But she had disappeared on February 17, as attested to by her parents and by the woman and her coachman who had seen Miss Semple leave in a buggy. That was a Wednesday, and, although there was no sure proof, they could not doubt that she had died on the same day.

When the story of Olivia Wharton had appeared, the time of her disappearance was placed on August 17, 1864, although her body was not found until five days later behind Saint Patrick's Catholic Church. The abduction and, they were sure, the killing as well had been on a Wednesday.

The last of the Washington murders was reported on May 19, 1865, when the body of Edna Krantz was found outside the Old Capitol Prison, having been left there during the night of May 17-18. She was last seen alive the preceding morning, a Wednesday.

In all of those years, from 1860 until 1866, the Butcher had struck down a victim every time that the seventeenth day of a month had fallen on a Wednesday, and only on those days. Charlie Brady's murder was the one exception, but then his death had been a matter of expedience for the Butcher, and could not be expected to fit the pattern of the other deaths. The Butcher had a logic of his own, just as they had predicted. In the morning James would send to Judge Barrett a telegram saying, "The fair was a success," the code they had agreed upon to let him know that they now had no doubt that the Butcher would strike again on the coming Wednesday.

It was in studying the documents this one final time that Jen noticed something she had seen before but had not realized its significance. It was in one of the handwritten testimonials in reference to the death of Theodora Miles.

"Look at this," she said to James, pointing to its last two sentences.

"I don't believe it!" he said. He read it again and slowly lowered the sheet.

"Well, fer Heaven's sake, Major," McBrien said, "are ye intending then to test the extent o' me patience? Or are ye going to say what it was ye seen in that sheet o' paper?"

"I'm sorry," James said. "Here — look at this. The last two sentences."

McBrien read them aloud: "The investigator was some new lieutenant in Baker's detective bureau — Gardner, I think, was his name. I never met him."

He was puzzled and clearly exasperated with the two of them.

"Well, then, what in the name o' God does it mean?" he asked.

"I apologize," Jen said, "I realize now the source of your confusion. We had told you about the Philadelphia policeman who had investigated the Conroy death and then later went to New York. We hoped to learn something from him, but we never found him. I think that we never told you his name. It was Gardner."

Gardner... Was it the same man? They had no proof, but it seemed too much to charge to coincidence. And so James had one more task to perform before the day ended. He must prepare a letter to ask Doctor Brownson to find out all he could about Samuel Gardner, including a physical description. Was it possible that Gardner was now in Penrose Valley under another name? And was he the Butcher? Or was he but one more person in pursuit of the Butcher? They would have the letter hand delivered by a conductor on the train so that an answer could be returned before Wednesday. They could not risk the telegraph.

If Gardner was the Butcher, and if Doctor Brownson could describe him for them, then they were on their way to ending his string of murders. But, as Jen pointed out, if he could not help, then they were baffled unless they could subscribe to the beliefs of the

Spiritualists and hold a conference with the dead. So far as they knew, their quarry had been clearly seen only by eleven pairs of eyes — all of them eyes now permanently closed.

Chapter XX: The One With the Gray Beard

Tis a naughty night to swim in.
>William Shakespeare (1564-1616)
>*King Lear* (1605) Act III, sc. 4

[Wednesday, October 17, 1866]

It was early, not yet six-thirty, and Jen was all alone in the kitchen. She had just added a scoop of coal to the stove, stirred up the fire to take some of the chill from the morning air, and was at the window looking up at the mountain. Actually, she was looking in the direction of the mountain, but its bulk was hidden in the morning fog. She crossed her arms, hugged herself with a little shudder, and huddled deeper into the warm woolen folds of the brilliant orange shawl she'd thrown over her shoulders, its brightness bringing some cheer to the morning gloom. It was a dank, dreary day, even though it had not yet actually begun to rain. What a miserable night it had been to camp out!

The coffee was almost ready. Its aroma filled the room, and she looked forward to a strong, hot cup. She cut two slices of bread from the loaf and put them into the wire toaster. She had to smile, because one of the slices was the heel of the loaf, which James and she both liked. Today she hadn't had to race him for it. The coals glowed brightly as she set aside one of the stove lids and put the toaster in its place.

She looked again toward the mountainside, wishing she could see the golds and scarlets that had given so much pleasure these past two weeks. The next day or two would probably reduce them to a drab brown. Summer was gone. Soon the branches would be bare and the dead leaves trampled underfoot. She shuddered again, but this time not from the cold. Today was the day, the Butcher's day, and they had no idea when or where he would strike, but none of them doubted that it would happen, and the thought chilled her. She examined the toasting bread. The first side was done. She flipped it over.

She was expecting a telegram and hoped it would not be long delayed. They had received one the day before from Judge Barrett. It had come quite early, just after the telegraph office had opened. James had torn open the envelope, looked at the message, and handed it to her. It was direct and to the point, no explanations offered:

DOCTOR DOUGHERTY. YOUR PRESENCE AND THAT OF MCBRIEN URGENTLY REQUIRED IN MAUCH CHUNK THIS EVENING. WILL EXPLAIN WHEN YOU ARRIVE. JUDGE BARRETT.

She had gone with them to the Hazle Creek Station and seen them off on the 2:45, hoping their return would be speedy. This day's first train from Mauch Chunk would arrive in Penrose Valley at 1:30. She buttered the toast, spread some of Mrs. Corrigan's elderberry jelly on it, and sat down to her breakfast.

It was 8:30 when the knock came at the kitchen door. She was in her special room reading and enjoying a final cup of coffee. Had anyone asked her at that moment, she could not have said what she was reading, so distracted was she by what they were sure was about to happen. She opened the door to a young lad, skinny as a rail, all knees and elbows, and known to one and all as Joey Beanpole. He held out the telegram tightly clutched in his right hand and removed his cap with the other. He looked so chilly.

"This just come in, Missus. Brung it here right away."

She thanked him and got him a few pennies and a handful of candy for his trouble and received the reward of a broad smile. As soon as he left, she tore open the envelope.

MUST BOTH REMAIN IN MAUCH CHUNK ONE MORE NIGHT. CANNOT BE AVOIDED. WILL RETURN TO PENROSE VALLEY THURSDAY FIRST TRAIN. JAMES.

So there was the latest word, probably conveyed to Captain Maddock before it had been to her. If Maddock had already seen this, and she was sure he had, what conclusions would he have drawn? That the killer of Evodia Zellner was not expected to strike in Penrose Valley? Would it cause him and his men to be more attentive to this day's events here at home? Or less? More additions to the ever growing list of questions, and none at all to the list of answers.

She spent the next two hours reading through the newspaper accounts one more time and finding in them nothing new. Then she reviewed a list they had drawn up a few days earlier. The town of Penrose Valley is not a large one and she had come to know many, if not all, of its people, especially during these past few months. The question in her mind was this: Who would the Butcher kill, if he killed in this town? And so they had made the list. Obviously, they could eliminate all the men. The Butcher had murdered Charlie Brady, but that was not his usual pattern. They removed from consideration women older than the mid-thirties and younger than eighteen or so. They also set aside those who were very tall, very heavy, or very thin, and those with other than dark hair — she hoped that her own red-brown hue would eliminate her. She had no way of being sure that the final list was complete, but she hoped they had thought of most of the possibilities. In this town of less than a thousand souls, there were, by her reckoning, fourteen who fit the requirements, including Catherine Corrigan, with her dark hair, fair skin, and full figure so preferred by the Butcher — and Jen had often enough remarked her youthful appearance. Mrs. Corrigan's resemblance to Mary Conroy had been evident from the first.

She thought the morning would never end. The silence of the house, usually so restful, was now oppressive. She did some housework, but it went all too quickly, and her heart wasn't really in it. She made some lunch and tried to eat slowly, until at last this endless morning actually did end, and she decided to walk to the station to see if there were any messages on the 1:30 train from Mauch Chunk. They had not yet had an answer from Doctor Brownson about Detective Samuel Gardner, and she hoped it might come today. It could reveal something crucial, even at this eleventh hour.

It was almost 1:30 when she set out for the station. The heavy morning fog had long since dissipated; but the day remained overcast and cool, so she put on her gray cloak and bonnet, realizing once she was outside just how much her choice fit the day's mood. There were few people about and she found herself wishing that James were with her.

McBrien's pharmacy was closed, the shades in the front windows pulled part way down. The day was dark enough that one might have expected to see lights, at least in the windows of the second floor where McBrien had his living quarters. Of course, there were none. At the side of the building were the steep stairs that led to the upper entrance. She didn't know why, but that flight of narrow wooden steps leading to that darkened apartment emphasized more than ever the sense of desolation that she had been feeling all day. Sometimes she was inclined to regret her overly active imagination.

There were lights in Mr. Beverley Arkwright's office at the mining company headquarters and someone glanced out the window as she went by. She couldn't tell who it was. On the first floor, clerks sat at their desks, heads bent over their work, all absorbed in the business of the company, no one speaking or paying attention to anyone else. There was light also in the windows of the police headquarters, but she could not see who was within. She wondered if Maddock had assigned anyone to guard the railroad station or anywhere else in town. He might well allow his disdain for James and McBrien to outweigh what should have been his most pressing concern.

As she drew near the station, she heard the double toot of the whistle and realized that the 1:30 had already come in and was now leaving on its way to Beaver Meadow. A lone figure emerged from the station, a carpet bag in one hand and a clumsy looking wooden sample case in the other. His posture bore witness to its considerable weight. He set it down for a moment to readjust his grip on its handle, caught his breath, and then picked it up again and stepped into the street, heading in the direction of the hotel. It was Mr. Michael Appelby, the surgical tool salesman, which explained the weight of the case.

She felt ashamed of herself as she did it, but she purposely slowed her pace and looked back over her shoulder as though waiting for someone to catch up to her. Not a very polite thing to do, she realized, but she was truly not of a mind to speak to him at the moment, and hoped that, with her cape and bonnet to disguise her, he would not recognize her. He was a pleasant enough fellow, even kindly, but he was a dedicated salesman and could talk a tin ear off a dead cat, and she was simply not in the mood for conversation. When she looked back in his direction, he was headed away from her toward the hotel. She imagined they would hear from him soon enough. She hoped that James would be back by the time he came to see them, so that the poor man would not think that James was purposely leaving town each time he came to sell something.

She felt a first touch of fine mist as she reached the station and knew they would have real rain before the afternoon was over. She opened the door and entered, just as Mr. Appelby entered the hotel across the street and shut the door behind him.

"Mrs. Dougherty! What a pleasure to see you. How are you today?"

"Fine, thank you, Mr. Canby, and I hope that you are, too."

Mr. Canby was the station master, a polite man with ever a pleasant greeting. He knew everyone in town, even those who seemed never to use the train. He was all alone at the moment.

"You weren't expecting the Doctor on this train, were you?" he asked.

"No, I wasn't. I came for another reason. I was hopeful that the conductor of the 1:30 might have brought a letter for my husband."

"That he did. Here it is."

He handed her the envelope addressed to James from Doctor Brownson. It was a real test of patience not to look at it on the spot; but she did not. Instead, she thanked him, put the envelope into the pocket of her cloak, and walked home at a ladylike pace, proud of her self-discipline — which ended the moment she shut the kitchen door, threw her cloak over the back of a chair, and ripped open the envelope.

> My dear Dougherty,
>
> My sincerest apology for the delay in responding to your query. It was my intention to respond by Monday, but what I took to be the acquisition of some straightforward information, eventuated in a task not easy at all.

You requested a physical description of Gardner. That proved simple enough, although not especially helpful. Two local policemen who knew him in 1860 said he was then in his thirties. But I examined his records at police headquarters and his year of birth was listed as 1834. If that is accurate, then he was 26 years of age in 1860, but looked older. But I doubt the truthfulness of that date for reasons that will be clear presently.

For now, allow me to continue with the description. He was near six feet in height and about 175 pounds in weight. His hair was dark, as were his eyes, and he had a moustache and, for a period of time just before he left for New York, a beard as well. He was of even disposition, interested in his work and good at it. There were occasions when his interrogation of suspects revealed an undercurrent of cruelty, but no more (perhaps even less) than one might discern in many of his co-workers. In sum, he was not so very different in looks or disposition from many others, with little physically or in any other way to distinguish him — a less than satisfactory description and the reason why I said that it was not especially helpful.

On the other hand, when I examined his personal records as received at the time of his hiring, what was most informative was that they offered, in the end, no information at all. He gave as his place of origin an address on South Street which he described as the home of his parents. No one there, however, has ever heard of him or them. The address he gave is real, but has for the past fifty years and more been inhabited by another family entirely.

He claimed to have been on the police forces in Boston and Pittsburgh, yet telegrams brought word that he had never been heard of in either. Hence, I do not know that we can trust even the date of birth or any of the information that he had so willingly supplied here in Philadelphia.

He also presented letters of reference from Boston and Pittsburgh, but they are now proven spurious and their signatories totally fictitious.

I contacted New York again and learned that he gave them as reference only Philadelphia, from which, of course, he was able to produce real letters. I contacted Washington and received nothing in return, not even a written refusal to answer. Typical government inefficiency — or arrogance!

The result is, therefore, unsatisfactory as to information; but most helpful in that it shows the man a charlatan. I had thought for a time, as I think you had also, that Gardner might have been in pursuit of the Butcher. I am now more inclined to the notion that he is the murderer, although I have not changed my opinion that he is with you in Penrose Valley and that he will strike there soon.

Please do me the great favor to convey to your charming spouse my best wishes and those of Mrs. Brownson as well, and be assured of the felicitations and continued willingness to assist in your endeavors of this,

                Yr. Obedient servant,
                Carl Gustavus Brownson

He was right about the physical description. It fit too many. She could think of a number of men in town who could be so described, including all but one of Maddock's men, and she was sure that more thought would produce more candidates. But she knew none of them well enough to know their dispositions, nor did she know what backgrounds they claimed.

So she was back to waiting. James had asked her to stay in the house for this day, and she had made an exception to go to the station. She saw no need to make another, even though she had run no risk so far as she could tell, apart from the possibility of being talked to death by poor Mr. Appelby.

She went back to her reading, with no more success than before. Suddenly she started as she heard a tap at the window and realized that she had dozed off. What she heard was the rain which had now begun in earnest and was being blown against the panes with enough force that it sounded like hail. The clock said four-thirty, but the heavy black clouds made it seem much later than that.

The kitchen was dark and the fire needed coal. She added it, then lit the lamp and decided it was time to think about supper. She was not especially hungry, but knew that she would be once she smelled food cooking. She took yesterday's beef stew from the icebox to heat in a saucepan. She filled the kettle for tea, sliced the bread, and covered it with a cloth to keep it soft.

When she heard the tapping at the door, it was so gentle that at first she took it for the rain again, but soon realized that someone was there. She opened the door to the last person she might have expected to see.

"Hello, Mrs. Dougherty. Our mom told us to come and see you for a while. She had to go somewhere and the men aren't home from the mines yet. Can we come in?"

The voice under the umbrella was that of Daniel Corrigan and, since there were four feet protruding from the bottom, she concluded that little Michael was under there, too.

"You certainly can," she said. "My goodness, your feet are all wet."

She helped them off with their shoes and set them by the stove to dry. She set out two more bowls for stew and cut some more bread. She took the butter from the icebox and put that on the table, too. And as she did so, she asked what had brought them here.

"It was because of the man," Daniel said.

"Yes," Michael said, "It was that man we don't like."

"What man?" she asked.

"You know," Michael said, "That mean one."

"He means the policeman," Daniel said.

"The policeman? Your mother went with one of the policemen?"

Jen knew that McBrien had not told Catherine the story of the Butcher, but he had certainly warned her to stay home for the day.

"Yes," Daniel said. "He came to the house to get her."

"Only he really didn't come to the house," Michael added.

"No," Daniel said, "he sent a boy to fetch her. He waited outside."

Her heart thumped. Her mind screamed, No, no, no — all the while trying to stay externally calm for the sake of the children.

"Do you know what he wanted?" she asked.

"He said she had to come, because Mr. McBrien was hurt and was asking for her, and that got her all upset," Daniel said.

McBrien hurt? McBrien was with James!

"She started to cry," Michael said, and his own eyes began to look wet. "She was scared."

"Did he say what happened?" she asked.

"No," Daniel said. "He sent the boy. He stayed in his carriage. I think he didn't want to get wet. His cape was all up around his face and he had a big hat. It was like that army hat Doctor Dougherty wears sometimes."

He meant the old slouch hat, the soft crowned hat so useful in weather like today's. The hat with the bullet hole that James was so proud of. The hat with the brim wide enough to conceal one's face.

"So you couldn't see which policeman it was?"

"Oh, yes, we could see," Michael said. "It was that mean one. That one that chases us away if we go near the police station. That one with the gray beard."

Dear Lord, she thought, this cannot be. Not Catherine...

"When did this happen?" she asked.

"Just now," Daniel said, "Just before we came over here. Mom got in his carriage and went with him, and we came straight here."

Jen knew she had to do something, but what?

"Boys," she said, "I am going to put your stew in bowls for you, and the bread and butter are right here. You may have as much as you like. I must go out for a while, but I will be back as soon as I can. Will you be all right here?"

They both nodded, perhaps a trifle unsurely, but she knew that they would be fine. It wouldn't be the first time they had been alone for a while, although it was the first time in this house and that probably made them uncertain. But she had to take the chance.

She got into her cloak, put a dark shawl over her head, and got an umbrella. She thought of taking Brady's gun from James's office, but decided against it. It would take too long to load and, besides, she was not so very good a shot. But she could not just stay here in the house and allow something terrible to happen. She had to find help, because she was sure that Catherine Corrigan was in mortal danger and she now knew that the Butcher was that "mean" policeman, Maddock, the one with the gray beard!

Chapter XXI: A Mistake

> The smylere with the knyfe under the cloke.
>   Geoffrey Chaucer (c. 1334-1400)
>   *The Canterbury Tales,* "The Knight's Tale" (1387)

[Wednesday, October 17, 1866]

It was after five and it was dark. The rain had begun to abate, the gusts of wind were fewer; but, although the clouds rushed eastward, there was nothing behind them but more clouds. There would be a half moon, but it would offer no illumination. She held her shawl clasped close at her chin with one hand and her umbrella with the other. Now that she was outside the cheerful warmth of the kitchen and into the wet and dark of night, it occurred to her that in her rush to do something about the plight of Catherine Corrigan, she really did not know just what she should do.

The first thing was to find them. She did not know where to begin, but she had notions about the places most likely. Near the railroad station perhaps? She went in that direction.

The houses were lighted, their inhabitants oblivious to the drama unfolding just beyond their doors. She moved slowly along the street, afraid to go too quickly lest she pass them by in the dark somewhere along the way. She peered into cross streets and alleys, her eyes straining to penetrate the blackness, past the occasional squares of pale light cast on the ground by a dim illumination coming from curtained windows. She was about halfway to the station when she heard movement in the alley off to her left. She went cautiously in that direction. The sound stopped. So did she. She waited, listening. There it was again. A rustling, a scraping. She went deeper into the dark. No windows faced onto this dead-end alley, no pale squares of light to encourage her, just deeper murk and wisps of fog that trailed along the ground like ghost fingers. Then, with a rush and a growl, a large black dog swept past her skirts, his teeth bared, his ears back, but his tail between his legs, more frightened of her than she was of him, although her shortness of breath told her that she had expected something far more fearful. She heard nothing else. She stood stock still, hardly trusting herself to move. Gradually her heart slowed. Her breathing returned to normal. She went back to Main Street, knees shaky, hands trembling.

There was no significant illumination nearer than the station, where the gaslights were, brightening only the first few blocks of Main Street, from the station to just past the mining company headquarters and the police station. She still saw nothing of interest, but then she was not likely to see what she was looking for out under the lights. If anywhere, they would be behind the buildings, in the dark shadows, watching. If she hoped to find them, she too must take to the shadows.

She saw the mining company's offices ahead of her. The whole first floor was shrouded in inky blackness, but a light burned behind the dark drapes of Mr. Beverley Arkwright's office windows, barely discernible from the street. Why, she wondered, was he still at work at this hour? It made no difference. She dismissed the question from her mind and turned left, into the alley. She edged into its depths, pausing, straining to hear.

She heard not a sound. He was quick, silent, efficient. The gloved hand closed over her mouth before she made the slightest noise. His other arm encircled her waist as he pulled her roughly into the deepest of the shadows. She felt his warm breath against the back of her neck and smelled the earthy odor of the wet wool coat whose coarseness scraped harshly against her cheek. She dropped the umbrella. Her shawl slipped away from her hair and the chill rain splashed onto her face. Drops ran down her neck from the brim of his slouch hat as he whispered her name. She went totally still.

* * *

It had seemed like a week, but it was actually not yet thirty-six hours since Judge Barrett's telegram had arrived summoning McBrien and Dougherty to Mauch Chunk. They were convinced that the Butcher would strike in Penrose Valley, and they knew full well that the telegram would get to Maddock as quickly as it came to them. Word of it might even find its way to the Butcher and their absence could become his license to run free on his chosen day. Leaving town was a great risk, but one did not take lightly a direct order from His Honor. The killer would realize that too, and would know that they had to go, like it or not. Dougherty had thought it best to be sure there was no misunderstanding. He asked McBrien to go to the telegraph office and send a message:

> JUDGE BARRETT. IS MAUCH CHUNK TRIP NECESSARY. QUERY. PLEASE CONFIRM. DOUGHERTY

McBrien had waited there looking out the window, his back toward Williams. Within ten minutes a wire confirmed the earlier message. The Judge must have been in his office, expecting to hear from them. A smirking Owen Williams wrote out the answer and handed it over, just itching to get rid of McBrien and deliver the news to Maddock.

> DOCTOR DOUGHERTY. MESSAGE CONFIRMED. MAUCH CHUNK THIS EVENING. BARRETT

There was no mistake. McBrien and Dougherty were scheduled to be in Mauch Chunk until at least the time of the Wednesday morning train. McBrien was barely out of sight, when Owen Williams put a note on the door indicating that he would back in a few minutes, and, with a furtive glance up and down the street, stepped over to the office of the Coal and Iron Police and slipped inside.

When Jen had gone with them to the station on Tuesday to see them off, they had seen Maddock. He never spoke to them, just paced the station platform in full uniform, his right hand on the butt of his holstered revolver. Dougherty hated the thought of leaving Jen in Penrose Valley alone, but he had to. He hoped that by the next day this whole business would be over and they could get back to their normal lives.

"I suppose he is here to see that Owen Williams told him the truth." Jen spoke quietly, indicating Maddock with a tilt of her head.

"Just good business sense, don't ye know," McBrien said, "See ye're getting full value fer yer investment. I doubt Owen Williams is performing this service out o' the goodness o' his heart. He's far too frugal fer that."

They were ready to leave, and Dougherty was full of misgivings. Should they stay here? Was Jen at risk if it was known that he was not in town? Was he doing the right thing? She must have read his mind, or at least seen it in his face.

"Don't worry. Everything will be fine. This must be done," she said, and took his hand in hers. "I will be perfectly safe."

"Tomorrow, Jen, don't go out of the house. Whatever happens, let it happen without you." Even as he said it, he knew that she would not be content simply to hide, but he was sure that there would be no reason for her to go out and she was not foolish. She nodded.

The train pulled out and she waved, just as she had in January before the Butcher's last murder. Maddock watched, then turned and left the station without so much as a glance in Jen's direction. The chugging engine picked up speed. The train would reach Weatherly shortly, and arrival in Mauch Chunk was scheduled for 4:25.

Ten minutes later they got off in Weatherly, bags in hand, and stayed in the depot until the train had pulled out without them. Once the station emptied, they put their overcoats and suit coats into their bags and withdrew haversacks and their old army overcoats, better suited to what they had to do. The bags they put in storage at the station and kept only the haversacks that held their revolvers and enough food to tide them over. Then they waited.

It was past 3:30 when they set out on foot along the railroad tracks back toward Penrose Valley. They made no effort to hurry, timing their arrival as planned. It was nearly dark as they approached Hazle Creek Station, but they left the tracks before the station was in sight. They avoided town, passing through the woods to the east and meeting Hazle Creek north of town, to follow it up along the sloping curve of the valley where no one was likely to be at this time of day. There they made camp for the night, a branch lean-to to ward off the damp, even though it offered no warmth. They lit no fire, but ate their food cold and drank water from the stream, fresh and clear here, above the corrupting influence of the waste from the mines.

"Do ye think this will work?" McBrien asked.

"I only wish I knew," Dougherty responded, as they lit their cigars and settled down to endure a long, cold night. They had been unable to take blankets. They simply took up too much room, and they wanted the bags to seem no more than what anyone would have taken for a single night; so they huddled in their coats and waited for morning.

Morning... It came with a damp that went right to the bones. Dawn crept up gradually, no burst of morning sun, just a blackness that faded slowly into lighter shades of gray. The fog kept them hidden and there was almost no likelihood that their position would be discovered. No one ever came this way to work and, on a day such as this, none of the town's boys would be here to play or gather wood. They decided that it was safe to build a fire. It might have been seen at some distance in the dark of the night, but not in this morning's fog. They had bread and cheese to tide them over and it would taste better toasted. They hunted up dry wood, shaved tinder, and soon had the first small flame bursting forth.

"Ye know, sir, I think I'm getting too old fer this camping out business."

McBrien was not yet forty and was in excellent physical condition, but Dougherty knew what he meant. Even at his age he felt the stiffness and knew it was going to take a while to get back to comfortable movement.

"So am I," Dougherty said. "A year of civilian life must have softened us."

For almost four years they had camped in far worse places than this, but it doesn't take long to get out of practice. The fire helped and so did the food. And then they waited. They were not far from town, but they saw nothing of it beyond the trees, even though, when the wind blew in their direction, they heard the fog-muffled sounds of the distant breaker machinery, the thunk-thunk of the steam engines, and the squeal of coal being crushed.

They were taking a chance, and they knew it, but it still seemed the best thing to do. The Butcher had struck before in broad daylight, and he might even now. But Dougherty did not think so. The town was too small; he would be too visible. He was more likely to wait for the coming of night. That meant that they must wait also. The day dragged on, each minute longer than the one before it. They did not begin their descent into the town until past four o'clock, timing their arrival to coincide with that of the night. So far as they knew, no one had seen them.

Where would they find him? His usual method was to convince his victim to come willingly and then to take her to a place where he could complete his task. He could go out of town, toward the mine or the breaker, but that, Dougherty thought, would be too risky. Since the strikes of the past summer, civilian guards still patrolled those areas at night to prevent sabotage. There were not many guards, but they moved about constantly and their presence was unpredictable. To go out there at night in a buggy would be to court discovery. In fact, to be seen or heard anywhere out of town in the dark on a night such as this could not fail to draw attention and suspicion. It was more likely that he would take his victim to some dark area of town, some place with the cover of woods, perhaps. For that reason, they intended to position themselves somewhere outside the area lighted by the gaslights, and there listen for the sound of a carriage.

The dark came quickly once it began. Even on a clear day, night moved in rapidly once the sun set behind the mountain to the town's west. With clouds and rain it was even faster, so they took up their positions later than they had intended. That bothered Dougherty, but it was too late to change anything. Still, what if he had already acted? It didn't bear thinking about.

He was on one side of Main Street, McBrien somewhere on the other. Now and again someone moved along the street, people they knew hurrying home, none of them in carriages, all of them thinking only of getting in out of this miserable weather. Now and again voices could be heard or sounds of laughter or argument coming from behind closed doors and windows.

"Jimmy! Paddy! Get in here fer yer supper! I'll not be telling yez again!"

"Ye shoulda seen it... Ye'd'a laughed out loud..."

"Don't sit there like a lump... I can use some help..."

"I seen Mamie today. She's looking a lot better..."

"The lazy bugger! He don't care if he does his share o' the work, but he damn well sees to it he gets the same pay as the rest of us..."

Bits and pieces of daily life. Snatches of conversation. No sounds of strife or fear, just family conversation, family arguments. Nothing to point to the Butcher. Then someone entered the alley, moving cautiously, taking a step then stopping to listen, someone not wanting to be heard. Dougherty drew back into the shadows and waited. He could not see who it was until they were no more than three or four feet away from each other. Recognition dawned and he acted.

He stepped from the shadows, put his arm around her waist to pull her deeper into the dark, and covered her mouth so that she would not make a noise and give away their position. Her umbrella fell to the ground as he whispered into her ear.

"Jen... It's James. Relax."

She went limp immediately, and he knew that she had, for a moment, been terrified. But she had recognized his voice and was still, although he could feel her shiver.

"Jen, what in the world are you doing here?" he whispered. "I thought that you were going to stay inside the house until this was over."

"I thought so, too," she answered as James retrieved her fallen umbrella. "Something made that impossible. Catherine Corrigan was taken from her home by a man in a carriage. That's why I came. I've been looking for you and McBrien, Thank God I've found you!"

"When was she taken?"

"I should say not more than a half hour ago. Her boys came to our house and told me. They are there now."

"Why did she go? Was it someone she knew?"

"The man in the carriage sent a boy to her door to tell her to get into the carriage, because something was wrong with McBrien. She went with him."

"Did Judge Barrett send the telegram this morning to say that we were to remain in Mauch Chunk?"

"He did," she said. "It came in a little after 8:00 this morning, just as he had agreed. I'm sure that word was passed to Maddock that neither of you would be home until tomorrow."

"Do you know who the man in the carriage was?"

"The boys said that it was the mean policeman, the one with the beard. They didn't see him clearly, but they knew he was a policeman, so he must have been in uniform. And they saw his beard, even though he had on a slouch hat and a cloak pulled up about himself. James, it was Maddock!"

"I'll find McBrien. He's somewhere in the alley on the other side of Main Street. You'll have to go home. The boys will be terrified if they are too long alone in a strange house. They'll need you to be with them if the worst happens. That's what we must try to prevent."

God bless her, he thought, she did not argue, she did not discuss the matter further. She knew the truth of what he said. She kissed him, told him to hurry, and then she headed back in the direction from which she had come, moving quickly and sticking to the shadows. He knew she would be frightened for him, but not a word of that did she speak, looking back only once, and then lost in the haze and the dark, as though never there at all.

He moved further from the lights, using the alley which ran parallel to Main Street, and crossed over only when he was relatively sure of not being seen. In the alley across the way, he moved slowly, quietly, waiting. He knew that McBrien would see him.

"I'm here, sir," the voice said out of a pocket of deep shadows between two sheds belonging to one of the stores that fronted on Main.

"Have ye seen something, then?"

"I saw Jen," he said, and told him all that she had said.

"I'll kill the bastard if anything happens to Catherine. What are we gonna do?"

"I have an idea," Dougherty said. "Do you still agree with what we decided earlier? That he won't risk leaving town in a carriage, and that he can't very well take her anywhere without one?"

"I'm surer of it the more I think about it," he said, "but where in the name o' God can we begin looking?"

"I've thought of one place," Dougherty said. "If I am right, then we have a good chance of saving her before he does any damage. I think that he takes his time and enjoys the anticipation of the act before he ever does anything. I suspect that he talks and watches, wanting to see their fear. That is why he needs a hidden place for what he does." He could not bring himself to say "kill" or "torture" or any of the words that did not need to be said anyway. They both knew what the Butcher did. Dougherty also knew that McBrien was as aware as was he of what it meant if his theory of the Butcher's location was in error.

"I'll go along with that, Major. We've got to do something, and no matter what it is, I know we could be wrong. We'll just pray that we're not."

"There is one building in town that Maddock knows without doubt will be empty, one building where he is not likely to be disturbed the whole night through."

"My God!" The comprehension dawned, and Dougherty could hear it in his voice even without being able to see his face. "Me own house, is it?"

"It is," Dougherty said, "and I think he would use it just to prove how clever he is and how stupid we are. Do we go there?"

"We do," he said.

They set out, moving quietly, but taking not nearly as much care to remain unseen. McBrien's store, which was also his house, was only a few blocks down the street. They were there in minutes. They stopped in the alley, behind the tool shed and outhouse and examined the area. A buggy stood in the shadows. The horse had a nose bag and munched contentedly, dry enough under the overhang of the outside stair. There were no lights to be seen, but of course that was to be expected. If he was here, he would certainly have come earlier and made sure that the windows were covered so that he could use lights undetected, and he would probably have gone to the upper story, since the first floor had the large store windows in the front and would have been entirely too risky, even with their shades drawn.

"How do ye want to go about this, sir?"

His voice shook, but he was ready to act and he would be in control of himself, as Dougherty knew from past experience in battle.

"I suggest that one of us go in through the kitchen door on the first floor and up the inside stairs. The other will go up the outside stairs to the door on the second floor. When we are both in place, we rush in as quickly and as loudly as possible and attack him from two sides. We'll have to be careful about shooting, so as not to hit Catherine or each other, but getting at him that way may confuse him and prevent his escape. Do you agree?"

"I do," he said, "and I think that I'd better be the one to go in through the kitchen. It'll be dark in there, and if ye ain't used to the place, yer liable to knock something over and warn him."

They both realized that if he heard them he might well kill her immediately and try to escape, and they had to stop that.

"That's what we'll do. We need to get into place and then both move at once. Does the door at the top of the inside stairs have a lock on it?"

"It does not," he said.

"The outside one has," Dougherty said. "Have you the key with you?"

He handed it over.

"I'll unlock the door as quietly as possible, but I'll first allow you enough time to get into place. Once I'm ready to go, I'll swing the door open and I'll shout as loudly as I can. You come in the other door at that moment. Are you ready?"

"I am."

Staying to the shadows, they headed for the doors. McBrien let himself into the kitchen just as Dougherty reached the side of the building and began moving quietly up the stairs. He stepped with care, placing each foot near the side of each tread to lessen the creaking, gently shifting his weight. The slowness of his progress tore at him, but he could risk no noise. The horse beneath the stairs simply ignored him. Finally, he was at the top. There was a faint odor of oil, the smell of a lamp burning, although no light could he see. At least he saw none until he was exactly at the door. There was a blanket fastened on the inside, covering the glass panes of the door, but he saw the smallest thread of light at one edge, and he knew that they had made the right decision. He took out the key and looked at the lock. It had already been opened. The door frame had been cracked with a crowbar or a chisel, and all he had to do was slam open the door. He waited, wanting to be sure that McBrien was at the other door, and knowing that he had to negotiate the kitchen and stairway more slowly so as to avoid any noise. Dougherty counted off what he thought was four or five minutes, and then, with a roar, threw open the door and leaped into the room, his revolver drawn.

This was McBrien's sitting room, and its furniture had all been pushed back against the walls. A lamp, turned low, sat on a table, its dim light picking out the figure of the still clothed Catherine Corrigan on her back in the middle of the floor, her hands and feet bound with strips of soft cloth. Even as Dougherty saw that, he knew why there had been no restraint marks on Evodia Zellner and no mention of them in any of the accounts. There was a gag in Catherine Corrigan's mouth, and her wide open eyes stared in his direction. Next to her on the floor lay three or four knives and a wooden handled length of thin rope — the garotte.

Her tormenter stood over her, a long knife in his hand, but Dougherty's shout had thrown him off. He turned to face his intruder. He wore a slouch hat and had the cloak pulled up to hide his face. His features were lost in shadow, but there was no mistaking the gray beard at the cloak's collar. He came at Dougherty with knife raised high, ready to plunge down. Dougherty fired point blank at his chest and heard only a loud click. The day's damp had gotten into the powder, in spite of his efforts to keep it dry. Dougherty watched the knife slash down at him.

* * *

Jen hated the very thought of leaving James and going back to the house. She knew he was right, but that did nothing to change the direction of her heart. Everything within her fought to turn around and go back to him. It was not even that she thought she could truly be of help in a physical conflict. It was the fear she had for him, the horrible premonition that he would be hurt, or even killed. She would rather run the risk with him than leave him to face it alone. She was almost home, when she made her decision. She turned around and began to retrace her steps.

She had gone but a few feet, when she stopped and weighed what she was about to do. She was being foolish. What she felt was exactly what she had felt so often during the war, when he went into battle and she and her mother were left behind, waiting for the wounded to pour in and dreading that he would be among them. Of course, she would rather face the danger with him than have him face it without her. She could not even imagine her life if he were taken from it. But she also knew what would happen if she went back. His whole attention would be given over to protecting her, and that would mean less attention to protecting himself and McBrien — or Catherine Corrigan. Her good intentions would produce precisely the wrong results. If that got him wounded or killed, she would never forgive herself. No. He was right, and she knew it, so again she turned in her tracks and went to where she could do the most good, wiping from her eyes the tears of frustration.

She moved faster as she saw the light in the kitchen and began to think of the boys, left alone to worry about where she had gone and where their mother was. They would be worse off if they were truly left alone without their mother at all. That, she prayed, would not happen. Surely James and McBrien would prevent it, without either of them being hurt. All she could do was rely on God's help and do what she had to do for the boys.

They sat together on the rocking chair near the stove. Daniel looked so relieved when he saw her, that she knew she had done the right thing. His little brother leaned against him, sound asleep. She hugged the two of them.

"Is our mom coming home now?" Daniel asked.

"Not right away," she said, "but I think that she will be here very soon."

"Was Mr. McBrien sick?" he asked.

"No," she said, "He is fine. He will be here soon, too."

He was satisfied. She lifted Michael from the chair, moved Daniel over a little, and then sat down with Michael on her lap, Daniel cuddling beside her, and an arm around each of them. They both looked so safe, and she hoped that it was not an illusion. Gradually Daniel drifted off to sleep, too, and she sat alone, waiting. Waiting.

* * *

The knife came flashing toward Dougherty as he tried to back away, but he was too close to the wall and had nowhere to go. He stumbled over his own feet. He raised his arms to fend off the attack. The gesture was automatic but, even as he made it, he knew how futile it was. He was about to be stabbed, maybe fatally, and he hoped that McBrien could accomplish what he could not.

That was when he heard a sound utterly out of place in this room. The sound that a baseball bat makes when it strikes a fast pitched ball. The Butcher's eyes opened wide, then glazed over and rolled back into his head. The knife dropped from his grasp as he slumped over on top of Dougherty, and they both crashed to the floor. Behind him stood McBrien, his six foot frame towering over them, his face contorted in rage. In his hand was a weapon Dougherty knew he possessed, but had never before seen him use. It was a strip of strong leather with two lead musket balls sewn into a pocket at the end. Its effect was immediate and gratifying. The killer was out cold, perhaps dead. McBrien helped Dougherty get out from under him, and then turned to Catherine Corrigan.

He took the gag from her mouth, used his jackknife to cut her bonds, and held her in his arms as she sobbed. She was almost incoherent, but they gathered that nothing had yet happened to her apart from threats. She was near hysteria, but she was safe. On the floor were more of the cloth strips he had used to bind her, and Dougherty used them to tie his arms and legs tightly and firmly. Next to him was the knife. Dougherty picked it up. It was a surgeon's amputating knife, a Tiemann surgical instrument, razor sharp, its blade well cared for, lovingly honed and polished. In fact, it had only one defect. There was a small piece missing from the very tip of the blade, and Dougherty had no doubt whatsoever that its jagged edge would fit perfectly the little triangle of metal that he had found wedged into the spine of Evodia Zellner. He felt for a pulse. The heartbeat was strong. He examined the back of the head for a soft spot where the musket ball would have damaged the skull. He found nothing. Unless there was serious internal damage, he would probably survive to meet the hangman. Only then did he roll him over.

Dougherty removed the slouch hat, opened the cloak, and, to his great surprise, found that in doing so he was also coming away with a handful of gray hair. The beard was not real! The killer was not Maddock, after all. In that they had made a mistake.

Chapter XXII: If I Am Not Mistaken

Quis custodiet ipsos custodes?
   Juvenal (60-130)
   Satires VI, 347

[Friday, November 2, 1866]

They'd gone to early Mass to pray for the dear departed on this chilly All Souls' Day, with its hint of first snow. The altar was stark, the vestments black, Father McGuire duly somber, and Sarah Carmody had sung the *Dies irae* — her high pitched voice, now in its eightieth year, wavered and quavered and was sufficient to bring to the eye of every listener a tear, whether of sorrow for the dead or of pain at notes sung so near what had been intended by the composer without ever actually getting there. There were more than enough deceased to pray for — so many innocent lives taken by a madman, and there was the Butcher himself, dead now these two weeks, since Friday, October 19.

After breakfast, Jen and James sat down to complete the task they had begun more than a week earlier: A full report for Judge Barrett. Evidence of the killer's guilt was clear cut and easily presented. He had acted precisely as predicted, verifying that he was the one who had killed all the earlier victims. Besides, they had found among the possessions in his hotel room, a diary of copybooks, that he had kept for years. What had begun as a plaint about a life of pain, had gradually become the insane resolve to rectify things by removing over and over again what he saw as the source of his endless anger.

"You were right," Jen said. "He was insane. There is no other explanation. There is no excusing what he did, but there is also no excusing what was done to him. I wonder if, without all the cruelty he bore, he would have turned out differently? Or would he still have been insane?"

"We shall never know the answer to that," James said.

The diary recounted each of the killings, the killer becoming ever more crazed as time went on. The broken blade of the knife with which he had attacked James was the perfect match for the broken point taken from the autopsy of Evodia Zellner. The garotte, marked with old bloodstains was there, next to Catherine Corrigan, waiting to be used on her. In his hotel room was a .22 caliber revolver, an Allen and Wheelock 7-shot side hammer, the sort of gun easily concealed but deadly at close range. It was probably with this that he had attempted to kill Charlie Brady. He had an army revolver when they captured him, but he had never drawn it. Dougherty guessed they had caught him completely off guard.

McBrien had remained with Catherine Corrigan and the Butcher while Dougherty had gone in search of Captain Maddock. He was patrolling the area about the depot, and it took some time for Dougherty to persuade him to come with him. They needed him, since his jail was the only place the killer could be kept until transported to Mauch Chunk, there to await trial, his eventual hanging almost a foregone conclusion. Maddock and Dougherty took him in, while McBrien took Mrs. Corrigan home and then went to fetch the boys. Maddock was with Dougherty — he insisted upon it — when he went to the hotel to examine their prisoner's room. That was where they gathered the evidence.

It was also where they gave a considerable fright to Mr. Michael Appelby, the surgical instrument salesman, whose room was across the hall from the one they had to enter by breaking the lock and waking all the guests on that floor. The desk clerk had no key. The occupant had insisted on that, caring for his own quarters and doing his own cleaning — something they allowed in the case of long term residents. When they struck the door with their shoulders, Mr. Appelby had popped out of his room in his nightshirt and cap, thinking that the building must be on fire.

"The poor man," Jen had said when Dougherty told her about it. "He is always so meek and mild. This must have given him second thoughts about ever visiting this town again." But her pity was lost in laughter at the notion of that very proper salesman ready to abandon the hotel in his nightshirt.

"The funniest part about it," James said, "was that Mr. Appelby said that he had taken that room purposely. It made him feel safe knowing that his next door neighbor was a policeman."

"Quis custodiet ipsos custodes?" she quoted, "Who will guard the guards?"

"By the way," he said, "You recall that Catherine Corrigan was concerned about Maddock observing her house? I asked him about that. He swears he never did it, and I believe him. I'm sure that it must have been Steven Carter doing it, in disguise. His diaries were full of references to his 'invisibility,' how his victims saw him and didn't see him. He had a talent for disguise, and he spent long times planning his crimes, examining his victims over and over before he abducted them."

He must have gone to Mauch Chunk on a number of occasions to prepare for his murder of Evodia Zellner, and he had accompanied Captain Morgan Maddock there in January when the Captain met with Judge Barrett, on the same day that McBrien and Dougherty were there. They had never seen him while they were there, and Maddock had never mentioned his presence — simply because he had never had reason to do so. But by the time Maddock had returned to Penrose Valley on January 18, Carter had been ready to return with him, with nothing to indicate what he had done the night before.

Steven Carter, the Butcher. The only one of Maddock's men who had appeared to be a real policeman, because he had actually been one all the while he had been a killer, finding a great enjoyment in being assigned to solve the very crimes for which he himself was responsible.

His real name was Samuel Gardner. The story of the killings and the capture of the murderer had appeared in the Philadelphia papers two days after his attempt on the life of Catherine Corrigan. It had been read by a woman named Wanda Carter. She had gone to the police with her story, and through them it had been brought to the attention of Doctor Brownson. He was the one who sent them a copy of the statement that she had prepared for the police.

> My name is Wanda Carter. I am the widow of Steven Carter. I am 72 years old. I wish to make a statement about the man who called

himself Steven Carter. His real name is Samuel Gardner. I knew him since his childhood. He lived near to my husband and me. After the tragedy he lived with us for three years. That must be why he took my husband's name as his own. We took him in those years ago because we felt so sorry at all he suffered.

Mrs. Carlotta Gardner came to live near us when her son was five years old. That was in 1839, in July. There was no Mr. Gardner. She claimed to be a widow, but no one believed it. She was a loose woman I regret to say. She had gentleman callers at all hours.

Samuel was a sad child. Her men friends were nasty to him. She never cared, not even when they beat him. She dressed in a manner some call flash, but I call slatternly. Her dresses showed too much. Her face was painted and her hair was overdone and she was too attentive to men. Even married men of the neighborhood. I do not include my Steven in that number. He had sense. Besides he knew I was not blind. She was seductive. I know no other word to describe her conduct. Her and her affectations. Rouge, and frills, and the loud striped stockings she thought showed off the graceful curves of her legs. Graceful curves, indeed!

The poor lad was the one that sorrowed me. All he wanted was his mother to pay him attention. He would do anything she wanted to that end. She treated him like a slave and not like a son.

I should not say this, but it is the truth so I will. The way she treated him was not natural. Not the way of a mother with a son. She had him combing her hair over and over again. She had long black hair she thought made her beautiful, and the poor boy would comb and brush it and drape it over her shoulders and back and cover her like a veil. It just wasn't natural, I'd say. It was a disgrace.

And the men. They just wanted him out of the way. The poor child was never let live like a normal child. She demanded his attention to her every whim. He had to make her happy, when all the while she was the mother and she should make her child happy.

It grieved me. The poor tyke would get upset about something and cry and she'd say, "Now that's enough of that. Stand up straight! Be a little soldier! Don't make me sad. Good boys don't do things like that. Make mommy smile. I don't know how such a child ever came from inside me!" I cannot imagine how a mother did not care a fig for that little boy, and how she could say things like that. It was so cruel! It still brings me tears to think of it.

I remember the tragedy. It was July 17 of 1850, near the lad's sixteenth birthday. It was Wednesday and I remember it because it was the day of our fortieth wedding anniversary. We didn't see the child all day long, nor the mother. There were two men there the night before and they left early in the morning. I swear I heard her say goodbye to them, but perhaps not. The police said she was dead before they left They said one of them killed her. They never did find them.

I have no idea who found her or the child. When they did, she was dead for hours. She was strangled with a cord. The boy sat beside the body and stared straight ahead. For two days he said nothing. When he did talk, all he said at first was "Make mommy smile" like she always said to him. He came out of it after a while, and had nowhere to go, so we took him in, we felt so bad for him. The police talked to us and to all the neighbors. No one could tell them when the murder happened and no one could describe the two men.

He stayed with us for three years, Samuel did, until October of 1853, and then he disappeared. He just up and left one day. Said not a word to us. We never heard from him again.

I don't like to say this, but it is true. He was a peculiar child when he lived with us. I guess it was how he was brought up. He tried to please, I guess, but it was like he really didn't want to. There was something strange in him, very distant. He never did us harm, but one time he really scared me. There was a little cat and he picked it up and it scratched him. He threw it against a fence and stomped on it. He hurt it real bad and left it to die. Tell the truth, when he left us I was glad.

When I saw the name in the papers, Steven Carter, and the report said that it was thought that his true name might be Samuel Gardner, I had no doubt that it was the same one. They showed me a photograph taken after his death. His face was horribly disfigured by a bullet and he was older, but it was Samuel. There could be no mistake about that. I am sorry for him and for what he did.

Dougherty doubted that the two men mentioned by Mrs. Carter were the killers of Carlotta Gardner. In his diary entry for the day he first saw Abiageal Conroy, Gardner wrote of having to kill her all over again, a clear indication that Abiageal's was not his first murder.

Perhaps that was the day when his insanity found its way out into the world around him instead of remaining trapped within. Dougherty could not prove it, but he was nonetheless convinced.

They never got to ask him, and now they never would. Maddock locked Carter in his new jail and refused to let Dougherty or anyone else see him the next day. He had regained full consciousness by the time they had put him in his cell; but he refused to speak, apart from one remark he made at least three times.

"That is the end. It is over."

Beyond that, he said nothing else in Dougherty's presence, and Maddock insisted that he had said nothing to him either from then until the time of his death. He just sat and stared, his eyes focused on nothing, and a tight little smile upon his lips.

On Friday morning, Maddock was to take Gardner to Mauch Chunk to consign him to Sheriff Ziegenfuss for incarceration in the county jail. Dougherty decided to walk to the station to see if the prisoner would speak — provided that Maddock and his men even allowed him to get near Gardner.

The morning was crisp, bright, alive — at odds with the events of the week and the activity of the day. There were people in the streets, but none seemed aware of the removal of the Butcher. Two of Maddock's men (neither of whom Dougherty had ever seen before) were in front of the depot and he wondered where Maddock was. The train had not yet arrived.

"Is Captain Maddock here?" he asked one of the two.

"Who wants to know?"

He told him who he was. The man was not impressed, but relented when he invoked Judge Barrett's name and he pointed him to the side of the station. Maddock was on the platform. Was Gardner with him? And, if so, why were these two here and not where the prisoner was? Dougherty was about to ask, when he heard the shot. He ran to the platform. The two policemen, he noticed, came after him, but did not run.

Maddock was down on one knee, his still smoking gun on the ground beside him. He was doing something to Gardner, who lay face down on the rough planks. Maddock looked over his shoulder at Dougherty and slipped into his coat pocket an object of which Dougherty had only a fleeting glimpse. He stood up and put the revolver into its holster.

Gardner did not move. A pool of bright red blood oozed onto the platform from beneath his head. His left arm dangled over the platform's edge, the handcuffs attached to it. His right arm was unshackled.

"Doctor! I am afraid that our prisoner is dead."

Dougherty knelt beside the body and looked. The ball had entered behind the right ear and exited just below the left eye producing a wound that had torn a large hole from the left eyeball to the level of the upper teeth. The hair above and behind the ear was singed, still smoking slightly, and the ear itself was black from the powder.

"He got his hand free and tried to run for it," Maddock said, his voice quiet and even, no trace of excitement. As cool a customer as ever Dougherty had seen. His subordinates, now arrived on the scene, said nothing, just stared at Dougherty as though daring him to contradict their chief's statement.

"How far did he get?" Dougherty asked.

"We were over there," Maddock said, pointing to a position at the far corner of the platform — a place not visible from where the two officers and Dougherty had had their earlier conversation. "He broke free and ran. I drew my gun and fired from there. He fell right where he now lies. As you can see, the handcuff is open."

The distance between the body and where Maddock claimed to have been standing when he fired the shot was perhaps fifteen or twenty feet. Dougherty looked again at the powder burns and touched the still warm hair.

"That is to say," he went on, "he may actually have been closer to me when I fired and, as he fell, his forward motion took him to where he is now. He had started to run, you see."

And so began the process of editing, the effort to cover his tracks. He was a quick study, this Captain Maddock, and Dougherty knew that he would never succeed in proving that he had just wilfully killed his own unarmed prisoner — especially since he had not seen the act take place and the two officers would surely support Maddock's version. But Dougherty's silence bothered Maddock, pushed him to try to justify himself.

"In the end, it's better this way, isn't it?"

"Is it?"

"Far better. Think about it and you'll have to agree. Justice has been done. A murderer is dead. You have no doubt that he was a murderer, do you? The only difference is between a bullet and a rope.

We saved the county the time and expense of a long trial that could come only to the same resolution. And it saves a great deal of pain. A trial was bound to bring hurt to everyone. The Zellner family... Even Mrs. Corrigan... It is all better this way. You've got to agree to that. Justice has been done, but it is a justice tempered better to the needs of the innocent. That's the ticket! A tender justice, I'd call that. And, in the end, probably better even for Gardner, although his welfare is of little concern to me."

And so it ended. The Butcher was gone, and there was nothing Dougherty could do about it. Nor did he think he could prove that what Maddock had slipped into his pocket on the platform that day was the key with which he had just unlocked the handcuff of the already dead Gardner, although he was himself certain of what he had seen no matter how fleetingly.

"Why did Maddock do it?" Jen asked him later, after he had told her the whole story. "Was he serious about avoiding pain to the innocent? Even so, that wouldn't justify what he did."

"The only pain Maddock was concerned about was his own... and possibly Arkwright's. It could do them no good at all to have one of their own Coal and Iron Police the subject of a notorious trial that might drag on for a long time and wouldn't go away until after the execution."

That was the last of the Butcher, but there were far better things to occupy their attention. Sean McBrien and Catherine Corrigan both came to the conclusion that life is too short to be wasted in prolonging a decision that is best made immediately, and so they spoke to Father McGuire and were preparing for a wedding in the Spring. Catherine spoke to Dougherty again about the money that Charlie Brady had left for her and she was adamant that it should be given to his aunt in Philadelphia, who, Dougherty was sure, could use it. It was sent to her.

"I am glad that it's all over," Jen said.

"It is hard to believe that it has been almost ten months since Charlie's body was discovered in the mines," he said, "and even harder to believe how much has happened since."

"And there is even more to come," she said.

"More? What else is there, now that the report is finished?"

"Names," she said, "we shall have to consider the names."

"Names?"

"Yes, names. I suppose we should be thinking of names for both boys and girls, wouldn't you say? And I should say that we had best begin soon. After all, we have only until about May to decide, if I am not mistaken."

Historical Note and Thanks

This book is a work of fiction, although mention is made of a number of historical persons. Most of the main characters, including the Butcher, are imaginary. The various towns mentioned are real, with the exception of the town of Penrose Valley. There is such a valley, between Beaver Meadows and Weatherly, in Carbon County, Pennsylvania (I used to hike there frequently as a schoolboy), but it never was the site of a town. However, Hazle Creek Bridge Station did exist at that location. It was built for the convenience of passengers from Hazleton and Buck Mountain, whose railroad lines there joined the Beaver Meadow Branch of the Lehigh Valley Railroad.

There are in the book references to a number of crimes apart from the fictional ones of the Butcher. All of those are real, and many of them played a part in the later trials of the Molly Maguires, although at the time they were committed no one could have proved that such an organization had anything to do with them; and, even later, it was never clear if they should all have been attributed to them or were merely used by the prosecutors of the Molly Maguires to make their point.

The newspaper accounts are all fictitious, with the exception of the excerpts from Benjamin Bannan's editorial in the *Miners Journal*, the tale of the Texas judge at the start of the book, and the story in Chapter IX from the *Carbon Democrat* describing the mysterious wild animal in Mauch Chunk. The story of the Mansion House Hotel handyman is perfectly accurate. Those events did occur during the winter of 1866, although I have moved them forward in time by a few months. As it got nearer to the Spring of that year, someone actually got a glimpse of the animal in the daylight. It was not a kangaroo, but a mountain lion.

In the book I consistently refer to the town of Beaver Meadows (which is where I was born) as Beaver Meadow (without the final "s"), since that is the way in which it was then known. I mention this because, even to me, the lack of that final "s" tends to grate upon my aesthetic susceptibilities and any inhabitants of Beaver Meadows who read this book may feel the same.

I must also thank a number of people who read various versions of the manuscript, commented upon it, proofread it, or encouraged me in the error of my ways in spending my time so frivolously. Among those people are: Harry W. Buchanan IV, M.D., Alice Holland, Cait Kokolus, Maria A. Loch, Monsignor Kevin T. McMahon, Eugene and Alice Mulligan, Edmund and Martha Mulligan, Mary Mulligan, Elizabeth M. Nagel, Mary Reiter, Vicki Sefranek and Karen Siegfried.

I also thank Maria A. Loch for her help in the typing of the original manuscript and the formatting of the final published versions.

I wish, finally, to offer a word of very special thanks to the staff of the Dimmick Memorial Library in Jim Thorpe (*olim* Mauch Chunk) for their assistance in finding books, maps, newspaper accounts, and some wonderful old photographs of Mauch Chunk.

Historical Characters

For those who are interested, the following is a list of historical persons mentioned in this book. Some are referred to merely in passing, others play some part in the story. I have tried to present them in ways true to what I could find out about them, but clearly their interaction with fictional characters is itself the product of my imagination. They are listed in the order in which they appear in the text.

Judge George R. Barrett
Associate Judge A.G. Brodhead, Jr.
Doctor John B. Longshore
Sheriff Reuben Ziegenfuss
Henry Dunne
O.W. Davis
Benjamin Bannan
Mrs. Maggie Walters
Doctor Wilson Packett
Mary Murrey
General Lafayette C. Baker
Provost Marshal General Marsena Patrick
Allan Pinkerton

General George B. McClellan
General Judson Kilpatrick
Reverend Father Jacob Walter
Secretary Edwin Stanton
Mrs. Rose Greenhow
Miss Belle Boyd
Dr. Rensselaer Leonard
Amelia Bloomer
Dr. Mary Walker
Mr. Lewis
Constable John B. Thomas
Mr. Joyce
Charlie Gallagher
The Dearing Family
Antoine Probst

Made in the USA
San Bernardino, CA
29 November 2013